THE
LAST
LEGIONNAIRE

Paul Fraser Collard

THE LAST LEGIONNAIRE

headline

First published in Great Britain in 2016 by
HEADLINE PUBLISHING GROUP

1

Cataloguing in Publication Data is available from the British Library

ISBN 978 1 4722 2275 6

Typeset in Sabon by Avon DataSet Ltd, Bidford-on-Avon, Warwickshire

Printed and bound by CPI Group (UK) Ltd, Croydon, CR0 4YY

FSC
www.fsc.org

MIX
Paper from
responsible sources
FSC® C104740

Headline's policy is to use papers that are natural, renewable and recyclable products and made from wood grown in well-managed forests and other controlled sources. The logging and manufacturing processes are expected to conform to the environmental regulations of the country of origin.

HEADLINE PUBLISHING GROUP
An Hachette UK Company
Carmelite House
50 Victoria Embankment
London EC4Y 0DZ

www.headline.co.uk
www.hachette.co.uk

For the Butterworths

Glossary

•◆•——◆——•◆•

arrack	native liquor/spirit
Buffs	nickname for the 3rd (East Kent) Regiment of Foot
bundook	slang for a rifle or musket
chechia	brimless cap with a tassel, similar to a fez
chokey	cholera
costermonger	man who sells produce such as fish, fruit or vegetables from a barrow or basket
en échiquier	French military tactic where infantry units advance as if each was on a separate square of a chessboard
furlough	period of leave from the army
hawa khana	to take the air (Urdu)
kepi	military cap with a flat circular top and visor
macadam	road surface made of tiny granite stones
munshi	language teacher

pandy	colloquial name for sepoy mutineers, derived from the name of Mangal Pandey of the 34th Bengal Native Infantry
particular	London fog
patterer	street vendor who sells their wares with speeches that have little regard for either truth or propriety
poker	knife or sword
rhino	money, cash
rookery	city slum
Rupert	slang for a British officer
sapeur de génie	French soldier of engineers
shako	military cap in the shape of a cone, with a peak, worn with a short coloured plume
tin	money, cash
Uhlans	Austrian light cavalry armed with lances
walk the chalk	withdraw, go away
Zouaves	French infantry unit famous for colourful uniform

NORTH-WEST ITALY (1859)

Bergamo

Brescia

Magenta
×
Novara • Milan
Vercelli
★ ★ Verona
Peschiera
Mortara
Solferino
Pavia ×

Turin
Casale
Valenza • Voghera
Mantua Legnago
★ ★
★ Piacenza
Alessandria

Genoa

★ Fortresses

○ Austrians ● French ◐ Piedmontese

THE BATTLE OF SOLFERINO

LAKE GARDA

Cucchiari
Lonato • Desenzano
Mollard
Durando
Peschiera

Morris

San Marino
Benedek

Montechiaro
Fanti
Salionze

Regnaud
Baraguey
Pozzolengo
Schlick

Partouneaux
Castiglione
Madonna della
Scoperta
Villafranca

Niel
Solferino
Stadion
Mensdorff

MacMahon
Cavriana
Valeggio

Carpenedolo

Canrobert
Volta
Clam Gallas
Zobel

Medole •
Guidizzola
Schwarzenberg

Visano
Ferri
Zedtwitz

Castel
Goffredo
Wimpffen • Roverbella

Goito
Weigl

Schaafsgottsche

❖ Imperial headquarters

○ Austrians ● French ◐ Sardinian

Chapter One

---◆---

London, March 1859

The alleyway stank to high heaven. The remains of a dead dog lay beside the officer's boots, its rotten corpse bloated and stinking. The stench rose up, the fetid miasma catching at the back of his throat, so he spat, scouring the bitterness from his mouth. The stink of the rookeries had not changed in the years he had been away.

He pulled his greatcoat a little tighter around him, then stepped over the matted fur of the dead dog. The streets far from London's more fashionable areas were familiar to him, despite the fact that he had not been there for nigh on a decade. The mean back-to-back houses of the slums were still pressed cheek by jowl. The same angry shouts of frustration came from the souls incarcerated within, the screams of their babies stirring memories of the place he had left so many years before.

He had long thought about this moment, the dream of his return sustaining him during his first weeks and months in the Queen's army. He had been forced to leave this place, a brutal fight denying him the right to live under his mother's roof. The army had taken him in. It had clothed him and fed him. It had trained him to be a redcoat, a killer of the Queen's many enemies, and it had given him a home when no one else would. Now he was back wearing the uniform of a captain in the 3rd Regiment of Foot. He was no longer the unwanted son, the boy who just wanted to be man. He was an officer, a man of station and importance. Or at least he was dressed as one.

The officer pressed on. He stuck to the alleyways; the narrow spaces that ran behind the tight rows of squalid housing. The main streets would be busy this close to dinner-time. The match sellers and the patterers would be working the crowd, and the costermongers would be looking to clear away the last of the day's stock from their barrows before they turned in for the night. The officer did not want the attention that he knew his presence would attract. The eager men, women and children who worked the streets of Whitechapel were certain to be keen to see him part with the shillings in his pockets, either willingly or not.

A young boy came rushing in the opposite direction. He was moving fast, his small feet sure and steady, his arms pumping hard as he ran. He only spotted the tall figure in the greatcoat at the last moment, and he skidded to a halt, his eyes darting this way and that as he tried to find a way past.

''Scuse me, mister.'

The officer smiled. He had spotted the boy's clenched fist, and could smell the aroma of the small meat pie even over the pungent stink of the alley. He fished in a pocket to pull out a coin before offering it up like a conjuror seeking to amaze his audience.

'You want to earn a sixpence, lad?'

The boy's face creased into a scowl. He could not have been more than ten years old, but he knew enough to be wary of gentlemen who hid in the shadows and flashed their money at small boys.

The officer saw the boy's expression. He wanted to laugh, but he kept his humour contained, just as he hid all his emotions away. 'Stand easy, lad. I've got a question, that's all.'

The look of suspicion did not change.

'The Counting House, do you know it?'

The boy bit his lip. His eyes were fixed on the sixpence.

The officer lifted the coin higher, further from the boy's reach. 'Do you know it?' he repeated.

The boy nodded, his scowl deepening as he realised he could not snatch the coin and escape.

'Who runs the place these days?'

'Old Maggie, of course.' The boy's answer was quick, his scorn at such a foolish question obvious.

'Maggie Lampkin?' The officer lowered the coin a fraction.

'Course. It has always been her place.'

'What about her old man? Is he still there?'

'You said one question.' The boy's eyes narrowed. 'Two questions cost a shilling.'

The officer could not help but smile. 'For a shilling, I'd want you to take me there.'

The boy flashed a smile of his own. He had never spent a single day at school, but he knew how to tally a man's worth. 'You lost, mister?'

'No.'

'Then why'd you want me to walk you?'

'Maybe I just want the company.' The officer watched the boy closely. It did not feel so long ago that it had been him filching meat pies from old Bartholomew's barrow.

'I ain't that kind of boy, mister.'

The officer's hand moved quicker than the boy's eyes could track. It cuffed him around the ear, the blow short and sharp. 'Shut your filthy muzzle.'

The boy lifted his chin to show the blow had not hurt. 'So what's your name, mister?'

The officer snorted. 'The going rate appears to be sixpence for a question, a shilling for two.'

The boy laughed. The sound came quick and easy. 'Fair enough.' This time it was his hand that moved fast, the purloined pie slipped into a pocket. 'I'll take you to the ginny.' He looked the officer in the eye. 'For that shilling of yours.'

The officer flicked the sixpence at his new guide. 'I don't want any trouble. You get me there nice and quiet and I might be inclined to be generous.'

The boy snatched the coin out of the air, making it disappear within the span of a single heartbeat. He contemplated the officer, his eyes narrowing as he assessed the options.

The officer saw it all. He raised a hand and pointed down the alley. 'Now walk your chalk. I'll follow you. And if you run, I'll come after you.'

'I won't peg it, mister.' The boy's fleeting smile hid the notion that he had been thinking of doing exactly that. 'I want your other sixpence.'

The officer did not respond to the choice reply. He waited for the boy to do as he had been instructed.

The boy took one last look at the scarred face and the hard grey eyes. The officer did not appear to be the sort to take kindly to being disobeyed, so he turned and set off down the alleyway.

The officer followed. He did not need the boy to show him the way, but he had not lied when he had said he wanted the company. He knew the paths he had to follow, but not who waited around the next corner. The boy would. The officer did not fear footpads; he had killed too many men for that. But he did not want to return here as a killer. There would be time enough to reveal his bitter talents, the skills that had kept him alive on the battlefields of the Crimea, Persia and India. For now, he wanted nothing more than to find out if he had a place that he could finally call home.

The officer held back as they emerged from the alley. The light was fading, but the three pairs of gas lamps on the wall of the gin palace burned brightly enough to cast a glow for yards in all directions. The blue-tinged light played across the display of gilded rosettes and sconces on the palace's garish facade, the gilt burners a beacon that summoned the thirsty congregation to their worship.

He stared at the great plate-glass window decorated with the image of a giant sun. He remembered the day the glass had arrived, the crowd that had gathered as the ancient windows were hacked out and replaced by the single glittering sheet. He savoured the memory, the glory of that day shimmering through the years. He had been proud then. Proud of his status, his position in the dark society of the rookery assured by his mother's ownership of the one place that offered the locals a respite from the never-ending drudgery of their sorry existence.

Yet that pride had not been his to savour. It had faded fast, quicker even than the purple and yellow bruises that marked his flesh as his mother's old man demonstrated just who owned what. He had not felt the same pride again until the day he had first pulled the heavy woollen red coat of a soldier on to his shoulders.

'Come on, mister. What you waiting for?' The boy turned to shake his head at the rum cove with the ready supply of tin. 'There it is. I saw you right, didn't I just.' The palm was held out. 'I reckon that's sixpence you owe me.'

The officer dipped a hand into the pocket of his greatcoat, then flipped out another coin. 'Easy money.'

This coin too disappeared quickly. 'You want me to wait to get you back to a cab?'

The officer smiled. 'No.'

'Staying for a bit, are you?' The boy smirked. He knew why men of a respectable kind would go out of their way to visit a back-street gin palace.

'Perhaps.' The officer knew what raised the boy's smile. 'Does Mary still work there?'

The smile was gone. The scowl that replaced it was fierce. 'She works there, but not like that. And she's too good for the likes of you.'

The officer was surprised by the strength of the reaction. He had once believed he had loved this girl called Mary. She had been a rare beauty, the kind that men would pay dearly for the right to be in her bed for an hour or two. The officer had never been granted such a delight, but the notion still sparked an itch in his groin that even nine years away had been unable to extinguish.

He looked at the boy carefully. 'What does she do now?'

The chin lifted. 'She helps Maggie run the place. Looks after it herself at times too.'

The officer took the news in. He wondered what else had changed in the years he had been away.

The boy sniffed, then wiped his nose on the cuff of his grey flannel shirt. 'You want anything else, mister? I know a place that might suit you better. It ain't far.'

'No.' The officer shivered. He felt the first fluttering of nervousness deep in his gut. It was like the moment before battle, the quiet time when the bravado stopped and each man was left alone with his fear. Angry at his reaction, he hid his emotions and stepped forward, the boy forgotten, making for the door that announced entry to the Counting House, the words etched deep into a plate of ground glass.

The air inside was thick with pipe smoke, and the stench of overripe bodies caught in his throat. The smell had not changed. The stink of piss and gin was just as he remembered.

His boots scuffed the sawdust spread on the floor. It needed changing; the scarred and stained floorboards were visible in wide patches. He ran his eyes around the room, the memories surging through him in a great unstoppable wave.

The early-evening crowd filled the place, men, women and children standing in docile lines as they waited for their turn at the great slab of mahogany that stretched across the far side of the room. He knew no one there, but the faces were just as he remembered, the same sea of sad, careworn expressions, passive in the expectation of relief.

He glanced behind the mahogany bar, his eyes roving over the complex arrangement of spiral brass pipes that led from a series of barrels lining the wall to a line of spirit taps that bore the names of the various brews. 'The Out and Out', 'The No Mistake', 'The Bairn's Favourite', 'The True Spirit', 'The Sit-Me-Down'; the bold names, and their even bolder claims, made him smile. He remembered the great vat in the yard behind the palace where the gin was watered down before it was fed into the barrels, the brew the same no matter what fanciful name it took.

'Billy! Where the devil have you been?' The question was

snapped out, the voice shrill and carrying easily over the chatter of the palace's patrons.

The officer started. He looked for the owner of the voice, a cold surge of nervous anticipation churning in his gut.

'Come here, you little scamp. I should tan your bleeding backside. You're late like bloody always.'

The officer was buffeted as the boy who had guided him to the palace pushed past.

'I'm here now, Maggie. I've been working.'

The officer noticed the approving smiles on the faces of the crowd, the boy's bold retort earning their approval. More than one hand reached out to ruffle his hair as he worked a seam, his passage to the bar made easy as men and women stepped out of his way.

'My eye, working, is it? You should've been working here, you little tyke.'

The officer scanned across the heads of the crowd, searching for the woman who had called to the boy, and whose voice had sent a shiver running down his spine.

'I'm here now, Maggie, so don't you fret; at your age it could be the death of you.' The boy beamed at the crowd's reaction, nodding at the smiles and winking at one of the girls in red stockings sitting on a stool near the fireplace. He stuck his thumbs under the lapels of his worn worsted jacket, his narrow chest puffed out. 'Where d'you want me?'

'There's piss in the parlour. Mop it up, there's a darling.'

The crowd chuckled. The palace's customers formed a willing audience to the show put on by the cocky lad and the loud bawd behind the counter. It was what they came for almost as much as the thin gin they bought by the pennyworth, the bright lights and the spectacle a relief from the dour greyness of their lives.

The officer did not join in. He hung back, his greatcoat wrapped tight around him, the fabulous scarlet of his uniform covered and his tall black shako pulled low over his eyes. He kept his face hidden. His own mother would not recognise him.

'Good evening, sir!' The woman the boy had addressed as Maggie spied the stranger's presence in her place. He was a head taller than most in the room and he stood out like a fox in a henhouse. 'There's a good seat in the parlour for a fine gentleman like you. No need to wait with this lot of sorry sods.'

The officer locked his eyes on the owner of the loud, hectoring voice as the crowd laughed off her insult. She was barely tall enough to see over the bar. The hair piled high on her head might once have been a fiery red, but now there was more grey than ginger. It sat like a pale and ancient cat above a florid jowly face with lips rouged to a bright red.

'Make way for the gentleman, you lazy buggers,' Maggie ordered. There were stares, and a fair few scowls, from the locals, who were immediately suspicious of a stranger. 'Make way, I say.'

The officer moved forward, towards the bar.

'The parlour, my love, it's just behind you on the right. That's the place for a fine gentleman like you. Young Billy here will come to see to you when you're settled.'

The officer paid the direction no heed. He moved closer, studying the woman's face. Unlike the palace, she had changed. Flesh and spirit had been eroded in a way carved wood and glass could never be. Yet the light in the puffy grey eyes was unaltered by the passage of time.

'Oh, you're a thirsty fellow, are you?' She shook her head, but still found a smile for the man who would pay at least triple the going rate for his drink. 'What'll it be then, sir? A touch of the good stuff for a fine gentleman like you, I shouldn't wonder? Why, I think I've got a bottle or two with your name on it down here. Better stuff than I serve the likes of these miserable bastards!'

The crowd reacted to their cue with mocking groans and hoots of disapproval.

'Hush, you lot. You knows your place!' The woman laughed off their grunts and growls, her eyes coming to rest on the tall officer who now stood directly in front of the proprietor of the Counting House, the finest gin palace this side of Petticoat Lane.

'What'll it be then, my love?'

The officer could see the suspicion in the woman's eyes. The slight flicker of fear as the stranger stayed silent.

The room fell quiet as the question hung heavy without a reply.

The officer pulled off his shako, his hand instinctively running through his close-cropped hair. He looked at the woman, whose eyes widened as she finally realised who had come back to her palace.

He offered a thin smile. 'Evening, Ma.'

The palace's owner stared back. Her mouth opened, but no sound came out.

Jack Lark let the flaps of his army greatcoat fall open. The scarlet officer's coatee was bright amidst the drab greys and browns around him. He had come a long way in the years he had been away. But now he was home.

Chapter Two

———◆———

'Where did you get that bigger one?'

Maggie's hand traced the thick scar on her son's left cheek. They sat together at one end of the table in the palace's back room, a space usually reserved for gambling, or for dealing with private business that needed to be conducted away from the prying eyes of the customers. Jack's greatcoat hung from a peg on the wall and his scarlet officer's coatee was draped across the back of his chair. He had removed his sword, but his holstered revolver stayed on his hip, the familiar weight reassuring.

'Delhi.'

'Delhi! Where the hell is that when it's at home?'

'It's in India, Ma.' The answer was given softly. Jack pulled away from her touch.

His mother's hand dropped. 'Was there fighting there, then?'

Jack shivered. He had been with the British soldiers when they first forced their way on to the ridge that overlooked the city of Delhi in the weeks after the native soldiers had mutinied against their white masters. He had still been there months later when the British finally launched an assault on the great city that had become the heart of the rebellion.

His mother sat back, her hands retreating to her lap. 'You look older.'

'So do you.' Jack tasted a moment's anger. He had not known what to expect when he finally completed the long journey that had started at a graveside outside Delhi all those months before, but now that the moment had finally arrived, he felt surprisingly little.

'It ain't been easy.'

There was awkwardness between them, the years a chasm that was not easily crossed.

'What about Lampkin?' It was hard not to sneer as he named his former master. Jack had lived under the man's sufferance, paying his board and lodging in work and in beatings. Until the day when he had fought back.

His mother snorted. 'He's a dead'un. He passed a few months after you left.' She was derisive. 'He was never the same after you did him over. Of course, the stupid bugger wouldn't admit it. He got in a fight with some fellows from down by the river. I don't know what it was about. He died.'

Jack remembered the fight that had led to his banishment. He remembered the young man who had fallen into Lampkin's clutches, but he could not recall the lad's name. Jack had arrived in time to attempt a rescue, but the fight had not been over the fate of a stranger. It had been coming ever since the day Lampkin arrived to claim the palace and its proprietor as his own.

'He never recovered. You hurt him bad that day, Jack.'

'He drew a knife.'

'And you beat him half to death for it.'

Jack felt little as he absorbed the news. Death had been his constant companion for years. He had seen so many friends die; lost so many of those that he had foolishly allowed to come close. Against that, the fate of his former master meant nothing. 'You chose him over me.'

'I couldn't turf him out. Not after all he did for us.'

'For you.'

'For us. We wouldn't have lasted a month after your fool of a father fucked off.'

'You still chose him over me at the end.'

'I had to.' Her reply was cold. 'I had no choice.' The words were bitter. She reached out to take his hand.

Jack was watching his mother closely. He had come to understand her better over the years. He had been almost a grown man when he had fought Lampkin. In the aftermath of the fight, he had made his mother choose between them and he had been the one discarded. Yet the life he had lived in the years he had been away had given him a different perspective to the one he had had that day. He knew he would not have stayed even if she had chosen him. He would have moved on, leaving his mother to face whatever fate had in store for her. Lampkin had been her choice. He was a vicious, bullying bastard, but he was her bastard and he would be there when her only son had long departed. Jack had forced her to choose, but he now knew that there had only been one option she could have taken.

'I know, and I survived.' He felt uncomfortable under her touch. Her hand was cold, the skin dry and chafed. It was the hand of a woman who worked hard for her living.

'And look at you! You came good.'

'This isn't real.' He had decided on total honesty. He had left his lies back in India. 'I stole it.'

For the first time, his mother smiled. 'You ain't a Rupert?'

'No. Not a real one. I have been, though.' Jack could not match her smile. He had been a British officer for a time. Or at least he had pretended to be one. He had stolen a rank far above his own, fighting in the Crimea as a charlatan captain, commanding a company of redcoats in the battle at the Alma river in the place of an officer who had died in the peace of the Kent countryside. 'I was even a general once.'

'A general!'

'I served an Indian maharajah. I saved his son. He gave me the title as a reward.' Jack could scarcely remember the months he had spent in the maharajah's court. It was if the memory belonged to someone else.

'What about all those Indian princesses? If you was a general, they must have swooned at the very sight of you!' His mother tried to tease him.

Jack thought about the one Indian princess he had known. 'No, they didn't swoon, Ma.'

'There must have been a girl or two out there.'

'One or two.'

'No one special?'

Jack found it hard to swallow. 'No, Ma, no one special.' He gave the lie badly. He felt the memories stir, the first tugs on the chains that kept them shackled in the shadows. He forced them away and steered the conversation back to his mother. 'No one to replace Lampkin?'

His mother's laugh was short. 'I'm an old woman, Jack.'

'An old woman with a palace.'

'Oh, men want that all right. They just don't want me.'

Jack saw a shadow flicker across her face.

'You've been a long way from home.' His mother looked down, her eyes following one of the many cracks in the table.

'I'm back now.' He could see that she was struggling to take it all in. He had a feeling that his words meant little; that his tale was barely registering. She looked up to stare at his face, searching it for something.

'So if you ain't an officer, what are you?'

'I don't know.'

'A runner?'

'No, I have my papers.' Jack thought of Ballard, the intelligence officer he had served under during the campaign against the shah. His reward had been a set of discharge papers that had given him back his own name. He had fought at Delhi as himself, his experience of war the only qualification he had needed in the turmoil that had gripped the country in the months after the mutiny.

'So are you staying? Are you back for good?'

'I reckon.' Jack was uncomfortable. His plan had been to return to the place where he had been brought up. He had not thought any further ahead than that. He had been an impostor and a thief, but now he had turned his back on all that. He no longer strove to be someone he was not, such ambition washed away by an ocean of blood. He didn't need to prove he was better than the fools and wastrels allowed to become officers simply by virtue of their birth. He craved something far simpler yet infinitely harder to find. He wanted a place to call home.

'You can stay if you like?' The offer was made with hesitation.

'I'd like that.' Jack felt the tremble in his mother's hands.

He realised she wanted him back but had feared he would not stay. 'So who helps you here?'

His mother smiled. She had the answer she wanted. 'Mary. She had a boy and I took her in. She works hard, bless her, I couldn't manage without her. Since you left she's become like a daughter to me. Now her boy helps out too. Did what you used to do. You met him tonight.'

It was Jack's turn to grin. The lad who had escorted him to the palace was Mary's son. 'He's a fine lad.'

'He's like you was. A little shit.'

Jack grunted in acknowledgement of the barb. Yet he did not believe everything his mother had told him. Two women and a boy could not hold on to a gin palace. The rookeries did not work like that. 'That's all?'

'We get by.'

'What about the father of Mary's nipper? Where's he?'

'God alone knows.' Jack's mother did not shirk from the facts. Whores were ten-a-penny in Whitechapel. Mary's story was hardly uncommon. Maggie offered a tight-lipped smile. 'You always liked her.'

'She looked out for me.' He could not resist the pointed comment. It had been Mary who had comforted him when he was alone, who he had gone to when the beatings were bad.

'You never did what you were told.' His mother offered a thin smile at the memory. 'You were always running off.'

The memory stirred nothing in Jack's heart. He tried to conjure an image from the past, but he found he could not do it. If he tried too hard to search his memories, he woke the faces of the dead that lived in the darkest recesses of his mind. He could not bear that, so he simply looked down at the table, his eyes roving across its scarred surface.

'Did the army teach you to obey orders?'

'For a bit.' Jack looked up and saw his mother staring at him. He sensed she wanted him to reveal more of his past, but his cold reaction was keeping her at bay. 'I wanted more than I was allowed.'

Again the tight smile. 'I ain't surprised. You always wanted more, even if it meant taking a hiding from my old man. So you became a redcoat and then a thief?'

Jack nodded. He had once thought of it in grander terms: a crusade to be the kind of officer the redcoats deserved, taking him to places he would never have believed possible. But such naive dreams meant nothing in war. 'I was good at being a soldier.' He revealed a little of his pride. It was all he had, the satisfaction at what he had become, the skills he had learned in battle the only true thing about him.

'But you came back here?'

'I had nowhere else to go.'

'Last knockings, are we?' His mother tried to laugh, but the sound died away. She pulled her hand free.

'I wanted to come.' His skin tingled, cold now the warmth of her hand was gone.

'I'm glad. You here to work?'

'I'll help you. If you'll have me.'

For the first time his mother looked unsure. 'Things are different now. We ain't had no man here since John passed.'

'So how did you keep hold of the palace?' Jack pressed her. His doubts returned. She was not telling him the whole story. An old woman, an ex-whore and a bastard child could not run something as fine as a gin palace by themselves.

'I pay.'

Jack did not reply at first. He was not surprised. Protection gangs had always been around. Lampkin had had no need of them, for no one in the rookery would have been brave enough to take him on. But without him around, Maggie had been forced to look elsewhere for security. 'How much?'

'Half of what we take.'

Jack felt a flicker of temper. That was not protection. It was extortion. He watched his mother closely. She was not ashamed of her decision. She looked up and caught him studying her. She lifted her chin, her eyes narrowing slightly as she waited for him to challenge her.

'If I stay, you won't need them any more.' He kept his tone neutral. He would not pay the bastards. He had brought all the protection he needed. His hand slipped down to touch the hilt of his revolver. He had fought on the walls of Delhi, had defended the British cantonment at Bhundapur and ridden with the Bombay Lights at Khoosh-ab. He had no need of anyone else.

'They're bad men, Jack.'

His mother matched his tone. He noticed she did not try to change his mind. He was her son and she did not doubt him. He felt something stir deep within him.

'They do not know me.' This time it was Jack who reached out. He took his mother's hand and held it tight.

'Maggie!' Mary's son, Billy, poked his head around the door. His young face betrayed his fear. 'Mr Shaw is here. He wants you. He's clearing the place out.'

Jack's mother did not move. She stayed still, her eyes locked on to her son's hand wrapped around her own.

'Is that him?' asked Jack.

Maggie nodded.

'Then I'll give him the good news myself.' He patted her

hand then got to his feet. He flashed a smile at Billy. 'You might want to stay back here, lad.'

'Why?' The answer was quick. 'You going to fight Mr Shaw?' The boy did not look horrified by the idea.

'No. Least I don't plan to.'

Young Billy's face fell. His eyes focused on the holstered revolver on Jack's hip. 'Can I take your gun for you?'

'No.' Jack saw the boy's eagerness 'But if you don't give me any shit for a week, I'll teach you how to clean it.'

'Deal.' The boy snapped the answer, then his face fell. 'You might not be alive in a week.'

Jack felt the stirrings of a smile. 'Is this Mr Shaw that bad?'

The boy bit his lip, then nodded.

'Well you had better take me to see this monster.' He gestured at the door. 'You go first, Ma. We don't want to alarm Mr Shaw.'

His mother rose to her feet and walked to the door, only pausing when she came level with her son. She looked up, her head tilted back as she studied his face.

'You know what you are doing, Jack?'

'No.' Jack found his smile. 'I never do.'

His mother grinned back. 'Well then. Let's get this done.' She turned and flapped a hand at young Billy. 'Get on with you, you little scamp. Let's go give Mr Shaw the happy news.'

She bustled out. Jack let her go. His hand slipped to his holster, his fingers deftly undoing the buckle on the flap to free the revolver within. He had lied to his mother. He knew exactly what he was doing.

Chapter Three

———◦•◦———

'About time, Maggie. I don't appreciate you keeping me waiting.'

Jack heard the arrogant tone in the voice that greeted his mother as he followed her into the bar. The palace was empty. A single figure was leaning against the counter, whilst a much larger man stood by the door that led to the street. He saw the silhouettes of the crowd milling around on the far side of the plate-glass window, waiting to be allowed back inside the palace. The two men had cleared the customers away so that their business could be conducted in private

'Good evening, Mr Shaw.'

There was fear in his mother's voice. It brought him up short. He did not think he had ever heard her sound truly frightened before. She had always greeted the world with a laugh and a smile, her blarney as much of a draw as the watery gin she served.

'Who's this?'

Jack had been spotted. The man called Shaw stood straight, staring at him. His heavy coat flapped open, revealing the thick cudgel held on a string attached to his belt.

'He's my son.' Maggie walked behind the bar. Some of her former confidence seemed to return as she took her usual place. 'You and your man want a nip of something?'

Shaw nodded by way of reply. He kept his eyes locked on Jack. Behind him, the second man stayed by the palace's door, cudgel in hand.

Jack returned Shaw's gaze calmly, but said nothing. He would let the other man play his hand first.

Shaw fixed Jack with a slow smile. It did not reach his eyes. 'What's your name?'

Still Jack said nothing. Shaw was a hard-looking man. His face was covered by a thin beard, and he bore three small scars in a row across one cheek. He stood an inch or two over six feet tall. Jack had noticed the way that he leaned against the bar with casual confidence, the kind that only came with the sure knowledge of being able to handle any man who came against him. He was a threatening fellow, and Jack understood his mother's fear, even if he did not share it himself.

Jack moved slowly, his eyes assessing the man by the door. He was big, but unlike Shaw, he did not have the build of a fighter. He was stout, with a large belly, and he carried a cudgel in his right hand, the thick foot-long oak shaft that was such a common weapon in the rookery. To Jack's eye he did not look dangerous. Not like Shaw.

Walking behind the bar, Jack took his place at his mother's side. He kept his eyes fixed on Shaw the whole time. He sensed the simmering anger in the man's gaze as his question remained unanswered.

'You know why I'm here, Maggie.' Shaw shifted his attention to Jack's mother.

'I've got your money, Mr Shaw. But by my tally you are a few days early.' Jack's mother placed a quart of gin in front of the man who had emptied her palace. She pushed another to the bar's far side for Shaw's henchman, who was watching on from his place by the door.

'No, you don't have that right.' Shaw slipped his pork pie hat from his head before placing it carefully on the counter. 'I would never make a mistake like that. The money *is* due.' The last sentence was delivered deadpan. Shaw's eyes flickered back to Jack, who still stood beside his mother, his face impassive. 'Are you going to stand there and stare at me all night, chum?'

Jack did not deign to answer. He knew Shaw's business well enough. Protection rackets had been going on as long as there had been men strong enough to deliver the threats that forced people like his mother to pay them. He did not recall Shaw from his time in the palace. When Lampkin had been master, there would have been no talk of protection, unless it had been his mother's old man making the demands.

'Who the hell are you?' He asked the question in a mild tone, keeping his eyes on Shaw as he pulled a glass from beneath the mahogany bar. He did not look down as he flicked a brass tap, snapping off a perfect measure that filled the glass to the brim.

'My, my.' Shaw smiled thinly. 'So you do have a voice. I was beginning to think you were a bit simple, like my Prussian friend over there.' He nodded towards the man still waiting by the door before turning his baleful gaze back to the counter. 'That's a bold lad you bred, Maggie. Shame you didn't teach him his manners.'

'He's back from the wars, Mr Shaw.' Jack's mother seemed

to have mastered her fear. Her reply was firm. 'He was a soldier.'

'Was he now?' Shaw looked Jack up and down. 'You still a lobster, chum, or are you a runner?'

Jack downed his gin without tasting it. 'I don't like asking a question twice, but seeing as how we just met, I'll give you the benefit of the doubt. So I repeat. Who the hell are you?'

This time Shaw laughed. He turned and looked back at his man. 'You hear that, Schmitty. Maggie's brat doesn't know who I am.' When he turned back to face the bar, the thick cudgel was in his hands. He swept it along the mahogany top, sending the two quarts flying. They shattered as they hit the floor, the gin splattering across the sawdust.

Shaw was not done. He smashed the cudgel down, slamming it violently into the counter, the sound of the impact like a gunshot. Then he pulled back, holding the cudgel upright, his face flushed and his body vibrating with an anger that was barely under control.

'You want to know who I am?' He spat on to the counter, then glared at Jack, the cudgel moving slowly back and forth in the air, held ready to lash out again. 'I'm your worst fucking nightmare.'

Jack had not so much as flinched, standing composed in the face of Shaw's violence even as his mother shuddered. And now he laughed. Shaw's bold claim amused him. The man was hard, even for the rookery, but he was most certainly nowhere close to the devils that inhabited Jack's nightmares. He had seen far too much to be frightened of a man with a stick.

'It's time you left.' He spoke softly before reaching out to lay a soothing hand on his mother's shoulder. He could feel her shaking. 'I'll clean up the mess, Ma.'

'Jack . . .'

She started to speak, but Jack hushed her by lifting a single finger.

'It's all right, Ma. Let me handle this.' He turned to look at Shaw, who still stood there, his cudgel ready to strike. 'Like I said, it's time you left.'

Shaw cackled. 'Give us what we are owed, or by Christ I'll tear this fucking place apart.' He turned to his enforcer. On cue, the stout Prussian took a step forward, ready to do his master's bidding.

Shaw turned back to face Jack. His mouth opened to say something, but the words never came out. He was staring straight into the muzzle of a Dean and Adams five-shot revolver.

'Now then.' Jack's tone lacked all emotion. 'I don't know what's been happening round these parts whilst I have been away, but I'm back now. This is my mother's place and I'm going to be staying here a while. That means I'll be looking after things from here on in. So I suggest you both leave.'

Shaw stood tall. He showed no fear, even with a hand-gun aimed at his face. 'You don't know who you are dealing with.'

'I don't give a shite.' Jack held the revolver stock-still. 'I don't reckon you're welcome here any more, *Mr* Shaw.' He made the name sound like an insult. 'I'm asking you one last time to leave.'

Shaw stared at Jack. then slowly lowered his cudgel. 'You're going to regret this, chum. You mark my words.'

'That's as maybe.' Jack lifted the revolver a fraction, filling the end of the barrel with Shaw's flushed face. 'But not half as much as you'll regret not fucking off right here and now.'

Shaw took a step backwards. He looked at Jack's mother,

who was holding on to the edge of the counter as if her world was spinning around her.

'Are you not going to set your lad straight, Maggie? You know who I am and what I'm capable of. You want to be a part of his malarkey? If I leave here tonight without my tin, then our arrangement is finished. I won't protect you no more.'

Maggie let go of the bar. 'I reckon it's time you left, Mr Shaw. My Jack is back now. We don't need your protection any more, not now we have a man about the place again.' She stood straighter, then glanced at her tall son before glaring at the man who had taken her money. 'I'll ask you kindly not to call on us again.'

Shaw started to laugh. 'Are you sure about this, Maggie? I don't want it said I didn't give you a chance to reconsider. We've been friends too long for that. You sure you know what you're doing?'

Jack's mother lifted her chin defiantly. 'I do.' Her voice wavered, but she stood firm.

'So be it.' Shaw nodded, acknowledging her decision. 'You had better be ready to face the consequences.' He glowered at Jack. 'Both of you.'

'Oh, we'll be ready, Mr Shaw.' Maggie was warming to her new role. 'This is my place. We managed well enough when my John was alive. My Jack is twice the man *he* ever was, so I reckon we'll be fine now he's back.'

'Very well.' Shaw reached forward and removed his pork pie hat from the bar. 'I'm right sorry it has come to this, but it is what it is.' He settled his hat on his head, then fixed his eyes on Maggie. 'As of now, you're no longer under my protection. You understand that you'll have to pay for making me leave without my tin. I can't let it pass. It wouldn't be good for my reputation, not good at all.' His expression hardened. 'I'll make you regret siding with your mongrel bastard, Maggie. By God, I swear you'll rue this day.'

He brought his simmering anger back under control with difficulty, then turned on his heel and strode towards the door. He paused on the threshold, his right hand on the doorknob, and turned back to look at Jack.

'Well met, Jack. I reckon we'll be seeing each other again.'

'Goodbye, Mr Shaw.' Jack still had his revolver levelled. 'Next time I see you, I'll put a bullet right between your eyes.' He had to give Shaw credit. The man was eerily calm even with a loaded revolver pointed at him. It meant he was either a brave fellow or else simply too dumb to recognise the danger.

Shaw laughed at Jack's threat. 'You know what, chum, I think you'll try. I shall look forward to our next meeting, indeed I shall.' He opened the door and left the palace, his Prussian henchman trailing in his wake.

'I bloody well hope you know what you are doing, Jack.' Maggie pulled out a damp cloth and used it to wipe over the counter, slicking away the thick gob of phlegm Shaw had spat on to its top and gathering together the shards of broken glass. Already the bravest of her customers had started to file back into the palace.

'I'm not going to see you pay your tin to a piece of shit like that. I meant what I said, Ma. I'm back now. Things are going to change.' Jack holstered his revolver, then looked down at his mother. He saw she was standing straighter. Her face had softened and she seemed younger. She was more like the woman he remembered.

He cocked an eyebrow at the first ancient crone who inched

closer to the bar. 'What'll it be?' It was a question he had once asked a hundred times a day.

He had meant every word. He was back. He would not leave again.

Chapter Four

———◆———

'For the love of God, is that really you, Jack?'

'Good morning, Mary.' Jack sat at the table in the back room. The remains of his breakfast lay in front of him, the grease from the thick slices of fatty bacon he had eaten staining the plate. He had been getting around his first mug of tea when the door to the scullery at the rear of the palace had opened to reveal a face he would have known anywhere.

He rose to his feet, then stood awkwardly as the woman he had once thought the most beautiful girl in the world paused in the doorway and stared at him.

'You're taller.' Mary stayed on the threshold.

'And you haven't changed.' Jack gave the lie easily. Mary was no longer the slim-hipped girl who had intoxicated him with desire. He saw that her figure was fuller; her waist thicker under her very proper dark skirt and her chest heavier beneath the demure blouse. Yet her face was just as he had remembered, and her wide-set blue eyes stared back at him with what he hoped was pleasure.

'My eye, you must have lost your sight when you was away.' Mary shook her head at his reply. She took off her hat, holding it in front of her, her own awkwardness obvious.

Jack shifted from foot to foot. 'It's been a fair while.'

'It has that.'

'You've been well?' Jack was struggling to know what to say. He had learned many of the ways of an officer, but polite conversation had not been one of them.

'Yes. Thank you for asking.'

'I hear you're a mother now. You've got a boy.'

'You've met my Billy?'

'Last night, although I cannot think why you didn't name him after me.' Jack flashed a smile.

'Hark at you!' Mary took a step into the room. 'After you indeed. Did you not remember my old dad's name was William?'

Jack laughed. 'No. I thought you might've missed me.'

Mary came closer. She was smiling. 'I did, Jack. I missed you. You didn't come to say goodbye.'

'I didn't have a choice.' Jack kept hold of his smile.

'No, I suppose you didn't. It would've been nice, though. It weren't the same after you left.'

'I'm back now.'

'To stay?'

'I reckon.'

'Things aren't the same here. You know that?' Mary bustled into the room to begin clearing away Jack's breakfast.

'They don't look that much different to me.' He reached forward to pull her hand away from the table. He held it, savouring the feel of her skin under his touch. He had been alone a long time. 'I'm not the boy I once was.'

Mary did not pull her hand away. She searched Jack's eyes. 'No. I can see that.'

Jack drew her closer. He could smell her. She didn't smell of French perfume like some of the women he had known. She smelled of carbolic soap, the simple aroma of a clean home. She moved into his arms, her head coming to rest on his chest. He held her then, his hand sliding to rest in the small of her back.

Mary pulled away sharply. She turned her back on him and busied herself clearing away.

'I met Mr Shaw.'

She went still for a moment, her body rigid. Then she carried on clearing. But Jack saw the tension that remained in her posture.

'You know him?' He asked the question of her back.

'Course. Everyone round here knows him.'

'I told him to sling his hook.'

He was met by silence. The only sound in the room was the scrape of a knife across a plate as Mary cleaned away the traces of his bacon.

'Why'd you do that?' The question came after a long pause.

'I'm back now. We don't need to pay some ruffian to keep us safe.'

Mary snorted. 'I hope you know what you're doing.'

'I reckon I do. We don't need a man like that. I'm here now. I'm all the protection we need. I'll keep us safe.'

'Why would you do that?' She turned to face him, his plate still in her hands, her expression twisted with distaste.

'It's my home.'

'No it isn't. It hasn't been that since you were a nipper. You remember what it was like, how you felt back then? It was never a place for you. It weren't then and it sure ain't now.' She shook her head at his foolish words. 'Look at you. You stroll in here like you own the damn place, turning our world upside down and putting us in danger.'

'In danger! You're not in danger.'

'Is that so?' Mary's cheeks were colouring now, her rising temper increasing the tempo of her words. 'You know that, do you? You know about Shaw, about how bloody dangerous he is?'

'I know that we don't need him or any other bugger who happens to take a shine to this place.'

'Why's that, Jack?' She tossed his plate on to the table. 'Are you staying around, then? Are you going to guard this place night and day? Because that's what it'll take to keep us safe from that bastard.'

'I'll do it. If that's what it takes.' He saw Mary take a deep breath as she brought herself back under control.

'You don't know the half of it. You don't know what that man is capable of, or what price he sets for protecting us. It ain't just your ma who pays. Oh no, we all dance to that bastard's tune.'

Jack had a fair idea what price Mary would be paying. It shamed him, but he felt his determination harden. None of them would dance to Shaw's tune any longer. 'I know Shaw's type. He's all piss and wind. He doesn't scare me.'

'Maybe he should.' Mary looked at him, searching his face for something.

'I've done things, Mary.' Jack looked away, unable to meet her gaze. He felt the iron shackles tighten, the protection against what he had seen strengthening once more. 'Shaw is just a man. I've killed many like him.' His voice tailed off. 'I'll take care of this place. You, Ma, your boy, you're all safe now.'

'You going to promise me now, Jack? Just like you did when you were a boy. You going to promise that you'll always be here, always looking after me?' Mary contained herself with difficulty, holding her temper in check. She turned away, then began to walk towards the scullery door.

'Stay where you are.' The order stopped her in her tracks. It was given with the snap of authority, the voice of a man used to being obeyed. 'You've had your say. Now you'll listen to me.'

Mary turned to face him, leaning against the doorway. She met his stare, her eyes defiant, her anger glimmering just beneath the surface.

Jack took a step towards her, and then another. 'You know nothing about me. What I've done. If you did, you would know that I'm not frightened of Shaw, or of any other thug that happens along. If you knew where I've been, the battles I've fought in . . .' He felt dizzy. He barely saw the woman in front of him. His memories were breaking free of their manacles and they surged through him. He saw them then, the faces of the men he had killed. In his mind he relived the moment when death came to claim them. Alongside them were the faces of those who had died around him, the friends struck down, the lovers lost.

'I'll keep you safe.' His voice changed. He sounded cruel, the bitterness of what he had seen, what he had done, now released. But still he walked towards her, his hands reaching out to take hold of her once again.

'Safe. There ain't no place safe round here, not with Shaw around.' There was no sympathy in her reply, only fear. 'You think that because you've been in the wars he's going to leave you alone? I've seen him at work. That man is a killer, and I reckon he enjoys it, too. You and him, why, you both look just the same to me.'

Jack took hold of her shoulders. Now that he was close to her, he could see the furrows in her skin, the dark patches on her cheeks half hidden under rouge, and the puffy grey pouches around her eyes. He let her go. He suddenly felt cold. He had summoned the memories, releasing them from their cage, and he found he could no longer speak. He walked away, his boots loud on the rough wooden boards.

Mary did not let him go in peace. 'I've got a boy now, Jack. My Billy is all that matters. I've got to give him some sort of a chance, some kind of a future. I cannot let you put that at risk.'

'I hear you.' Jack did not turn to look at her. He picked up his sword, which he had propped against the wall behind his chair. It was the weapon he had taken into the breach at Delhi. It felt snug in his hand, the feel of the hilt under his fingers familiar. Acting on instinct, he drew the blade, the steel whispering out of the leather scabbard that kept its edges sharp.

He turned then, the blade alive in his grip. He looked back at Mary and saw the fear on her face as she faced him. He revelled in the feeling. He wanted to show her what he was, what manner of man he had become. He was a killer, returned from war, and he was frightened of no man alive.

He saw Mary step away, as if he was about to strike her down with the sword that he held with such ease. He sheathed the blade, and closed his eyes. He heard the door open, then close, and once again he was alone.

Chapter Five

———◆———

'What'll it be?'

'Half-quart, please, mister.' The young girl was too small to see over the bar. She held up a glass jar, balancing it precariously on the counter and following it with three grubby pennies.

Jack put the jar under the tap, the action instinctive, and looked down at the blue eyes peering up at him. The girl could not have been much more than six years old, but she was old enough to be sent out to fetch gin to see her mother through the night.

He glanced outside. He could not see to the other side of the street. The particular was bad that night, the fog smothering the city in a dirty yellow shroud.

'You got far to go, love?'

The girl sniffed. Her nose dripped and she used a corner of the grubby grey shawl that engulfed her tiny frame to smear it away. 'Nope.' The answer was wary. Even a child knew to evade such a question.

Jack smiled at the answer. The girl could not live far from

the palace and he reckoned she would be all right. It was too early for the footpads, and the other denizens of the night-time streets too would be waiting before they came out to ply their trade, targeting anyone foolish enough to be abroad in the rookery when darkness set it.

'Hurry home, love.' Jack filled the jar, then flicked its stopper back in place. 'Don't you dawdle now.'

'I won't, mister.' The girl's hands reached up to steal the bottle away.

The crowd was thin enough for Jack to see her stop to steal a sly sip from the bottle before she wrapped her mother's old shawl around her shoulders and left the palace.

'She's a good girl, that Eve. Her sister is that trollop Abigail that my Billy moons after.'

Jack smiled at the mention of Abigail. He had seen her around the palace of an evening. She was attractive, in a dark, feral fashion. He had noticed Billy's infatuation with her. It reminded him of his own youth, and the hours he had spent dreaming of a life with Mary.

'Now that Abigail works, young Eve looks after her old ma.' Mary kept up her tale even as she served another customer. 'She got the chokey last winter; God alone knows how she survived. She's a tough old bird, but it's hard on her kids. Still, they look after each other well enough.'

Jack grunted. Mary knew everyone's story. He did not care to hear each sorry tale. 'It's quiet tonight.'

'Particular's bad.' Mary reached to pull across the wicker basket containing the small dark cakes that young Billy laced with salt each morning. She inspected the contents, poking one with a finger, before pushing the basket back to the far side of the bar. 'Best give everyone a bun. They won't last till the morrow. They might keep a few of the buggers back for another pennyworth.'

Jack shook his head at the mercenary tactic. He was slowly getting used to the running of the palace and the long hours spent standing behind the counter. He had been back nearly a month and had worked every day, taking his meals in the back room and sleeping in the attic bedroom that had once been his. Life was becoming routine.

He had not completely forgotten his former trade. He looked across to the shelf that ran beneath the counter to check that the holster, and the revolver it contained, was in place. He had not forgotten the man Shaw, either. The weapon was loaded every day and unloaded every night. He kept it to hand, ready for the day when Shaw would return. He did not fear the inevitable encounter; in fact he looked forward to it. He found himself glancing up when the bell above the palace's door jingled. He felt the same pang of disappointment every time he saw it was just another punter, another lost soul come to claim the liquor that dulled their senses enough for them to endure another day of their miserable existence.

He willed Shaw to come. The days were beginning to blur together. There was little to separate them, the grinding and monotonous routine of running the palace the kind of drudgery he had not known since his first weeks in the army. There was little chance of change, his future suddenly mapped out and ordered. Shaw's reappearance would give him the chance to show his worth and reveal his darkest talents. And it would put an end to the tedium.

The bell rang. Jack's head snapped up on cue. He sighed. It was a fat-hipped woman and her friend, the sound of their gossiping just about loud enough to carry over and grate on his ears.

'What's wrong with you? You waiting for someone?' Mary had not missed his reaction. 'What'll it be, my loves? A pennyworth each of the Bairn's Favourite, if I'm not mistaken.'

Jack glanced away, reluctant to witness the look of pleasure on the women's faces as Mary remembered their favoured choice of gin.

'We need more glasses.'

Mary made the request sweetly enough, yet Jack still bristled. He was discovering that the role of potboy was not much to his liking. He had been an officer, a man others looked to in the bleakest moments of battle. Now he took orders from a former whore, his tasks the same ones he had learned as a child.

Still, he did as he was told, squatting to the floor to begin pulling glasses from the back of the deep shelf hidden under the bar. The bell rang again. It was a constant sound in the palace. A large number of their clientele took their gin away with them to drink on the street or back in their homes. He presumed the pair of gossips Mary had served had slipped away. He did not get up, but kept at his task, pulling the stacks of glasses closer to the front edge of the shelf so that they would be readily to hand.

'Jack.' Mary said his name very quietly. There was no mistaking her tone.

'Good evening, Mary, what a fine night for mischief.'

He recognised the voice at once. His wish had been granted. Mr Shaw had returned.

The patrons of the palace were no strangers to violence, or to the men that orchestrated it. They bustled out, Shaw's Prussian escort pushing at a body here and there to speed their exit, his heavy oak cudgel held ready, the silent threat enough to make even the old scurry away. Not one person stayed behind to help. It was the way of the rookery. Survival was all.

'Where is he?' Shaw snapped the order. He did not come close to the mahogany counter, but held back, his enforcer moving to stand behind him, covering his back.

Mary's hand pushed down on Jack's shoulder, an attempt to hold him in place out of sight.

'I don't know where—'

He cut her off by rising to his feet. 'I told you not to come back.' He kept his tone even, as if asking what measure of gin Shaw required. He was oddly pleased that Mary's first instinct had been to keep him safe. It proved that her affection for him had not totally crumbled away.

'Hiding behind a woman's skirts, are we, chum? That's not what I expected of a man like you.'

'I suggest you leave.' Jack felt the tension in the air. Violence had crept into the palace in Shaw's shadow.

Shaw ignored the order. 'Of course, Mary's behind is a fine hiding place for a man.' He leered at her. 'I reckon I'll be paying you a visit later tonight, my girl. I fancy a little comforting.'

Jack glanced at Mary. Her reaction to the vulgar reference was well hidden.

Shaw tried to provoke a better response. 'You weren't complaining last time I had you on your back, were you, Mary? Screaming to the rooftops you were. Why, I think I still have the marks.' He made a ploy of looking over his shoulder, as if he were able to inspect his own back.

'Shut your mouth.' Jack felt the first stirrings of anger. He swallowed it down and kept it bottled tight. He would not release it. Not yet.

Shaw laughed, a humourless bark. 'You make a lot of demands for a cove who's just arrived round here. I'd hoped you would've learned who you were dealing with by now. Maybe even learned a little respect.'

Jack held himself in check. He recognised the feeling that Shaw was awakening. It came to him in battle. It was the madness that drove him into the worst of the fight and kept him alive when any sane man would have given in to the slaughter. The memory of what he became thrilled through him. He felt the temptation to release it, to give the madness its head. He wanted to show Mary what he was, what he could become. Yet somehow he stayed still, holding the emotion under tight rein.

'I'll tell you one last time. This is our place. Always was. Always will be. We don't need your kind.' He was pleased his voice came out with an even tone.

'My kind.' Shaw cocked his head to one side. 'Why, I don't think you like me. I don't think you like me at all. Not like old Mary there. She likes a taste of me, don't you, love? Aye, there you go, blushing like a fucking virgin, as if you don't know what I'm talking about. But you know all right, you know what we gets up to, what you like to do when there isn't anyone look—'

'Enough!' Jack reached down to slip a single glass into his hand. His holstered revolver was on the far edge of the shelf to Mary's right, well out of his reach. 'Now get out!' He barked the order, his hand tightening around the glass. He did not expect to be obeyed.

'No.' Shaw lifted the cudgel and pointed it at Jack. 'That's not how this goes. We don't take orders from a mewling prick like you.' He nodded to his man.

The bulky Prussian moved swiftly to obey. The oak shaft he carried was a simple but effective weapon. He made straight for the fireplace, lashing out the moment he was in range, his cudgel driving against the mirror on the wall above the mantel. It smashed into a thousand pieces that rained down in a spectacular, chinking shower. He swept the weapon along the mantel, sending a pair of brass candlesticks flying, before turning away with a great snort and kicking out with his heavy boots, smashing the simple stools lined against the far wall for those punters that wanted to stop to sip at their gin. In one quick movement, he seized the nearest table and hurled it against the wall, the wood splintering, the broken shards falling noisily to the floor.

Shaw strode forward, his face twisted in a snarl. 'This is what happens when you cross us. You see it!' Again the cudgel jabbed out to point at Jack's breast, and Shaw cackled as his man continued to smash anything he could find, his delight at the violence obvious. 'And there ain't nothing you can fucking do to stop it.'

Jack was moving before a plan of action had fully formed in his head. He felt a flash of elation as the chains fell away to release the demons they held in check. He bounded over the bar, his backside sliding across its top, glasses knocked flying by his flailing boots, adding to the sound of chaos unleashed.

The Prussian had left his graveyard of furniture and was already approaching the bar, his cudgel ready to smash the glasses strewn on its top. He came at Jack as soon as he leaped across the counter.

Jack ducked away the moment his feet hit the floor, and the wild, sweeping blow scythed above his head. He heard the explosive grunt as the man missed his target, the heavyset body jerking as the Prussian sought to bring his weapon back down on to the crown of his opponent's head.

Jack was slow. He had not fought for months and his instincts were buried so deep that they came out creaking and protesting. But he had time to dash the rim of the glass hard against the bar's edge before he tried to spin away. He nearly made it, his body starting to come to life, but the cudgel caught him on the shoulder and he fell, his body thumping heavily into the wooden floorboards.

'Jack!' He heard Mary scream his name as he went down, followed by Shaw's roar of delight at seeing him beaten so easily. The Prussian grunted again as he recovered from the impact, and readied another blow.

Jack scrabbled on the floor, his dignity forgotten. His knees scuffed across the wood, his motions frantic and barely controlled. It was the big Prussian's turn to laugh as he lifted the cudgel above his head, readying the crushing blow that would put an end to the farce. The heavy oak shaft whistled down, the powerful strike rushed but still vicious enough to stave in Jack's skull.

It missed.

Jack was moving faster now. He had seen the blow coming, so he stayed low, then twisted his body to one side. As the cudgel slid down past his right hip, he rose to his feet roaring like an inmate of Bedlam. The shard of glass in his hand was viciously sharp, and he drove upwards with all his strength, the improvised weapon cutting deep into the Prussian's belly. He had aimed true, the ragged glass piercing the soft flesh above the big man's groin.

The Prussian screamed, an inhuman roar of agony and

shock. Jack drove the glass deeper, twisting his wrist to gouge through fat and gristle. He released his weapon, then pushed the Prussian backwards, the glass buried deep. The man staggered away, both hands clutched to the tear in his flesh six inches above his balls. Blood was pulsing over his clasping fingers, a great wave that smothered his arms to the elbow. Then he crumpled, his scream trailing off to little more than a pathetic whimper as he curled around his wound.

Jack stood back. He could feel the heat of the Prussian's blood on his hand. He took a deep breath, caring nothing for the gore that splattered the sawdust-covered floor. He pointed a single bloodied finger at Shaw, who had stood transfixed as his henchman was struck down in the passage of no more than a dozen heartbeats.

'Time to dance.'

He took a second breath, then did what he always did.

He attacked.

Chapter Six

———•◦•———

Shaw rallied fast. He bellowed as Jack came at him, then lashed out with the cudgel, the blow short and sharp.

'Come on then!' he cackled, his face twisted with delight. 'You fucking want some!'

Jack stayed silent as he kept out of range, the madness of his wild rush for the moment contained. Shaw had reacted instinctively, even as his henchman writhed in a pool of his own blood. Jack's first opinion had been proven correct: the man was a fighter, and much more of a danger than the bigger Prussian he had already cut down.

He kept his eyes on Shaw even as he darted away. His opponent used the cudgel well. It would be no easy thing to take the man down with no weapon save his bare hands. He glanced back at the bar. Mary was staring at him, her hands clasped to her face.

'Mary!' he shouted. 'Get the gun!'

Shaw laughed. 'You stay where you are, Mary!' He snapped his own instruction. 'You help this merry little fucker and so help me I swear I'll break your fucking neck.' He laughed as he met Jack's gaze. 'She ain't going to help you, chum. Useless bint she is, just a washed-up fucking doxy. Only good for one thing, and to be honest, she ain't even that good a fuck.'

Jack let the insults flow by. He had killed harder men than Shaw. 'Mary.' He spoke calmly. 'Get the gun. Then throw it to me or shoot the bastard yourself, I don't care which you choose.'

Shaw whooped with delight. 'Kill me, is it? How the fuck are you going to do that?' He slapped the cudgel down into the palm of his free hand, repeating the action for a second and then a third time. Then he stepped forward, swinging the weapon down and aiming a blow at Jack's shoulder.

Jack saw it coming and swayed back, letting the oak shaft skim his front. He released his fist the moment it was past, darting a punch at Shaw's face, the swift rising blow aimed squarely at the man's nose.

Shaw was too quick. He recovered fast and ducked away, staying low so that Jack's fist scraped off his scalp. Then he counter-attacked, driving the cudgel end first into Jack's gut and knocking him backwards, a wild cackle escaping his lips as he landed the first telling hit.

Jack staggered back, his breath forced from his lungs so that he gasped and sucked for air. Shaw gave him no respite and came at him again, the cudgel now held in both hands. He swung the shaft, catching Jack under the chin and snapping his head back, then drove him backwards, legs pumping as he slammed him into the wall. He pressed his weight forward, grinding the cudgel into Jack's throat, his face no more than a single inch from Jack's own.

'Not so fucking hard now, are you, chum?' The words were spat out, and Jack felt the wash of Shaw's sour breath on his skin.

The pain came on brutally fast as his throat was crushed, the wooden shaft cutting into the soft flesh. Jack twisted his body in an attempt to get free. Shaw saw the effort and laughed, pressing his own weight forward, holding Jack in place, his delight at inflicting pain shining in his eyes.

But Jack was not done. His shoulders and arms were pinned back but his hands were free. Even as his vision started to grey, he turned his wrist then lunged his right hand forward and grabbed Shaw's balls, the tender flesh soft under his fingers. He took firm hold, then pulled as hard as he could.

Shaw yelped with the sudden pain. He tried to get away, but Jack held him fast, twisting his wrist cruelly, his fingers holding Shaw tight.

The yelp turned into a scream. With his balls on the point of being ripped free of his body, there was no way Shaw could keep Jack pinned to the wall. He dropped the cudgel, his hands clawing at his assailant in a desperate attempt to release the merciless grip.

The pressure on Jack's upper body disappeared as Shaw's weapon fell away. He sucked a single breath into his tortured lungs, then slammed his head forward into Shaw's unprotected face. It was a brutal blow, and it forced Shaw away, tearing his balls from Jack's grasping fingers. The taller man staggered, blood beginning to pour from his nose. His sneer was gone.

Jack stepped forward. He took two more quick breaths, his throat burning as the air rushed into his grateful lungs. Then he lashed out, stepping into the blow that he aimed at Shaw's gut. Shaw was hurting, and he could do nothing to escape the attack. Jack followed the gut punch with a second that caught his opponent on the side of the head.

'Come on!' He released his fury and roared with triumph as

Shaw's head came down. He smashed his knee forward, catching Shaw full in the face, then kept after the bigger man as he staggered backwards, punching and kicking, each blow landing true. The salvo hammered into Shaw's body until finally he could take no more and he fell, hitting the floor in front of the fireplace like a sack of shit.

'Jack! Stop!'

Mary was screaming at him to end the merciless battering. He barely heard her and cared nothing for the command. He kicked Shaw in the throat, then stamped down hard, grinding the fallen man's hand into the floor, the sound of bones breaking barely registering under the roar of his anger.

'Step away or so help me I'll shoot you down.'

The threat registered. With an effort of will he staggered to one side, his breath coming in laboured gasps. He saw Mary clutching his revolver, the firearm large in her small hands. And it was pointed at him.

'What the hell are you doing?'

'Stand away.' Mary lifted the weapon. 'You're killing him.'

Jack did not have the breath for any more words. He bent double, his hands on his knees as he hauled in painful lungfuls of air. He was struggling to understand what was happening.

'Keep back!' Mary shouted, the revolver waving in Jack's direction. 'You hear me? Keep back!'

Jack did as he was told. He managed to lift his head and saw Mary's flushed face, her eyes wide over the barrel of the gun that still pointed at his skull. He could not believe she was coming to Shaw's defence after hearing the filth that had poured out of the man's mouth.

He waved a hand at the gun, trying to push it away. But Mary was already turning, hands shaking as she changed her point of aim.

He had been wrong. She was not saving Shaw. She was going to kill him.

He noticed the revolver go still in her grip. He straightened up painfully, his breathing slowly returning to something like normal. He stepped forward, coming to stand at her side as she aimed the barrel of the gun at the man who lay unmoving on the floor.

'You bastard!' She spat out the words, holding the revolver steady, her finger curling instinctively around the trigger.

Shaw's face came up slowly. It was smothered in blood, a gory mask that split and cracked as he sneered at the woman standing over him. 'You bitch.'

Mary laughed once, then pulled the trigger.

The revolver roared. In the empty palace, the sound was deafening.

Shaw screamed. He rose from the ground, his mouth stretched wide in a dreadful wail. Mary had been knocked back by the power of the revolver's recoil, but she gamely brought the gun back down and fired again, her own shriek of terror lost as the second round roared out.

Jack flinched, his body acting on instinct. He sensed Shaw moving fast, the big man somehow finding the strength to run.

'Shoot him!' he bellowed, his hand slapping his thigh in frustration.

Mary brought the gun around and fired off a third shot, screaming again as she did so.

Shaw was still on his feet. Jack had no idea if he had been

hit, but he did not dare move. He saw how wild Mary was with the gun and he knew that to go after Shaw was to risk taking a bullet in the neck.

'Shoot him, for Christ's sake,' he urged, but Mary's strength was failing, and the gun drooped.

Shaw made it to the door. He hauled it open, half tearing it off its hinges in his panic to escape. The moment it was wide enough, he charged out, lurching away from the threat of the bullets.

Jack and Mary stood in silence. In the aftermath of the fight, the only sounds came from the bloodied Prussian, who whimpered as he lay curled in a ball on the floor.

'Did I hit him?' Mary's question broke the spell. She still held the gun, pointing it at the door.

'No.' Jack fought the urge to spit. The familiar rotten-egg stink of powder smoke was thick in his nostrils.

'I missed?'

Jack snorted. 'You missed.' He reached out to take the revolver from her hands. He noticed the tremble in her fingers. 'You should've let me finish him.'

Mary scowled. She did not seem upset by the violence. 'I wanted to kill the bastard myself.'

Jack slipped the still hot revolver into the waistband of his trousers. 'It sounded to me as if you rather liked him.'

'Don't be a fool. You think I enjoyed letting him do those things to me?' Mary looked ready to start another fight. She faced Jack, hands on hips, her chin lifted in defiance.

'I don't know what to think.' Jack looked across at the bloodied Prussian. He had not moved, and Jack decided he posed little threat.

'You know what I was. You think he didn't know that too?'

Mary's anger simmered. 'We paid him off with more than bloody rhino.'

'I thought all that was in the past.'

'So did I.' Mary tossed her head. 'You know what they say. Once a whore, always a damn whore.' She did not bother to hide her bitterness.

'I don't think of you like that.' Jack winced as his body reminded him of the bruises he had taken. His throat was raw and every breath burned.

'Then you came back from the wars a fool. I did what I had to do to keep this place safe. I'm not proud of it, but I ain't ashamed of it neither.'

He heard the hardness in her words. 'I'm not judging you, Mary. I know what life is like.'

'Then you know why I did what I did. I had to keep this place for my Billy. He needs a home. You can understand that, I reckon.'

Jack nodded. His own mother had made hard choices to keep a roof over her son's head; decisions he had not understood until he was long gone. Mary had done the same for her son. He had not lied. He was the last person who could ever judge another's sins.

'You did what you had to. Now, are you going to help me with this Prussian arsehole, or are you going to stand tossing your head around like a nervous damn filly?'

'You've become one mean bastard, Jack Lark.'

'I know.' Jack took a tentative step towards the Prussian, who had gone worryingly silent. 'And I bet right now you're damn glad I did.'

Mary didn't answer. They stood over Shaw's henchman in silence.

'Is he a dead'un?' Mary spoke first. She did not sound concerned by the notion.

'No, at least I don't think so.' Jack went gingerly down on to his haunches and peered closer at the Prussian. He did not look dead.

'Shame. It would've made things easier.' Mary came to crouch at Jack's side. 'We could've tossed him in the Thames and that would've been that.'

A pair of pale blue eyes turned their way. The Prussian was alive. Jack had the feeling he had understood Mary perfectly well.

'Help me.' The words came out as little more than a whisper.

Mary tutted, then looked at Jack. 'You going to kill him?'

'No.' Jack could not help but shake his head at the suggestion. Mary was harder than he had given her credit for. 'Is there someone who can help him?'

'There's no doctors around here. Mrs O'Fallon might help. She does for the girls when they have their babes. She could stitch him up.'

'Get your Billy to fetch her.' Jack stood up and pulled off his shirt. 'Let's at least try to keep him alive until she gets here.'

He was about to squat back down when he saw Mary staring at him.

'You have been in the wars.'

Jack looked down. He was used to the scars. From the thick weal on the left side of his torso to the ridge of raised flesh on his right shoulder, his body bore the reminders of the battles he had fought. He shrugged, then knelt at the Prussian's side. He felt a prick of shame at letting Mary see him half naked. Once he would have stripped off in front of her gladly. Now he just felt awkward.

'Lie still, you,' he whispered to the Prussian, who stared back in silence, his eyes fixed open in a mute appeal for aid. Jack glanced back at Mary, who had shown no sign of moving. 'Don't just bloody stand there. Send for that woman.'

As she left, he returned his attention to the man he had cut down. He winced as he saw the gaping hole half hidden under the Prussian's hands. He folded his shirt and held it gently over the wound. There was a lot of blood, but he had seen worse.

'I reckon you'll be all right, mate.'

The Prussian said nothing.

'Sorry I had to do that.' Jack rocked back on to his heels. He had never sat with a man he had wounded. Men fell all the time in battle, those he cut down dropping away with their last shrieks of horror ringing in his ears. He remembered many of their faces, the shock and terror reflected in their eyes as they realised they were about to die. But that was all. They were gone quickly, their passing fleeting. Now he sat with a man bleeding from a wound he had inflicted, and he did not know what he felt.

'*Danke.*' The word came with a hiss of pain.

Jack did not know how to reply, so he simply sat there.

'Why are you helping me?' The silence had stretched thin before the Prussian murmured the question.

'I can't just leave you to bleed to death. That wouldn't be right.' Jack smiled at his own words. He had been in battles when the killing had stopped suddenly. One minute he had been in the thick of the fighting, surrounded by men clawing at one another in a desperate bid to kill or be killed. The next, each man realised that the fighting was done. He remembered the embarrassed looks as they moved apart, the odd sense of uneasy camaraderie that built even as they stood over the bodies of their fallen mates.

'Fucking English.' The Prussian was lying on his side. He tried to spit, but only succeeded in dribbling a glob of phlegm on to his chin.

'I'd shut your mouth if I were you.' Jack tried not to laugh at the insult. The Prussian was bleeding like a stuck pig, yet still he had the nerve to abuse the man who held his life in his hands. Jack thought it an admirable trait.

'Why do you work for that bastard Shaw?' He settled into a more comfortable position. He had done all he could. The Prussian would live or die at fate's hand now.

'*Geld*. Money. Why else?' The Prussian closed his eyes against the pain.

'That's it?' Jack was oddly disappointed.

'*Ja*. What else is there?'

'Loyalty?' Jack looked round for Mary. He wished she would hurry.

'You cannot eat loyalty.'

Jack grinned. He was beginning to like the Prussian. 'So that's all you want?'

The Prussian did not reply. His eyes were closed as he fought against the pain. It was some time before he opened them again. '*Nein*. But it's all I can get.'

Jack nodded at the honest answer. 'So what now? I reckon your mate Shaw left you for dead.'

'Fuck Shaw.'

'Fair enough.'

Jack heard a commotion coming from the rear of the palace. He felt relief. Mary's Irishwoman had arrived. He got to his feet. He could not help but look down at the man he had half killed. He reckoned Shaw had it wrong. The Prussian was no simpleton.

'I tell you what.' He spoke loudly enough for the Prussian to hear him over the bustle. He saw the blue eyes look up. 'If you live, I'll give you a job. You can work here.'

The Prussian's eyes closed. 'Fucking English,' he whispered. He said nothing more as Mrs O'Fallon bent over him and got to work.

Chapter Seven

—◆∙◆∙◆—

'He won't be back.' Jack leaned forward and looked at his mother. They were sitting at the table in the room behind the bar. Mary was there, but her son was already busy in the yard behind the scullery, preparing for the weekly delivery of gin that was due that morning.

'How can you be sure of that?' Maggie poured scorn on the notion. 'I know Shaw. He won't leave you be after what you did.'

'He'll have to. I hurt him and his Prussian chum. The whole world will know it. He won't risk another shaming.'

'You don't know him.' His mother shook her head. She sat at the far end of the table, a mug of fresh tea steaming in front of her. 'He's an evil bastard.'

'So am I.'

'He's right.' Mary sat next to Jack. 'He beat them both, Maggie. You should've seen it. He took them down in the time it takes you and me to change a bloody barrel.' There was no sense of praise in her words. She made the verdict sound like she was damning him.

Jack's mother still shook her head. 'I know men like Shaw. They don't walk away from a fight. I tell you now, he won't just waltz back in here looking for another scrap. He'll take you quietly, when you're alone, when he can get you on his terms. There ain't no fair rights round here.'

Jack refused to be warned. 'If he does try it then I'll just have to beat him again. I'm not going to live in fear of him or anyone else like him. This is our place and I aim to keep it that way.'

'By hiring Shaw's Prussian bully?' Mary made her opinion of Jack's odd choice clear.

'He'll do. If he lives.'

'Mrs O'Fallon reckons he will. She says he bled no more than a woman with her first child.' Maggie gave the latest news. The Prussian lay upstairs in Jack's bed. Jack had been to see him and had repeated the offer of a less vicious employment. This time the Prussian had accepted in a more traditional way.

'Lucky us.' Mary was scathing.

'He'll keep this place safe. I thought that's what you wanted.' Jack tried not to snap.

'And where will the money come from?'

'I'll pay him.'

'Will you now? You rich enough to hire servants?'

'Rich enough.' Jack met Mary's stare. 'You want a lady's maid?'

'You can keep your money. Just make sure you keep your promises too.'

Jack thought he saw a fleeting hint of a smile on Mary's face at the fanciful idea. He had been only half joking. He was not a rich man, not by any standards, but he was not a poor one either. His attempts to better himself had sustained his ambition whilst he had it. But he was a boy from Whitechapel. There were always ways to get some rhino, and he had not been shy of taking the opportunities when they had come his way.

'So you're master here now?' Mary mocked him. 'Hiring staff and running the damn place.'

'No.' He scoffed at the idea.

'Then what the hell *are* you doing?' Mary's eyes were hard. Any notion of good humour had clearly beaten a hasty retreat.

'I have no idea,' Jack answered with total honesty.

'No. I figured that much.' Mary shook her head at his foolishness. 'Yet still you're willing to destroy everything we have just so you can prove that you are a hard man now, that you're not that little boy who ran off.'

Jack glowered. 'It's not like that.'

'No?' Mary was cruel. 'I reckon this is all one great game for you. No one else wanted you, so you came back here. You turn up looking like some fine toff, but in truth you're just another bloody man who reckons it's his God-given right to do whatever the hell he pleases.'

Jack rose to his feet. 'I fought for this place. I didn't have to.'

'Really? I reckon you wanted that scrap.' Mary's eyes blazed up at him. 'I reckon it was the best thing could've happened to you. You were bored shitless, we all saw it. I reckon the fight with Shaw suited you very nicely.'

'You really believe that?' Jack's voice was like ice.

'Yes, I bloody well do.' Mary did not back down. 'Men like you are ten-a-penny round here.'

'Men like me?'

'Mary!' Jack's mother reached across to try to land a

calming hand on Mary's forearm, but she shrugged it off and rose to her own feet.

'Yes, men like you.' She spat out the words. 'Men who think nothing of killing. Men who fight rather than using their bloody heads. Men who do what the fuck they want without any thought of the damn consequences.'

'You have no idea.' Jack snapped the reply.

'I have every idea. You think you're special, that you're different because you fought in the wars.' She made her voice sound wheedling as she mocked him. 'You're nothing special, Jack Lark. Your life isn't all that different to any one of ours.'

'Is that so? Have you killed a man? Have you watched him die with your sword buried in his guts?' He was shaking now. 'Have you sat with a young lad and said nothing as the poor bastard dies in your arms? You know nothing.' As he spoke, the images flooded into his mind. The faces of the dead mocked him, taunting him with their hollow, glazed eyes.

'I know you're a fraud!' Mary was shouting now. 'You're just a common bloody trickster.'

'And you're just a doxy who doesn't know shit.'

Mary slapped him. The blow came hard, the sound of the impact like a gunshot.

Jack laughed then, mocking her attempt to hurt him. He saw her hand tense as she readied another blow. It had barely travelled an inch before he reached forward to grab her forearm, his fingers digging into the flesh around her wrist. He pulled her towards him, dragging her forward so that her face was close to his own.

'Do not tell me what I am.' He spoke softly, every word as hard as steel. 'I know what I have become.'

He threw her away then, not caring that he hurt her. He did

not look at either of the two women again as he stormed from the room.

He would not be left to go in peace.

'That's it. Turn your back.' Mary's voice harangued him. His rough handling had done nothing to quench her anger. 'I know you, Jack Lark. I know what you are. So you slope off, just like you always do. That suits us nicely. We don't bloody want you.' Her voice was cruel and her face changed as she spoke. It twisted, her mouth ugly, as if she was sucking on something sour.

Jack slammed the door behind him and stood behind it, slowing his breathing. He was in the main room of the palace. The stink of sour gin caught in his nose as he controlled his anger. The smell sickened him.

The collar was stiff. His fingers were clumsy and out of practice, but he forced the final button into its hole. The fit was tight around his neck, the high collar forcing his chin up so that he looked down his nose at the world around him, just as an officer should.

He stood back from the window, then smoothed down the fabric of the scarlet coatee. It was slightly rumpled from its time in the chest where he kept his things. He had not worn it since the day he had arrived back in Whitechapel nearly a month before, his role as potboy not requiring the dress of an officer of the Queen. But the snug fit of the captain's uniform coat felt good on his back.

He pulled on his kidskin gloves, taking time to ensure that each was smooth against his skin, then reached for the tall black shako with its stubby plume. He kept it tucked under his arm as he checked his reflection in the room's small window, which acted as a mirror now that darkness had fallen outside.

He liked what he saw. He straightened his back, instinctively adopting the posture of an officer. His fingers traced the crown and star embroidered on the collar of his uniform jacket in golden thread. The rank of captain sat well with him. It was the first rank he had assumed, and the one he felt most at home with.

The fight with Mary had cleared his mind. He was going back to what he had always been. He had returned to the one place he had thought of as home in an attempt to build a new life on the foundations of the past. He had been wrong. He was no longer the boy who had worked at his mother's beck and call. He was a soldier, a redcoat. He did not belong in a gin palace. He belonged on the battlefield, where his talents had a rightful place.

He had tried to deny who he was. He would not do so again.

Chapter Eight

'Good evening, sir, welcome to the Army and Navy Club.'

Jack slipped the shako off his head and handed it to a liveried servant standing ready near the entrance to the officers-only club. He nodded to acknowledge the man's greeting, his hand running over his close-cropped hair as he ran his eyes around the room.

The club was busy. He had chosen the date with care. There were a number of events being hosted that night, the combination of two regimental dinners and a birthday celebration certain to fill the place with enough unfamiliar faces that one more should not stand out.

Once or twice he had felt like he had been followed from the rookery, but he had stopped and checked behind him, and was confident that the feeling was nothing more than a twinge of unfamiliarity at once again taking on the role of a redcoat officer.

'Are you here for Lord Butterworth's celebration, sir?' The frock-coated servant sought to guide the newly arrived officer to the correct event. Already an officer and his lady were entering the club behind Jack, and the sound of a hackney cab carried inside as still more guests pulled up to the kerb on the corner of George Street.

'Yes, indeed. It is upstairs?' Jack offered a smile to the man charged with greeting the guests. He made the guess easily. He had already spied a group of three officers making their way up the grand staircase that swept into the hall. None was escorting a lady, and their uniforms came from three different regiments, the identification a simple matter of glancing at the coloured facings on their jackets.

'Yes, sir. Lord Butterworth and his guests are in the library.' The servant nodded before ushering Jack forward, his white-gloved hand gesturing for him to walk on.

Jack needed no more invitation. He walked towards the staircase, his heartbeat barely increasing as he returned to the world he had inhabited for so long. It was almost too easy. A man presenting himself in the correct uniform, with passable manners and the right accent, was rarely questioned. Once that fact had astonished Jack. Now he barely paid it any heed.

He ascended the stairs at a leisurely pace, following behind another pair of officers slowly making their way upstairs to the club's evening rooms. Officers did not rush. The staircase wrapped itself around the corners of the hall, the great glass panels on the ceiling dark now that night had fallen. It was grandeur on a vast scale. The club was not quite a decade old, but it had the feel of an opulent Italian palazzo, or so Jack heard the officer in front of him proclaim to his companion.

He paused at the top of the stairs, taking a moment to straighten his jacket. A grim-faced, grey-moustachioed general stared down at him from a gold-framed portrait, his face cast into an eternal scowl of disapproval, as if he could see the impostor now standing before him. The notion made Jack smile as he moved on. The weight of the officer's uniform felt good on his shoulders; the contrast to the green apron of a potboy could not have been starker. He felt he was starting to understand what he was, what he had become. He had come back to London thinking to end his time as a pretender. Instead he had simply taken on a new role, masquerading as a son returned and a man reclaiming a former life. The fight with Shaw, and the less violent but more powerful one that had followed with Mary, had focused his mind.

'Good evening.' A man dressed in a black frock coat nodded a friendly greeting as he passed Jack by.

Jack returned the comment with a smile. He took a deep breath, then pressed on, heading towards an elegant salon just off the first-floor landing, from where he heard the sounds of polite conversation.

'Take him down!'

Jack dived, grunting with pain as the body he was tackling drove hard into his shoulder. He fell away but kept his arms wrapped around the man's legs, binding them tight so that the two of them came down together in one breathless heap.

'I say, good tackle, old man.'

The breathless voice was loud in his ear, and he felt the scratch of whiskers on the side of his face as his target twisted round. He would have laughed at the turn of phrase if the man had not been lying on his chest. He wriggled free in time to see another man in shirtsleeves bound close by to snatch up the teapot that had been knocked from the tackled man's grasp when he hit the floor.

'Over here, Sir John!' More voices bellowed for attention, the other members of Jack's team calling for the teapot to be passed to them. With a loud hoot, the man in possession obliged by sending it spinning towards a teammate, the pass executed across the front of an opposing player about to make a tackle.

Jack rolled painfully to his feet, his hands instinctively pressing the small of his back to knead away the dull ache that had not been improved by the collision with the coffee room's wooden floor. The pain was a nagging reminder of a youth spent in the gin palace hauling barrels. Years on campaign had done little to rid him of its constant presence, and now it felt like the devil himself was sitting on his shoulders jabbing a fiery trident into the small of his back. Yet still he managed to grin as he watched three members of his team rampage across the enormous room, the delicate china teapot thrown from one to the other as they swept towards the line of laughing officers who defended the far side.

'I say, old man, lend us a hand.' The man Jack had tackled lifted a hand in his direction.

Jack bent down to haul his victim to his feet, laughing at the exaggerated expression of pain on the man's face. 'Sorry about that.'

'No need to apologise, old man, all part of the game.' The man's mutton chops were in disarray, and he raised a hand to his face to smooth them back into place. 'It was a splendid tackle. Why, I thought I was going to make it.'

'You very nearly did.' Jack winced as his back twinged. 'What say we leave this game to those fools and go get ourselves a drink?'

'I think that is as fine a notion as I have ever heard.' The man groaned as he took his first steps. 'I am getting too old for such goings-on.' He smiled at Jack, then offered his hand. 'Augustus White.'

'Arthur Sloames.' Jack gave the false identity as he shook hands. It was a nod to the captain he had once served and whose untimely death had provided him with his first opportunity to become an impostor.

The two officers walked slowly from the field of play that had been cleared in the centre of the room. A great cheer went up from its far end as a vigorous tackle upended one of Jack's teammates.

'That's the spirit. Play up, Butterworth, play up!' Augustus roared his encouragement before taking a firm grip on Jack's elbow. 'Let's make ourselves scarce before that damn teapot comes back this way.'

Jack let himself be led. He was enjoying himself. The group of officers had welcomed him into their midst, not once bothering to interrogate him as to who he was. They had invited him to join their dinner, and the only question he had been asked had been an enquiry as to which position he preferred to play in the impromptu game of indoor rugby.

The two officers walked towards their coats, draped over the chairs that had been pushed to one side to make space for the rugby field. Augustus groaned theatrically as he pulled his over his shoulders.

'You tackle hard, old man. I expect I shall be bruised for a week.'

'Let me get you a drink to make amends.' Jack glanced across at his companion's uniform as he pulled on his own, noticing the bright yellow facings and the single crown embroidered on the collar. Augustus was a major in the 15th

Regiment of Foot, a regiment that Jack had not come across before.

'Now that is a capital notion.' Augustus finished doing up his buttons before raising a hand to usher Jack towards a corner of the room far from the raucous game of rugby.

The players had brought a phalanx of wine bottles into the room with them. Jack let Augustus select one whilst he picked out two clean glasses from a neatly arranged collection that had been put in place by the club's servants.

'Shall we sit down over there? I rather think I need a rest.' Augustus picked up a second bottle and motioned towards a seat close by.

Jack slumped into the club chair with relief. 'I am not sure I am cut out for indoor rugby.'

Augustus snorted as he poured the dark red wine. 'You and me both, old man.' He glanced up at Jack as he handed over a glass, then picked up his own and raised it in front of him. 'I propose a toast. Foolish games for foolish folk.'

Jack raised his own glass and chinked it against his companion's. 'I can drink to that.' He took a mouthful of the wine. It tasted better than gin.

Augustus placed his glass on the small table that sat between them, then slumped back in his chair. He lifted a hand and gestured at Jack's face. 'That's a nasty blighter of a scar.'

Jack resisted the urge to run his fingers across the raised welt of flesh on his cheek. 'Nature of the job.' He used a tone that he knew would divert Augustus's attention elsewhere.

'I apologise. I know one shouldn't mention these things. What with events in the Crimea, then those beastly affairs out in India, it's a wonder any of us are quite whole.'

Jack hid a scowl. He did not think the 15th had been

anywhere near the fighting in either conflict. 'So what brings an officer of the 15th to London?' He tried to set the conversation on a sounder footing. He was enjoying his freedom, and he wanted to know what was going on in the wider world.

'I serve with our 1st Battalion down at Portsmouth. We brought up a draft of men to Chatham. It seemed a waste to come all this way and not engage in a little diversion on the way back.' Augustus drained his glass before leaning forward to top them both up. 'If you will forgive me asking the same question, what's an officer from the Buffs doing here? I thought your mob was all overseas?'

Jack had chosen his borrowed regiment with care. The 3rd East Kents were known as the Buffs due to the colour of the facings on their uniform. The regiment had two battalions. One was stationed in the East Indies, the other in Malta. It made it unlikely that Jack would bump into any of its serving officers during the few hours that he passed dressed as one of their captains. He had stolen the uniform on his way back from the East, lifted from an officer's trunk that he had come across at Waterloo station.

'I'm on furlough.'

'You lucky bugger. How long?'

'A year.' Jack made sure he caught the major's eye. 'I was wounded at Delhi.'

'Enough said, old man.' Augustus sat back, his discomfort at being faced with a fighting officer obvious as he fidgeted under Jack's gaze. 'Is that where you got the . . .' He paused and used his glass to gesture at Jack's face.

Jack nodded before draining a large measure of his wine.

'I see.' Augustus wiped his hand across his mutton chops. 'It was a beastly affair, absolutely beastly. There were rumours back at the depot that we would be sent out as reinforcements.'

Jack sensed this would not have been to Major Augustus White's liking at all. 'It was hard fighting.' He could not resist tweaking his companion's tail. 'You have to give the pandies credit. They didn't cave in as easily as you might have been led to believe. They nearly had us at Badli-ki-Serai, and the assault on Delhi was a damned close-run thing.' He dropped the names, watching for a reaction.

'You were at both?'

'I was in Delhi when the first mutineers rode in. I was there when we kicked them out again.' Jack spoke in a deadpan tone, but he was struggling to hide a smile. Augustus was looking at him as if he were some kind of hero.

'My dear fellow, I cannot start—'

'No,' Jack cut him dead, 'I do not imagine that you can.'

A commotion from the far side of the room took his attention. He had enjoyed landing the barb, but for a reason he could not fathom, he sensed the arrival of danger.

Augustus was still talking. 'I read about the siege in the papers. What you fellows achieved, why, it was nothing short of miraculous. I have often said as much to my fellow officers back at the depot . . .'

Jack barely heard him. He was watching a group of newly arrived officers, who were picking their way through the debris caused by the rugby match. From their faces, it was clear they were not amused to find the usually dignified salon filled with roaring and sweaty officers treating the place with disdain.

'Those pandies, well, they deserved everything they got. The papers were full of their atrocities. I curse my luck daily that the 15th were not given a chance to pay the blackguards back for what they did . . .'

Jack paid no attention to Augustus's meaningless wittering. His eyes were riveted on the face of one of the officers as they arranged a circle of armchairs on the far edge of the temporary rugby pitch. It was a face that had no right to be there. He had last seen it in a dank alleyway a few days after the British expeditionary force had beaten the army of the Shah of Persia at the battle of Khoosh-ab. Jack had just committed a murder, the killing of an enemy spy the last act he had carried out on the orders of the man who had unravelled his identity.

There were over two dozen officers in the coffee room, with at least the same number of servants, yet for some reason Jack saw the officer turn to look straight in his direction. He found himself staring into the calm and knowing gaze of Major John Ballard, one of the army's finest intelligence officers, and one of the few people alive who knew who Jack Lark really was.

Chapter Nine

—◦•◦—

'I say. Do you mind if we leave?' Jack cut off Augustus's windy ramblings. He rose to his feet hastily, his knees catching against the table in front of his chair, nearly knocking over the half-drunk glasses of wine.

'Let's hold here a moment, old man. There's plenty of time for a little diversion later on. Let's drink these first.'

'Sorry, chum.' Jack was regretting the evening's consumption. The wine was making him slow. 'I've got to get out of here.'

Augustus half rose. 'I say, are you quite all right, old man? You look rather peaky.'

Jack paid him no heed. He had his eyes fixed on Ballard. The intelligence officer had not changed in the two years since Jack had last seen him. Thin as a rake, he still wore the dark blue uniform of the hussars and sported the same narrow moustache on an otherwise clean-shaven face. Jack was appalled to see him making his excuses to the rest of his group as he turned away from them.

'Shit.' He hesitated, unsure of what to do. For a moment he

considered brazening it out and holding to his story. But this
was Ballard. He had already seen through one of Jack's
charades, and that had been before they had spent months
together on campaign.

'I say, what's that, old man?' Augustus had heard the oath
and his face had creased into a scowl. 'I hardly think that is
appropriate language. This is a respectable establishment
and—'

'Sit down and shut the fuck up.' Jack snapped the order. He
was already moving away, his eyes searching for a way out.
He barely heard Augustus's reaction to the pithy command.
The game of rugby surged closer and he slipped back into the
fray.

'I'd take your jacket off if you are coming back out.' A hand
pushed at Jack as an officer rushed past, his face flushed with
sweat.

Jack kept moving, ignoring the players even as he was
buffeted by another officer, the game in full flow around him.
He kept his eyes on Ballard, who now stood staring at the space
next to Augustus that Jack had just vacated.

There was the sound of porcelain smashing, followed by a
great cheer. Jack ducked behind the press of bodies that had
piled up as the players charged into one enormous ruck. He
kept low, taking care only to straighten up as the players began
to stand around him. He stayed in the melee, enduring his
own share of back-slapping as the game broke up, the sweaty
officers around him barking with good humour.

Ballard was on the move. He approached the far side of the
crowd, his small frame nearly completely hidden by the beefier
bodies of the officers leaving the field of play to recover their
uniforms. His head turned briskly this way and that as he

searched the faces. To Jack's mind he looked like a sparrow who had found his way into a parliament of rooks.

Jack was fast running out of crowd. The players were dispersing quickly, their chatter loud as they relived their part in the game. He darted away, keeping close to a pair of officers walking off together. To his dismay, they stopped when they reached their discarded jackets. He could only stop with them, hoping against hope that Ballard would not spot him for a second time. He made a play of dusting down his own coat, and even attempted a hearty slap on one of the officer's backs before his sangfroid deserted him. He glanced back. Ballard was staring straight at him.

For the span of a single heartbeat he met the other man's gaze. Then he ran.

The club was busy. Jack rushed along the landing, caring nothing for the disapproving glares and hoarsely whispered rebukes sent his way.

'I say. Steady as she goes.' An officer in the dark green uniform of the Rifle Brigade snapped at him as he blundered past, the contents of a half-filled glass of claret slopping dangerously close to his uniform.

Jack broke free, then galloped down a quieter landing, skidding around a corner, and headed for the stairs. He thought he heard someone running after him, but it was not the time to turn and look. He made it to the top of the stairs and charged down, taking them three at a time, his breath already rasping in his lungs, his boots loud on the stone steps.

Faces lifted towards him as those in the lower hall looked up at the commotion. Jack leaped the last half-dozen steps, but his boots slipped on the polished marbled and he fell awkwardly, hitting the floor with his hip then sprawling forward, arms outstretched to break his fall. He came to a halt in an ignominious heap at the feet of the servant who took the officers' hats.

'Fucking hell.' He picked himself up painfully.

'Are you quite all right, sir?' The servant was trying to stifle a smile. 'Would you like me to retrieve your shako?'

Jack was in no mood for mockery. He pushed the servant away, using the poor man as leverage as he made for the door. Now that he was about to escape, he risked a glance back, a flicker of excitement at the madcap dash through the club firing in his gut.

The officers in the hall were staring at him like pigeons in a coop who had suddenly spotted an eagle sitting calmly amongst them. But Jack had no interest in their scowls and disapproving glares. His eyes were drawn upwards, to the landing on the first floor.

Ballard was leaning against the banister, his chest heaving with the exertion of the chase. But his eyes were sharp as he stared directly at Jack.

Jack stood there catching his breath. He was relieved to see Ballard far enough away to pose no threat. He waved.

He did not wait to see how Ballard would react.

The streets were dark when Jack left the public house. He had been sitting in a quiet corner drinking steadily, drowning the shock of seeing Ballard, his mind dwelling on the time when he had worked for the intelligence officer.

Ballard was a tie to his past, one that he had tried hard to leave behind him. Seeing the intelligence officer in the Army and Navy Club had caused his new world to collide with the old. He had served Ballard well and they had parted on reasonable terms, but he would not allow himself to be drawn back into the man's orbit. Only death and killing lay in that direction, and he had had his fill of both, just as he had had his fill of taking orders. He was his own man now. He would not go back to being the person he had once been.

He staggered out on to the street, gasping as the cold air hit him. He was half-cut, but alert enough to pause and peer into the darkness, wary of the shadows even in his befuddled state. He saw nothing ominous, so he resolved to walk. He was no more than quarter of a mile from the gin palace, and he felt sober enough to make it back more or less in one piece.

He pulled his uniform coat tight around him as he felt the first chill. The effects of the beer he had sunk made themselves felt as the heat of the public house was replaced by the cold night-time air, and he paused, taking firm hold on the wall of the nearest house to steady himself.

He caught a glimpse of a shadowy figure sliding past on the far side of the street. It was a warning, and he forced himself to stand straighter. He took a few tentative steps, assessing his state of drunkenness. To his satisfaction, he felt half-decent. The beer's presence was noticeable, but he was not about to topple over.

He stifled a belch and walked on. His officer's coatee flapped open, but he did not have the inclination to work the buttons back into their place. It was easy enough to amble along the centre of the street, which was pretty much empty this late. But he was not completely alone. Even in the gloom he could see a huddle of blankets in the doorway of a dressmaker's shop. It was not an uncommon sight on the streets near the gin palace. There were plenty of folk unable to find any better accommodation.

'Oi, mate, got a penny?' The voice came from deep within the mound.

Jack slowed, but did not stop. He was on the outskirts of the rookery, and even slightly the worse for wear he knew better than to make himself an easy target.

He was about to pass the vagrant by when he saw a familiar sight balanced on the macadam near what he presumed was the sleeping figure's head. It was an upturned army-issue Albert shako, the type that the red-coated soldiers had worn when they had invaded the Crimean peninsula in what would prove to be a long and wearing campaign to capture the Russian naval port of Sevastopol.

'Got a penny, mate?' the vagrant called out for a second time. The voice was thick with phlegm. Jack heard the man's throat gurgle as he noisily sucked down the contents of his nose.

'What regiment?'

The blankets stirred. A corner was pulled back and Jack caught the glimmer of a single eye glaring up at him. 'Give me a shilling, mate, and I'll give you my whole fucking life story.'

Jack was finding it hard to stand still. He contemplated the eye, then fumbled in his coat. He did not carry much money with him – he was not that foolish – and the night's drinking had cleared out most of his pocket book, but he still had a handful of coins, which he pulled out and deposited in the man's shako.

'I've paid my dues.' He fixed his gaze on the single eye. 'Answer my question. What regiment?' He delivered the command with some of the snap of an officer.

'The 7th.' The reply was given grudgingly. A little more of the blanket was pulled back to reveal a heavily bearded face. It was hard to see much in the gloom, but Jack got the impression that the man was looking at him with something other than annoyance.

'I know the 7th. I was with the King's Royal Fusiliers at the Alma.'

Either the face betrayed nothing, or else Jack missed it.

'I was at the Alma.' The man spoke the words as if saying them for the first time in a long while. 'We saved your sorry arses.'

Jack was sobering fast as he remembered leading a company of redcoats in the assault on the Russian redoubt on the far side of the Alma river. The King's Royal Fusiliers had led the way, whilst the other regiments in its division, including the 7th Fusiliers, had been drawn into vicious fights with enormous Russian columns sent to throw the British division back over the river.

It had been his first taste of battle. He had done little save go forward with his stolen company and take his place in the line when it finally stormed the redoubt. They had lost many men in the long assault, with dozens struck down by the Russian artillerymen. He shivered as he remembered what it had been like to walk up that slope on that bloody day so many years before.

'It was a hard fight.' The man Jack had disturbed broke the silence.

Jack did not know how long he had stood there without speaking. He forced the memory back into its cage. 'What happened to you?'

'I got hit. Invalided out. I was one of the lucky ones.'

'You came out of Scutari?' The main British hospital had become a byword for the worst conditions of filth and squalor, thanks to the reports sent to the British press by the reporter William Russell. Jack had found himself there after the battle. Somehow he had recovered, his body healing well enough to let him find a way out.

'Fucking shithole that was.' The man pulled the blanket back over his face. There was the sound of footsteps on the street behind them, but Jack stayed where he was. He looked down at the heap of blankets for a long while. He did not know if the man knew he was still there, but it was clear that their conversation, if it could be called that, was over.

It was hard not to picture himself in the man's place. It was the fate of so many soldiers, the army quick to cast out any who could no longer serve the colours. He did not know how he had survived for as long as he had. He had taken enough wounds along the way, but never one serious enough to leave him nothing more than a cripple dumped on the street and left to fend for himself.

He sighed, then resumed his weary walk back to the ginny. There was nothing more he could do for the ex-soldier. The few pennies would have to suffice.

The man hidden under the blankets waited for Jack to get a few dozen yards away before he rose slowly to his feet, casting away the filthy coverings with a sneer of distaste. It took but a second to ease the seventeen-inch bayonet from the sheath on his belt as he began to walk, his movements awkward after so long lying on the cold macadam.

He spat, then whistled once, the sound sharp in the quiet. He saw a figure step out of the shadows on the far side of the street. There were no gas lamps in this part of town, but there was sufficient moonlight for the man – who had not lied about his days in the 7th Fusiliers – to see the firm nod of the head as the identification was confirmed.

The old soldier started to move quicker, the sharpened bayonet held low in his right hand. A second and then a third man joined him, their footsteps sounding quick and sharp. The figure who had made the identification slid back into the shadows as the trio he had hired broke into a run, their paths converging on the back of the man dressed in the uniform of a British army captain.

Chapter Ten

———◦•◉•◦———

*J*ack froze when he heard the silence broken by the staccato rhythm of boots hitting the ground in unison. The evening of drinking had dulled his senses, but the sudden flare of danger still registered in his fuddled mind. He was running before he had any idea of a plan. His officer's coatee billowed around him as he pumped his legs, forcing the pace.

'Get him!'

The sound of the boots picking up speed reached his ears as he pounded past a draper's wagon left empty outside its owner's shop. He darted behind it, then doubled back, reaching out to take a firm hold on the wagon's side as he changed direction then hurtled up the narrow gap between the vehicle and the wall of the shop.

He saw them then. He was no longer running away but towards the men who were chasing him, and there was time enough to make out the three dark figures spread wide across the street. The one directly in his path skidded to a halt as his quarry suddenly turned and ran straight at him. Jack saw the man set himself, the glint of a weapon held low at his right side. There was no time to plan, or to give his other two pursuers a moment's thought. He just rushed at the man in his path, his boots hammering hard on the macadam.

The man lunged as Jack came at him. It was a vicious blow, the bayonet held in his right hand staying low as he punched it towards Jack's gut. But Jack saw it coming. He jumped, then lashed out with his boot, catching the underside of the bayonet and kicking it skyward. His attacker's arm was thrown backwards with such force that the man was knocked on to his backside.

Off balance, but still moving fast, Jack collided with the man who had thought to spill his guts on to the quiet back street. He let his weight go and fell hard, making sure his body came crashing down on top of his attacker, his knees planted firmly on the other man's chest, ruthlessly crushing his ribs and driving the breath from his body.

There was no time to stay and fight. Jack's hands clawed at the ground, his palms slipping across the macadam, his feet lashing out as he used the man's body for purchase. He felt his right boot catch the fallen body in the face, then he was up and running, his arms starting to pump hard, the other two pursuers already on his tail.

He felt a moment's joy as he galloped away from his assailants. There was madness in the uneven fight, a delight in having already knocked down one of the men who had come for him. He did not stop to wonder who they worked for, or why he had been singled out. He had known that the moment he heard the footsteps chasing after him.

He hurtled around a corner, taking the dangerous race into a narrower street. It led away from the palace, but he had no intention of heading back there until he was alone. He pounded on, ignoring the burn in his chest. The narrow street turned left, then right, and then left again before running behind a newly constructed warehouse not far from the sugar factory. It was near pitch black behind the tall brick building. He darted into an alleyway that led along the back of a row of houses and stopped, holding his breath, forcing his body to obey even though he wanted nothing more than to bend double and suck down huge draughts of air to ease the pain in his tortured lungs.

As the first pursuer stormed past, panting heavily, Jack stepped out of his hiding place and directly into the path of the second, slower man. There was just enough moonlight to let him see the shock on the man's face before he thrust his elbow forward into his throat. The pursuer's momentum drove him on even as his hobnailed boots skidded in a futile attempt to stop, and he went down hard, his legs taken from beneath him as the blow snapped his upper body backwards.

Jack skipped to one side to avoid the man's flailing arms and legs. His pursuer lay on the cobbles, his hands lifted to cradle the ruin of his throat, which was making nasty choking, sobbing sounds as he tried to breathe.

Jack's legs felt wobbly, but he forced them to pick up the pace as he sprinted back the way he had come. He heard the commotion as the last ambusher turned and ran back past the man with the broken throat, who was thrashing wildly and gargling for attention.

He was no more than ten yards from the end of the narrow street when a fourth figure moved into his path. Even in the darkness there was no mistaking the pork pie hat that was pulled low over a face contorted with anger. Nor was it hard for Jack to recognise the barrel of the Colt revolver held ready to fire and aimed at his head.

Mr Shaw had come to finish the job.

'Well met, Jack Lark.' Shaw stepped forward, the gun lifting as Jack floundered to a halt just five yards from its muzzle. 'Didn't I say we would meet again?'

Jack forced himself to stand tall. His lungs burned, but he would not give Shaw the satisfaction of seeing any weakness. He heard movement behind him as the last of his pursuers finally lumbered into place.

'That was a pitiful display, Bird, and not at all what you promised.' Shaw's tone was glacial.

'I'm right sorry, Mr Shaw, sir, that I am. But this here heathen cove didn't fight fair.'

Jack recognised the voice. It belonged to the man he had supposed to be a vagrant. He glanced over his shoulder and took in the heavily bearded face, and the moonlight glinting off the bayonet held in his ambusher's hand.

'Of course he don't fight fair, Bird.' Shaw's voice was laced with derision. 'No sane man does.' He cackled, clearly well pleased with how his hand had played out.

'I'll stick him now, Mr Shaw, if it pleases you.' Bird, anxious to appease his paymaster, stepped forward.

Jack's shoulder blades twitched as he imagined the cold steel sliding into his flesh. He brought his breathing under control and tried to think of a way out. He was trapped like an eel in a barrel waiting for the cold touch of the fishmonger's knife.

'No, no, no.' Shaw shook his head and kept his eyes fixed on Jack. 'Where is the fun in that? I'm of a mind to make our mutual friend here pay a price for what he did to me.'

He lifted his left hand, rotating it slowly so that Jack's eye was drawn towards it. The hand was twisted, with three of the fingers held at impossibly stiff angles. Jack remembered the fight in the palace, and the feel of bones breaking under the heel of his army-issue boot.

'You see that, don't you, my old chum? It ain't a pretty sight and it hurts like a bastard.'

Shaw stalked forward, keeping the revolver aimed at Jack's head.

'Give me your hand, Jack.' His voice was deadpan. 'Now, if you please.'

The revolver lifted, the barrel inched forward so that it touched Jack's forehead.

'Give me your fucking hand,' hissed Shaw, jerking the gun so that the point of the barrel ground into Jack's flesh.

Jack was powerless. He lifted his left hand, moving it slowly and carefully so as not to startle the man who held his life at the tip of his trigger finger.

Shaw gave another cackle. He took Jack's hand, his touch cold, and caressed it, sliding his twisted fingers up and down.

'You feel that? You feel the broken bones.' The hand stopped moving. Clumsily it forced Jack's ring finger into an awkward grip. 'You know how much they hurt, Jack? Every fucking minute of every fucking day they remind me of what you did.'

Shaw's face twitched and went still. He looked down at his hand gripping Jack's. Then he gave it an almighty twist.

Jack's trapped finger snapped like a dry twig caught under a heavy boot. He howled then, the sound escaping his lips as a fiery poker of pain lanced through him.

'Keep fucking still!' Shaw bellowed the order. Jack had

flinched as his finger was broken, but Shaw had been ready for it, and now he pressed the gun forward, breaking the skin on Jack's forehead.

'Oh, that hurts, doesn't it, chum? Fucking burns, doesn't it just?' Shaw shifted his hand, taking Jack's middle finger in the same clumsy grip. 'You've got ten fucking fingers and I am going to break every single fucking one.' He cackled with delight at the horror he saw reflected in Jack's eyes.

Jack bit hard on his tongue as Shaw adjusted his grip, the bones of his broken finger grating under the unwieldy touch. He could not allow Shaw to carry on. He closed his eyes, summoning the will to attack. He felt the press of the revolver on the broken skin above his eye, and sensed the razor-sharp tip of Bird's bayonet held close to his kidneys.

He tensed, then took a final breath.

'What's going on there?'

The shout came so suddenly that Jack nearly jerked backwards into the bayonet.

'You, sir. Let that man go free.'

Jack froze. He held every muscle still. He felt Shaw's hand twitch, then let go of his.

'Move yourself.' A second voice joined the first and a heavy-set figure loomed into Jack's line of sight, a Colt revolver held in a great paw of a hand. He caught a glimpse of dark tweed, and a pugnacious and scarred face underneath a deerstalker hat. 'You too, chum.' The revolver twitched so that it pointed over Jack's shoulder. 'And I'd put that fucking poker away if you know what's good for you.'

Jack could scarcely credit who was in front of him. He knew that if he possessed an ounce of sense, he would turn and run right at that moment. Risking a bullet in the back was nothing when compared to what he knew would happen if he stayed where he was.

'Wise fellow.' The man in the deerstalker grinned at Bird. It was not a pleasant expression. 'Move back, slowly now.' He turned to Shaw. 'Give me that.' A second great paw rose up to close around Shaw's own revolver. 'Right dangerous these things are. What say I look after this, keep it safe like?'

The man possessed an aura of calm, as if interceding in torture was an everyday event. Knowing him as Jack did, that was actually more than likely. Shaw backed away, glaring at the newcomer who had curtailed his enjoyment, stepping carefully past Jack until he stood next to a shaking Bird.

Only then did the man in the deerstalker turn to wink at Jack. 'Evening, Jack. Bet you didn't expect to see me.'

Jack was saved from forming a reply as the man who had first intervened strode into view.

'Good work, Palmer.' Major John Ballard of the army's intelligence department came to stand at Jack's side. 'Would you be so kind as to take these two fellows away? Make sure they understand what will happen to them if we see them again. Oh, and have them pick up that poor chap lying down over there. I don't think he is so very badly hurt, but we really should not leave him lying in such a place as this.'

'Yes, sir.' Palmer nodded to show he understood the order. 'Very well, gentlemen, walk this way if you please.' He used his revolver to gesture down the street away from Jack. 'I wouldn't stop if I were you. These new Colts are temperamental sons of bitches. Why, they have been known to go off just like that.'

Palmer ushered his charges away, walking two yards behind them, with both revolvers held ready to fire. Jack watched them depart. Only when he saw them pause to collect their half-suffocated ally did he turn to face the man who had come to his rescue.

'I didn't expect to bump into you.' He delivered the line with as much sangfroid as he could summon.

'Ha!' Ballard smiled thinly as he watched Palmer moving away, the fingers of his right hand stroking his moustache. Finally he looked at Jack, as if noticing him for the first time. 'I'll wager you thought you had given me the slip with those antics of yours back at the club.' His blue eyes were icy cold. 'It is good to see you, Jack.'

'I wish I could say the same.' Jack found he was smiling despite his words. The man known as the Devil had come back into his life and he knew with utter certainty that it would no longer be the same. He felt the hand of fate take hold around his soul. Ballard had saved him, but he would not have done so without first calculating what Jack could do for him.

He laughed aloud at the notion, earning him his first glare from his former master. Ballard must have need of his services. Jack did not think he would be bored any longer.

Chapter Eleven

'Ouch! That bloody hurts.'

'I am doing the best I can,' Ballard snapped back as he bound the broken finger on Jack's left hand to its neighbour with a length of twine he had found on the ground.

'Well take care. Hell's teeth,' Jack hissed as Ballard tugged his knot tight. 'I bet you are bloody enjoying yourself.'

'Oh absolutely. There is nothing I like better than being dragged away from a good dinner to chase a miscreant in the dark. There, that will have to suffice for the moment.' Ballard stepped away, clearly pleased with his handiwork.

'A miscreant?' Jack lifted his hand to study the temporary binding. It was as neat and precise as he had expected. Ballard did not have it in him to do anything in an untidy fashion. 'Is that what I am?'

'I am being kind.' Ballard smiled.

Jack did his best not to grimace at the expression that sat so badly on Ballard's face. The last two years had passed swiftly, and it did not seem so long since Jack had left him in a dark alley, the body of the man he had just murdered at

Ballard's command lying on the ground in front of him.

'You look awful, Jack.' Ballard had been giving Jack's face the same level of scrutiny. 'Clearly life has not been agreeing with you.'

Jack bristled. He knew Ballard had seen the scar on his cheek, the legacy of a mutineer's sword. 'I was at Delhi.'

'Ah.' Ballard understood. 'I see.'

'Where were you?' Jack fired the question, unable to withhold the accusatory tone.

'Bombay. I have only just returned to these shores. I have some pressing family matters to attend to.'

'I see.' There had been no fighting in Bombay. Ballard would have been spared from witnessing the full horror of the mutiny.

Ballard's eyes narrowed, but the uncomfortable conversation was ended by the sound of footsteps coming towards them. Both men turned and saw the hefty form of Palmer, Ballard's bodyguard, enforcer and general ne'er-do-well walking towards them.

'Did you deal with them?' Ballard spoke first.

Palmer nodded, then looked down as he carefully replaced his revolver into the waistband wrapped around his not inconsiderable middle. He still held the one he had taken from Shaw.

'What did you do to them?' Jack fired off a question of his own. He knew Palmer.

'I let them go.'

'You what?' Jack did not believe the answer.

'Oh, they know not to bother you again.' Palmer was smug.

Jack felt a rush of fear. It raced through him, every nerve jangling. 'You're a fucking idiot. Men like Shaw don't give a shit for a warning. Now get out of my way before I knock you down.' His fear was taking hold. He knew what Shaw would do the moment he was free.

'Now, Jack. I am sure—'

Jack cut Ballard off by using both hands to shove Palmer out of his way. He was running before the larger man could react.

He knew where Shaw would go. He just hoped he would not be too late.

Jack's boots pounded into the macadam, the sound echoing off the silent houses that lined the street. The night dwellers who roamed the rookery stayed in the shadows, not one willing to risk taking down the lean-faced villain who charged through the night.

Jack forced himself to think of nothing other than his footing. The fear was bright, but he held it close, refusing to let it dominate him. He ran hard, ignoring the pain in his hand and the burning in his chest. He had gone soft, the weeks he had spent travelling and working in the gin palace leaving him short of breath, and with limbs that trembled with the effort of keeping him upright. But he had long mastered his body, his mind refusing to listen to its complaints.

The ground passed swiftly under his boots as he hurtled along, thumping out the yards as he ran through streets he had known since he was a boy. They were as familiar as his own flesh, and he thought only of his destination, his path taken without hesitation.

He heard the commotion long before he saw it. The rookery was usually quiet at night, its wiser denizens content to sit behind locked and barred doors, the streets left to the night villains who owned the darkened alleyways and hidden corners where they plied their trade. But there were a few things that could entice the good citizens from their homes. A fight would do it, or perhaps a ruckus created by brawling whores.

Or a fire.

The crowd was dense, the men, women and children drawn to the spectacle by the promise of drama. It was a lure few could resist, even though the first pickpockets would already be cutting the purses of the unwary and inattentive.

'Let me through!' Jack shouted to be heard. The onlookers were noisy, whoops of excitement greeting a flash of flames as the roof of the palace went up with a great whoosh. 'Let me through.'

He worked through the crowd, using his elbows freely to force a passage. Many of the watchers recognised him, his weeks behind the palace's counter earning him a place amongst the rookeries better-known coves.

'Let him through! Let Lark through.' The call changed, the instruction delivered with glee as one of the night's prime performers pushed on to the stage.

Jack wormed his way forward. The crowd made it easy then, parting for him and letting him pass as if he were a modern Moses. He staggered as he emerged from their midst, his footing failing him at the last.

He felt the heat on his face. He recovered his balance, but still he floundered, his urgent pace faltering as he confronted the very sight he had feared.

'Where's Maggie?' He whirled around to grab the closest person, a man of ancient vintage he recognised well enough. 'Where is she?'

The man recoiled from the venom in Jack's voice. He lifted a wavering arm, a single finger pointing towards the inferno.

Jack felt his strength flag as he turned to face the flames. They daunted him as they roared and surged through the building. He felt the fear then, the terror of what he must do. The blaze mocked him, a gout of fire choosing that moment to break through the slates on the roof and fountain into the sky, the great column greeted with the coos and cries of a crowd revelling in their entertainment.

'Jack! Jack!'

A surge of relief rushed through him. It was so strong that he felt his balance totter. It was Mary. Not all was lost.

'He's in there! He's in there!'

The fear returned with a vengeance. Mary ran at him, her face streaked with the black touch of smoke. Her skirt was singed, the hem torn so that it flapped around her calves.

'My Billy! He's in there!' She threw herself at him, fingers like claws as she pulled at him.

Still he hesitated. He knew what she wanted, what she was begging him to do. Yet his well of courage had run dry.

Mary dragged him forward, moving him towards the heat that was like a solid wall in front of him. 'My boy! My boy!'

Voices in the crowd wailed as they heard the desperate cry. There were few in the rookery who would not react to the threat to a child, if only to add to the drama, and to the delicious horror of the treat they were watching with such rapt fascination.

'Jack!'

He saw her properly then. She was not his Mary. She had not been for years. She was old, the soot stuck in the cracks and crevices time had wrought on her skin. And she was terrified. More terrified than any person he had ever seen. Not even on the worst battlefield, or in the bitter street fighting in the narrow alleys of Delhi, had he seen such abject horror.

He moved then. Her eyes had shamed him, her fear for her son more than he could bear. He took the first steps towards the flames, summoning the courage he would need.

The great window shattered. Ten thousand shards of glass exploded outwards, the glass submitting to the power of the flames that raged within. The crowd roared, a sudden flare of panic replaced with a cheer that only such wanton destruction could inspire.

It was the last sound he heard before he ran into the flames.

Chapter Twelve

---•◆•---

The heat hit Jack hard. It slammed against him, driving him backwards, stopping his charge as surely as if he had run into a brick wall. He lifted his hands, flinching from its power, his boots skidding to a halt amidst the shards of glass littering the ground.

Inside, the fire raged, the main room well ablaze. Flames licked across the ceiling, great fingers of red and yellow moving with a speed that he could barely track. Yet he saw a path, a few yards of floorboards not yet engulfed.

It would be the last time he hesitated.

He ran at the open window, his hands lifted in front of him as if they could ward off the flames. He jumped, bounding over the windowsill, his boots catching at vicious shards of glass that stood upright like so many bayonets. Then he was through. Bright white flashes of pain seared across his skin as the flames licked him, their fiery tendrils sending up sparks as they lashed around his boots. He went forward, trying to find a path, his eyes in agony as the flames burned them dry. He could feel the raw power of the fire, every inch of him crying out in revulsion as it touched him, but he saw there was a gap, a channel through the heart of the flames, and he took it even as his boots began to smoke and burn.

The door to the back room was closed. Flames licked around its edges, the frame well alight. He kicked it open without a thought. It crashed on to its hinges and a great black cloud of smoke rushed out to smother him. He staggered, choking, the soot and smoke filling his mouth so that he gagged on the fumes. He could see almost nothing. Yet the flames were thinner to his front, so he went forward, his back bent as if he walked into the teeth of a gale.

His boots caught on something lying just inside the door. He nearly fell, but saved himself by grabbing at the door frame. He screamed then, the pain lancing into his palm as flames licked across his hand. With his flesh on fire, he could not hold on. His balance failed the instant he let go, and he fell to his knees, landing on a body.

The horror stuck in his throat. He could see nearly nothing, so he reached down, his good hand acting faster than he could think, the need to know overriding the fear at what his questing fingers might discover.

His hand ran over the body. It was a man, not a woman or a boy. He knew who it was immediately. There was no time to think, or to feel grief for the Prussian he had employed to protect his mother's palace. There was just the relief, the sudden guilty stab of joy that the body belonged to a near stranger, to a man who meant nothing to him.

He got to his feet, clumsy in the dark, and clambered awkwardly over the body, his right hand useless and burned. Yet he knew where he was and he stumbled forward, his damaged left hand with its broken finger reaching for the table he knew would be to his front.

'Ma!' He screamed the word, the smoke burning his throat the moment his mouth opened. 'Ma!' He cared nothing for the pain, and he called again even as the smog choked him.

'Jack!'

He barely heard her at first. Flames flickered across the ceiling, scorching and burning. With a great roar a huge piece fell, a pulsing mass of flames that thundered down, sealing off the door that led to the back yard.

'Ma!' He moved, seeing nothing, groping in the darkness. His boot thumped against wood, fallen plates and glasses crunching underneath his smouldering soles. Then he saw her, lying on the floor under the table. She was curled into a ball, her body wrapped around something that he could not see. It hurt him to see her so, helpless and vulnerable, her pride meaning nothing against the fire that he had started as surely as if he had lit the match himself.

It took him no time to get to her. He reached for her, his only thought to pull her to safety. But she swatted him away with her arm, the gesture awkward and feeble.

'Take him!'

For the first time he saw what it was his mother was curled around. It was Mary's boy, and he was either dead or dying, the smoke as effective a killer as a cannon loaded with canister. She pushed the small body towards him.

There was no time to think. Another great wave of flame engulfed the ceiling, filling the room with still more choking smoke. Jack took hold of the boy.

'Go!' From somewhere his mother found breath. She screamed at him, urging him away. 'Get out!'

He scrabbled backwards, dragging the boy with him. He

couldn't breathe, and his chest was burning, as if it too were on fire. Somehow he got to his feet, his legs shaking with the effort. The boy weighed little, but still he staggered, tottering away from his mother like some ancient crone.

He took no more than a single step before he turned. The desire to run was fierce, the need to suck in the clean night air nearly more than he could resist. But he would not leave her. Not for a second time.

'Come on!' He spat out the words as he balanced the boy's weight in his arms. He could not beckon to her, could not summon her to him. He could do nothing but stand there, the still body of the boy held tight, his head bowed as he struggled to see her through the blackness.

'Get out!'

Her last words came as a screech. He barely made them out before there was a great groan from the ceiling. It fell in one enormous burning mass, the flames searing through the dense cloud of smoke, sparks thrown up in a wicked explosion. It engulfed her, burying her beneath the inferno, her final command cut off.

Jack forced himself to move away. There was no thought in his mind save the desire to live. It lent him the strength to place one foot after the other, his lungs burning as his throat closed completely. He refused to die, to let himself fall. It would not end here.

He felt a strong hand pulling at his shoulder. He staggered, not understanding. Somehow he kept his footing as he was dragged through the doorway, his awkward burden threatening to fall at any moment.

In the light of the flames, he saw that it was Palmer who had followed him into the fire. The larger man took him by the arm and hauled him on, both of them crouching as the flames rushed around them. Palmer got them moving quicker, and they stumbled away, ducking and twisting through the flames. When they reached the window, Palmer turned, half lifting, half pulling Jack and the boy he carried over the sill and out.

Jack's legs gave way and he sprawled to the ground, the boy dumped without ceremony amidst the shards of glass. He lay there, the pain surging through him, until he could bear it no more. He jackknifed, his legs curling into his stomach as he retched and coughed in a fit that refused to end. It went on and on, his body fighting to breathe as he spewed filthy black muck on to the ground.

No one came to his aid. He could hear the crowd, their shouts and cries; he sensed people around him, boots clattering past as someone ran for the boy he had dropped. The fit went on, the coughs racking him. He was powerless against them, his strength spent, and he lay there covered in filth as he puked out the contents of his stomach.

'Drink this.'

Something was pressed to his lips. Liquid poured into his open mouth, filling it, scouring away the bile. He coughed, then spluttered, then puked again on to the boots of the man holding the bottle to his face. More liquid came, filling his mouth, the ginger beer grabbed from a street seller overwhelming his senses. Somehow he swallowed, choking down the vile crud that was suffocating him. He opened his mouth, desperate for more, and snatched the bottle, gulping down the liquid it contained with the desperation of a starving newborn. Then he collapsed, his face hitting the ground.

He lay there then, his breath coming in painful shallow gasps. The macadam was blissfully cool on his cheek, and he felt the first chill of the night air seep into his scorched body. He had nothing left, and he went still, his eyes shut against the pain.

He had no idea how long he lay there before they came for him. Strong hands turned him on to his back, then eased him into a sitting position. His head lolled forward, but he forced himself to look up. It hurt, his eyes two orbs of pain, but he recognised the face that was in front of him.

Ballard rocked back on his haunches. 'Are you alive, then?'

'No.' The single word was followed by another bout of coughing.

Ballard shook his head. 'I thought you were dead.'

Jack did not try to speak. He just looked at Ballard. The officer's face was streaked with soot, his pristine uniform filthy.

'Here, drink some more of this.' Ballard held another glass bottle to Jack's lips.

He drank gratefully. Only when the bottle was drained did he stop. For the first time he noticed the flap of skin hanging from the palm of his right hand, which was covered with grotesque yellow blisters.

'The boy?' The words hurt him. But he had to know.

'He lives, Jack. The boy lives. You saved him.'

Jack shook his head in denial. 'No. It's all my fault.' The drink was reviving him. From somewhere he summoned the will to do more than lie on the road. He reached awkwardly with his left hand, using Ballard's arm to help lever himself to his feet. His head swam and his vision greyed, but somehow he stayed there, his fingers clasped firmly on the sleeve of Ballard's jacket.

The crowd cooed as they saw him rise. He could not tell if it was in approval or disappointment, but he did not care. He thought only of the small body lying no more than a yard away, and the woman who sat beside it.

'Mary?' He called to her, the words coming out as little more than a croak.

She turned at her name, staring at him as if he were a stranger, just a man from the crowd drawn like an oversized moth to the flames. Then her eyes narrowed and she looked away. But there had been enough time for him to see the loathing in the flat gaze.

Chapter Thirteen

———•◆•———

Jack stared at the wreckage. It was no longer smoking, the persistence of the constant thin rain that had arrived in the small hours of the morning enough to dampen the last signs of the blaze that had destroyed the palace. The scorched timbers mocked him, the tumbled-down walls all that was left of his mother's pride. There was little else left standing, the fire raging uncontrolled until the rain had come. The gaudy splendour of the palace had been consumed by the inferno that not one soul doubted was no accident.

Her body was gone, as was that of the Prussian, Schmitt. Jack had not spared himself the sight. He had stood with the rest of the onlookers as the husks had been dragged out, the twin lumps of twisted charcoal bearing no resemblance to the people they had been only the previous day. He had not intervened as they were taken away. His final glimpse of the woman who had given him life was a singed and blackened claw protruding from underneath the hemp sack that had been used to hide the hideous sight of her corpse from the dozens of children drawn to the wreckage.

The crowd had melted away now that the drama was long finished. Even the most persistent of the street sellers had packed up and gone, the opportunity to make a penny or two from working the crowd now past. Ballard and Palmer had left with them. They had spoken to Jack, he knew that, but their words were forgotten. He did not know where they had gone, or if they would return.

He heard the footsteps of someone coming to stand beside him. He had been left alone, the dispersing crowd steering a wide path around the man in the tattered officer's scarlet. One kind soul, a woman he recognised as a regular of the palace, had come to him and bound strips of cloth around his raw and blistered right hand. She had departed, but still he did not move; he simply stood and stared, his mind empty of every thought except one.

'You need to come away.' Mary spoke with a voice devoid of compassion. 'You're doing nothing standing there.'

Jack did not acknowledge her presence. He continued his lonely vigil, his eyes tracing a path over the destruction.

'You should be doing something. Not standing here in the rain.'

Jack could find nothing to say. He held his emotions close, already starting the process of burying them away.

'You killed her. Near killed my boy, too.'

'It's my fault.' The words hurt him. They were the first he had said for an age, and they tore through the ruined lining of his throat like razor blades.

'Of course it's your fault. I told you . . .' Mary's voice wavered, but her eyes blazed with a barely controlled anger. 'I told you what would happen. But that didn't stop you, because you knew better. You, with your fucking red coat, and your sword, and your bloody toy gun. You, the fucking war hero, knew better than me, a washed-up doxy with a bastard boy.' Her hand rose, a single finger pointing towards the smouldering rubble. 'You take a good long look at that. You see what you brought here. What you did.'

'I know.' Jack did not hide from the accusation. He told himself it meant nothing, the price that others had paid for his decisions just another notch alongside the hundreds already cut deep into his soul.

'I said you were a cold bastard, Jack Lark. Your own mother dead and you don't even shed a single damn tear.' Mary's lips twisted as she spoke, as if she were chewing on something foul.

Jack stayed silent. He knew death. They stood there side by side in the rain.

'You killed your own mother.' Mary broke the silence. 'The one person in this world who loved you, and you killed her.'

Jack did not reply, but the words etched themselves deep in his soul. His mother had done her duty, had done the right thing by him. Hers had been a tough love; a love that was delivered with smacks and cuffs around the ear as much as with anything more caring. But she *had* loved him. It was why he had come back, and he had seen it again every day since he had returned. At least, he thought he had.

The grief settled. He stored it away, locking it up with the rest, his mind building the barriers around it that would keep it shackled and hidden. It would stay there, festering in the darkness, never forgotten, but at least constrained.

'What are you going to do?' Mary pulled at his arm, making him look at her. 'Where will you go?'

Jack met her gaze. 'I'm going to find him.'

'Him? Shaw?' Mary's hand dropped to her side. 'It's over, Jack. He won. Look over there if you don't believe it.'

Jack shrugged. He tasted the desire for revenge. It was flavoured with smoke, and with burning.

Mary's gaze did not leave his face. 'I have to get back.'

'Where's Billy?'

'Maud took us in.'

Jack remembered that Maud was the woman who had bandaged his hand. She lived opposite the ginny, coming in a dozen times a day. His mother had sometimes let her help tidy up, even though the old lady was past doing anything useful for more than a few minutes at a stretch.

'We can't stay there,' Mary continued. 'The old dear hasn't got two farthings. I need to find us a place, thanks to you.'

Jack shook his head, wincing in pain as he did so. 'I'll take care of you.'

'Like you did before?' The words came laced with scorn.

Jack could not meet her gaze. 'I'll see you right.'

'You will.' It was a statement, not a question.

Jack felt the exhaustion then. The need to find a place to rest was making itself known in every battered fibre of his being. He wanted to hide away, to bury himself somewhere until he could breathe without such agony.

'I'm going back to my boy. I'll wait for you to send for us. Like it or not, we are your responsibility now. You threw away everything we had, so you are going to make it right. You have to.'

Jack understood the anger behind her words. Yet he heard something else. He heard fear. Mary had lost her employment and her home. In the rookeries, that was enough to start a decline that would end on the streets. Without money, life became unsustainable. If she could not find work, then the only option was the living death of the poorhouse. Her child would be taken from her, severing the tie between them for life. Mary's world had been shattered by the events of that evening; events that Jack had set in motion the minute he had taken his first step over the threshold of the palace all those weeks before.

'I'll do what is right.' He gave the promise. He saw her chin lift, her battered, sorry pride still there.

'You had better.' She spoke firmly. There was no trace of grief, no hint of the approach of tears. Her words were as hard as iron.

He saw her head turn as someone approached them, the first to dare to do so. It was Palmer, his deerstalker held in front of his belly. His thick tweeds were covered with black smoke marks, but his face had been recently cleaned, although inky streaks remained behind his ears and under his chin.

'Good evening, love.' The large man addressed himself to Mary. 'Is your boy recovering?'

'He is,' Mary replied with surprising politeness. 'Thank you for what you did.'

'It was nothing.'

Jack scowled. He saw Palmer look at the ground as he spoke to Mary. The older man appeared uncomfortable.

Mary smiled. 'You saved him. I owe you my son's life.'

'I bloody saved him.' Jack spat out the words, even though they hurt like the very devil.

'You bloody put him there.' Mary turned on him, her thin smile twisting to a sneer.

'It's not Jack's fault, love.'

It surprised Jack that Palmer would speak up for him. He tried to read the man's expression. Palmer's features showed the wear of his years. His broad nose had clearly been broken a number of times. The rest of the face was fleshy and covered with fine pockmarks, the legacy of some childhood illness. Jack had never seen him look anything other than composed, no matter the situation. Yet now he seemed as awkward as a boy asking to hold a whore's tits for the first time.

'It bloody well is his fault.' The sharpness returned to Mary's tongue. 'I warned him what would happen, but he is too bottle-head stupid to listen. Now his own mother is dead, and her blood is on his hands as surely as if he had cut her throat himself.'

Palmer winced at the tirade. He did not argue his point and turned instead to face Jack. 'The major told me to tell you that he has found you lodgings.' He dipped his head as he looked at Mary. 'For you too, love, and your lad. I am to take you there.'

'Now?'

'Now. It's not far.' Palmer addressed himself to Mary. 'You want me to help with the boy?'

Mary nodded. 'He's not got the strength. Not yet. You'll have to carry him.'

'All right.' Palmer was unconcerned.

'Is this place clean?' Mary asked, a hint of uncertainty in her voice.

'It's clean enough.'

'I'll go get him ready.' She flicked a finger in Jack's direction. 'That useless loaf can show you where we are.' She did not bother to look at him, but lifted her tattered skirt and walked quickly away to prepare her son for the move.

'She doesn't like you very much.' Palmer made the observation when Mary was far enough away not to hear him.

'No. Not any more.'

'Pity. She's a tidy one.'

Jack had no interest in Palmer's opinion. 'You need to find him.'

'Who's that then?'

'The man who did this. The man you let go.'

Palmer barked with laughter. 'What? You wanted me to snuff him out?'

'Why not?'

'I'm not a murderer. I leave that to you.' Palmer's eyes narrowed as he spoke.

'Unless the Devil tells you to.'

'Aye. Maybe.' Palmer did not bat an eyelid at the accusation.

'So find him.'

'Only if the major tells me to.'

Jack felt the first stirrings of anger. 'Why's that? Can't you do anything without his say-so?'

'I reckon I know what I'm about.' Palmer's voice did not change. 'I don't need you telling me what's what.'

'So that's it? Don't you have a mind of your own?'

Palmer said nothing.

'Fuck me.' Jack sagged. He felt broken. 'You're nothing but a useless fucking toady.'

Palmer laughed off the accusation. 'And you ain't nothing but a mewling turd. I'll let you off, for the moment. I reckon that smoke addled your wits, such as you had.' He leaned forward, his face looming towards Jack's. 'But call me that again and so help me I'll rip your fucking throat out.'

He pulled away and stood straight. 'You'd better show me this house where that poor woman's boy is laid up. Then you can follow me.' He gave Jack a grim smile, then gestured with his hand to encourage him to move.

Jack looked at the calmness in Palmer's eyes. They both knew the older man could make good on his threat with one hand tied behind his back. He did what he was told and went to find Mary and her boy.

Chapter Fourteen

---◆◆◆---

The garret room smelled. The damp was all-pervading, the room chill and miserable. Mould smothered the walls and much of the floor, the dark blue-black smudges all the decoration the place offered. The room could have been warmed, the fireplace ready to be stoked with fuel, but its occupant had no desire to see any more flames, even controlled and safe. So it was left undefended against the conquest of the damp and the mould, invaders as efficient as any British political officer at taking ownership of a land not rightfully their own.

Jack lay on the single bed and stared at the ceiling. The days had gone by, one after another, their passing unremarked and barely noticed. He was almost recovered, the days of inactivity doing much to ease the pain of the worst of his burns, and to allow for the muck he had inhaled to be spewed into the pisspot by his bed.

His right hand was still bandaged, whilst the left had a splint against his broken finger. With both hands damaged, he was unable to tend to his wounds himself, and was forced to rely on Mary to change his dressings. She spoke little when she ventured upstairs from her room on the floor below. Not even the garret's musty chill could match her icy reserve. She dealt with him out of duty, nothing more, any compassion burned to a charcoal husk by the same flames that had taken both her place of employment and the woman she had thought of as a mother.

Jack stared at the ceiling and conjured a face from a patch of mould above his head. It was the face of the man he would kill, no matter how long it took. One day Shaw would be found. Then he would die, the simple fact a small comfort as Jack let his body recover.

Shaw dominated his thoughts, with much of his time spent imagining the man's death. Jack had seen many men die, had watched as the final flicker of life departed their eyes. He fed his determination with the image of Shaw's soul fleeing his broken carcass. It was a good image, the kind that could help a man find his strength, the kind that could give purpose to a life bereft of one once again.

A knock at the door brought him to his feet. He crossed the room quickly before snatching it open, expecting to see Mary come to perform her duty as nurse.

'Good afternoon, Jack.' Ballard could not hide the hint of a flinch at the force with which the door was opened.

'You.'

'I am glad to see you on your feet.' Ballard attempted something that could be construed as a smile.

Jack made no attempt to invite his former master into the room. His body was healing, but his soul was still blackened. He was not ready to discover what plans Ballard had for his future.

'I can return tomorrow.' Ballard took half a step backwards.

'No.' Jack closed his eyes as he summoned the strength he would need. He could not hide away for ever. 'You can come in, but I give you fair warning that you may regret it.'

Ballard looked past Jack's shoulder. His thin moustache twitched as he saw what waited for him. 'It would be best if we have this conversation somewhere private.' He sniffed as he finished speaking, his distaste obvious. 'I have left Palmer downstairs. He does not need to hear this.'

'You'd best come in then.' Jack stood back and gestured for Ballard to enter. He noted the reference to Palmer's presence in the building, Ballard cautious enough around Jack to have brought his bodyguard. 'Sit wherever you want. I would recommend the chest by the window, but you run the risk of getting a splinter in your arse, so perhaps choose the bed; the spot there by the wall is the driest.'

Ballard's nose twitched as he ran his eyes over the choices Jack had indicated. Neither appealed. He offered a thin-lipped smile to his host, then approached the chest. 'Could you not be bothered to light the damned fire? It's colder than a convent in here.'

Jack snorted at the comparison. 'I wouldn't know, as I've not had the pleasure of visiting one.' He felt a flicker of enjoyment at Ballard's discomfort. The major was a staff officer, his wars fought in comfort and far from the dirty business of the battlefield where Jack had found his place.

'They are not the jolliest of places, Jack. I do not recommend you finding one to visit. Knowing you, you would probably steal away one of the novices, or else convince the Mother Superior to take you to her bed. Deflowering a bride of Christ would not be good for your soul.'

Jack shook his head at such foolishness. 'I doubt it would matter.'

'No, perhaps not.' Ballard sat down with exaggerated care. He paused, clearly waiting for something sharp to stab him. When it didn't, he summoned a smile and gestured for Jack to sit too.

'Will this take long?'

'It depends how difficult you are.'

Jack growled at the barb, then plonked himself on the bed, leaning carefully against the rusty bedstead. His back was painful, the pit of his spine a constant wearing ache that had not been helped by his recent misadventures.

'How are you?' Ballard had seen the wince.

'How do you think?'

'Your hands?'

Jack held them up towards Ballard as an answer. The splint used to hold his broken finger in place stuck up like a miniature flagpole.

'Still sore?'

'No, they fucking hurt.'

Ballard winced at the invective. 'I am sure that will pass. Keep the dressings clean.'

Jack had no time for any more of Ballard's doctoring. 'Have you found Shaw?'

'No, not yet. Palmer is looking for him.'

Jack grunted. 'He won't find him.'

'You would be surprised. Palmer is like a bloodhound. He can sniff out a troublemaker at a thousand yards.'

'He's not that bloody good. He let the bastard go.'

'Really, Jack. You must not blame Palmer.'

'Why not?'

'We cannot kill everyone who crosses our path. As convenient as that may be.'

'Why not?' Jack repeated. He knew he was being difficult, but he did not care. 'I'm going to kill that bastard when I find him, and I don't care who sees.'

'I am sure that is true. But I'm afraid it will have to wait.'

'No it won't. I am going to find him and then I am going to kill him.'

'Time has not softened you then, Jack? You are still the same man I found masquerading as a dead officer in Bombay?'

'Perhaps.' Jack refused to be shamed. He knew the manner of man he was. To his surprise, Ballard had looked pleased as he asked the question. Seeing such an expression on the face of the Devil made him wary.

'I am glad to hear it. You are a man of unique talents, Jack Lark. They make you a useful fellow to have in one's corner.'

'I am not in anyone's corner. Not any more.'

'Is that so? I suspect you are keen to find employment, to find a place where you can belong.' Ballard's tone changed as he replied. He spoke softly, letting the words hang between them.

Jack's mouth opened to denounce the notion. But he saw the way Ballard was looking at him. The intelligence officer knew him well. Too well, it seemed, for he had spoken a truth that Jack was trying hard to ignore. He had been searching for a place ever since he had walked away from that funeral on a dusty hillside outside the broken walls of Delhi.

'I'm a free man. I can do as I choose.' Jack matched Ballard's quiet tone.

'Are you?' Ballard studied him closely. 'Are you truly free? Or do you carry your past with you everywhere you go?'

Jack could no longer meet Ballard's stare. He glanced up, finding the patch of mould where he had discovered Shaw's face earlier, but the image had gone, the swirling patterns nothing more than the smudges of decay.

'It's not your fault, Jack. None of it.' Ballard kept his eyes on him. 'No man controls his own fate. Not you. Not I. Not even uncompromising fellows like Palmer.' He tried to inject some humour, but his voice tailed off as he saw Jack's reaction.

'I do.' Jack broke the silence, clearing his throat noisily before leaning forward to spit a wad of blackish phlegm into the pot by the bed. 'I got my name back. That was my reward, remember?'

'The papers weren't destroyed in the fire, then?'

'No.' For the first time in a while, Jack glanced across at Ballard, who sat easily on the wooden chest, his hands folded neatly in his lap. 'I'm not that foolish.'

'Where are they?'

'Cox and Cox.'

'Along with a rather juicy deposit of funds, I expect.' Ballard preened at the jibe, his fingers rising to stroke his moustache. 'We never did look into quite how you managed to get hold of that casket.'

Jack barked a bitter, humourless laugh. 'That is long in the past. Not even you would stoop to dredging up such ancient history. I'm a discharged soldier with papers to prove it. I doubt I'm the only redcoat to come back from India with a penny or two to his name.'

Ballard's hand stopped moving as he contemplated Jack. 'Those discharge papers of yours.' His fingers resumed their motion, moving back and forth over his moustache like a cat wiping its paw across its ears. 'Did you ever look at them? I mean, really look at them? They are a valuable commodity to a man like you. A man keen to leave his past behind him.'

Jack scowled. He did not like the change in Ballard's tone. 'I looked at them.'

'Did you take a peek at the signature?' Ballard goaded him.

'Stalker signed them.' Jack had checked his papers a dozen times. Ballard always had his own agenda. He did what suited him and nothing more. Jack had learned that the major's mind concocted schemes that others had no chance of understanding. His fellow officers on the staff had given him the nickname of 'the Devil', a moniker that Jack had deemed perfectly fitting from the moment he had first heard it. With Ballard, nothing was certain, his scheming brain working at a different speed to that of mere mortals. But Jack was certain of one thing. General Stalker had signed his discharge papers. Stalker had been the commander of the division he had served in during the campaign against the Shah of Persia. He had died shortly after the battle outside the village of Khoosh-ab, killed by his own hand, a sad and ignominious end for a fine career soldier.

'Did he now? Why, that truly is an amazing feat.'

Jack felt Ballard's grip closing as surely as if he had placed his fingers around his throat. 'Why?' He choked on the single word.

'Well, the poor fellow had been dead at least a whole day. A corpse signing a set of discharge papers, well, that is nothing short of miraculous!'

'What do you mean?'

Ballard smiled. It was like a fox spotting the door of the henhouse left ajar. 'The date, Jack, the date! Did you check the date of the signature?'

Jack closed his eyes against the pain. 'No.'

Ballard rocked back. His hands moved as if to clap, but stopped halfway when he saw the look on Jack's face. He composed himself. 'They were dated after poor Stalker had killed himself. They are fake, Jack. Fake papers for an impostor; even you must see how fitting that is.'

Jack let his head fall back so that it rested against the wall behind the bed. Ballard had humbugged him.

'The devil really is in the detail, Jack.' Ballard could not resist aiming the barb, using his own nickname with relish.

'So what do you want?' Jack did not bother to hide the bitterness in his reply. Ballard held all the cards, just as he always had. He had given Jack back his name. At the time it had been everything Jack had wanted. Now it appeared to be nothing more than a trickster's sleight of hand.

'I want *you*, Jack.' Ballard leaned forward as he replied. 'I told you once before that I do not care for petty crimes. I am involved in other affairs. Affairs that need not worry about such details. I have a new mission, one where you would be of much use to me, if not invaluable. I want you to come back to work for me.'

'And if I refuse?'

Ballard sat back, the chest creaking as he shifted his weight. 'Then there is the small matter of some funds at Cox and Cox deposited in the name of a certain Jack Lark, a man the army believes died back in '54. If an army agent, especially one as respectable as Cox and Cox, were to discover that a sizeable deposit had been made in the name of a dead soldier, well, they would have no choice but to freeze that account. Should a man then present himself claiming to be that very same soldier, then I am sure our good and respectable friends at Cox and Cox would be duty bound to have him reported, and I suspect his fate would look rather bleak. Especially when he is found in possession of a set of forged discharge papers.'

Jack knew his former master was more than capable of making good on the threat. Then he would have nothing. No home, no money and not even a name. He kept his eyes on Ballard, who sat no more than a yard away. It would be an easy thing to kill him, to throttle the life out of the man who appeared to have his fate tucked safely in a pocket. If Ballard were no longer around, there would be no one who knew the truth of Jack's discharge. The money he had stolen and placed at Cox and Cox would still be his, and no one would be any the wiser. His last link to his past would be severed the moment Ballard drew his final breath.

Ballard kept his eyes on him. This time he did not smile. 'Palmer is just down the stairs, Jack.'

'You think I would kill you?' Jack snorted even as Ballard read his mind.

'I think you would contemplate it. You would not be the man I know you to be if you did not.' Ballard paused. 'I notice you did not say *try* to kill me. Do you believe it would be so easy?'

For the first time, Jack managed a tight-lipped smile. 'Yes.'

Ballard reacted with mock surprise. 'You have seen me in action.'

'That's why I know it would be easy.' Jack had seen Ballard fight; indeed, the major had once saved his life. But Ballard was no warrior.

'Yet you have not so much as moved a muscle.'

'I am thinking.'

'So you *have* changed.' Ballard smirked at his quick retort.

'I do not recall you being very good at thinking before you act. Remember the munshi?'

'No.'

'You don't recall that man you captured.' Ballard lifted a finger and gestured at Jack's face. 'He gave you the smaller of your two scars.'

Jack's hand rose on instinct to touch the blemish. The larger one, the gift from Delhi, hid most of it. 'No. I don't recall.' He gave the lie easily.

Ballard read him well enough not to say anything further. Instead he got to his feet, tugging hard on his uniform trousers to smooth out the creases that had formed as he sat.

'I shall send Palmer to collect you tomorrow morning at eight.'

'I have not agreed to work for you yet.'

'You and I both know that you will.' He looked straight at Jack. 'You have no choice.'

Jack let his eyes bore into the major's. His blackened soul felt empty. 'I am done serving.'

'What about Mary and her boy?' Ballard spoke softly.

'What about them?'

'Without me you have nothing.' Ballard played his last card. There was no sense of triumph in his tone. He was in control, just as he always was. 'How will you look after them without money?'

Jack lowered his gaze. Ballard was correct. If he could not access the funds deposited at the army agent, then he truly was penniless. His actions had destroyed Mary's home and her employment. If he did not take care of her and her son, their future was as bleak as his own. He summoned the will to look up and face Ballard again. 'I have no choice then.'

'No, Jack, you really do not, but do not feel bad about that.' Ballard's expression was one of concern, not victory. 'I want you to help me. Do that and all this will be forgotten.'

Jack searched Ballard's face. He did not know if the major spoke the truth. But he found it did not matter. 'They cannot stay here. I will have to find them somewhere better to live. Or do you have plans for them too?'

'Now that is your first sensible question.' Ballard paused as he pondered. 'They could be useful.' The decision was made quickly. 'She can come with us, her boy too.'

'So where are we going?' Jack asked the question that he knew Ballard wanted to hear.

'Why, my dear, Jack, I thought you would have guessed. We are going on a little journey.' Ballard gave his best attempt at a smile. 'We are going back to war.'

Chapter Fifteen

———•◆•———

*J*ack was bored. He threw the previous day's *Times* back on to the drum table at the side of his chair before getting up to walk to the window. The rain beat steadily against the glass, the staccato rhythm echoing through the small anteroom that he had sat in for the last two hours. At least the room was warm, a fire burning away merrily in the corner fireplace. The flames still made Jack uncomfortable, but the warmth was pleasant and he was glad to be indoors on such a filthy day. As much as he chafed at the waiting, he could not deny how good it was to be somewhere that felt significant.

Palmer had collected him at eight, just as Ballard had ordered. Jack had been brought to Ballard's offices by hackney carriage, and there he had been left to kick his heels until Ballard returned from a meeting somewhere else in the labyrinthine building not far from Trafalgar Square. The journey with Palmer had been completed in silence.

Jack had told Mary where he was going, and that he had found them all employment. The conversation had taken place through a barely open door. Mary was reluctant to admit him into the room she shared with her son. Billy was recovering, but it would still be days before he was well enough to be up and about. Jack had glimpsed the boy over Mary's shoulder, his guilt flaring as he saw the lively urchin laid up under blankets, his eyes dull and listless.

'Good morning, my dear Jack! Good morning indeed!' The door to the room was thrown open and Ballard bustled in, a look of satisfaction plastered across his face.

'Good afternoon.'

'Now, now, do not start our day together with such churlishness,' Ballard admonished. 'I have enjoyed a successful meeting with our sponsor and I will not allow you to sully my mood.'

'Our sponsor?'

'I shall tell you more, indeed I shall. But this is not the time. Tell me what you know of the northernmost Italian provinces.'

The request took Jack off guard. It was typical of Ballard to assume that everyone else's mind could perform the same mental somersaults as his own.

'A little.' The habit of not admitting a lack of knowledge was buried deep. His mother had taught him to read and write passably well, but he had not enjoyed more than a rudimentary education. Much of what he had learned had come from his first regiment, whose colonel had allowed his brighter soldiers a few hours a week in the regimental library. His career as a charlatan officer had made him adept at dodging questions about matters that he did not know a thing about, although in truth, very few of his fellow officers had asked him much at all, their education, more often than not, as patchy and as scant as his own.

'Shall we sit?' Ballard gestured at the club chair Jack had

recently vacated before taking another for himself. 'Our friend Napoleon has sparked something of a crisis in the region.' He raised an eyebrow as he looked at Jack. 'You have heard of Napoleon III, Emperor of France?'

'Of course,' Jack replied as he sat. In truth, he knew little, but he assumed Ballard would be unable to resist giving a lecture, so he doubted that his lack of knowledge would matter.

'Good man, you are not totally hopeless then. So our friend Napoleon – I suppose we must call him a friend after the Crimea – has created something of a situation. Reports coming from Paris indicate that he and his new best friend, Vittorio Emanuele III of Sardinia, are cooking up trouble for the poor Habsburgs. If what we have discovered is correct, Vittorio and Napoleon have hatched a plan to turf the Austrians out of Lombardy and Venice. Once their aim is achieved, that kingdom will be added to that of Sardinia, in return for Vittorio ceding the French-speaking areas of Savoy and Nice back to Napoleon. I don't know how much you know of this area, but it is made up of a messy hotchpotch of tiny states with more petty jealousies than a girls' boarding dormitory. They have this damnable notion of unifying together. "Italy for the Italians", they say. 'Italy' means nothing, of course, just a geographical term if you ask me, but they believe in it, the stupid fools. One only has to look at the uprisings back in '48 to see how touchy half of Europe is about such things.' Ballard scowled as he saw Jack struggling to keep up. 'Are you quite well, Jack? You look like you are sucking on a lemon.'

Jack shifted in his seat. 'Perhaps you could go a little slower?'

'My dear Jack, we have much to do and I cannot waste time. The chase is on.'

'What chase?'

Ballard preened as Jack snapped at the lure. 'Now is not the time for your questions. So, you are familiar with the area of which I speak?'

'No.'

Ballard rocked back in his chair and clapped his hands before giving his odd bark of a laugh. 'You are priceless, Jack, absolutely priceless. The kingdom of Sardinia is to be found in an area south of the Alps, in the passes of Savoy and the plains of Piedmont, in what some would call the north of Italy.'

Jack felt the burn of embarrassment on his cheeks, but he did his best to ignore it. He could not help but be intrigued, and Ballard was a good lecturer, even if he did go a little too fast.

'Vittorio Emanuele has risen up against the Austrians before.' Ballard kindly overlooked Jack's blushes and carried on. 'The last time was in '48, when half of Europe smelled the miasma of revolution. A fellow called Graf Johann Radetzky, Austria's viceroy in Milan, crushed the revolt rather brutally. There were two battles, one at Custozza and one at Novara. The poor Sardinians took a beating, but that didn't stop them from helping us in the Crimea.' Ballard paused and frowned. 'I almost forgot. You were there, were you not? Perhaps you saw them?' He raised an eyebrow in Jack's direction.

'No.' Jack saw the flash of annoyance in Ballard's eyes. The major had discovered much of Jack's past, but not all. Jack had never revealed anything about his time in the Crimea, something that vexed the intelligence officer immensely.

Ballard's brow furrowed deeper. 'I still don't know your whole story, do I, you damned rogue, and I see that you plan to keep it that way.' He sniffed as Jack stayed silent. 'One day you will tell me everything.'

'One day you will learn to keep your beak out of business that doesn't concern you.'

'I doubt that!' Ballard laughed off the belligerent reply. 'If I ever become that dull, you have permission to shoot me.'

'Very well.' Jack kept his reply cool.

'Ha! I do not doubt that you would.' Ballard shook his head slowly. 'I missed you, Jack; I never realised until this moment quite how much.'

'I didn't miss you.' Jack fought the urge to smile.

'You are not a very convincing liar. I am astonished that you could last so long as an impostor.' Ballard's eyes twinkled. 'So, back to the matter in hand. Vittorio helped us in the Crimea and that earned him a seat at the peace conference that followed. That in turn gave him the opportunity to put this whole Italian problem on the table. Not even Palmerston could ignore something slapped right in front of his damn face, though I expect the old fellow was too distracted by being awarded the Order of the Garter to mind for long.'

Ballard offered his tight-lipped smile as he spotted Jack hanging on his every word. 'Now, as I said, Napoleon and Vittorio have been plotting, and our sources tell us that their preparations for war are well under way. The Sardinian army, such as it is, has mobilised and is now massing on the border with Lombardy. Vittorio has called up all his reservists and the French are manufacturing like mad. Napoleon is just like his bloody uncle in that he thinks the artillery can win battles all by themselves. The man's factories cannot make cannon fast enough.'

'He's wrong. It's the infantry who win battles.' Jack could not hold back the comment.

'I agree.' Ballard nodded, encouraging Jack's involvement.

'Although if I recall correctly, the cavalry nearly managed the whole affair in Persia.'

'Perhaps. But the Persians didn't hang around long enough to make it a proper fight.'

'You sound disappointed.'

'No. It's what happened.' Jack had ridden with the cavalry that day. 'If their line had stood their ground, the outcome could have been very different.'

'You are correct, I am sure.' Ballard ceded the point to Jack. 'It will be interesting to see how these Sardinians stand.'

Jack heard the first clue as to what Ballard was planning. 'You will be there?'

Ballard waved the comment away. 'Everything in its time, Jack, everything in its time. The French and Sardinians are not standing alone. Even the bloody revolutionaries are getting involved. Have you heard of a chap called Garibaldi?' He gave Jack no time to reply. 'The man is a bloody pain in the backside. He wants to create a state of Italy, can you believe. He has about as much chance of that as I do of becoming prime minster, but for the moment his interests are aligned with those of Vittorio, and so he has turned his own private army over to strengthen the allied force.

'Of course, if we know this, then so do the Austrians. The emperor has reinforced his forces in the region, and some sixty-five thousand men have been recalled from furlough. The Habsburgs have huge resources to call on. The empire has thrived in the years since the Congress of Vienna back in '15. It now consists of Upper and Lower Austria, Salzburg, Tyrol, Carinthia, Carniola, Littoral, Bohemia, Moravia Silesia, Galicia and Lodomeria, Hungary, Croatia, Slavonia, Dalmatia, Transylvania, the voivodeship of Serbia and the banat of

Temeswar, and of course Lombardy and Venetia.' Ballard took a sharp intake of breath as he finished reeling off the long list of duchies and kingdoms that formed a part of the enormous territory.

'What are we going to do?' Jack asked the question. 'We fought alongside the French and the Sardinians in the Crimea. Will we do so again now?'

'No, at least I don't think so. Things with the French are a little frosty after that Orsini affair. I have no idea why Napoleon is so shocked that someone would try to assassinate him, but he is certain that we had our finger in that particular pie. Even though Palmerston tried to appease him by introducing a Bill to make it a felony to plot here to murder someone abroad, Napoleon still won't trust us. Of course, that Bill is what got Palmerston kicked out of office, and even though it is looking quite possible that he will return as prime minister after all this messing about with the election, I would think we would keep out of this one and leave it to the French. But that does not mean there is not a role for us to play, albeit a minor one.'

Jack was starting to understand the situation. 'Go on.'

Ballard sat back in his chair, his fingers lifting to toy with his moustache. 'Have you heard of the practice of sending observers to a foreign war?'

'I have.' Jack nodded.

'That is to be our role.' Ballard smacked his hand on to his knee and sat forward quickly. 'What say you to that?'

'We're just going to watch?'

'You have it exactly.'

Jack thought he saw something hidden in Ballard's expression, as if he were not telling the whole story. But the idea of going to Italy as an observer made sense, and it gave Jack a reason for being there. He might not be political, but he knew war. The notion of observing intrigued him. It would be a relief to stay on the sidelines as three armies slugged it out. There would be no fighting, no sucking up the courage to lead men into battle and no bowel-wrenching fear.

'You want me to come with you?' Jack kept his voice level, as if the notion neither interested nor pleased him.

'I do. Palmer will be with me, but I like to be prepared, and I have a fancy that somewhere along the line you will be useful to me. The woman and her boy can come with us too. We shall not strictly be on campaign, so I think we can allow ourselves a little comfort. I imagine she will be able to take care of us rather nicely.'

Jack tried not to guffaw. Ballard was the shrewdest man he had ever met, but in some ways he was most definitely an innocent. 'I am sure Mary will be more than capable. Her lad, too.'

'Very good! We shall be a merry little party indeed.' Ballard's eyes narrowed as he thought on his plans. 'You can keep your name. No one but I knows the truth about that, and it will be too complicated to change it now.'

'That is very good of you.'

'Capital.' Ballard missed the dollop of sarcasm. 'I shall sort out the paperwork this afternoon. We do not have long.'

'Why's that?'

'We must be on our way. The Austrian foreign minister, Graf – they are all some sort of bloody graf – Ferdinand von Buol-Schauenstein, just issued an ultimatum to Vittorio demanding Sardinia's immediate, unilateral disarmament.'

'Surely they won't agree.'

'We will make a statesman of you yet. No, Vittorio will not

agree, not with Napoleon whispering sweet nothings in his ear. He is certain to refuse.'

'Which means?'

'Which means, my dear Jack, that Europe is about to go to war.' Ballard ran a single finger across his moustache, then smiled. 'And that means that so are we.'

Chapter Sixteen

Paris, May 1859

*J*ack eased off his boots then tossed them to the ground, a sigh of pleasure escaping his lips even as their pungent aroma caught his nose. It had been a long day, and he was tired. The small walled courtyard behind the house where they were lodging was a wonderful haven tucked away from the bustle of the city. He could smell the lavender that rambled near the rear wall, its scent a delicate balm against his own stink. He sat at a small metal table, his feet resting on gravel, relishing the peace and the shade. It felt good to sit in the cool, and his breathing slowed as the frustration of the day began to leave him.

'What the devil is wrong with you?' Mary had seen him arrive, and now she bustled out into the courtyard, her face creased into a scowl as she saw him sitting at ease.

Jack spotted that she had a mug in her hand. 'If that tea is for me, then I shall marry you this instant.'

Mary snorted. 'Don't flatter yourself.' She held out the battered tin mug. 'You can have it, I suppose.'

Jack took it gratefully. He had failed to win Mary over. She still treated him with icy disdain. Not that he blamed her. He had ruined her world, her current employment little reward for everything she had lost. He had not forgotten Shaw. But the choice he had faced had been simple. Accept Ballard's offer and give both him and Mary a place, or spurn it and spend days, or weeks, hunting for revenge. There was only one thing he could do, and so Shaw was left in peace, for the moment at least.

'Thank you.' He cradled the hot mug in both hands. His right was still bandaged, but the splint had been removed from his broken finger. It was crooked and hurt like the devil if he caught it at the wrong angle, but it served as a reminder of a debt left unpaid.

'You can bring the mug back in when you go for a wash.' The ever-present scowl on Mary's face deepened a fraction as her nose wrinkled at the smell coming from Jack's bootless feet.

'It's been a hard day. I think I'll rest here a while.'

'A hard day! I think you have forgotten what a hard day's work is really like.'

Jack did not rise to the bait. He took a first tentative sip of the steaming liquid, closing his eyes as the taste of it filled his mouth. When he opened them again, he caught Mary staring at him. She looked away quickly when she saw him notice her scrutiny.

'Did you get everything on the list I gave you?' The question was snapped at him.

'Some of it.'

'Some? You've been gone hours, yet you didn't get everything?'

'It was hard.'

'Hard! What is hard about spending Mr Ballard's money on a few necessities?'

Jack was too tired to argue. 'It's not London.'

'Is that so?' Mary's sarcasm was biting. 'Well I'm right glad you told me. I thought I was still in bloody Whitechapel.'

Jack laid his head back. Most of the courtyard was in shade, but he felt a single beam of sunlight wander pleasantly across his face. He could also feel Mary's eyes boring into him.

'So are you just going to sit there?'

'Only if I'm left in peace.'

'There's work to be done. You know how Mr Ballard likes everything ready when he returns.'

Jack kept his eyes closed even as he mocked her. '*Mr Ballard*,' he imbued the honorific with a liberal dose of scorn, 'can go take a running jump. I've done enough for one day.'

'And what have you done exactly?' She did not give him a chance to reply. 'Wandered around gawping when you should have been grafting, that's what.'

'It wasn't like that.' Jack rocked forward, opening his eyes so he could glare at Mary. 'This bloody city is full of lunatics. All they do is shout and wave their bloody arms.'

'Is that why you didn't get half the things you was told to? Because someone raised their voice and waved their arms at you?'

Jack could not help but smile as Mary gesticulated in a parody of his description. He could still see the girl he had once loved underneath the scowl. 'I got what I could.'

'And it ain't enough. I can't feed me and my boy on what you brought, let alone Mr Ballard and his man.'

'Then you go and get something. None of the buggers speak

English. You have to shout and point, and even then you still don't get what you bloody want.' Jack let some of his frustration show. 'It wasn't this hard in India.'

'I got plenty to do already, thank you very much.' She placed her hands on her hips and stared at Jack. 'You've got to go back out.'

'No I don't.'

'We need more meat. There's a boochery or whatever they call it just down the road.'

'I went there. The man is a maniac.'

'I don't care. I can't feed us all on three slices of ham.'

Jack did not answer. He closed his eyes and wondered where he might find some peace. He heard the sound of a door slamming, and then footsteps. It appeared that peace would prove to be elusive that afternoon.

'Good day to you both.'

Jack did not bother to open his eyes as Ballard came into the courtyard. He heard the major's boots on the gravel, his short, quick steps as identifiable as his voice.

'Good afternoon, sir.' Mary's voice welcomed her master.

'My dear Mary, what a day. I say, is that tea I spy?'

'Let me fetch you a cup, sir. Just brewed, it is.'

'That would be magnificent.'

Jack grimaced at the interaction between the two, the formality grating. He opened his eyes to see Ballard standing with his hand on the back of the chair where Jack's feet were currently resting.

'Move your feet, there's a good fellow.'

He slowly eased himself into a more upright position.

'You look exhausted, Jack. Has Mary been working you hard?'

Jack scowled, an expression that deepened as he heard Mary's loud and derisive snort from somewhere indoors.

'I have news.' Ballard sat down quickly.

Jack sat straighter. The major was full of beans, which usually meant he had something of note to tell. 'Go on.'

Ballard offered a half-smile at Jack's interest. 'A moment, if you will. I have dust in my throat.'

'Have mine.' Jack pushed his tea towards the major.

Ballard's smile widened. 'I wouldn't dream of coming between you and your tea. We can wait a moment, I am sure Mary will not be long.' He made a show of settling into his chair.

Jack bit his tongue, then drank his tea. He knew Ballard would keep him waiting simply because he could, so it was best not to show that it bothered him.

'Napoleon has left the city.' The major finally broke the silence just as Mary approached with a tray. In contrast to Jack's battered tin mug, Ballard's tea had been served in a fine bone-china cup with a matching saucer. 'Thank you, my dear.' He nodded his thanks to Mary before turning back to look Jack in the eye. 'Everyone who is anyone is on their way to Piedmont.'

Jack's feigned indifference had ended the moment Ballard started to speak. 'So it begins.'

Ballard sat forward, his childish game forgotten. 'Indeed, although it appears Napoleon may already be too late. The Sardinian army stands alone until the French forces can get to the theatre of war. The Austrians outnumber them by at least two to their every one. If the Austrians go for the Sardinians' throat, it could all be over before it has truly begun.'

'How long until the French get there?'

'It should be soon, but quite frankly, the French are in something of a mess. They knew this thing was coming, but they were still not ready. At least now that the order to mobilise has come they are getting on with it, and their first divisions are already on the move. There are trains from Paris that go directly to Toulon or Marseilles. From there it is but a short sea crossing to Genoa. There is also a second route by train from Paris to Saint-Jean-de-Maurienne, followed by a quick march through the Alps to Susa in Piedmont. Even as we speak, some four thousand labourers are working around the clock to keep the passes through the Alps clear.' Ballard spoke briskly as he detailed the French movements. 'The railways are making all the difference. Journeys that would take days on foot can now be done in a few hours. This is a modern war, Jack, using all the advances that have been made. Imagine what the first Napoleon could have done if he were alive today. Why, I fear we would all be speaking French within a year.'

Jack hid a smile. It was rare to see Ballard so animated. 'When are we off?'

Ballard beamed with pleasure at Jack's question. He fished in a pocket and pulled out a small pile of tickets, which he brandished at Jack. 'We leave first thing in the morning for Marseilles. I got you, Palmer and the boy second-class tickets. Mary will join me in first. I would not feel happy leaving her with such company as inhabits a second-class carriage.'

Jack did his best not to spit out his tea. Ballard clearly had no idea of Mary's past. Jack had no intention of altering that. It was much more fun to see the major treat her as if she were a shy wallflower. He remembered Mary in her heyday, with her bright red stockings and the wild mane of hair that had intoxicated many a punter. If Ballard saw her as she had been then, Jack had no doubt that his rose-tinted image would change in an instant.

The major sipped from his cup. 'I say, this tea really is rather delicious. Mary certain knows how to handle a teapot.'

'She's a girl of many talents.'

'Indeed.'

'She needs a husband.' Jack smiled as he teased his commander.

Ballard frowned at the notion. 'I rather assumed she had one. At least, had once had one.' He looked at Jack. 'Her boy.'

'Ah.' Jack understood. 'No, sir, he's a bastard all right.'

'I see.' Ballard hid his expression behind another sip of tea. When the cup was lowered, a scowl was firmly in place. 'That is hard on Billy. A boy needs a father, even if he cannot play as full a part in his child's life as he might wish.'

'What would you know?' The mockery escaped Jack's lips before he could hold it back. He heard something in the major's tone that he had not noticed before.

Ballard did not look at him. 'I have a son.' He made the admission quietly.

'I had no idea.'

'I cannot see him as much as I would like.' Ballard's eyes were still averted. 'After his mother passed away, I sent him to reside with my cousin until he was of an age to attend school. We were in India at the time, and it seemed the wisest course of action.' His eyes lifted to look at Jack. 'You know what it is like in India. It is not a place for a child without a mother.'

Jack tried not to squirm. Seeing Ballard uncomfortable was like seeing a mother stare at a much younger man with lust in her eyes. 'No, perhaps not.'

Ballard drank the last of his tea. 'Life is not always what we would choose it to be.' He fixed Jack with his firm stare. 'But sometimes the choice of action is clear. When something needs to be done, one must simply do it. Is that not right, Jack?'

Jack did not fully understand the question. 'I suppose.'

'A meek answer! I did not expect that of you.' Ballard placed his empty cup forcefully into its saucer. 'Come, we have much to do if we are to leave in the morning.' He got to his feet, nodding to Jack before bustling away.

Jack did not know what to make of Ballard's revelations. But the major was correct. There was plenty to be done before the morning, so he drained his mug and bent forward to retrieve his boots.

Chapter Seventeen

'*I* reckon I can walk faster than this.' Mary's son Billy offered the comment, his nose pressed hard against the glass of the second-class carriage's smoke-streaked window.

'Shut your damn muzzle,' growled Palmer, his deerstalker pulled low over his face as he tried to sleep. He was sitting next to the youngster and so had to endure the worst of the boy's constant fidgeting. 'And for Christ's sake sit still.'

'Keep your voice down.' Jack sat on the other side of Palmer. He found the boy's constant moans just as wearing, but he could not resist taking the boy's side, if only to goad the bigger man.

Palmer looked at Jack out of the corner of his eye. The compartment was cramped. Palmer took up most of Billy's space as well as his own, and his large knees pressed close to the French soldier sitting on the bench opposite.

Jack caught Palmer's glance, then nodded towards the three men on the opposite side of the compartment. 'Keep it down. I doubt they want to hear you bawling the boy out.'

'Like I give a shit.' Palmer looked at the three men opposite. Two were trying to sleep, but the man in the middle seat was staring balefully at the three English travellers. All three were dressed in uniform, one Jack half recognised. There was something familiar about the dark blue jacket with long tails, the green epaulettes with red crescents, the baggy, lightweight white campaign trousers and the jaunty red kepi, but he could not place the regiment. The man starting at them had a tanned, lean face, and Jack guessed he was in his early twenties. His uniform bore the red stripe of a sergeant on the lower part of his sleeve near the cuff, as did those of his two companions.

'Where you from?' Jack asked the question as he caught the Frenchman's eye, hoping the man would be able to speak English. In truth, he was as bored as Billy. The train had started with bustling purpose, and had flashed through the outskirts of Paris at a terrific rate. But after just over an hour, the locomotive's speed had slowed to barely a crawl. They had been creaking and rolling along at a walking pace for the past two hours, and the slow progress was stretching everyone's nerves.

'Boston.' The answer was given without enthusiasm. The soldier's expression did not change.

'You're American?' Jack blurted the inevitable question. He had not known what answer to expect, but the sergeant's accent had still taken him by surprise.

The Bostonian shrugged. It was all the answer he gave.

'Leave the man alone.' Palmer spoke out of the side of his mouth. 'He doesn't want to talk. Especially not to you.'

Jack gave Palmer's advice no heed. 'What's an American doing in the French army?' He looked more closely at the sergeant. He wore his hair long and tucked behind his ears, and sported a small goatee that framed a mouth bearing a hint of smile.

'Fighting, mainly.' The man's eyes moved between Jack and Palmer. His accent was strong.

'What regiment are you from?' Jack wanted to know.

'Le Douzième Régiment Étranger.'

Jack recognised the name. He had seen one of the French Foreign Legion's regiments in the Crimea, and it had been the subject of many conversations between the British officers.

There were many tales about the Legion, and even more about the men who served in it. Its ranks were filled with the flotsam and jetsam of Europe, the regiment content to recruit any man who came to them. Those who joined were given a choice. They could keep their identity and the past that came with it, or they could abandon everything about the person they had been and let the Legion give them a new name. Rumour had it that many chose the second option.

'Were you in the Crimea?' He watched the American carefully as he asked the question.

'Yes.'

'The Alma?'

The man nodded. 'And after. At Sevastopol.' He was watching Jack just as closely. 'You were there.' It was a statement, not a question.

'The Alma.'

Again the silent nod as the man contemplated Jack, his eyes boring into his for an uncomfortably long period of time. Then he reached up to the knapsack on the shelf above his head, his fingers searching for something. He gave a short snort as he found what he was looking for, pulling out a dark green bottle.

'Have you been to India?'

'Yes.' Jack watched as the man uncorked the bottle.

'Then you'll like this.' The American lifted the bottle to his nose to inhale the aroma coming from the open top. He paused, lifting it towards Jack as if making a toast, then took a long swig, his eyes closing in silent ecstasy. When they opened again, he was smiling for the first time. 'Here.' He held it out to Jack. 'Drink.'

Jack took the bottle and gave it a circumspect sniff. He noticed young Billy watching him closely, and even Palmer had half opened a single eye. The smell coming from the bottle made his eyes water, but he recognised it well enough. 'Arrack?'

The American tilted his head to one side in acknowledgement of the guess. 'Not quite, but it's similar. Give it a try.' The instruction sounded more like an order than an offer.

Jack did as he was told. The liquid hit the back of his throat, the burn and the rush of fumes just as he remembered. He swallowed, the fire sliding down his gullet to burn in the depths of his stomach. It took a moment to control the heady rush before he could hand the bottle back. 'It's good.' The words came out as a hoarse whisper.

This time the American sergeant laughed. 'No, it's goddam awful, but I find it does the trick.'

Jack laughed with him. 'It does that.' He made a play of wincing and shaking his head, making the sergeant laugh loud enough to wake up his two companions.

'What are your names?' Jack's throat still burned, but he managed to sound more normal as he asked the question.

'That is Marsaud.' The American nudged the man on his left. 'He's Swiss. By rights he should be in the First Regiment, but the man is a fool and so got stuck with us in the Old Second.' He shook his head, the name he had give his own regiment clearly not agreeing with him. 'The fat oaf by the window is Baranowski, and my name is Kearney.'

'Ah! You started without me!' Marsaud saw the bottle in Kearney's hand and immediately reached for it. He too spoke in English, but with a heavy accent.

Kearney nodded towards Jack. 'My new friend fought in the Crimea.'

Marsaud swigged a good measure of the powerful liquor, then glanced at Jack over the bottle. 'Then you earned a drink. It was hard fighting out there.'

'It was.' Jack held out a hand.

Marsaud smirked, then handed him the bottle. 'We found that English officer there. You remember him, Kearney?' He used his elbow to prompt the man sitting to his right. 'The one with a hole in his guts.'

Kearney's face changed as he searched his memory, then split into a smile as he found what his comrade was referring to. 'Ah yes! The one who told us he was quite fine even though we could see his backbone through his stomach.'

'Yes! That is the one.' Marsaud gave Jack an encouraging smile as he took a second measure of the arrack. 'You like it?'

'No.'

'No, me neither.' Marsaud shrugged. 'But it's cheap and it does what it's meant to do.' He reached over and retrieved the bottle, then nudged the sergeant on the far side of Kearney with its base. The man took it but said nothing.

Kearney saw Jack look across at the man by the window. 'Don't mind him. He's a Pole. He doesn't speak English.' He nodded to his comrade as the bottle was passed back.

'You cannot get the chance to speak English very often.'

'We have Englishmen. They don't find it so easy to learn French.'

'How many Englishmen are there in your ranks?'

Kearney moved his lips as he contemplated the question. 'Not so many. We don't ask about a man's past in the Legion. Who he is now is all that matters to us. We concern ourselves with what he becomes, not what he was.'

'Sounds like my kind of place.' Jack saw Billy hanging on their every word, so he reached across and took the bottle from Kearney, then handed it to the boy. 'Taste that, lad. It'll put hairs on your chest.'

The three sergeants from the Legion all beamed as Billy took hold of the bottle before raising it to his lips. He drank, the liquid sloshing loudly. His eyes widened, then he choked. Tears streamed down his face as he half threw the bottle back to Jack before clutching his hands to his throat.

The men laughed at the display. Even Palmer managed a smile.

As if on cue, the locomotive jolted heavily before lurching forward, finally picking up speed. The French countryside began to slide past the window at an ever-increasing rate as the troop train resumed its former clattering rhythm.

Jack saw the Legion sergeants share a look. They were men going to war, and he felt a pang at being the outsider, at not sharing their feelings.

He would have no place on the battlefield, but he sensed that he would not avoid becoming involved in the conflict that was drawing in men by the thousand. There would be war in Europe, and he knew with utter certainty that he would be a part of it.

Chapter Eighteen

Genoa, May 1859

'Nothing?'

Jack grimaced as he squeezed through the crowd. 'Nothing.'

'Damnation!' Ballard's frustration was getting the better of him.

The quayside was bedlam. Ballard's party was pressed together at the end of the quay, their luggage piled around their feet. Hundreds of troops were disembarking from the transport ship, the ranks of French infantry filling every inch of space as they filed past, their sergeants and corporals swearing and shouting at their charges to move quicker.

Jack stumbled as he emerged from the scrimmage, ducking under a musket that was being carried balanced over a Frenchman's shoulder. He had been sent to try to locate some porters to help get the party away from the dock. There was no one save for swarms of onlookers who had thronged to the port to see the French troops arrive. Palmer had gone with him, but had left Jack to report back to Ballard whilst he tried to find them some kind of conveyance to get them to a place where they could stay.

'We'll have to shift for ourselves.' Jack wiped the sleeve of his jacket across his sweat-streaked face.

'Do not tell me the damned obvious.' Ballard was the only one of the group in uniform. He still wore the dark blue of the 15th Hussars, even though it was many years since he had served in the regiment's ranks. Jack and Palmer were dressed in civilian clothes, their heavy jackets and thick trousers ill suited to the heat that had assailed them the moment they had disembarked.

'Well get on with it then.' Jack was in no mood for Ballard's waspishness. He bent low to pull the largest trunk towards him. 'Bloody hell, whose is this?'

'That is mine.' Ballard knocked Jack's hands off the trunk. 'I shall take it. Help the others.'

'What have you got in there? That bloody thing weighs a ton.'

'Necessities, nothing more. Now get out of my way.' Ballard shouldered Jack to one side, then took hold of the trunk's handles. With a grunt and a strain he just about managed to lift it. 'Get on with it!' he exhorted Jack before taking a first awkward step, the trunk banging painfully against his knees as he did so.

Jack grabbed his own knapsack and slung it on to his shoulder before starting to collect the valises and portmanteaus that contained the rest of their possessions.

'Give us a bloody hand, boy,' he growled at Billy, picking up a valise and tucking it under his arm.

'Don't take it out on him.' Mary pulled her own bag from the ground. 'Ain't his fault.'

Jack gritted his teeth. He was already carrying three bags and was trying to slide another up the side of his body so he could tuck it under his right arm. Somehow he managed the trick. Mary and Billy gathered the rest. With his back bent, he crabbed his way after Ballard. It was not a great start to their campaign.

'Have you ever seen anything like it?'

'No.' Jack answered Palmer's question honestly. The pair stood at the window in their room, looking out over the street. The room was large but completely empty save for their luggage. It was the only accommodation Palmer had been able to find, and all five of them would have to share the one space.

The wide boulevard outside the window led directly down to the docks. It was the main thoroughfare through Genoa, and it was packed solid with the French army, as what looked to be an entire army division picked its way through the city. Everywhere Jack looked he saw infantrymen bowed low under the weight of their campaign equipment. Behind them came a dozen guns, the large cannon followed by limbers and wagons full of ammunition.

The noise was constant. The sound of countless pairs of boots hitting the ground echoed along the street as the troops marched as best they could in the melee. All the while, shouts and orders were bellowed, the men charged with maintaining order fighting against the difficulties of moving so many soldiers in such a confined space.

Jack turned to face the room. Mary was doing her best to organise the chaos of the luggage that had been dumped here, there and everywhere. Billy had disappeared the moment they had arrived, keen to explore his new surroundings. Ballard had left them too, eager to find someone in authority who could provide him with the papers he would need to requisition some transport so that they could accompany the army when it left Genoa.

'My eye.' Palmer spoke quietly, his gaze still riveted on the scene outside. 'Those things look evil.' He was looking at the artillery battery filing past below the window.

'I bloody hate cannons.'

Palmer caught Jack's eye. 'Don't we all, chum.'

'You served?' He knew little of Palmer's past, but he recognised the look in his gaze.

Palmer nodded. 'Before your time.'

Jack was intrigued. He had no idea how old Palmer was, so he made a guess. 'India?'

'For a bit.'

'Against the Sikhs?'

'Maybe.' Palmer refused to be drawn.

Jack wanted to press, but he knew what it was to have demons. There had been hard fighting in India in the years before he had journeyed to its shores. He guessed Palmer was around ten to fifteen years older than he was. That meant he could easily have seen action against the Sikhs, or the Afghans; maybe both and others besides. 'Makes you want a drink.'

'Doesn't it just.'

Jack still wanted to know more. It was the closest thing to a proper conversation he had ever had with Palmer. It was worth celebrating, so he turned to call across to Mary. 'We got anything to drink, love?'

'I ain't your love. And no, we haven't.'

Jack heard Palmer grunt in sympathy.

'In my pack.'

Jack turned sharply. The other man had spoken so softly that he had barely heard the words.

'In my pack.' The instruction was repeated as Palmer kept his vigil at the window.

Jack needed no more of an invitation. He walked to Palmer's knapsack, ignoring the disapproving glare on Mary's face. It was heavy, so he squatted on his haunches, pulling open the straps. He saw the bottle of brandy immediately. It was three-quarters full. The sight made him smile. He had never seen Palmer drinking, but it was clear that Ballard's man enjoyed a nip here and there.

He pulled out the bottle and was about to stand when he saw something bright half hidden beneath a spare shirt. He glanced at Palmer, but the man was paying him no attention, his gaze still fixed on the column passing by in the street below. Jack slipped his fingers underneath the shirt and took hold of the object that had caught his attention. He checked that Palmer was still looking away, then took a glance at what he had found.

It was an oval picture frame, no bigger than the palm of his hand. He looked down at the smiling image of a small girl about eight or nine years old. She was a pretty thing, with blonde hair and a pair of bright blue eyes. It was a simple picture, the kind that would cost a proud parent a few shillings. But the artist had still captured something of the child, a quirky half-smile on her face that was quite captivating.

He looked up to see Mary staring at him. She shook her head but said nothing, her opinion of his prying obvious. He slipped the portrait back into its place underneath the clean shirt, then fastened the straps on the knapsack before straightening up and taking the brandy across to the window.

'This what you wanted?'

Palmer glanced down and nodded. 'Aye. A man needs to be prepared.' He reached for the bottle. 'You saw her then?' He asked the question without looking at Jack.

For a moment Jack thought about lying. But he did not sense anything in Palmer's tone that made him wary, so he answered truthfully. 'Yes.'

'My daughter.' Still Palmer did not look at him. 'Elisabeth.'

'She's a pretty child.' From where he stood at the man's side, Jack could see that Palmer was no longer looking at the French troops, but was instead staring straight into the sky.

'She is.' Palmer smiled as he spoke. 'She's as pretty as an angel.'

Despite the warmth in the room, Jack shivered. The image of Palmer's daughter reminded him of another child, another face that only appeared in his nightmares. That child had died in a back alley in Delhi, murdered in front of his eyes. For an instant he was there and he froze, the image searing into his mind with such force that it sent a shudder surging through him.

'Here.'

Jack looked up to see that Palmer was offering him the brandy.

'Have a dram or two.'

Jack reached gratefully for the bottle. He felt no shame that Palmer had surely spotted his reaction. He had seen the same look reflected in the big man's eyes. They stood and drank, neither speaking as they watched the horde passing by, the long procession of men and wagons crawling along

'I just do not understand it.' Ballard swept into the room. His voice rose as he vented his frustration. 'These damn people.

Do they not care that I represent the British government?' He walked briskly across to dump a thick wedge of paper on top of his travelling trunk before standing still, one hand on his hip, the other clasped theatrically to his head.

'What's the matter, sir?' Jack asked the question dutifully.

'The British government is being ignored!' Ballard shook his head as if disbelieving his own words. 'These damnable Frenchies are doing nothing, and I mean nothing, to assist me.'

'Are no wagons available, sir?' Palmer asked deadpan.

'No, no, there are none. Nor are there any horses, or even a single damn mule!' Ballard's voice kept rising. 'Everything is in a state of utter chaos. The French, damn their eyes, did not bother to think what they would need. Now they are here, and lo and behold there are not enough supplies to equip a single battalion, yet alone an entire army!'

Jack was not surprised by Ballard's discovery. The French army had swamped Genoa. Thousands of men had already passed through before they had arrived, and the French com-missariat had stripped the town bare of anything even remotely useful. He was about to tweak Ballard's tail and remind him of these salient facts when he spied Mary studying the British major. He had not seen that particular expression on her face for nearly a decade. It was a look of appraisal, the same look she had once given a man as she assessed his worth and calculated the price he would pay for her services.

'What do you think we need?' Jack was put out enough by Mary's expression to forget the need to tease his commander.

'There is transport, for starters.' Ballard maintained his theatrical pose, but raised his eyes to the ceiling as if searching it for inspiration. 'An agent of the Crown cannot be expected to march like a common soldier. Then we will need supplies;

there is no knowing what we will be able to find once we are on the move.' He lowered his gaze and scowled at Jack. 'The list is endless. I have no idea how we will manage.'

'Can you write it all down for me?' Jack greeted his master's despair with a calm smile.

'Of course, but do give me some credit, Jack. I do not think they will listen to you when you ask. They will ignore you as surely as they ignored me.'

Jack's smile broadened. 'I am sure you are right, sir.' He glanced across at Mary, who was still staring at Ballard. 'But then I don't intend to be doing any asking.'

Ballard's eyes widened. 'You mean to steal what we need?'

'Yes.'

Ballard gave one of his own rare, wolfish smiles. 'What a capital notion.'

Chapter Nineteen

The two men and one boy moved quickly. They had waited until night had fallen, the near full moon casting enough light for them not to have to worry about being able to see. They had left the lodging shortly after a late supper, a light meal of bread and cheese the best Mary had been able to provide given their straitened circumstances.

Jack's stomach growled, earning him a glare from Palmer. The three of them were in the alley to the side of the tall town house where they had rented a room. Ballard had not felt the need to offer to accompany them, but he had been forced to overrule Mary, who did not want her son to join the venture. The boy had been brought up in Whitechapel. He knew how to move quietly and how to make sure the right objects ended up in the correct pockets.

'Looks quiet.' Jack was leading the way. He craned his neck so that he could see around the corner of the building. The street was nearly empty. With so many foreign soldiers in the town, the local population was wisely staying indoors, their windows and doors bolted tight in case their allies felt the need to fill their pockets and knapsacks before they left. 'No, wait.' He held up a hand and the three of them shrank back into the shadows, faces lowered, as a group of French non-commissioned officers sauntered past, their voices loud in the night-time quiet.

Jack let them go past. He had no idea what they would encounter on the streets now that night had fallen, but he wanted to be cautious. None of them spoke French. Any inter-action with the French soldiery would be difficult, and should be avoided at all costs.

'All right, let's move.' He led them out of the shadows, with Billy tucked behind him and Palmer bringing up the rear. They walked quickly, their boots loud on the cobbles as they crossed the street. Palmer had suggested they head back towards the docks, so Jack led them downhill. They were not the only ones abroad. A few groups of French soldiers went by, but none gave the three of them more than a cursory glance. Still Jack led them at a brisk pace until he spotted what they were looking for.

He brought them to a halt, then turned to face Palmer. 'Do you see those wagons?' He had spotted a line of them parked in a small square just off the main thoroughfare.

Palmer nodded. He pushed his thumbs through the straps of his knapsack. 'Let's get it done.'

Jack nodded. 'Wait here while I check them out.'

There was nothing else to be said. He walked away, leaving the other two behind. As he passed the road that led towards the wagons, he spotted a single pair of sentries. They were standing together, their muskets on their shoulders as they talked. He knew they would not expect any real trouble, their presence alone enough to safeguard the supplies from their own side, or from any of the local population attempting to make off with anything.

He took a moment to check no one was watching before turning and going back the way he had come. This time he saw what he wanted on the side of the square opposite the two sentries. He kept walking, his head turning from side to as he checked for any hidden scrutiny.

'You look like a bloody felon.' Palmer greeted his return with a hoarse rebuke.

Jack ignored the criticism. 'There's an alley way on the far side of the square. We can use that to get close.' He looked at Billy. 'You up for this, lad?'

The boy nodded. 'Course I am, Jack.'

Jack smiled at the bravado. He made one last check up and down the street to be certain that no one was watching the oddly matched trio. He saw nothing untoward.

'Right.' He grinned at the boy looking up at him. 'Follow me.'

'My eye! What's that bloody stink?' Billy hissed the words as they crept cautiously through the dark alley Jack had spotted.

'It's the bloody French.' It was Palmer who replied. 'Shit anywhere they will.'

'The dirty bastards.'

Jack bit back the urge to laugh. There was something in the way the boy uttered the insult that he found funny. But there was no time to enjoy it. They had reached the end of the alleyway. The wagons were just ahead.

'You ready, lad?' He took Billy's shoulder before guiding him forward.

Billy nodded, his lips pressed tightly together.

Jack checked round swiftly, then took firm hold of the boy and hoisted him on to the back of the closest wagon. 'Be quick,' he whispered before shrinking back into the shadows.

Billy did not need to be told twice. Bending low, he got to work.

Jack cocked an ear. He heard the gentle creak of a crate being opened. It was far too loud not to be missed. He inched out of the alley to take up position behind the wagon. Palmer followed, the pair working together to cover both flanks. Both had the reassuring solidity of a Colt revolver pressed against their spine. They had no intention of drawing the handguns. They were amongst an allied army. If they were caught, they could hardly shoot their way free. Any scuffle would be fought the old-fashioned way, with fists and boots rather than bullets.

'Here.' Jack started as Billy hissed down at him. 'Stop lollygagging and take these.'

Jack snorted at the boy's quick tongue, but still reached up for the bottles he was being passed. He recognised the feel at once.

'Open your knapsack,' he whispered to Palmer.

'What has he found?'

'Brandy.'

'I told he's a good lad.' Palmer held out his knapsack and Jack slipped the bottles inside.

'You want more?' asked Billy, his voice too loud.

'No. Shit, come on.' Jack heard sounds of movement, the noise of boots coming towards them. 'Get down.'

Billy slid down almost immediately, landing surely on his feet next to Jack.

'Let's go.' Jack would not push their luck.

The three scuttled away, disappearing into the darkness of the alley moments before the first sentry stuck his head around the back of the wagon they had just ransacked.

* * *

'You know what to get?' Jack pushed his mouth close to the boy's ear.

Billy nodded. He looked up at Jack, his eyes eager.

'Get it done.' Jack half pushed the boy away and watched him slip through the back door of the tall town house before returning to where Palmer waited behind a wooden outhouse.

'Is this worth it?' Palmer greeted Jack with a scowl.

'I want a sword. A good one, too.' Jack offered the explanation as he took up position where he could watch the house. They had discovered that a number of French officers were billeted there and had tailed a clutch of young subalterns back to the building, surmising from their wandering gait and loud, bawdy conversations that the group had been out for an evening's drinking. The trio had waited a full hour before letting Billy loose, until Jack was reasonably certain that enough time had passed for the half-cut officers to have fallen into a stupor.

'Waste of bloody effort, if you ask me.' Palmer made his feelings clear.

'I didn't.'

Palmer snorted. 'You still think you're a Rupert?' He shook his head at the folly of Jack's desire. 'You don't want a poker. A bundook and a bayonet, that's all a man needs in a fight.'

Jack noted Palmer's use of the slang for a rifle, a term used by redcoats who had served in India. It gave more clues to the man's past, as did his preference for a bayonet. 'You were a redcoat then?'

'Once.'

'When?'

'Watch the damn house.'

Jack did as he was told. He knew Palmer would say nothing more.

The minutes dragged by. Jack stayed in the shadows and began to worry. Billy had been gone too long.

'You think we should go and get him?' he hissed over his shoulder at Palmer, who had chosen to sit on the ground and leave the watching to Jack.

'He'll be back. If he ain't, well, you were the dolt who wanted a bloody poker.'

Jack bit his tongue. He turned back to resume his vigil and found himself staring into Billy's glowing face.

'Where the hell did you come from?' He had not heard the boy approach.

'Where d'you think?' Billy came close, his arms full. 'Here you go.' He pressed a sword into Jack's gut. 'Good enough for you?'

Jack grasped the sword in both hands. It had the curve of a sabre and it was reassuringly heavy. 'You little bugger, that's perfect.'

The boy held something else out. 'You might want these too.'

Jack took the second object clumsily, the sword still in his hands. He recognised the feel of the leather carrying case instantly. 'Blow me tight.'

'Thought you'd like them.' Billy beamed. 'So what next?'

Jack laughed quietly. Mary's son had provided him with a new sword and a pair of field glasses. He glanced up at the sky. It was starting to get lighter. They had dealt with his priorities, but they still had to get the things on Ballard's list. He cocked an ear as he heard a sound that would do the job nicely.

He turned to Palmer. 'You hear that?'

'Aye,' the larger man replied, then slowly eased himself to

his feet. 'It came from just over yonder.' He nodded towards the shadowy buildings at the rear of the yard behind the officers' lodging.

'Shall we take it?' Billy asked the question, his eagerness obvious.

'Oh yes.' Palmer smiled at his companions. 'That'll suit the major very nicely indeed.'

The mule was noisy, too noisy, and it clearly objected to the two strangers who bustled around it, piling on sacks and panniers from the wagon left outside the stable.

'Look alive-o. We don't have long,' admonished Billy, who was on lookout whilst Jack and Palmer loaded up the mule.

'Hush yourself,' snapped Jack, then had to snatch his arm away from the mule, which had just tried to bite him. He moved away quickly to grab another sack, which smelled like it contained cheese. The pile they were quickly depleting must have comprised the officers' private stash of provisions. Jack felt no compassion for them. The men under their command would enjoy no such treats. Now neither would the officers.

'*Qui vive?*'

Jack stopped in his tracks, a heavy sack that he guessed contained flour in his arms.

'*C'est vous, Maxime?*'

Again the voice came. Jack did not understand the words, but he knew they were in trouble.

'Frenchies!' Billy called out a belated warning.

'Shit.' Jack bundled the sack he was holding on to the back of the mule, balancing it precariously on one of the already bulging panniers.

'Leave them to me.' Palmer strode outside.

Billy rushed to Jack's side, his voice breathless with excitement. 'Will Mr Palmer fight them?'

'Shut your muzzle.' Jack pushed the eager boy to one side, then reached for the mule's tether. As he untied it, he heard loud voices outside, a flurry of fast French greeting Palmer's appearance. 'Come on, lad, hold this and come with me.'

Billy grabbed hold of the tether. Together they hauled the mule's head around, ignoring the loud braying that announced the animal's protest to the world.

'Come on!' urged Jack, pulling hard. Finally the reluctant animal started to move. They emerged from the stable to see Palmer standing in front of three dishevelled French officers, roused from sleep by the noises coming from behind their lodging.

'*Mais qu'est ce que tu fais, bordel?*' The shortest of the three Frenchmen strode towards Palmer, gesticulating wildly.

Palmer ignored him. Instead he looked over his shoulder at Jack and Billy, who were dragging the mule and its load towards the side passage of the house.

'You boys ready?'

It was getting brighter, the approach of dawn lightening the sky. Jack saw Palmer's face crease into a smile as he posed the question.

'Hit him, Mr Palmer!' Billy sang out before Jack could reply.

Palmer's smile broadened at the high-pitched command. He turned on his heel to see the Frenchman close behind him, his mouth spewing out a tirade of protest at being ignored.

'Oh shut your mewling,' bellowed Palmer, his deep voice cutting the Frenchman off. He gave him no time to gather his thoughts. His fist moved fast, hitting the officer full in the mouth.

'Shit.' Jack muttered the word under his breath before turning back to the mule and pulling hard on the lead rope, forcing the animal to pick up the pace.

'Hit him, Mr Palmer! Hit him!' Billy bounced against Jack's side, his eyes riveted on Ballard's bodyguard.

The Frenchman sat on his backside, his hand raised to his mouth. Blood seeped through his fingers to drip down the front of his white shirt. His companions glanced at each other, and the first went for Palmer, his fists flailing towards the taller man's head. Palmer saw him coming and had time to laugh before he ducked away, dodging under the blows before coming up punching. His fists pounded the Frenchman's gut, one after the other, a series of half a dozen blows coming so fast the French officer could do nothing but absorb them before his feet gave way beneath him. He fell back, hitting the ground hard before curling into a ball around his battered stomach.

'Get on now, Jack.' Palmer snapped the command, his breathing unaltered.

Jack did not need to be told twice. He was forcing the pace and had managed to get the mule into something that resembled a trot. He glanced back just in time to see Palmer turn to face the remaining Frenchman, his fists lifting into a fighting stance.

The last Frenchman was less keen to fight. His head whipped around as he searched for a weapon.

'Come on now, monsewer.' Palmer took a step towards him. 'Let's get it over with, shall we?'

The Frenchman made a desperate grab for a shovel left propped against the wall of the outhouse.

'Aye, we can do it that way if you like.' Palmer took another pace forward.

Jack reached the side of the house, losing sight of Palmer as he and Billy made for the main road to the front of the officers' lodging.

'Wait!' Billy screeched in protest, desperate to witness the fight about to take place.

'Shut up.' Jack had no intention of waiting. He had the mule moving and he knew that if they stopped, they would have the devil's own job getting it going again.

As they emerged from the passage, he pulled the animal's head around, aiming it in the direction of their own lodging.

'Come on, you bastard.' The animal fought against their control, and Jack's boots skidded on the ground as he wrestled the beast after him. He just about had them going in the right direction when Palmer jogged out of the passageway, his head turning quickly from side to side before he spotted them.

He ran over to them, his face bearing the slightest hint of a flush.

'Did you get him, Mr Palmer, did you knock him down?' Billy dropped the lead rope as he ran towards Palmer.

'Come on, lad, no time for that now.' Palmer lowered a heavy arm around the boy and pushed him forward.

He trotted alongside the mule and flashed Jack a smile before slapping the animal hard on the flank. The mule responded by immediately charging forward. Jack stumbled and nearly lost his footing at the rapid increase in pace. Palmer laughed at the sight before easing himself into a run to keep up with the beast.

The two men, one boy and a single mule pounded through the quiet streets in the last of the night. They had all they needed.

Chapter Twenty

---◆---

Novara, June 1859

The tricolours were bright in the late afternoon sunshine as the tired French column marched into Novara. To the dusty and footsore soldiers it appeared that every inhabitant of the town had turned out to wave a flag in greeting. The huge crowd welcomed them with enthusiasm, their cheers and shouts accompanying the orchestra set up in the town square, which was blasting out 'Partant pour la Syrie', Napoleon's favoured choice of national anthem.

Jack grimaced as he forced away a plump middle-aged woman who had grabbed his cheeks before trying to kiss him full on the lips. She laughed, her mouth opening wide to cheer even as she stumbled backwards.

Ballard's little party marched in between two regiments of chasseurs, their single mule led by Billy, who had declared himself the animal's owner. They were all suffering from the heat and the dust, the long days of marching made all the more miserable by constant delays that left them exposed to the relentless sun for hour upon hour.

'Go away.' Jack used his palm to push away a young boy trying to hug his legs. He turned to Ballard. 'This is madness.'

The major marched at Jack's right. With Palmer on his other side, he was being spared much of the crowd's attention. 'It is a good madness, Jack. Do not be such a sourpuss.'

Jack only managed to growl in reply. The crowd's cheers doubled as they spotted a body of cavalry arriving behind the chasseurs. Jack did not think he had ever seen so many people in one place. A crowd dozens deep lined the streets. Every window was open, and townsfolk leaned out to wave their tricolours and halloo the troops marching below. The grander houses sported balconies, on which hordes of better-dressed citizens gathered, their cheers and waves no less enthusiastic than those coming from the dirtiest rascals cavorting in the gutters. The women tossed down rose petals, showering the heads of the crowd and the soldiers alike, their daughters blowing kisses to the more handsome in the ranks, their laughter unaffected by the ribald suggestions shouted back their way.

Another stout matron stepped forward. She collided with Jack, pressing against his arm before succeeding in planting a wet kiss on his cheek. She tried to reach Ballard, but Jack fended her away. He watched her carefully as she pirouetted to one side, a small tricolour brandished over her head like a trophy.

The column's pace had slowed to barely a crawl. The French soldiers were enjoying their role in the spectacle, and to a man they played to the crowd. Many raised their kepis on the barrels of their rifles, holding them high over the heads of the marching column. The locals thronged around them, the men grabbing hands whilst the women kissed any they could reach.

'Do try to enjoy yourself, Jack.' Ballard was forced to lean close so that his words could be heard over the tumult. 'I fancy it is not often a soldier is greeted thus.'

Jack was tempted to forcibly switch places with his commander and see how the major liked the attention. The idea died as the column came to a complete halt.

'For God's—' His curse was cut off as yet another woman came at him. He lifted a hand to push her away, but she was too quick and slipped into his arms before he could fend her off. She nuzzled against him, her face and hair pressing against his neck, her lithe body writhing against his hip. He slipped his arm around her waist and held her close. She smelled of soap and rose water, and with his hand circled around her hip, he could tell that she was slim. Encouraged, he risked a glance at her face. She was pretty, with dark brown eyes that sparkled as she cheered loudly in his ear. She laughed as she saw him looking at her, her head thrown back to reveal a long, slender neck.

'Now you like it better, I fancy,' Ballard shouted gleefully as he saw Jack entwined with his attractive admirer.

Jack said nothing. It had been a long time since he had held a girl. The crowd was now pressing forward to engulf the stationary column. His companion reached down to take hold of his hands. She pulled him from Ballard's side and he could do nothing but go with her.

The gap was immediately filled with more well-wishers. Jack could not help laughing as an older woman swept in and grabbed Ballard's cheeks before planting a series of loud kisses across them. The girl laughed with him, then pressed her own face forward, kissing him lingeringly on the lips. Her eyes were open, and she laughed as she pulled away, her cheeks tinted pink at what she saw reflected in his gaze.

She backed away, pulling Jack after her, easing him through the crowd. He went with her, the life in her eyes captivating him. She leaned forward to kiss him again before twisting away to haul him into the depths of the throng.

Jack turned to glance at his companions. Ballard and Palmer were both surrounded, and a stout matron was smothering Billy. Mary was at the boy's side. Someone had planted a flower in her hair, and she was laughing as a man kissed her hand.

Jack lost sight of them as his companion tugged him after her. They were in the thick of the crowd now. Men and women clapped him on the back, or tried to kiss his face, and he was buffeted from side to side as his partner cavorted in from of him. Eventually she found a space large enough to dance in. Those around them whooped with delight as they saw what she intended, many starting to clap and sing in encouragement.

Jack gave up any notion of fighting free and let himself be led into the dance. He would do what Ballard had suggested and try to enjoy himself.

'Wipe that smirk off your face, if you please, Jack,' Ballard snapped the moment Jack approached the small fire that would warm their camp that night.

He did his best to obey, hiding his face from his commander. Night was falling. Ballard and the others had not gone far. The column had taken several hours to clear Novara, and they would be spending the night in a field only half a mile from the town.

'Did you not enjoy the celebrations?' Jack could not resist the jibe.

'No, I did not.' Ballard was waspish. 'It was a trial, and one made all the harder by your absence.'

'You told me to enjoy it.'

'I did not mean by yourself. I did not bring you all this way to abandon me.'

'I did not abandon you.' Jack sat down on the ground opposite Ballard, their meagre fire between them. Palmer was off to one side, busying himself with a jug of beer that had been given to him by the good citizens of Novara. He seemed content to leave Jack and Ballard to their conversation, but Jack was sure that he would have at least one ear on what was said. Mary and Billy were curled up together under a blanket a few yards away, exhausted by the day.

'So whilst you were cavorting with that local girl—'

'I wasn't cavorting with her,' Jack interrupted his commander. His time with the girl had been rather enjoyable, but it had come to an end rather abruptly when her father had arrived to reclaim her. There had not been time for anything untoward to occur, but for the first time in a long while, he had been tempted by a woman. He shook the notion away. That was a complication he did not need. He had spent the next few hours trying to get back to his party. It had been a tiresome experience, but he had no intention of admitting that to Ballard.

'Did you hear what I just said?'

Jack focused his attention back on the major, who was staring at him across the fire. The flames lit his face with an orange glow that flickered across his features and cast his eyes into shadow.

'I'm sorry.' He offered a rueful half-smile. 'Do you mind repeating it for me?'

Ballard shook his head slowly. 'I give you news of the greatest import, yet your mind dwells on some skinny girl who dared to give you a kiss.'

'She wasn't all that skinny.' He might only have danced with her, but he had been left in no doubt as to what curves had been hidden under her thin summer dress. 'So what news?'

Ballard's lips pursed. 'I am of half a mind not to tell you.'

'I apologise, sir.' Jack tried to sound contrite. 'I'm all ears, I promise.'

'Very well.' Ballard needed no further urging. 'The Sardinians have won the first battle of the campaign.'

Jack laughed, thinking that he was being mocked. He caught a glimpse of Ballard's face in the firelight and it was enough to stop the laughter. 'You're serious?'

'I am always serious, Jack, I would have thought you had learned that much by now.' Ballard's finger lifted to toy with his moustache. 'Vittorio Emanuele may not need Napoleon's assistance after all. If what I hear is correct, the Austrians have been repulsed by a Sardinian attack. There are even tales of Vittorio himself fighting in the front line.'

Jack gave a single grunt in response. 'So it was a big battle, then?'

'So they claim. But the Sardinians would claim a dancing master wrestling with a stray dog to be a pitched battle, so we should not believe all I have been told. Whatever the facts, it is clear that the Austrians are dithering. I confess I cannot think why. They should be pressing home the advantage of their numbers whilst the allied army is still disjointed. If they let the French and the Sardinians combine, they will have made their task twice as difficult.'

Jack was listening carefully now. He understood Ballard's point. Together, the French and Sardinian armies would be more than a match for the Austrian force. If the Austrians had any nous, they would throw everything they had at the

Sardinians before the French arrived. He shook his head as he considered their folly. 'They are making Napoleon's task too easy. Once the armies are joined together, he can go on the offensive.'

Ballard offered one of his rare smiles. 'He is thinking bigger.'

Jack scowled. As ever, Ballard was withholding some of the information he had discovered. 'Go on.'

'Orders to march have already been given. The French are being bold. Napoleon has decided upon a flank march directly across the face of the enemy.' Ballard looked across to check that he had Jack's full attention. 'Come closer so I can explain.'

Jack did as he was bid and shuffled around the fire so that he sat next to his commander.

'We are here.' Ballard used a finger to draw a circle in the dusty soil. 'The enemy are spread across their lines of communication, but the bulk of their force is here.' He drew a second circle to the right and slightly above the first. 'The Sardinians are above us over here.' A third circle was drawn above the first and to the left of the one that denoted the Austrian force. 'If I understand correctly, the French are going to change the direction of their march and swing up and around to join the Sardinians in their current position.' He drew a line to join the two allied circles.

Jack frowned. He saw the plan immediately. It was as bold as Ballard had claimed. The French army would march northwards, directly across the front of the enemy forces. It would allow the two allied armies to combine whilst changing the direction of their attack. But it was full of risk. If the Austrians knew what was happening, all they had to do was advance and strike the French in the flank.

'It's a hell of a risk. That march will take days, if not a full week.' Jack had seen the danger to the French's army's open right flank. Moving an army was a slow business. The Austrians would have men keeping them in touch with both allied forces. They could not fail to see what was developing right in front of them. They would have plenty of time to organise their attack.

Ballard was slowly shaking his head. 'There is ninety-six kilometres of railway line running from Voghera to Vercelli.' He drew two small circles between the two allied armies. 'A march that would have taken four to five days can now be done in just one.' He raised an eyebrow. 'The world has changed, Jack. This is the modern age.' He slapped one hand into the palm of the other. 'We must grasp the potential that all these wonderful advances have presented to us.'

Jack heard the change in Ballard's tone. He was clearly impressed by the thinking of the French commanders. 'Their flank is still open.'

'By the time the dullards in the Austrian high command see the opportunity, it will be past.' Ballard leaned forward. 'This is modern war. Napoleon has grasped that fact; the Austrians have not. The Sardinians will launch a diversionary attack in the north, which should keep the enemy guessing for long enough for the French to move.' He shook his head before looking Jack firmly in the eye. 'The Austrians' timidity invites such a move, and I am pleased to say that we shall have the opportunity to see just how this hand plays out. I have found us a place.'

Jack held Ballard's gaze. 'Where?'

'With General MacMahon. He commands II Corps.'

'A corps commander, is that all? I would have supposed you would want to be with Napoleon himself.'

'I thought you would prefer to be closer to the action.'

Jack saw a flicker of unease in Ballard's eyes. It was hard to read his expression, especially in the firelight, but he had an inkling that the major was holding something back. 'You're not telling me everything.'

'Why do you say that?' Ballard scowled.

'I know you.' Jack had spotted the way Ballard's eyes narrowed as he absorbed the accusation. 'We are not just here to observe. You would never have accepted a place with a mere corps commander unless you had reasons for doing so.'

'It was all I could get.'

Jack snorted. 'You're a terrible liar.'

'You would know.' Ballard looked away and stared into the flames.

The silence stretched thin. Jack let it build, certain that it would defeat Ballard more surely than any argument he could concoct. He did not have to wait long to be proven correct.

'I suppose I should tell you.' Ballard glanced across at Palmer, who returned his stare as calmly as ever. 'You are correct, Jack.' He looked at Jack as he made his confession. 'There is something else we are here to do.'

'You devious bastard, I knew it.' Jack could not hold back the comment. He considered the interplay between Ballard and his bodyguard . 'Palmer knows this already, I take it?'

Ballard nodded.

'You couldn't trust me?'

'It is not a matter of trust, Jack. I would trust you with my life, I think you know that.'

'But not with this, whatever it is.'

'There was no value in you knowing.'

'So what has changed?' Jack searched Ballard's face for the truth. He did not know if he would ever find it.

'We are close now. You will need to know what you are looking for.' Ballard paused, then offered a tight-lipped smile. '*Who* you are looking for.'

Jack heard the confession being made. 'I see. So we came all this way to find someone?'

Ballard nodded. 'A young man whose father is keen for him to return home.'

'What's he doing here?'

'The young man in question fancies himself as something of an adventurer. He ran away from home to join the French forces. Now he is here, but his father wants him back.'

Jack absorbed the facts. 'This lad's father, he must someone important if he is willing to bankroll us.'

'He is a man of means, yes. I cannot reveal his identity to you, but I shall say that I trust his judgement completely.'

'And here you are. Ready to do his bidding.' Jack's first instinct was to mock.

'Do you not approve?' Ballard's eyes narrowed at the comment, yet he answered pleasantly enough.

Jack considered the question. 'No, I don't think I do. But I doubt either you or this rich old bastard, whoever he is, would think to ask my opinion.' He laughed at his own pomposity, then looked across to see Palmer's reaction, but the older man's face was carved from granite and gave nothing away.

He thought on Ballard's announcement. 'It's all rather convenient,' he was thinking and talking at the same time, 'you being in the right place and all. I take it that this man we are after is in MacMahon's division?'

'Yes.'

'A coincidence?'

'Please, Jack.' Ballard pouted at the very idea. 'Do you really think I would rely on chance?'

'So this has all been arranged?'

'Of course. Nothing happens by chance, do you see that now? It is all part of a design.' He stared at Jack. 'My design.'

'I see.' Jack tried not to let Ballard detect how impressed he was. He should have known that the major would have had everything planned down to the last detail.

'So what are we to do,' he asked the only question that seemed relevant, 'when we find this young miscreant?'

'It is very simple.' Ballard appeared to try to find another smile. He failed, and his expression looked much closer to a grimace than anything warmer. 'When we find him, we have only one course of action.' He looked Jack straight in the eye. 'We kidnap him.'

Chapter Twenty-one

---◆·◆·◆---

The day was the hottest yet. The line of march was littered with fallen treasures, the French soldiers abandoning the souvenirs they had brought with them from Novara. Jack scanned the debris. He saw nothing of value, at least not in military terms. The French army might have dumped anything that weighed them down, but they were not discarding any of their equipment. Their discipline was holding, even as they attempted to steal a march on their enemy.

The train ride from Voghera to Vercelli had taken Ballard's small party the best part of a whole day and half a night. It had been slower than anticipated, but they had still travelled the ninety-six miles in less time than even the fastest forced march. There had been no sign of the Austrians, even when they left Vercelli far behind and set out again on foot, their single mule still their only form of transport.

They had been on the road since dawn, marching in the dust of the troops ahead, and stopping only for an hour when the sun was at its height. Now the afternoon was drawing to a close and the cooler air of evening was providing a welcome respite.

The march had given Jack time to think on Ballard's mission. He examined his feelings to see if he liked the sound of this boy they had come so far to find. The lad had thrown off the shackles of his old life and found himself a new one, one that his family clearly did not approve of. In that way, this young rebel was very much like Jack himself. But Jack had embarked on his first charade out of desperation, his future bleak and without much in the way of hope. This boy's life was different. It would have been one of privilege and ease, a thousand options his for the taking. He had spurned such advantage, and to Jack's mind that made him just another callow fool with more money than sense.

'You look like you need a good shit.'

Jack grunted as Palmer aimed the barb. They were walking side by side at the head of their little column. The regiment in front had fallen out of the line of march, but Ballard had ordered his party to continue, the French soldiers' rest allowing the small group to march on without breathing in the persistent cloud of dust kicked up by their boots. It was not hard to agree with the decision, and the long, dreary trudge had been dramatically improved by their being able to breathe without choking.

'What do you reckon about this mission of ours?'

Palmer did not answer. His gaze was fixed on the scenery. The countryside they were passing through was lush and green, the rolling fields stretching away as far as the eye could see.

'Do you mind?' Jack broke the silence. He wanted Palmer's opinion.

'Do I mind what exactly?'

'Coming all this way for some little shit who has about as much sense as a dead sparrow?'

Palmer grunted at Jack's choice of words. 'No.'

'Truly? So you agree that it's worth this effort just to bring this posh boy home?'

Palmer's eyebrows knitted together. 'Mr Ballard thinks it is. That's good enough for me.'

'That's it?' Jack shook his head at the dull answer. 'Ballard says do it so that's enough?' He looked over his shoulder. Ballard was walking behind Billy and the mule. He was deep in conversation with Mary and would not overhear them.

'Aye. It's enough for me.' Palmer returned his gaze to the fields on either side of the lane they were tramping along. It was narrower than the main road they had followed for much of the day, its course meandering down the side of a hill towards a thin copse of trees.

'What a loyal fellow you are.' Jack tried to get a rise out of Palmer. He had never had such blind faith, not even when he was a raw recruit finding his way in the Queen's army. Such independent spirit had cost him, but he could not deny that part of his character. 'His hold over you must be pretty damned strong to have secured such devotion.'

Palmer glared at Jack for a moment before looking away, his expression guarded. 'You ask too many questions.' He made a play of glancing around them. 'Now I've got one for you.'

'What is it?'

'Where the fuck are we?'

Jack copied Palmer in scanning their surroundings. He saw no one and nothing, save for mile upon mile of empty country-side. They had been marching in the midst of an entire army, yet it appeared they had managed to get lost.

'Shit.' He ambled to a halt.

'Shit indeed,' Palmer agreed. 'We must've taken a wrong turn when we left those Frenchies.'

'We'll have to go back. We cannot have gone that far.' Jack turned and waited for Ballard to catch up.

'What is it?' Ballard called as he came closer.

'We took a wrong turn,' Jack answered.

'And how did *we* do that?' Ballard was clearly not impressed.

'It was Palmer's fault. He hasn't stopped talking since we left those French chasseurs. He didn't see the turn.' Jack tried to make light of the situation.

Ballard gave a derisive snort. 'There appears to be a hamlet ahead. Perhaps we will be able to find someone there who can do a better job of guiding us. You two walk ahead and see what is what. I'll follow with the others.'

Jack nodded in acknowledgement of the order. He could just about make out the top of the buildings Ballard had spotted. The hamlet was half hidden behind the copse of cypress trees they had been walking towards. On its far side, the ground sloped down sharply so that only a handful of red-tiled rooftops were visible. As far as he could make out, there could be no more than a couple of dozen dwellings at most.

As the two of them started to walk again, he felt an odd sensation, as though a cold hand had just brushed against the hairs on the back of his neck. It was late afternoon and all was quiet, the only sound, other than their boots and the hooves of the mule, the birdsong coming from the trees. Yet as they moved into the group of trees that straddled the lane, he began to feel uneasy.

The air grew cooler as the two men walked through the copse. Jack could smell the trees now they were underneath their canopy, the damp odour of a wood in summer. The feeling of unease was growing. He held out an arm and stopped Palmer in his tracks, then closed his eyes as he strained his hearing.

'What is it?'

Jack lifted a single finger to hush Palmer. He listened for a moment more, then opened his eyes once again. 'It's too quiet.'

Palmer said nothing, neither agreeing nor disagreeing with the observation. But he stood still and allowed Jack to listen.

The rest of the party came into the shadow of the trees.

'What is it now?' Ballard was close enough to snap the question.

Jack gave up his attempt to hear something. 'We need to get off the road.'

Ballard scowled. 'Why would we do that? I do not hear anything.'

'Then listen.'

'Come now, Jack. This is not the time. It's been a long day—'

'Be quiet, all of you. He's listening.' It was Mary who came to Jack's aid. 'He knows what he's about. You carry on, Jack.'

Jack caught her eye, but it was not the time to dwell on her support, even if it was the nicest thing she had said to him in weeks.

'Well, do you hear something or not?' Ballard fired off the question after a moment's pause, his voice tetchy. 'We can hardly stand here all day.'

'Hush.' This time Jack was sure there had been something. He raised a finger to silence any more questions, holding his breath as he tried to focus on the sound. It did not take long for him to know what he heard.

'Off the road. Now.' He hissed the command, then walked quickly to take the mule's lead rein out of Billy's hand. The animal brayed loudly in protest as he hauled it off the lane and deeper into the trees. 'Keep this bloody thing quiet,' he snapped as he handed the reins back to Billy, who was looking up at him with wide, excited eyes.

'What is it, Jack?' The boy was eager to know what had spooked him.

'Hush. Stay here. Look after your ma.' He turned to make sure the others had obeyed. 'Sir, stay here. I'll go ahead.' He looked at Palmer. 'You had better stay too.'

'Can't I come with you, Jack?' Billy made his plea quickly.

'No.' Ballard was quick to take charge. 'Jack, I'll follow you. Palmer will stay here.' He glanced sharply at Billy. 'As will you, William.' He looked back at Jack. 'What did you hear?'

Jack offered a thin smile. 'Horses, lots of them. And I wager they don't belong to the Frogs.'

Jack lay on the ground. It was damp, the undergrowth at the edge of the copse spongy beneath his chest. He had moved quickly through the last of the trees before going down on his belly to worm his way into the dense tangle of foliage at the copse's edge. He had chosen his spot with care, giving himself a clear view out of the trees whilst still being half hidden from view.

The ground sloped away sharply. The lane they had been following meandered downhill in a series of gentle curves towards the small hamlet that Ballard had spotted. It was not much of a place. The buildings that lined the lane were simple peasant houses interspersed with barns and outhouses. Most were made of stone, with small windows and wooden shutters, and none was of a size or grandeur to imply that anyone other than local farm workers lived there.

Jack eased himself into position, then pulled his field glasses from their leather case. The brass was cool in his hands as he readied them for use. He knew he owed Billy a coin or two for having the sense, and the deft fingers, to steal them for him.

The hamlet was quiet. He pressed the glasses to his eyes and panned slowly across the buildings. He saw no one. The silence pressed around him. Even the birds had gone quiet, the only sound the noise of branches and foliage moving in the gentle breeze wafting across the higher ground.

He focused on one of the larger houses near the centre of the village. He frowned. The shutters were closed, something that he found odd. It was late in the afternoon, the time for men to be returning from work in the fields, and for their womenfolk to be greeting them with food and drink. Instead he saw nothing and no one.

The sound he had heard earlier returned. It was louder, and this time he had no doubt what it was. He swung the glasses towards the far edge of the village. He saw what he expected to find almost immediately.

The Austrian cavalrymen were in no hurry. They entered the village at a gentle trot, their sabres sheathed. Clearly they were not expecting trouble, even this far from their own lines. Jack supposed they were a lightly armed patrol, the kind sent out far from the main body of the army to discover the location of the enemy forces. They were dressed as hussars, their uniform not dissimilar from that of the 15th Hussars that Major Ballard wore. But where Ballard's was dark blue, the Austrians' tunics were sky blue, with a green-faced shako with matching plume.

He kept his eyes on the cavalrymen as they rode into the village. They were close enough now for him to be able to pick out their voices and hear their laughter. They slowed their pace to a walk before coming to a full halt. He could make out the individual words as their leader gave the order to dismount. He did not understand what was said, but it was clear they intended to stay a while.

The Austrian commander's voice was not the only thing he heard. He lowered his field glasses, then eased on to one side so that he could look behind him. It sounded like a whole company of skirmishers was coming towards him, the noise of boots thrashing through the undergrowth loud enough to drown out the orders being shouted by the Austrians.

'For God's sake, keep it down!' he hissed.

Ballard emerged from the last of the trees. 'What can you see?'

Jack winced at his commander's loud voice. 'Get down before they see you.'

'Who will see me?' Ballard finally matched Jack's hushed tone. He crouched low, then scurried forward before dropping to the ground at his side.

'Austrian light cavalry. Probably just a patrol meant to establish where the French outposts are.' Jack gave the description in clipped, quiet tones.

'May I?' Ballard held out his hand.

Jack handed over his field glasses, then waited as Ballard made his own study of the enemy troops.

'Fine work, Jack.' Ballard finished his inspection quickly, then handed the glasses back. 'I knew I was right to bring you, even if it is your fault we are here in the first place.' The major's brow furrowed as he came to a decision. 'Well, we are lost, so perhaps they are too. Whichever it may be, I think our decision is clear. We will go back the way we came. There is no sense getting involved with these fellows.'

Jack nodded. He was in full agreement. Their party were ostensibly neutrals, but he did not want to explain the niceties of their presence to a group of Austrian cavalrymen.

Then the first scream shattered the quiet.

The sound undulated, overly loud in the still afternoon air. It was a dreadful noise, a banshee wail of horror that had no place being there.

Jack froze. The scream echoed through the buildings, rising in pitch before being shut off abruptly.

The quiet pressed back over them. It was as if the sound had never been, the scream a product of their imagination. He scanned the hamlet with his field glasses, searching for the source of the unholy noise. He saw nothing.

The Austrians had dismounted. He saw several of them walking easily down the hamlet's single lane. Some carried carbines, the shorter version of an infantryman's rifle. As he watched, a pair of them approached the door to one of the houses. They did not stop to knock, but simply battered it open with a combination of carbine stocks and boots. The door burst back on its hinges and they plunged inside, their carbines held ready to counter anyone who stood against them.

'The bastards.' He hissed the oath under his breath, then pulled the field glasses from his face. He had seen enough.

Another scream came. It was as dreadful as the first, but shorter, the sound cut off before it reached its crescendo. He looked up and saw Ballard watching him closely.

'What is happening?' The major spoke softly.

Jack was saved from giving a reply by the sound of a

commotion. He raised the glasses to his face in time to see a young girl burst out of a house and tear down the lane as if the very hounds of hell were on her tail. She was the first local he had seen, and he tracked her instinctively, his breath catching in his throat as he recognised her fear.

The girl ran hard, her skirts bunched in one hand. He caught the bright flash of a pale ankle as she tried to escape the two men who ran after her, their shouts of anger loud. She never stood a chance. She was running as fast as she could, but her pursuers were quicker. They caught her as she turned to run down the lane that led to the copse where Jack and Ballard lay watching.

One of the Austrian cavalrymen slapped the girl hard, the sound of the impact like a distant gunshot. Still she tried to get away. Jack saw her writhe back and forth in an attempt to free herself from their clutches. She was slapped again for her trouble, whilst the other man danced around her before darting forward to tear away her skirt.

For a moment Jack thought they would take her there and then. The fight had left the girl, and she did not resist as the men started to drag her away, their intent obvious.

A local man came out of the closest house. His shouts carried clearly to the British agents. He carried a long knife, the kind a peasant would use to carve bread or any haunches of meat that came his way.

The Austrian holding the girl laughed away the interruption before barking an instruction at his comrade, who immediately slipped his carbine from his shoulder.

The local cared nothing for the threat. He ran towards the pair of Austrian cavalrymen, bellowing in fury. Even from a distance, Jack heard the desperate anger in his voice, his horror at bearing witness to the girl's torment obvious.

He was still shouting when the closer of the two Austrians shot him.

Jack lowered the field glasses. Ballard was staring directly at him. There was a warning in his eyes.

Jack met the gaze evenly. He tried to deny the emotions that had been surging through his veins since the moment he had seen the girl attempt her desperate flight.

'The cowardly curs.' Ballard spoke softly, clearly appalled by what he was seeing. 'They are soldiers!'

Still Jack said nothing. He forced his breathing to slow, to counter the urge to act. He tried to convince himself that he had seen nothing more than the reflection of his nightmares. It was not his fight. The girl was not his concern, her honour and her soul not his to protect.

The scream came again. It was louder than before. It rose higher, the pitch pushing to a crescendo that went on and on, the sound wavering but left to echo through the silent hamlet.

'Jack!' Ballard's voice quivered with emotion. 'It is a shameful thing. It is despicable that soldiers would act in this way.' He paused to make sure he had Jack's full attention, speaking slowly and clearly. 'But we have a job to do. Do not put that in jeopardy.'

Jack kept his gaze riveted on Ballard's face, his eyes locked on to the coldness he saw reflected in the other man's stare.

He was up and running before the scream ended.

Chapter Twenty-two

———◆•◆———

*J*ack's breath echoed in his ears. It was all he could hear as he ran. Everything was focused on what was to come, on what he would unleash on the men who brought war to the innocent.

The ground flashed past under his boots, yards disappearing in seconds. He freed his weapons as he pounded on, the hilt of his stolen sabre snug in his right hand, the Colt revolver solid and sure in his left. The girl had been dragged from sight, so he concentrated his attention on the nearest house, his body thrilling with the promise of the violence to come. It was time to be who he was meant to be.

He hit the first door hard and went in fast. It took no more than a single heartbeat for his eyes to adjust to the gloomy interior. An Austrian cavalryman came staggering out of a rear room, his arms filled with a heavy sack of flour. Jack saw surprise register on the man's face before the sabre took his throat. The soldier hit the floor face down, his body thumping on to the sack, which burst on impact, filling the air with an explosion of white dust. He lay where he fell, his blood turning the spilled flour to red paste.

Jack felt nothing. He was already turning away, gore dripping from the sabre. Outside, he paused, glancing from side to side for no longer than a second before he was moving again.

He ran hard, bounding over a low wall as he made for the place he had seen the Austrians leave their horses. Two of their number came out of a house twenty yards to his front. They took one look at him before they dropped their haul of earthenware jugs and drew their swords.

He ran straight at them. He did not think of the odds, or of the risk to his blackened soul. He paid no attention to the sound of breaking pottery as the jugs smashed, their precious liquid spilling to darken the dusty soil.

The two Austrians were no raw recruits. They came at him with measured purpose, moving apart, clearing room for their sword arms as they prepared to cut down the blood-splattered madman charging towards them.

Jack saw their intent and skidded to a halt, his boots scrabbling for purchase. He spotted the flicker of alarm on the two faces now no more than ten yards away. There was time for the hint of a smile before he covered the first face with the barrel of his revolver.

The gun roared.

The first Austrian crumpled as the bullet tore into his chest. He fell without a sound, his body seeming to roll over itself as it tumbled forward.

The second man bellowed, raising the alarm, before the Colt's second bullet took him in the centre of his face.

Jack lurched back into motion, his eyes roving across the silent houses, searching for the one where the two Austrians had taken the girl.

A door to his right opened. He saw the frightened face of a young Austrian cavalryman roused by his companion's shout. It was not one of the men Jack was searching for, so he turned and vaulted over a low stone wall that ran alongside the lane.

Voices chased after him. More cavalrymen emerged to shout in alarm as they spotted the man who had come amongst them. He ignored them and kept moving, instinct driving him onwards.

Another door swung open. A man stepped outside, the sword in his hand incongruous against his naked legs. Jack recognised him in an instant.

The Austrian saw him coming. Unlike his comrades, he did not seek a fight. Instead he twisted away, making a grab for the door handle.

Jack knew what was intended. He forced his legs to work harder, straining for every last scrap of speed. Three paces on and he knew he would not make it. The door was already moving, the Austrian's face twisted with sudden fear as he tried to slam it shut.

Jack raised his revolver, his left arm braced. He fired as he ran. The first bullet chewed a thick splinter of wood an inch away from the Austrian's hand. The second hit the ancient wood half an inch below the first. The third took the Austrian in the throat.

Jack shouted then, the first sound he had made since he had left Ballard. He released the madness, the joy of rediscovering his bitter talent. He was aware that other men were chasing after him, but he paid them no heed. He thought only of the girl he raced to save. The man he had shot blocked the doorway, the door pressed hard against his bare legs. His shirt had rucked up as he fell, revealing his private parts. Jack barely noticed them as he leaped over the body and into the gloomy interior.

A sword came at him out of the darkness. He did not know what saved him. Instincts buried deep unleashed a parry that blocked the blade an instant before it sliced into his neck. His eyes adjusted to the gloom and he located his assailant before the sword came at him again.

This time the parry was easy. He swatted the blade aside, then countered with a strike of his own. He felt nothing as it was knocked away. It was simple to sway back, then let the inevitable counter flash past his chest. He held back his next stroke, instead twisting away from the door. He did not want the open entrance at his back, the men coming after him sure to be only too willing to slide a blade into his unprotected spine.

It was as he moved that he saw the other bodies in the room. One was dead, a gaping chasm where a throat had been. He was an old man, his grey beard now blackened with blood.

The second body was still very much alive. The girl he had watched being taken away was sliding backwards on the floor, the tattered remains of her dress clutched around her. He caught a glimpse of her naked chest, but her lower clothes appeared intact, and his heart sang as he realised he had arrived in time.

'Come on then!' He fanned the flames of his own fury. The sight of the abused girl spurred him on, and he attacked the enemy soldier, his stolen sabre moving fast. The sword blurred through the air, flowing through the blows, one coming after the other without thought. The Austrian whimpered as he fought, a cry escaping his lips every time he managed to block another attack.

Jack began to laugh. He taunted the Austrian, his superiority revealed with every hammering blow he struck. He was still laughing as he knocked the man's sword wide, then stepped forward and punched his sabre into the man's chest, pushing his weight behind it, driving the blade deep.

He came close to the man he was killing, his face no more than an inch from the Austrian's nose. He sneered as the would-be rapist died in front of him, the feel of his blood hot and sticky on his hands. He did not shirk from the horror he saw reflected in his opponent's eyes, the final glimmer of terror unleashed. Then with a great roar he threw the man away, forcing the corpse from his blade and freeing it ready for the fight he knew was still to come.

The door was yanked open. The rest of the cavalrymen had arrived.

Jack lifted his left hand. He fired his last bullet, the shot catching the arm of the first man through the door. He let the gun fall from his hand, then attacked with his sabre, his first, desperate blow forcing the wounded man to a take a step backwards.

He snarled as he fought now, his sabre battering away the wounded Austrian's weak counter-stroke. The man did not try again. Instead he slipped to one side, making space for a second cavalryman to step forward.

Jack cared nothing for the new arrival. He parried the Austrian's first thrust, then drove his sword hard at the man's gut. He felt the tip score into flesh before the Austrian brought his own sword back in a desperate parry. Jack recovered the blade, then slashed it at the man's face, a triumphant bellow escaping his lips as he saw it slice through his cheek.

He stepped backwards quickly, twisting to one side as the second sword came for him. He had no choice but to give ground and was forced back. A third then a fourth cavalryman pushed their way into the room, come to exact their revenge.

Revenge they would never get.

The crash of the revolver was loud enough to drown out the pants and bellows of the fighting men. The Austrian nearest the door fell, his hands clasped to his back. The three men left standing whirled around. They had time to see a figure fill the doorway before the revolver fired again. In such an enclosed space, it was as easy as knifing eels in a barrel, and not one bullet missed. The last three Austrians died within the span of few heartbeats, the revolver used with unerring accuracy.

Jack watched as the men died in front of him. It was only when the gunfire stopped that he finally lowered his bloodied blade.

'You're a fucking fool.' Palmer strode into the slaughter-house, his nose twitching at the taint of blood and gun smoke that lingered in the air.

'And you were damned slow in getting here.' Jack bent down to retrieve his revolver from the floor, then sheathed his blood-smeared sabre. He did not look at the bodies. He turned instead to face the girl he had come to rescue. She huddled in the shadows, wrapping her torn clothes around her, looking back at Jack with eyes wide with terror.

'It's all right, love. We're not like them.' Jack tried to smile. The girl looked anything but reassured. 'It's okay.' He held up a hand. It was covered with gore. He saw the girl cringe away from him like a child recoiling from the image of a monster in a fairy tale.

'Shit.' He spat out the word, then turned away. He felt tired. He looked at Palmer. 'I'll fetch Mary. She'll know what to do.'

Palmer grunted. He was checking the bodies, prodding each

one with the toe of his boot to check they were truly dead. Satisfied, he glanced at the girl. 'You did all this for her?'

Jack made a play of checking over his revolver in lieu of answer.

'Was that the reason?' Palmer repeated his question.

Jack looked up. 'Yes.'

Palmer held his gaze for a good while. Then he nodded. He did not say anything more.

Chapter Twenty-three

———•◆•———

Dawn came quickly. The night had passed peacefully, the men and women of the small hamlet providing the best they could for the foreigners who had fought and killed on their behalf. Food had been produced, and a raw red wine had washed down the evening's dinner that for once they had not had to cook for themselves.

Jack walked out of the house where he had been given a bed. He had slept like the dead. He had been exhausted; the fight had drained him of every scrap of strength. He was out of condition, soft after so long sleeping in warm beds. He was not concerned. The toughness would come fast, the hard days and bitter nights of a campaign sure to harden his flesh until he could march all day and still fight at the end of it.

The birds were singing, so he paused on the threshold of the house to listen to their song. The air was chill, but the sun was warm on his face, its heat dancing across his skin to leave it tingling. He closed his eyes to savour the sensation.

Hearing the soft scuff of footsteps, he opened his eyes, blinking hard as the sun seared into them. He saw Mary walking towards him, a tin mug in her hands.

'God save me, but tell me that is tea.' Jack lifted a hand to shelter his eyes. He saw Mary smile at his greeting. The sight surprised him. He could not recall when he had last earned such a reward.

'You're in luck. But it's the last of the leaves, so you'd better enjoy it whilst you can.'

Jack drank in Mary's appearance as she walked towards him. He had not looked at her properly for some time, and now he glimpsed the girl he had once doted on in the woman coming towards him. She was dressed in a simple cotton dress in a warm blue fabric, a gift from the locals, and her hair was pulled back and tied behind her head. She looked clean and fresh and he felt the stirring of an old desire.

'Stop staring,' Mary told him, but the rebuke was delivered with little force. She came close enough to hand over the tea.

'Thank you.' Jack cradled the mug, luxuriating in the warmth that seeped into his hands. 'Is this really the last of it?'

'It is. Don't tell Mr Ballard that I let you have it.'

'Then I must thank you.'

'You did a good thing. You deserve a reward.'

'Do I?' Jack took a sip of the tea, closing his eyes as he savoured the taste. He would miss it. The French officers drank tart green coffee by the sackload. It was not a patch on a mug of good thick, tarry tea.

'Of course.' Mary came to stand at his side so that the sun was on her face. 'You saved that poor girl.' She looked up at him, her eyes screwed almost shut against the sun. 'It was a brave thing to do.'

'I doubt your precious Mr Ballard would agree.'

'Those bastards had it coming. You gave it to them.' Mary

scowled. 'They deserved to die for what they were doing.'

Jack snorted at her fierce words. They reminded him that Mary was harder than he gave her credit for. 'I'm glad I did something right for once.'

'For once you did.' She turned her scowl on him. 'My Billy thinks you're quite the hero.'

'The lad might be right.'

'No, he's not.' Mary was firm on the matter. She sighed. 'He's an impressionable young boy who's never had anyone to look up to, not a man at least.'

'And he looks up to me?'

'He won't for long. I'll make sure of that.'

'He might not listen to you.'

'Oh, he will. You did right to save that girl, but it doesn't make up for what happened in London.' Her words were sharp.

'I know that.'

Mary shook her head. 'I don't reckon you can ever make up for that.'

'So I'm damned for all eternity?'

'Yes.' Mary's scowl softened, and she sighed. 'But then we're all damned, aren't we?'

Jack understood that was all the concession he was going to get. 'Then at least I'll have some company.'

'You will that.' Mary almost smiled. 'We'll all be down there right alongside you.'

'Well, that's all right then. At least I won't be alone.'

'You will always be alone, Jack Lark.' Mary shook her head slowly as she looked up at him. 'You won't ever let anyone get close to you.'

Jack heard the truth in her words. It shamed him into silence.

They stood together in the sun, each alone with their thoughts. The silence was only broken when they heard the sound of someone else approaching, and the girl Jack had rescued came into view carrying two buckets of water. The hamlet was attempting to return to normal after the traumatic events of the previous day. Mary raised a hand to wave in greeting. She was rewarded with a fleeting smile.

Jack watched as the girl walked past. He might have tried to hide it, but he could not deny the pride he felt at what he done. Had he not intervened, her life would have ended in blood, pain and fear. Instead she was up and about almost as if nothing had happened. She had not been spared completely, and he was certain she would be troubled by nightmares for a long time to come. But it was a small price to pay to have avoided the fate she had faced at the hands of the Austrian cavalrymen.

'She'll live.'

Jack looked at Mary sharply. Her words were hard, yet he did not want to risk an argument, not after the progress they had made, so he said nothing and contented himself with watching the girl. She walked slowly, her heavy load slowing her pace. The morning sun was behind her, and he could make out the shape of her legs through her simple cotton shift. He supposed she was beautiful, in a winsome, girlish sort of way. She was the kind of girl a young lad could happily fall in love with.

His reverie was brought to an abrupt halt when Mary rapped him on the arm. 'Don't stare so. She's too young for you.'

Jack laughed. 'Am I old, then?'

'Too old for a girl like that.'

'She's not to my taste. She's too thin. I prefer my women

with a bit of meat on their bones.' He reached across and poked Mary in the side of her stomach. His hand was slapped away. But he saw the smile sneak unbidden on to her face.

'Don't even think about it.'

'I wasn't.'

'Of course you were.' Mary snorted. 'You've been wanting to get into my drawers ever since you got hair on your balls.'

Jack guffawed at her turn of phrase. 'So I'm not good enough for your bed?'

'No. Never was and never will be.'

'Harsh.'

'But true.'

'So you like men with a bit more gravitas?' He caught her eye. 'Do you like the Devil, then?'

Mary laughed the idea away. 'Of course not. He wouldn't have the likes of me.'

Jack heard a trace of nervousness behind the laugh. 'It happens.'

'Not to folk like me.'

'I've seen it.' Jack thought back to his previous adventure with Ballard. There had been a woman then. Her name was Sarah and she came from a background not wholly dissimilar to Mary's. She had married well and had taken the rewards it had brought her.

'Fairy tales don't count, Jack. They ain't real.'

'It wasn't a fairy tale.' He reflected on how Sarah's life had played out. It was not something he would recommend. 'But I'm sure you're right. It's not for the likes of you.'

Mary opened her mouth to reply. Whatever she was about to say was lost as a sound like thunder echoed along the horizon.

'What the hell is that?' she asked in the silence that followed.

The sound came again before he could reply. This time it lasted for longer, rolling out and growing louder before stopping abruptly. Jack was already moving, calling for Palmer as he went.

The bodyguard, who had been staying in the same house as Jack, came out quickly, blinking in the bright sunshine.

'You hear that?' Jack snapped the question as the noise returned, louder than before.

Palmer nodded. He said nothing.

'Get the mule ready.' Jack gave the order before turning back to Mary. 'Find Billy. We need to get moving.'

Mary looked from one man to the other. 'Will one of you kindly tell me what the devil that is?' she demanded, hands on hips.

Palmer ignored her and went off to find the mule. Mary grabbed Jack's arm, making him face her.

'What is it?' she repeated.

'Guns. Artillery, anyway,' Jack replied. 'Someone has just started a battle.'

They had left quickly. The locals had not seen them off. Jack got the sense they were relieved at their departure. They might have saved one of their girls from being ravaged, but they were still strangers. Their presence was tolerated, but they were a reminder of a day the villagers would spend years trying to forget.

'What do you make of it?'

Ballard walked at Jack's side. His legs were shorter than Jack's, so he was forced to move them quickly to keep pace.

'It's no skirmish.' Jack cocked an ear. The noise of the guns was constant now, intensifying the closer they got. He felt a part of himself awakening at the sound.

'Then we must move quickly.'

'We are.' Jack heard the anxiety in Ballard's voice. He did not recall seeing his commander this tense.

'Well, we must keep up the pace. We shall not stop, not for anything.'

'Then save your breath for marching.' Jack's reply was waspish. It earned him a scowl.

'Do not forget why we are here.' Ballard ignored Jack's advice. 'I have not forgotten your actions.'

'You think I did the wrong thing?' Jack scoffed at his master's words.

'You disobeyed me.'

'I saved that girl.'

Ballard did not reply immediately. When he did, his voice was like ice. 'We have a duty to find this boy. I vowed to his father that we would keep him safe. I intend to keep my word.'

'We might not even find him. A battle is a bloody big place. We have a whole army to search through.'

'Nonsense.' Ballard's reply was immediate. 'I know his regiment. It will be a simple enough task to find them.'

'And then what?' Jack felt his breath catch in his chest. They were walking briskly, and the advice to save their breath had not been solely for Ballard's benefit.

'Then you keep him safe. When the opportunity arises, you take him away.'

'What, we ask him to come with us?' Jack mocked his commander. 'Swan in there and pluck him out of their bloody line? You think they'll just let him go?'

'Of course not, but I am sure a man of your talents will be

able to find a way. Until then, you will keep him safe. You and Palmer know how to fight. Use that knowledge to protect the boy.'

Jack bit off a sharp retort. He was tweaking the tail of the Devil, and he would do well to mind his tongue. Ballard was not a man to cross. 'Let's find him first. Then we can decide what to do next.' He tried to mollify his commander.

'You will do more than that.' Ballard snapped his reply. 'I brought you here for this, and this alone. When you find him, you will protect him in any way you can, no matter what it takes.'

Jack understood the tone. There was no need to reply, so he saved his breath for what was to come.

Chapter Twenty-four

The French army was on the move. The enemy had finally been forced into action. Now Napoleon had the chance to test the mettle of his troops on the field of battle. His II Corps, commanded by Général de Division MacMahon, was marching to take up position to make an attack.

Ballard's small party was caught up in the rush. They had left the hamlet behind and marched towards the sound of the guns. Within an hour they were back in the midst of the French army as it manoeuvred towards the Austrian force. The road was clogged with men, horses and wagons. Progress was slow, and the column they followed was frequently forced to stand idle in the sun as the road ahead became blocked.

'This is chaos.' Ballard made his verdict on the continued delays clear.

Jack looked around. To his mind, the column was as ordered as it could be. The French army was reacting well and moving at a decent pace. 'It's not so bad. Don't panic.'

'Panic indeed.' Ballard glared at him, his face flushed. 'Ah, Jack, quickly now, stop that fellow.' The major had spotted a rider trying to force a passage through the column.

Jack did as he was told. It was easy enough to wait for the rider to get close. Then it was a simple matter of grabbing his bridle and tugging him to a halt.

'*Monsieur!*' Ballard stepped up to the man's stirrup before he could snap at Jack to release his bridle. 'Major Ballard, British Intelligence, attached to General MacMahon.' He shouted the fleeting introduction.

The French officer looked anything but impressed. 'What do you want? Be quick now, I have an urgent dispatch for Général de Castagny.' His English was good.

'Where is General MacMahon's headquarters?'

The Frenchman scowled. 'A mile ahead, perhaps less. They spent the night bivouacked around Turbigo. Now please let go of my bridle.'

'What has happened?' Ballard clearly did not care for the Frenchman's supercilious attitude.

'The Austrians happened, *monsieur*. They hold the high ground around Magenta.'

'You did not expect them to be so far north, did you?'

'Perhaps not, but now we have them and we can bring them to battle.'

'What of their numbers?'

'Forty thousand, perhaps more.' The French officer's horse tossed its head, forcing Jack to wrestle with it to maintain his hold. '*Monsieur*, I must get on.'

'One last question. What are your orders?'

'To attack the enemy, as quickly as we can.'

Ballard stood back, then gestured for Jack to let the man's bridle go. He had learned enough. The second major engagement of the campaign had begun.

* * *

The man's arm was gone. All that was left was a bloody stump liberally swathed in bandages now soaked with gore. Yet he still found the strength to wave at Mary as the cart he was on went past, his face creasing into a smile as he spotted her blue cotton dress amidst the sea of uniforms.

They had been walking for hours, and it was now early afternoon. They had crossed the River Ticino on a pontoon bridge at Turbigo before passing through another village called Robecchetto as they tried to catch up with MacMahon's II Corps. The number of casualties coming back the other way had increased with every mile. The French were well organised, and so far all the wounded they had seen were being taken away from the front line in ambulances and wagons standing ready for just that purpose.

'Poor bastards.' Jack stood back to let the next cart pass. Six men were on board. All were wounded, their faces bearing the strain of being maimed in the opening salvos of the battle.

'They're the lucky ones.' Palmer stood grim-faced at his side.

'Come along.' It was Ballard who geed them up. 'We must get going.'

Palmer caught Jack's eye and shrugged. He moved away, quick to obey. Jack took one last look at the cart full of wounded soldiers making slow progress against the tide of fresh troops marching the other way, then he followed the others.

They made their way into a small town that a few quick questions allowed them to identify as Cuggiono. The column they had attached themselves to pressed on, the men marching quicker now. The noise of the artillery fire had increased, the sound pounding out without pause, the air shaking with every salvo. Jack could smell the battlefield in the whiff of powder smoke drifting on the breeze, and in the tang of blood as each wagon ground its way past.

They passed silent houses, their windows shuttered and doors barred. Any inhabitants were hiding away deep inside, those foolish enough not to have fled at the sound of the first guns now at least wise enough to stay out of sight. Tricolours hung from empty balconies, forlorn and abandoned. The hasty celebrations that had marked the arrival of the French army had been quickly forgotten as the locals realised they were on the front line of a battle.

Orders came faster now. Riders rushed past the slow-moving column, their faces flushed and excited as they galloped between senior officers, passing commands and information, their horses snorting and whinnying as they were ridden hard.

Ballard pulled out a little black leather notebook and scribbled a quick series of notes with a pencil. They were now on the eastern flank of the Ticino river, at the western edge of the Lombard plain, a great plateau that stretched for miles until it reached a far line of hills. The ground closest to the river was poor, and Jack saw that the flooded fields would be a nightmare for the infantry. The plateau itself was largely unbroken open ground, save for a scattering of dense patches of fruit trees. The fields to either side of the road were planted to crops, and he could see the lead battalion of the column flattening a field of wheat as they manoeuvred.

'Where are the enemy?' Ballard came close to Jack's side and bellowed the question in his ear. Orders were being shouted back and forth as the troops in front of them deployed off the road, marching to the right to clear the way for the men in the battalion behind.

'Over there!' Jack waved an arm to point ahead. He was

trying to make sense of what he was seeing. The French battalions were forming up in line at right angles to the road. A large number of French artillery pieces were already there, massed in a single enormous battery facing south. They were firing fast, the gunners sweating around their heavy cannon.

'I see.' Ballard was making quick sketches in his little book. 'Once we are re-formed, will we sweep forward?'

'No.' Jack shook his head. He understood the French formation better than his commander. 'The Frogs are going on the defensive.'

Ballard's face creased into a scowl. 'How so?'

'If they were going to attack, they would be staying in column.' Jack looked up and down the French line. 'This is a defensive formation,'

'Which means what precisely?'

'Which means they reckon the bloody Austrians are coming this way. The French are preparing for defeat.'

'Are you sure?' Ballard's disbelief was obvious.

'Yes. They are preparing to cover a retreat.'

As if to emphasise the notion, the French guns fired another salvo.

'There is still fighting ahead.' Ballard jabbed a finger.

'And it looks like the Frenchies are taking a pounding.' Palmer made the announcement as he came to stand at their side.

Jack looked where Palmer was indicating. A stream of fresh casualties was swarming back along the road. Some were in ambulances, whilst others came alone or walking in pairs. There were many more than they had seen already, the fighting getting heavier and more destructive. Most were making for a first aid post set up on the edge of the town. The post flew a black flag, to let both sides know that it was a place of refuge and not a target.

'Keep the boy away.' Ballard snapped the order at Mary. Billy had led the mule forward with his mother, and now the lad was staring at the sad procession of broken bodies.

'I ain't bothered,' Billy protested. 'I've seen worse.'

'Come on, never mind the lad, we need to get off the road.' Jack spied another battalion of French infantrymen advancing behind them.

'Good idea.' Ballard scanned around. 'Head towards the aid station. I shall endeavour to find the commander of this battalion. With luck he can tell me where our man might be. Palmer, stay with me. Jack, take the others.' He gave his orders quickly. It was time to try to make sense of the confusion, and find their target.

'I have news.' Ballard made the announcement as he bustled over to where his small party waited for his return, not far from the first aid post. 'No one quite knows where anyone is.' He shook his head as he came to stand in front of Jack. 'You would think a damned general would know where his own men might be.'

'It's a battle. This is what they are like.' Jack snorted at Ballard's crass comment. He nodded to a grim-faced Palmer, who trailed dutifully in his master's wake.

'Well, it should be more organised. I am certain Wellington knew better.'

'I'm sure he didn't.'

Ballard glared at Jack, but Palmer laughed, earning a sharp look of his own.

'That's enough.' Ballard pulled out his notebook and flicked through to the last page. 'Now listen carefully. The enemy are about two miles ahead. MacMahon's corps was advancing on two fronts, but it appears the divisions have become separated. His right division under Général de la Motte-Rouge is at a place called Boffalora, a couple of miles to the south of here. They had nearly reached the town's bridge when MacMahon ordered them to hold their ground. We are with his reserve column. They have been ordered to consolidate here with the bulk of his artillery.'

Jack nodded. It made sense of what he could see around him. The general had ordered his reserve column to join his artillery so as to provide a solid defensive position to anchor the attack should his two main divisions be forced to pull back. That still begged the obvious question.

'So the first division is at Boffalora. The reserves are here. Where is the second division?'

'The second division under Espinasse was advancing out on the left. MacMahon lost contact with them a couple of hours ago.'

'So where's our man?' Jack opted not to pass comment on the skill of a general who somehow managed to lose a whole division.

'We know that he serves in the French Foreign Legion. They form a part of Espinasse's division.'

'And no one knows where they are.' Jack absorbed the news.

'No.' Ballard spotted something in Jack's reaction that led him to purse his lips, but he did not let it stop him continuing with his news. 'There are reports that the second division's lead regiment was also advancing on Boffalora shortly before the first division got there. Others say they are held up at a place called Marcallo, a mile or so to the left of our advance.' He looked up. 'That must be over there to the east.'

'What is your good friend the general doing to find his men?' Jack tried to make sense of the conflicting reports. It was clear that the truth of the matter was that no one knew where the second division had gone.

'He has patrols scouring the area. However, the Austrians are now counter-attacking all along the line, and MacMahon is worried that his men will be pushed back. If the Austrians can force their way into the gap between his two divisions, there will be no one to stop them crushing the whole French flank.'

'So it's a bloody mess?'

'The situation is rather fluid, yes.'

'And what do we do?'

Ballard's eyes narrowed at the question. 'There is only one thing to do, Jack. We go and get our man.'

'We?'

Ballard gave one of his rare smiles. It was not reassuring. 'You and Palmer are the best men for this job. As much as I may wish it were otherwise, I know I would only slow you down. We will stay here. I want you to head east. Find this village called Marcallo. It is as good a place for you to start as any.'

Jack glanced at Palmer. The big man's face was impassive. 'So be it.' He looked back at Ballard. 'So what's this bugger's name then?'

'His name is not important.' Ballard scowled at the question.

Jack was not deterred by his commander's expression. 'Of course it is. How else are we to find him?'

'I don't know his name.' Ballard gave the admission through gritted teeth. 'At least, what name he is using currently.'

'You don't know?' Jack could not help the smile creeping

on his face. 'You don't know?' he repeated the question with relish.

'No, Jack, I do not.'

'So what does he look like then? We need something to go on, or are we supposed to interrogate every man we find to see if he is someone's son and heir?'

Ballard did his best to ignore the barb. He dug in a pocket and pulled out a miniature portrait, which he handed to Jack.

'This is the image I was given of the boy.'

Jack looked at the portrait. The face of a boy stared back at him. He could not have been more than ten or eleven years old. He had a shock of blond hair, and bright blue eyes.

'Blow me, are we looking for a nipper?'

'It is a little out of date, I grant you. But his features are recognisable enough.'

Jack snorted. It was not much to go on. 'How old is he now?'

'Twenty-two.'

'And where did you get this?'

'His father gave it to me. Now, you have your orders and you know what must be done.' Ballard moved the conversation along briskly. 'Your first task is to keep the boy safe, no matter what it takes. Then, when the opportunity occurs, you will bring him to me.' He turned away, his orders given.

Jack caught Palmer's eye. The big man shrugged. Jack wanted to say something to Mary, but she was already fussing over Ballard and did not look his way. So he did what he was told and followed Palmer to war.

Chapter Twenty-five

———◆———

Jack and Palmer stepped off the road to walk in the ditch at its side. The traffic coming the other way was heavy, with a large number of wounded troops making their way to the rear.

They had left Ballard and the others behind, heading east across country in search of the men of MacMahon's second division. Twice they had been forced to go to ground as large bodies of Austrian Uhlans and skirmishers probed the gap between the French general's two divisions. Their nerves had been stretched thin as they hid away, but eventually they had found their way on to a road heading south that they hoped would lead them to the village of Marcallo.

Jack looked over the men coming back the other way along the road. The French infantrymen had clearly been in a hard fight. Their dark blue uniforms were streaked with dust, and several had lost the light kepis from their heads. Many wore light blue neck scarves, a new addition to their uniform that most of the French army had picked up in Genoa, and a number of these had been pressed into action as temporary bandages.

Most of the wounded walked past with their heads bowed and their eyes averted. But a few looked at the two men in civilian clothes going the wrong way. One, an officer sporting a blue sash around his waist and an open waistcoat that revealed a white shirt streaked with blood, paused long enough to call across to them.

'*Messieurs, vous allez dans le mauvais sens.*'

'What's that?' Jack had no idea what he was being told.

'He says we are going the wrong way,' Palmer replied. He ignored the French officer.

'You understand Frog?'

Palmer shrugged.

'*Vous devriez faire demi-tour,*' the officer called over his shoulder. '*Si vous tenez à votre vie.*'

'What does he say?' Jack asked as the last of the battalion passed them by.

'He says it's fine. Nothing to worry about.'

'Bullshit.'

Palmer shrugged. 'It doesn't matter what he says. We have our orders.'

Jack did not bother to reply. He followed Palmer, heading towards the battle that they could hear raging ahead. They kept to the ditch, leaving the road to the wounded French soldiers.

'Poor buggers,' Jack observed.

'They're well out it.' Palmer glanced down at the revolver on Jack's hip. 'You loaded?'

Jack nodded. He had prepared the firearm while he was waiting for Palmer and Ballard to return. He let his hand fall to his holster and unbuckled the flap.

He could see a village directly ahead. It was wreathed in

powder smoke, and the only French troops in evidence were those coming towards them, away from the fighting.

'You think that's Marcallo?' he asked.

'Aye. We'd better get a move on. Looks to me like the Frenchies aren't going to stand there for long.'

'We could wait here. Ask after our man as they come back.'

Palmer laughed off the notion. 'Come on, Jack. You frightened?'

'Of course.' Jack's right hand took hold of the hilt of his sabre. 'But that's because I am not bottle-head stupid. Not like some.'

Palmer ignored the reply and moved off at a trot. Jack went with him. They moved quickly. The traffic on the road had reduced to a trickle, only a handful of Frenchmen now making their way away from the fighting. Both the road and the ditch were littered with discarded equipment, and Jack's boots kicked a discarded kepi as he scrambled back up on to the road as it entered the outskirts of the village.

The houses in front of them bore the scars of the fighting. Walls were cracked and pockmarked, the ground around them piled with rubble. The air was full of dust and powder smoke, the smell catching in Jack's throat. The sound of rifle fire echoed down the street. Somewhere ahead a French unit was heavily engaged with the enemy.

Jack saw two French officers run into a house just to their right. He guessed the building had been turned into a command post, and that made it a wise choice of destination.

'Quick, in there.' He led Palmer across the road and into the house.

It was noisy inside. Raised voices shouted and bellowed as half a dozen officers tried to make sense of the fight. A scarred kitchen table had been dragged to the centre of the room and pressed into service. A single map was on its top, and the two officers Jack had followed inside were busy pointing at various spots as they made a report to an older officer standing on the far side of the table.

Jack could understand nothing. The French officers were talking loudly and quickly. One of them turned to push past as he made his way back out. If he was surprised to see two civilians, he did not wait around long enough to show it.

'Ask them where we can find the Legion.' Jack shouted the instruction into Palmer's ear.

Palmer nodded in agreement, then pressed forward, using his elbows freely to force his passage. Jack had seen enough so made his way back outside.

Palmer was not long in joining him.

'They're not here.'

'Then where the hell are they?' Jack was not impressed.

'No one knows. These fellows are from the same division, but they've no idea where the Legion has got to.'

'Shit.' Jack spat out the single word.

Before Palmer could say anything further, a great roar rose from just ahead and a wave of French infantrymen came running towards them, their ranks in disarray. Some stopped to turn and discharge their rifles, but most just kept going. More soldiers followed them, at least a hundred now, every man's eyes bright white in his powder-streaked face.

The French officers came rushing out of their command post. Orders were shouted as they ran towards their men. Already some were stopping, the retreat losing its impetus as the officers started to regain command of the frightened infantrymen.

'Come on.' Palmer grabbed Jack's arm, pulling him away.

'We should help.' Jack shook off the grip.

'And do what?' Palmer snapped. 'They will hold or they won't. We won't make a difference.'

Jack ignored him and strode into the melee. The French officers were trying to form their men up into line. Most were slow to obey, their expressions revealing their fear. Jack snatched his revolver from its holster and forced himself into the press of bodies.

'Form line!' he shouted, not caring if he was understood or not. 'Form line, damn your eyes.' He hauled a man around, forcing him into place at his side. Around him the French officers were doing the same, and slowly a formed line began to emerge from out of the chaos. Other soldiers saw what was being done and joined in, filling out the line so that it stretched from one side of the road to the other.

'Face front.' Jack could not help bellowing the order. He stood in the centre of the front rank. The pants and gasps of the breathless French infantrymen around him were subsiding, their fear now held in check as their officers brought them back under control.

'*Ils arrivent!*'

Voices cried out in warning, the sound just about audible over the shouts of the officers.

Jack saw the flood of white-uniformed soldiers come charging into view. There was no time to dwell on his first sight of the Austrian army, and he raised his revolver, filling the space over the end of the barrel with the face of an enemy soldier.

'*Feu!*'

'Fire!' Jack bellowed at the men around him as he pulled the trigger. Those French soldiers with a loaded weapon opened fire. This was no organised volley, yet it still cut down the leading ranks of Austrian troops.

Jack fired again and then again, emptying the revolver's chambers without pause. Around him, French infantrymen were reloading as fast as they could, their hands moving with desperate haste.

The command to fire came for a second time. This time more men were ready and the volley had more effect. Dozens of bullets flayed the advancing Austrian ranks, knocking over those leading the charge.

It would be enough. The Austrian infantry had pushed the French back from the far side of the village, but the impetus of their attack was spent. It was their turn to retreat, the loud shouts of the officers calling the battered ranks away.

The French had held, and now their officers shouted orders of their own as they prepared to advance once again. Jack pushed his way out of the line and returned to find Palmer sitting calmly on a low wall to the front of the command post. He was paying the fighting no heed, and was using a lock pin to clean under his nails. From somewhere he had secured a French rifle, and he had slung an ammunition pouch over his shoulder and attached a cap box to his belt. A bayonet tipped the rifle, a thin smear of blood on the blade showing that it had already seen use that day.

'Are you done now?' The question was delivered with a fair dollop of sarcasm.

'Shut your mouth.' Jack did not appreciate Palmer's tone. He strode past, not caring if the man followed him or not.

Chapter Twenty-six

———◆—◆—◆———

'So where to next?' Jack posed the question as they picked their way through the debris spread across the road. The sun was low in the sky to the west as the two Englishmen left the village behind.

Palmer had slung his borrowed rifle over his shoulder, and now walked with his thumb poked comfortably under its sling. 'You're the one with those fancy field glasses. Why don't you take a look-see?'

'That's it? That's all you can suggest?'

'What else do you want?'

'It would be nice if you could be bothered to help.'

'Like you did back there?'

'What do you mean by that?' Jack was struggling to hold his temper in check. He had seen what was needed, and had done his best to make it happen.

'It weren't our fight.' Palmer's voice was unchanged.

'We were there.'

'So? We could have walked away. Got on with our mission. Instead you wanted to play the hero.'

'I did not.' Jack's anger was simmering now. 'I did what had to be done.'

'Why? Did you think those Frenchies couldn't manage without you being there to hold their hand?'

'Those men were running. They had to be stopped.'

'Aye, that's right enough. But why by you?'

'Because I was there.'

Palmer shook his head at such folly. 'You still love it.'

'Love what?' Jack spat out the reply.

'Battle.'

'You think that? You think I want to fight?'

'No. I *know* you do.'

'You're mad.' Jack felt his anger wane. He had denied Palmer's accusation, but in truth he knew the older man was correct. He would not admit it aloud, for to do so would be to reveal the rotten core to his soul, and that he would not do, not to anyone. Instead he sat down at the road's edge and began the laborious task of reloading his revolver.

'I've seen men like you before.' Palmer broke the silence. 'They survive a battle or two, so they start to believe that they're good at fighting, that they have a talent for it.' He watched Jack pull out the small pot of grease that he used to seal each freshly loaded chamber on his revolver. 'Truth is they were just lucky. One day that luck runs out, and they're just as dead as the poor bastard who died in the first minutes of his first battle.'

Jack stopped what he was doing and met Palmer's flat stare. 'And you're different, I suppose?'

Palmer shrugged. 'I do what has to be done, nothing more, nothing less. I know that one day my luck will run out. I don't see the point in trying to make that day come along any quicker than it needs to.'

Jack's anger had disappeared. He could not argue against the truth. He returned his attention to his revolver. Only when he had finished loading it did he look at Palmer again. 'What about that lucky man? What if his luck holds? What if he goes on surviving?'

'Then I pity the poor bastard.'

The way he said the words made Jack laugh. 'You know what I think?'

'I don't care what you think.'

'I think,' Jack continued anyway, 'that we need to find this man Ballard wants.'

'So take those field glasses of yours and see what you can see.'

Jack nodded. 'You'd better stay there. I don't want you getting too tired. Your old bones can't take it.'

He got to his feet and thrust his handgun back into its holster before fishing out the glasses. He left Palmer behind and clambered on to a low rise on the western side of the road. Only when he reached the top did he put the glasses to his face.

At first there was little to see. To the west was MacMahon's reserve division and the black flag of the first aid post where he had left Ballard. He panned south. The ground there was covered by a great expanse of woodland that went on for what looked to be a good half-mile before it pressed against a ridge of higher ground. On top of the ridge was an area that was more built up, the houses larger and grander than in the other villages he had seen. A tall church tower stood proud from the other buildings, dominating the surroundings.

Here at last he spotted movement. He could not help a sharp intake of breath as he made out the Austrian infantrymen occupying the buildings around the foot of the tower, their bright white uniforms making them stand out against the dull stone at their backs. They were plainly expecting a French advance. Prepared defences lined the outer reaches of the village, with wooden palisades blocking the main approach.

Jack panned back towards the woods. This time he saw French soldiers. And they were fighting.

As far as he could tell, what looked to be an entire French brigade was advancing along a road that cut straight through the dense woodland. They were heavily engaged with Austrian troops. Much of the fighting was happening in the woods to either side of the road, and he could see little more than rolling clouds of powder smoke, and occasional flashes of musket fire.

He took a deep breath. He guessed the French were over a mile away. It was a fair distance, but he could just about make out their uniforms. He lowered the glasses. Palmer was looking at him, waiting patiently for news.

'There are French troops about a mile to the south-west,' Jack called across to his companion with a smile on his face. 'I think I just found the Legion.'

The French brigade had re-formed into two marching columns by the time Palmer and Jack reached them. There was no sign of the Austrians, other than the bodies strewn across the road and in the woodland to either side. The fight had been short and sharp, the French beating back the Austrian attack with rifle volleys and bayonets.

The French officers appeared to be in no hurry to resume their advance. They fussed over the ranks as they prepared their men for the assault on the Austrian-held town on the high ground away to the far side of the woodland that Jack had seen through his field glasses.

As the two British agents ran up, a French general and his staff were parading past. The infantry cheered as they spotted their commander, whilst Jack and Palmer were forced to one side by the gaggle of officers following dutifully behind their general.

Jack took the opportunity to look at the men who would assault the heavily defended town. Those to his front wore the fabulous Turkish-style uniform of the Zouaves. He had seen men like these in the Crimea. They were immediately identifiable in their baggy off-white linen trousers and short dark blue jackets edged in red. On their heads they wore red chechias with a dark blue tassel. They were a splendid-looking regiment, but there was more to the Zouaves than a fancy uniform. The dour-faced men in the ranks had earned a reputation as hard fighters, the regiment's long experience in North Africa giving them plenty of opportunities to learn their trade.

Now they showed the scars of the recent fighting. A fair number bore wounds, bound up with neckerchiefs or temporary dressings made from undershirts. Their clothing was stained with blood, their faces streaked with powder marks, and they bore the determined stares of men who had fought hard but who knew the battle was not yet done.

'So have you found the Legion?' Palmer stood red-faced at Jack's side. They had run for over a mile, and both were hot and sweaty.

'No.' Jack had no breath for more. The French general was heading to the front of the Zouaves, so Jack followed the twenty or so mounted staff officers who trailed in his wake. The two men were forced to run again to keep up, but they got close enough to hear the general shout out in triumph as he rounded the front of the regiment.

'*Voici la Légion! L'affaire est dans le sac!*'

Jack pushed through the horses so that he could see just what the French general had spotted. It was only as he stepped past the last officer that he saw the regiment at the front of the second column.

He drew in a sharp intake of breath. The men were wearing long blue tunics with green epaulettes over baggy white trousers paired with white garters. The French general had seen them first, and it had been his words that had given Jack hope that their search had come to an end.

They had found the Legion.

The French marched with a great fanfare. They had re-formed from the column of march into two groups of four battalions arranged in mixed order. In each formation, two battalions formed into line, whilst the other two moved into battalion column, one on each flank. The two battalions in line provided enough firepower to overwhelm the enemy, whilst those on the flanks gave the column depth and strength.

Each regiment's colours led the way, the bright tricolours lifted high so that every man in the ranks could see them. Deep in the formations, drummers beat out the staccato rhythm of the march, the young boys charged with taking the instruments into battle driving the great columns forward.

Jack and Palmer stood and watched as the regiment they had sought for hours went on the attack against the town to the south of their current position. From what Jack had seen, the Austrians were there in good numbers. They had been given enough time to prepare a series of fixed defences, and the garden walls and squat stone buildings would offer them a dozen strongpoints from which to fight off the French attack. It was a solid defensive position, and the French would have to fight hard to force the Austrian infantry to retreat.

It took several long minutes for the two assault formations to pass them by. As the last ranks marched past, Jack and Palmer forced their tired bodies into motion. The Legion was marching in battalion column on the right flank of the advance, and so the two Englishmen took up a position behind its rearmost company.

No one told them to go away, or asked them why they were there. Jack quickly gave up trying to see if the man they sought was in the ranks ahead of him. All they could do was tag along, and hope to find their target in the chaos of the assault.

It was not much of a plan, but it was the best they had.

Chapter Twenty-seven

───◆──◆───

The French marched to the hypnotic rhythm of the drums. It was the *pas de charge*, the same nerve-rending beat that had driven the great French columns against the enemies of the first Napoleon.

Jack walked at the rear of the formation, yet he still felt the mesmerising power of the drumbeat. He wondered at the bravery of Wellington's men in red coats who had stood in their two-man-deep line waiting for the ponderous columns to come against them. The French must have seemed unstoppable, the massed ranks certain to swamp the thin red line that stood in its path. Yet the British had held their ground, the power of their battalion volleys bludgeoning the great columns to a halt.

Now the French army had come back to a European battlefield. Jack did not know if MacMahon had finally located his second division, or if its commander was acting independently. Either way, one of them had ordered an entire brigade to assault the Austrian-held town ahead. It was a test of their bravery as much as of their musketry, and not one French soldier doubted that the Austrians would fail to stand against them.

Whoever was in command had ordered every gun they could find to take up a position to support the attack. The batteries had been massed together on a railway embankment, the raised ground giving them a good line of fire. Jack counted thirty-nine guns, all aimed at the barricaded streets and wooden palisades behind which the Austrian infantry waited, ready to turn back the massive formations coming towards them.

As one, the cannon opened fire. The heavy shells seared towards the Austrian defences. They landed in one dreadful, apocalyptic storm, ploughing up roads, smashing walls and ripping through the houses in which hundreds of Austrian reserves sheltered. More shells landed within moments, every one pounding into the defences. The wooden palisades were torn apart, and red-hot shards of shrapnel ricocheted in every direction. The heavy shells wrought a dreadful destruction on the densely packed ranks. Limbs were torn from bodies, flesh ripped apart as the French artillery threw the defences into chaos.

The infantry cheered as their gunners pounded the town. The new rifled cannon were unerringly accurate, and the cheers doubled in intensity as the gunners began to fire at will, great gouts of flames leaping from the barrels.

Jack could not help but flinch as another massive volley ripped through the sky. He knew what it was to endure such a barrage; the Russian gunners holding the Great Redoubt on the banks of the Alma river had created similar carnage in the British ranks marching towards them. He could not bring himself to cheer as the shells ground the Austrian defences into so much dust.

He had heard something of the La Hitte system the French used to convert the smoothbore cannon they had at their disposal. The rifling inside the barrel doubled the cannon's range, vastly increasing their accuracy. The system did for cannon what the new rifling and Minié bullets had done for the infantry's rifles. Now the Austrians were on the receiving end of an artillery barrage the like of which had never been seen on any battlefield. And it was decisive.

Under such devastating fire, no infantry could hope to survive, and the Austrians manning the palisades and barricades broke. They jammed the streets in their haste to escape, unwittingly making the French gunners' job all the easier. The artillery poured on the fire without mercy, their new conical shells gouging great holes in the enemy's broken ranks. The streets were littered with the dead and the dying, the living trampling both into the dirt as they tried to get away.

The French infantry pressed on, covering the sloping ground quickly. Their gunners fired without pause, the roar of the concentrated artillery fire loud enough to drown out the beat of the drum so that the columns appeared to advance in silence.

They reached the outskirts without taking a single casualty. Still the French gunners continued, the flatter trajectory of the new rifled cannon allowing them to fire over the heads of the advancing infantry.

Even from his place in the rear of the Legion's column, Jack could hear the dreadful sound of the exploding shells, the meaty slap of shrapnel hitting piles of bodies and the higher-pitched crack as it ricocheted off trees and buildings.

With a great cheer, the French charged. The ground was littered with bodies and broken weapons. The Frenchmen pounded over it all, their callous boots crushing any wounded man left lying in their path.

Jack went with them, driving into the rearmost ranks as the men stormed into the narrow streets. He ploughed ahead, feeling nothing as his boots thumped into a headless corpse left lying on the ground. He had no idea where Palmer was, but he did not care. He freed his weapons as he ran, pulling his sabre from its scabbard and hefting his revolver into his left hand. He was not there to fight, but he would not be unprepared.

The Legion's column was breaking up fast. Men ran in every direction as they hurtled into the narrow streets that led into the heart of the town. Already rifles were cracking out, the first shots being fired as the French troops started to find Austrian soldiers hiding in the closest houses.

Jack went with one group. He tried to look at their faces, but they were going too fast and he had no choice but to go with them.

The artillery barrage stopped. The French gunners could no longer fire without risking hitting their own men, and so the infantry were left to clear the town with nothing more than their rifles and bayonets.

More rifle and musket fire crashed out from the street that Jack was running down. He saw men fall just ahead, a handful of legionnaires paying the price for being brave enough to lead the attack.

'Come on!' He roared encouragement as the men around him charged on. They burst around a corner and saw half a dozen white-coated Austrian soldiers formed into a makeshift line. The Austrians had fired the volley that had killed the legionnaires' comrades, and now they were frantically reloading.

They would not get the chance.

The men with Jack cheered, then stormed forward. They hit the Austrian line hard, their bayonets thrusting forward as soon as they were close enough to attack. The Frenchmen fought with vicious intensity. Not one Austrian landed a blow before they were all cut down dead.

Almost immediately the legionnaires came under fire. Muskets were thrust out of upper-floor windows and fired down into the street. A man in front of Jack spun around, his hands clasped to his ruined face. Another cursed as a musket ball gouged a crevice in his upper arm, the blood spurting from between his clutching fingers.

'Off the street!' Jack shouted the order. He grabbed the wounded man and threw him to one side. 'Follow me!'

He did not know if the legionnaires understood him or not. He ran towards one of the houses he had spotted musket fire coming from. He saw a door so ran at it, kicking it open with his boot the moment he was in range.

The door crashed back on its hinges. He caught a glimpse of a terrified Austrian soldier before a musket was fired almost directly into his own face. He screamed then, the cry torn from him in a moment of pure terror. The ball spat past so close that he felt the wind of its passing on his cheek.

There was no time to dwell on the near miss. The Austrian soldier shouted in defiance, then thrust his bayonet at the man he had so nearly shot down. Jack battered it away. He heard the Austrian's howl of frustration turn into a shout of horror as he shoved the barrel of his revolver into the man's face. He didn't stop to think. He did not care that it was not his fight, that he had no place being in the thick of the action. He saw only a man trying to kill him.

He pulled the trigger. The tip of the barrel was so close to the man's face that the jet of flame spat out as it fired and licked against his skin before the bullet half tore his head from his shoulders. He fell away, his scream cut off.

Jack was pushed forward by men desperate to escape from the musket balls being fired down into the street. His boots caught on the body of the man he had killed. He stumbled, and only caught his balance as he was propelled on to a flight of stairs that led to an upper storey.

He cried out, fear surging through him as he imagined his own death. The Austrians upstairs had to know what was coming. His boots pounded on the wooden treads. With every pace he expected to see a musket barrel being aimed towards him. This time he knew they would not miss, and he bellowed as he went, his sword flailing out in front of him in a futile attempt to keep himself safe.

He lost his footing as he went over the last stair and fell forward, pain flashing through him as his knees hit the wooden floor. He was still scrabbling on the ground when the volley reached him.

The Austrians on the upper floor had held their fire for this moment. They waited for the first few Frenchmen to arrive, and then they fired. At such close range their muskets were dreadfully effective. The two legionnaires driving Jack ahead of them died in an instant, their flesh torn by the multiple impacts.

Jack felt the touch of split blood on his skin, but it was not his, and his delight at still being alive drove him into the fight. He saw nothing but a target for his sword, and he got to his feet then drove his weapon into an Austrian's gut.

The man clutched at the blade buried in his flesh. Jack

withdrew it sharply, slicing through the grasping fingers, half severing them. The man staggered away, and Jack backhanded the sword, slicing at a white-coated Austrian driving a bayonet at his side. The sword went wide, but it forced the Austrian to twist away sharply enough to save Jack from his attack.

In the cramped confines of the upper room, there was little opportunity for finesse. He drove forward, throwing himself against the nearest Austrian, hitting the man with his shoulder, the contact jarring through him. The man staggered backwards, giving Jack enough space to level his revolver.

The handgun pressed against a man's side and he pulled the trigger instantly. The sound barely registered over the roars of men fighting for their lives, but he heard his target scream as the heavy bullet tore through his flesh.

More Frenchmen came up the stairs. This time there was no volley to greet them, and they threw themselves into the melee.

The fighting was vicious. Jack saw one legionnaire tumble back down the stairs, a bayonet striking him through an eye socket. An Austrian died as a Frenchman disembowelled him, his guts blue and pulsating as they spilt into his hands.

One of the Austrians swung his rifle butt at Jack's head. He saw the blow coming so ducked underneath it. A heartbeat later, the man thrust his bayonet at him, the bloodied steel whispering past his face. He stayed low, then rose quickly, driving his sword into the Austrian's groin. It was a cruel blow and the steel went deep before he twisted his wrist, gouging away the man's life as he prevented the sword getting stuck fast in the suction of the dying man's flesh.

He cried out as the man fell against him. He feared for his life, his backside puckering as he waited for the cold touch of a knife. But the Austrian was already dying, and he slid down Jack's front, sinking first to his knees then on to the floor.

The Frenchmen cheered as the last Austrian fell. Jack bent double and sucked in a huge lungful of air, only to gag on it. The rotten egg stink of spent powder mixed with the smell of blood and shit to create the evil miasma of battle. Even as he choked down another breath, the fight replayed in his mind. The closeness of his own death appalled him. He thought about what Palmer had said. He had believed that he had a talent for battle, his skill at killing the one honest thing about him. He shivered as he thought of the musket ball that had seared past his face, and the volley that had missed him only because he had stumbled. He lived because he had been lucky. Not because he was quick, or brave, or cruel. His skill at battle meant nothing.

The notion that there was nothing he could do to escape his destiny sickened him. He had struggled for years against the future that fate had allotted to him. He had refused to accept that there was just one path for him to follow, and he had fought, and killed, to prove his worth to a world that neither knew nor cared that he was capable of so much more than he was allowed.

He felt his determination return. It did not matter if Palmer was right or if he was wrong. Jack could do nothing to control chance, but he did control his own actions. If he was not a soldier, he had nothing. He would not stop fighting. Not now. Not ever.

'Move!' he bellowed. The Frenchmen were lingering in the blood-splattered room. They were no different to the redcoats he had led before. They were as brave as any and would fight hard when the need arose. But without leadership, they would do only what came naturally, and no sane man walked willingly back into battle.

He had given the order expecting to be obeyed. He was roundly ignored, many of the men in the upper room simply staring at the foreigner in their midst, any earlier cooperation forgotten. A handful tried to leave of their own accord, but the stairs were blocked. Jack sheathed his bloody sabre, then shoved his revolver back into its holster before pushing forward to find out what was causing the delay.

At least half a dozen legionnaires milled around in the room below, blocking the exit.

'For God's sake, get out of the way,' Jack shouted, trying to get them to move. He was pushed backwards, the legionnaires refusing to listen to a civilian. One of the faces that turned to glare up at him belonged to a blond-haired soldier wearing the blue of the Legion.

It was a face Jack recognised at once, its likeness to a decade-old portrait startling.

He had found Ballard's man.

Chapter Twenty-eight

'Stay right fucking there.' Jack jabbed a finger at the man with fair hair, who stared back at him, his mouth opening in surprise as he became the centre of attention.

Jack pushed his way through the crowd of legionnaires. It was not easy, and he had to use his elbows to force a passage downstairs. The blond soldier had ignored the bellowed instruction and was already halfway out of the door when Jack reached the last step.

'I told you to stay there.' Jack lunged forward and managed to grab his shoulder.

'Who the devil do you think you are?' The man spun on his heel and shouted the question into Jack's face.

'I've been ordered to find you.' Jack kept a firm grip on his shoulder. The legionnaires were trying to leave the house, and those behind him were buffeting him as he got in their way. 'Your father sent us.'

'My father!' The blond-haired man spat the words out like an oath.

Jack winced as an elbow caught the pit of his spine. 'Come on, let's get out of here.'

Outside, the sounds of fighting were coming from every direction. Men screamed, whilst others shouted orders. Rifle shots rang out constantly. The Austrians had taken heavy casualties, but they were not giving up the town without a fight.

'Say whatever it is you have to say and say it quickly,' snapped the legionnaire.

'Your father wants you kept out of harm's way.'

'What the hell does he care?' The man scowled. 'I haven't clapped eyes on the miserable bastard for years.'

Jack felt a surge of relief. He had found his man. He would not have to go into any more houses, or fight any more Austrians. Whatever ration of luck he had left would be saved for another day.

'I am not going anywhere.' The Englishman's face twisted with distaste at the idea. 'I have my duty.'

'You don't have a fucking choice, chum.' Jack would not let his quarry escape.

'Do not dare to tell me what to do.'

'I'm sorry, I really am.' Jack offered a smile. 'But I have my orders.' The Colt slipped into his left hand with practised ease. He pressed the barrel into the blond-haired legionnaire's gut. 'You don't have much of a say in the matter.'

The man looked at the gun poking into the soft flesh above his navel. He contemplated it for a moment, then raised his eyes so that he was looking Jack directly in the eye. 'Go to hell.'

He turned his head away and shouted, his French fast and fluent. Jack had no idea what was being said, but he knew it was not going to help his cause.

'Shut up!' He snarled the words, his spittle flecking the man's cheeks.

He was roundly ignored, the Englishman continuing to shout for aid, so he did the only thing he could think of. He slammed his fist directly into the man's mouth. The legionnaire fell, hitting the ground on his backside, his shouts cut off in an instant.

Jack was given no time to celebrate his success.

'Drop the gun, my friend, or by God I will spread your brains all over the street.'

It was Jack's turn to feel the press of a gun barrel against his flesh. The man holding it was directly behind him, so he could not see who threatened him. The barrel was pushed forward with more purpose. 'Do it now.'

He thought about trying to fight. But the voice behind him was calm and devoid of emotion. He did not think a man who possessed a voice like that in the midst of a battle would fail to make good on such a threat, so he let his Colt fall from his hand.

'You bastard.' The man he had knocked on to his arse snapped the insult as he saw the gun fall away. He smeared the back of his hand across his mouth, glancing down at the blood that smothered it before pushing himself to his feet.

Jack lifted his chin and braced himself for the blow that he saw in the man's eyes.

'Hold it right there!' The man behind Jack snapped the command as he saw the same thing.

The blond legionnaire obeyed instantly. But still he leaned forward, pressing his bloodied face into Jack's. 'Who the hell do you think you are?'

'The man saving your sorry skin.'

'And who the hell says I need my skin saving?'

'Enough!' The man behind Jack put an end to the argument, then shoved Jack hard in the back, spinning him around.

Jack found himself staring into the face of Sergeant Kearney, the American he had shared a train compartment with on the way out of Paris.

'Ah, I thought I knew you.' Kearney had recognised Jack at the same moment. 'What the hell are you doing here?'

'I'm not here to fight.' He pointed a finger at the blond-haired man. 'But I am going to take him with me.'

Kearney laughed. 'No you're not. He belongs to the Legion.'

Jack's hand slipped to the handle of his sabre. 'He's English. His father sent me out here to take him back to England. That is what I intend to do.'

'Are you sure?' Kearney laughed again. He gestured around him. 'You going to fight us all, then?'

Jack had kept his eyes fixed on the American sergeant. Now he took a moment to see what was going on around him. They were not alone. At least a dozen legionnaires were watching the confrontation. Each was armed, and now every rifle was pointed towards Jack.

Jack's hand fell away from his sabre.

'You're a wise fellow.' Kearney cocked an ear. The sound of fighting was louder than ever. 'Now, we have a battle to fight.' He looked past Jack. 'Fleming, rejoin your group.'

The blond-haired legionnaire snapped to attention, then did as he was told, his obedience immediate.

Kearney nodded once to Jack. 'Do not try to interfere.' He waved to his men. '*En place!*'

The legionnaires formed up around their sergeant quickly and without a second word of command. Within moments they had moved off towards the fighting, the man Jack had knocked to the ground safely in their midst.

Jack followed them doggedly. He had come a long way to find the man that Kearney had addressed as Fleming. He would not let him go so easily.

The Frenchmen moved fast. The town was filled with the roar of battle, which grew steadily louder as they advanced. The fighting was brutal, with every street a battlefield, every building a strongpoint. The Austrians were making the French army pay in blood for every yard they captured.

Bodies littered the ground. The dead and the dying lay amidst the rubble, while those with lighter wounds needed no urging to head to the rear, a steady procession of wounded men working their way away from the fighting. Kearney's legionnaires pressed on through it all. Jack stayed with them, keeping his eyes on Fleming, the glimpse of blond hair he could see underneath his kepi making it easy enough to keep him in sight.

'*Ici! Ici!*'

The legionnaires turned a corner and were immediately summoned into the fight. A party of twenty to thirty Zouaves were trying to force their way past a pair of massive wooden gates that blocked the entrance to a courtyard. The air was filled with the noise of their rifles hammering against the wood.

The smallest of gaps opened in the massive timbers, and immediately musket fire spurted out through the opening. Two Zouaves were cut down, their bodies falling back into the men behind them. The French soldiers roared with anger. Those nearest to the doors thrust their own rifles into the gap, returning fire as best they could.

More French soldiers arrived from the opposite direction, their dark blue uniforms and green epaulettes identifying them as chasseurs. The fresh men joined the melee at the gate, adding their numbers to the press of bodies trying to fight their way inside.

The legionnaires swarmed forward. Jack went with them. His boots caught a body, and he looked down into the staring eyes of an Austrian corpse. The man had been shot in the breast, and his white tunic was smothered in blood. For an instant, an image of Jack's own face replaced that of the stranger, his skin tainted with the same waxy grey sheen of death, his sightless, lifeless eyes staring at nothing.

The thought shocked him, and he shivered. It was a glimpse into the future that waited for him, perhaps in just a minute's time. The notion sent a surge of ice surging into his gut. Fear followed, rabid, powerful and churning deep in his bowels.

Orders were being shouted over the chaos. The French general that Jack had seen earlier rode into the melee, the gold braid on his uniform making him stand out like a whore in a convent. He dismounted, ignoring the aides who were trying to grab his bridle and pull him away.

Jack shook away his fear once again, refusing to let it master him. He pushed his way towards the gate. He would not hide from his fate.

Galvanised by the presence of their general, the French pressed forward. The gap between the two massive doors was wider now. Jack could see dozens of Austrian musket barrels rammed through it. Flames shot from the barrels as the defenders opened fire. At such close range, none could miss. Half a dozen French soldiers went down amidst the boots of their comrades, their deaths callously ignored by the men still trying to force their way into the courtyard.

The French general charged forward, surrounded by

Zouaves, legionnaires and chasseurs. Rifles opened fire at the gap between the gates. The defenders had no intention of yielding and fired back, their musket balls searing into the attackers, knocking them over like skittles at the fair.

A great groan echoed through the French soldiers. The general had been hit. He fell backwards, his chest doused in blood. Willing hands hauled him away from the fighting. The sight goaded the attackers. Fresh men rushed the gates, their ranks packed deep as they sought to force their way in. Many fell, the Austrian defenders firing without pause.

A tall French *sapeur de génie* arrived. He carried a huge axe, which he slammed into the edge of the left-hand gate. He worked fast, ignoring the musket balls that zipped past him, tearing away the wood at the edge of the half-open gate. Another *sapeur* joined him. Together they hammered at the wood, whilst the men around them fired their rifles through the gap.

The second *sapeur* was felled as a musket ball took him in the throat. A Zouave picked up the axe and took his place, attacking the gate with great wild swings. The men around him cheered, the noise building in intensity even as the Zouave went down, a bayonet thrust through the gap to take him in the chest.

The American legionnaire sergeant, Kearney, reached the gate. He grabbed a splintered plank of wood and ripped it away, screaming at his men to do the same. Dozens of pairs of hands followed suit, some men even dropping their rifles as they tore at the gates with their bare hands.

The Austrians were still trying to hold their ground. The French soldiers gunned them down where they stood, dozens of rifles opening fire every time the gap widened. The screams were terrible as the French poured on the fire, the crowd of soldiers around the gate finally able to exact revenge for the men who had died.

The surviving *sapeur* tore a whole plank away from its supports. It was ripped away by Kearney, who threw it at the defenders. Again and again the two men attacked the gate until an entire section splintered then gave way.

With a great roar, the French soldiers stormed into the opening.

Still the Austrians fought on. Some had managed to reload, and now the leading Frenchmen fell as close-range musket fire tore into their packed ranks. But the defenders were horribly outnumbered, and the French cheered as the Austrian line disappeared under a frenzy of bayonet thrusts.

Jack went with the main rush. He stumbled over a dead Zouave and lost sight of Fleming. His head came up in time to see an Austrian counter-attack surging towards the gate. The French saw it too and rushed towards it, the courtyard on the far side of the gates now a battlefield.

The cobblestones were slick with spilt blood, and more than one man went down as his footing gave way. Jack could do nothing but press on as the mob of French soldiers surged forward. The man to his front died, an Austrian bayonet taking his throat, and Jack found himself in the front rank. He lunged, acting on instinct, his sabre darting forward to snatch away a man's eyes.

Another Austrian came against him. The man screamed, his lips pulled back in an animal snarl as he tried to slide his bayonet into Jack's gut. He was still snarling as Jack sidestepped the bayonet then drove his sabre through the man's throat, the sharpened steel gouging through the gristle with ease.

'Come on!' Jack felt the battle madness grow. The fight was breaking up around him as the two sides became intermingled. A bayonet slid past his side, tearing through the hem of his jacket. He turned, his sabre slashing at the man who had nearly killed him. The blow missed, but the Austrian died as a legionnaire buried his bayonet in the man's chest.

Jack spied an Austrian officer leading a fresh group of men into the fight. He stamped forward, his boots catching a dying man in the face, and parried the enemy officer's first blow. The man glared at him, then his gaze turned to the legionnaire at Jack's side. The Frenchman's bayonet was still buried in the man he had struck down. The Austrian officer spotted the opportunity. He thrust his sword forward, towards the legionnaire's unprotected heart.

Jack saw the blow coming. He was at the wrong angle to try to block it with his own sword, so he threw himself at the Austrian officer, hitting the man hard with his shoulder, driving the attack wide.

The two men went down in a jumble of arms and legs, both hitting the ground hard. Jack's breath was driven from his body, but he punched his sword hilt down regardless. He felt the blow land, so he followed it with another, then another. The Austrian officer was writhing underneath him. Jack felt a fist slam into the side of his head. It hurt, but he punched down again, then battered his head forward, driving it into the centre of the Austrian's face. He felt something break underneath his forehead, so he pulled his head back then slammed it forward again, all the while still punching with his sword.

The body underneath him went limp. Jack staggered upright. His head throbbed and his vision greyed, but he still held his sabre ready to attack.

There was no one left to fight.

The French soldiers cheered. Some lifted their kepis, or thrust their bloodied bayonets to the sky as they celebrated their bitter victory. The courtyard was like a butcher's yard. Bodies carpeted the ground, the white uniforms of the Austrians bright amidst the dark blue of the French. Some still moved, whilst others lay motionless, their bodies twisted into the impossible poses of the dead, their blood blackening the cobbles beneath.

Jack stood straighter. He turned towards the man he had saved, and found himself looking at the blood-splattered face of the blond-haired legionnaire, Fleming.

'It had to be you.' Fleming spoke through gritted teeth. 'Are you badly hurt?'

Jack shook his head, wincing as the action sent a spasm of pain cascading through his skull. He took a deep breath, then pointed his bloody sabre at the man Ballard wanted so badly.

'Don't go anywhere.'

The legionnaire grimaced at such belligerence. 'Don't worry.' He looked around him. 'I don't think any of us are going anywhere for the moment.'

Jack followed his gaze. The surviving French soldiers were moving between the heaps of bodies as they began the bitter task of sorting the living from the dead. The sounds of fighting were dying away, the last of the Austrian defenders pulling out.

The French had captured the town.

Chapter Twenty-nine

*J*ack sucked gratefully on a canteen of water as he sat on the ground with his back against the wall of the courtyard. He let his head fall back so that it rested on the wall. The stone was cool against his scalp, and he closed his eyes as he savoured the momentary peace.

He sat amongst the legionnaires. Sergeant Kearney was still there, but only half of the men he had led into the bitter fight were left standing.

'So who are you?' Fleming sat at his side. It was his square canteen that Jack was drinking from, the pair sitting in wary silence as the survivors of the fight slumped on whatever ground they could find that was not occupied by a corpse or a dying man.

'Jack Lark.' Jack drank again, swilling the water around his mouth before he swallowed it. Try as he might, he could not lose the taste of spent powder.

'Well met, Jack Lark.' Fleming looked down at his hand, then, after a moment's thought, offered it to Jack. 'My name is

James Fleming. Although most of these buggers insist on calling me Jacques.'

'Is that your real name?' Jack summoned the energy to shake Fleming's hand.

'Does it matter?'

'No, I suppose not.' Jack was bone weary, and the head butts he had thrown in the fight made it feel as if he had cracked his skull. He did not care what the man he had come for was called.

'You've put us all to a great deal of trouble.' He handed back the canteen.

'I never asked for that. I never asked for you to come.'

'But we came anyway. Your father is keen for you to return to England. He wants you to be safe.'

'My father.' Fleming scoffed. 'My father wanted nothing to do with me for years. His precious career came first. Can you understand what that feels like? To know that your father is more concerned about his bloody job than he is about his only son.'

'I don't care.' Jack rested his head against the wall again to lessen the odds of it falling from his shoulders. 'You're still coming with me.'

Fleming gave a short bark of a laugh. 'You can stop that nonsense; it really is getting rather tiresome. I'm not leaving.'

'I'll make you, if I have to.'

Fleming laughed again, louder this time. 'Look around you, Jack. One word from me, and any one of these bastards will slit your throat without so much as batting an eyelid. It wouldn't be the first time, and I very much doubt that it would be the last.'

Jack opened his eyes and looked around. Sergeant Kearney

was sitting with his legionnaires. All were keeping a careful eye on the man in civilian clothes who had fought like a devil and who now sat in their midst.

'I will give you a message, though.' Fleming caught Jack's eye and offered a tight-lipped smile. 'One you can pass on to that dear old father of mine.' The smile disappeared. 'Tell him to go to hell.'

Jack saw the passion in the younger man's face. He did not doubt the sincerity behind the message that he would have to give to Ballard.

'Jack!' The voice came from the entrance to the courtyard.

For a moment Jack held Fleming's gaze, only looking away when the voice called again.

'I can see you sitting there on your great fat arse, Mr Jack fucking Lark!'

The easily recognisable form of Palmer was standing in the broken gateway. With a groan, Jack got to his feet. He waved a greeting at Palmer, then looked down at the legionnaire he had followed into battle. 'This isn't over.'

'Yes it is.' The reply was given through gritted teeth.

There was nothing else to be said. Jack forced his abused body into motion and went to give Ballard the news.

'What the devil do you mean?'

Ballard shouted the words into Jack's face with such force that flecks of spittle landed on his cheeks. It was dusk, and they stood alone on the roadway a dozen or so yards from the first aid station where Jack had left the rest of the party. Palmer had gone to round up Mary and Billy, leaving Jack to face Ballard alone.

'I found him. He refused to come with me.' Jack had no strength left for temper.

'I didn't expect you to damn well ask him.'

'What did you think would happen?' Jack's voice kept its even tone. 'You wanted me to fight a dozen legionnaires?'

'If that is what it would have taken to bring the boy to me, then yes, that is exactly what I would have expected you to do.'

'Well, more fool you.'

'Be careful who you call fool.' Ballard snapped at the lure.

'I'm calling you a fool for sending me on a fool's errand.' Jack fired the words back with icy venom. 'I found your man and I gave him the fucking message. If you want to go and get him, then be my bloody guest. See if you have any more luck convincing his mates to let him go than I did.'

'You should not have given them the choice.' Ballard did not back down.

Jack bit his tongue. 'I saw no other way.'

'No, you never do. For that would involve thinking.' Ballard's eyes narrowed as he glared at Jack. 'I see that you are only capable of obeying an exact order.' He pushed his face closer to Jack's. 'The next time, you will do exactly what I tell you to do. You will not deviate from those orders even if the Archangel Gabriel himself arrives and begs you to do otherwise. Is that clear?'

'Yes, sir.'

'Good.' Ballard said the word with difficulty. He composed himself with a visible effort. 'This is not over.'

'The lad doesn't want to go home.' Jack could not hold his tongue, even if it meant tweaking the tail of the Devil himself. 'He told me to give his father a message.'

'What was it?' Ballard's words were chilled.

'To leave him alone.' Jack did not shirk from the major's gaze.

Ballard's expression was unreadable. 'It changes nothing. We must still take this boy to his father.'

'He's no boy. He's a man, doing what he thinks is right.'

'He is a boy who knows nothing.' Ballard shouted the words. 'There is no discussion on this matter.' He managed to bring his temper under control, but said nothing else before he turned sharply on his heel and stormed away, leaving Jack to stare silently at his back.

He stood there for several minutes until he heard footsteps approach. He looked over his shoulder to see Palmer and Mary coming towards him.

'You found him then?' Palmer spoke first. There was mockery in his tone.

'I did.'

'But you didn't think to keep hold of the bugger?'

'No.' Jack sighed. 'I should've let you try. You might've had more luck.'

'I doubt it.' Palmer grunted his reply.

'Where were you?' Jack could not help the question sounding like an accusation.

'I was busy.'

Jack looked down at Palmer's hands. There was black blood under his nails, and a series of deep scratches across one cheek and behind his left ear. They looked like claw marks. He did not doubt the larger man's assertion.

'Is he worth it?' It was Mary who asked the question. She stood between the two men, looking at them both in turn.

'Worth what, exactly?'

'You. Both of you. Both of your lives.'

Jack looked Palmer up and down. 'He's certainly worth Palmer's life. I'm not so bloody sure about mine.'

Mary tutted at the glib reply. 'I mean it. What makes one of him worth the two of you?'

The two men shared a look.

Jack answered for them both, trying to make light of the question. 'He's a rich boy, from a rich family. That makes him worth a dozen of the likes of us.'

'Maybe Jack's right, maybe he isn't,' Palmer gave his own answer earnestly, 'but the major says this man is worth it, so that's good enough for me.'

'Jesus Christ.' Jack winced at the response. It was the second time Palmer had made such a simple assertion, and it did not grate on Jack any less for the repetition. 'I would never have put you down as a lickspittle.'

'Jack!' Mary snapped the warning.

'All right.' Jack held up a hand, acknowledging her words. He looked at Palmer. 'Whatever he has on you, it must be bloody good.'

Palmer grunted. 'You have no idea.'

'No, that's not right.' Mary laid a hand on Palmer's arm. 'We have every idea. I'm a washed-up doxy, and he's . . .' she paused to flap her hand in Jack's direction, 'he's just a dolt who thinks he's clever enough to fool the world, when really the only person he's fooling is himself.' She turned her attention on Palmer. 'Whatever it is, I'm certain it won't shock the likes of us.'

Palmer offered her a grim smile. 'We make a fine team. A fool, a whore and a murderer.'

'So who did you kill?' Jack wanted to know what drove a man like Palmer into such blind obedience.

'Just a man.' Palmer sighed. 'He deserved it, I know that for sure, but that wouldn't have stopped them stretching my neck for it.' He looked up, searching the sky as he continued. 'You see, the problem for me was that the bastard was rich. He liked a drink, this fine fellow of mine, and he liked to race his damn carriage about like he owned the streets of London. One night he had an accident. Nothing serious. Just broke a wheel on his carriage and knocked over a bench. Not enough to bother a great lord like that. Except for the fact that he killed someone.' Palmer looked down. 'He killed my wife, and no one gave a shit. Just an accident, they said. Just one of those things.' He vibrated with passion. 'So I killed the bastard in cold blood, and I said her name over and over so it was the last thing he ever heard.'

He took a deep breath before he continued, the words flowing out of him now that he had let them free. 'I was found out by a friend of the man I killed, an officer in army intelligence. I would've hung, but this man, well, he offered me a way out. My daughter . . .' He choked on the word. 'I was all she had. If I'd let them take me away, she would've had nothing. You know what happens to girls like that.' He looked up at Mary as he made the statement. 'Mr Ballard found her a place. She's a good girl and she's doing well now. Thanks to Mr Ballard.'

He glanced down, his eyes moist. 'You understand now?' He shook his head, as if annoyed to have given away so much about himself, then looked Jack hard in the eye. 'I owe him everything.' He turned his wet eyes back on the sky, searching for a glimpse of the stars that watched over them all with such serenity.

Jack absorbed the confession. 'Is that all?' The glib reply fell flat.

Mary placed her hand back on Palmer's arm. 'Your daughter has a fine future ahead of her. That's a good thing.'

'I hope so.' Palmer sucked air through his teeth. 'By God, I hope it's enough.'

Mary kept her hand in place. 'It's everything. I would do anything for my Billy to give him a good future, anything at all.'

Jack heard the feeling behind her words. He could not share her sentiments. She and Palmer had children, people they loved and who loved them in turn.

He had no one.

Ballard bustled into the small camp, a hemp sack in each hand.

No one had said much following Palmer's confession. They had set up camp where they were, waiting dutifully for the major to return. Dusk had turned into night. They had eaten a meal of bread and cheese as they sat on the ground, and made themselves as comfortable as they could so close to a field of battle.

Ballard walked close to the fire that Jack had got going with powder from a cartridge from his revolver. He dumped one sack in front of Jack and the other in front of Palmer.

'What's this? Presents?' Jack tried to read his commander's face in the light cast by the fire. He failed. Ballard's habitual assured expression was firmly back in place.

'There is a new plan.' The reply was clipped.

'Go on.' Jack could not help but sound dubious.

'Open it.' Ballard turned to make sure Palmer was also paying attention.

Jack did as he was told. He pulled out a uniform coatee, the fabric coarse under his fingers. He held it towards the firelight and recognised it immediately. It was the uniform jacket of the French Foreign Legion, the men he had fought alongside that afternoon.

'You want us to join the Legion?' He posed the question as he dug deeper into the sack. His fingers felt the shape of a French kepi, along with trousers and what he thought to be gaiters.

'No, Jack, I don't want you to *join* the Legion.' Ballard made sure that both men were looking at him before he continued. 'But the next time, you will not ask our target's permission. These uniforms will get you close. When the time is right, you will strike him down and take him away. No one will question two men dragging a wounded comrade to safety.' His eyes glimmered in the firelight. 'There are just two rules. You keep him alive, and you bring him to me, no matter what it takes.'

'No matter the cost?'

'Yes, Jack, no matter the cost.' Ballard glowered at him. 'You will not fail me twice.'

Chapter Thirty

*J*ack was bored. He kicked at a stone and watched it skitter across the road until it cracked against a tree. The sound made the mule start, and it brayed in protest until Billy managed to calm it.

It was the third draining day of marching. None had been particularly long, but the French advance was slowed by frequent halts that left the men, and the small party of British agents in their midst, to endure hour after hour in the relentless sun, choking on dust and kicking their heels.

The Austrians were retreating faster than the French could advance. They destroyed every bridge after they had crossed it, forcing the French to build a series of pontoon bridges, each of which only added to the maddeningly long halts. So far they had crossed four rain-swollen rivers, and there were many more between them and Milan, the Austrian-held capital of Lombardy.

Jack wiped a hand across his sweat-streaked face. He had shed his outer layers, so walked in only a loose shirt and breeches, yet he still felt disgusting. He smiled as Palmer stood in stoic silence at his side. Ballard's man still wore his thick tweeds, as if going for a day's hunting in the wilds of Scotland rather than tramping across the Lombard plain.

There was little news to brighten the tiresome march. A reconnaissance force of French cavalry had clashed with the Austrian rearguard at a place called Melginano. The skirmish had escalated quickly, but neither the French I Corps nor MacMahon's II Corps could get to the front fast enough to turn it into a major engagement. I Corps managed to reach the fighting late in the afternoon, but succeeded only in providing some target practice for the Austrian artillery.

The battle had done little to improve either side's prospects of a convincing victory. Jack and Palmer had been given no opportunity to don their new uniforms and try to abduct their target in the chaos of a skirmish, something that vexed Ballard no end. The major had taken to spending more and more of his time with the staff officers who served the newly promoted Maréchal MacMahon. He returned only rarely to remind Jack and Palmer of their duty. The only person he had a kind word for was Mary, his mood improving markedly when he passed a moment or two engaging her in conversation.

The column they were following started to move off. Jack forced his tired feet into motion. He marched like a redcoat, his mind idling through the interminable hours, his world reduced to the ground beneath his boots and the backs of the infantry-men in the regiment to his front.

'For God's sake.' He could not help but swear as the column ground to yet another halt. He doubted they had covered more than five hundred yards since the last stop.

'Stop your whining.' Mary walked alongside him. She still had enough energy to chastise him. She too had reduced her layers of clothing, so that she walked in just a simple cotton shift. She was still hot and sweaty, and the dress clung to her in ways that Jack found altogether too distracting.

'I've got a bone to pick with you.' Her tone was glacial.

'What have I done now?' Jack found his eyes lingering on the shape of Mary's figure. He forced them away with reluctance. Her expression made it clear that she had spotted his scrutiny, and that it was not appreciated.

'You've been teaching Billy to use that damn gun of yours.'

'Is that all?' Jack had expected worse.

'What the hell are you thinking?'

'It's nothing.'

'It flaming well is not *nothing*.' Mary's temper was firing. 'You leave my boy alone. He already wants to be like you. Don't bloody well encourage him.'

Jack barked with laughter, but cut it short when he saw the glare in her eyes. It was flattering to think that Billy had taken a shine to him. 'He wanted to learn. He's a bright lad.' He tried to mollify her.

'Which is why I don't want you filling his head with all sorts of nonsense about becoming a bloody redcoat.'

'It was good enough for me.'

'Being a street sweeper was good enough for you. You leave Billy alone.'

'He might need to know how—'

'No.' Mary cut him short. 'He's not here to fight. You keep him out of harm's way, you hear me, Jack? That boy is here only because of you. So you keep him safe and stop trying to make him like you.'

Jack sighed. 'I'll do my best.'

'You had better do more than that.'

'Jesus Christ, Mary.' Jack was trying hard to bite his tongue. 'I can't help it if the boy looks up to me.'

Mary's eyes narrowed. 'Don't worry. I'll tell him what you're really like. Just make sure you do your bit and leave him well alone.'

'All right.'

The simple agreement took some of the wind out of Mary's sails. 'You make sure you do.'

'Is that all?'

'For now.'

'Good.' Jack snapped the answer as an idea formed in his mind. He wanted a change of company. And he knew where to go to find it.

Jack picked his way through the soldiers' encampment. The Legion was well drilled and used to setting up a temporary home at the end of the day's march. General MacMahon had ordered his II Corps to a halt as the sun set, another long day of little progress coming to an end.

He was impressed by what he saw. Even though the column had only been halted for half an hour, they had already laid out their three-man tents in an ordered grid of parallel lines. With that done, the legionnaires had settled to their dinner. Jack's stomach rumbled as he walked past cauldron after cauldron filled with rice, onions and bacon. Some of the soldiers were sitting playing lotto, the legionnaires' favourite pastime, and he felt a strong sense of longing to be back with men for whom a campfire like this was home.

He had come to the army when he had nothing else. He had never expected to find the camaraderie that made his life in the ranks so enjoyable. The days with his mates were some of the rare memories that did not haunt him. A large part of him yearned to be able to return to the simple life of a redcoat, a life not burdened by responsibility, or the bounds of ambition. There were times when he felt like a fool for having walked away from it, his decision to try to climb above his station costing him in so many more ways than he could ever have imagined.

'What the hell do you want with us now?'

Jack was startled out his reverie. He had been spotted.

'Sergeant Kearney.' He nodded a greeting at the Legion sergeant, who had spied him wandering close to his fire.

Kearney shook his head. 'Don't you ever give up?'

'No. Not as a rule. Is he about?'

Kearney nodded at a fire a dozen yards away. 'He's just over there, but I doubt he'll appreciate your visit.'

'Like I give a shit.'

Kearney chuckled at the belligerent reply. 'You two should get along fine. You're very much alike.'

Jack snorted at the idea. 'I doubt it.'

'Then you would be wrong.' The sergeant was sitting comfortably on the ground, and now he stretched his legs out in front of him, totally at ease with his surroundings. 'But I reckon you don't listen too well, so I'll hold my peace.'

Jack grinned. He liked Kearney. The man was at one with his place in the world. He had a sureness about him that Jack had seen in the best non-commissioned officers. Men needed that calming influence in battle. It held them steady so much more effectively than even the harshest disciplinarian ever could.

'Now that's the first wise thing I've heard you say.' He dawdled at Kearney's fire. 'You're a long way from home, Sergeant.'

Kearney shrugged. 'I am home.' He gestured around him. 'I belong here more than I belong in Boston.'

Jack understood the feeling. 'Still, it's a strange place to find an American.'

'It's the Legion. We all came from somewhere and we all found our way here. We do our duty and we learn not to ask about a man's past.'

Jack heard the warning in the words. 'So do you mind if I talk to your chum?'

'So long as that's all it is.' Kearney smiled. 'If I hear anything else, so help me I'll slit your throat myself.'

Jack laughed at the certainty behind the words. 'I hope it never comes to that.' He was not joking. He did not fancy the notion of fighting Kearney.

'Then don't let it.' Kearney grinned. 'Stop by on your way back. I reckon I've still got some of that arrack somewhere.'

'I'll do that.' Jack nodded his thanks and went to find his man.

'Would it make a difference if I damned your eyes and told you to bugger off?' Fleming greeted Jack as soon as he approached the legionnaire's fire. He sat with one other man, the two of them staring silently at a small cauldron filled with simmering water as they waited for it to soften up the day's ration of bacon enough to make it edible.

'No.' Jack had decided on total honesty. 'Mind if I sit down?'

'Yes.'

'That's not very civil.' He sat down regardless. 'Smells good.'

'It won't taste it. It's more gristle than meat. But if we boil it long enough it should be all right. If not, we'll leave the bloody thing cooking overnight then eat in the morning.'

Jack smiled at the experienced opinion. Many would-be soldiers joined the ranks for little more than the promise of regular food. But even the hungriest soldier quickly tired of the basic rations all armies fed their men, the rancid meat possessing little to recommend it.

'You can share our dinner. Save it going to waste.' Fleming sat forward and gave the stew a half-hearted stir. His messmate peered inside the cauldron, then shook his head before getting up and disappearing inside the tent, leaving Jack and Fleming alone by the fire.

'That's good of you. I won't say no.' Jack nodded his thanks for the offer. He had not failed to notice that there were just two men sharing the food, whilst three sat round most of the other campfires. He was not enough of a fool to ask where the third man might be. The recent fighting had claimed plenty of lives, and the Legion had lost its fair share.

'Why are you here?' Fleming gave up stirring the pot and looked keenly at Jack.

'I was going to ask you the same question.'

'Then this will be a dull conversation.' Fleming shook his head at the idea, then sighed. 'I am here because I was tired of being in the way.' He kept his eyes on Jack as he offered the explanation. 'I do not expect you to understand.'

'I don't.' Jack's reply was sharp. 'Most men join the ranks because life has shat on them so badly that being a soldier looks better than the cruddy existence they face outside. You had everything they could ever have dreamt of; more, even. Yet here you are, eating the same vile grub and fighting anyone you're told to. It doesn't make much sense to me.'

'No, put like that it doesn't make sense to me either.' Fleming chuckled at Jack's description. 'But I wouldn't change it. I belong here now. I chose this life. I don't want to give it up.' His eyes narrowed. 'I *won't* give it up.'

'You like it that much?'

'No, not all the time, but I have found I have a taste for this life. My old one was all mapped out for me. What schools I would attend, what career I would follow, even what woman I should marry. I wasn't given a say in any of it.' His deepening scowl was replaced by a smile. 'So I buggered off to come here. The Legion took me in. They didn't ask me whose son I was, or what school I had attended. I gave them a made-up name and they accepted me, no questions asked.'

Jack listened carefully. He knew only a little about the Legion; soldiers' rumours and campfire gossip rather than anything factual. Fleming's tale was intriguing, and Jack found himself feeling almost envious. It was a tempting option to become someone new. A man's past could be lost and might possibly even be forgotten.

'So your life was terrible?' He wanted to know more, to try to understand what drove a man who had every advantage in life to give it all up for a place as a common soldier in the service of a foreign power.

'I hated not having a choice.' Fleming offered a thin smile at the admission. 'I'm sure you don't understand, but I could not bear to sit there and just plod my way along the path they had set out for me. It is my life. I will choose how I live it. I shall not be told. Not by my family, not by my father, and most certainly, Jack, not by you.'

Jack smiled at such determination. He came from a very different world, the rookeries of London bearing no comparison to the life of a rich man's son. Yet much of what Fleming said could have come from his own mouth. Fate had chosen a path for him and he had rejected it, becoming an impostor to prove that he could be so much more than he was allowed. Such naïve ambition had been washed away in the blood of the battlefield, but he could well remember the burning desire to fight against his fate.

'So I cannot convince you to come with me?' His smile widened as he spoke.

'No. You will have to kill me first.' The bold challenge was made with a grin.

'Is that all? You should've said.' Jack laughed. 'Then I could have shot your bollocks off the first time I saw you and we wouldn't be having this dull conversation.'

Fleming guffawed. 'I like you, Jack. You're full of shit, but I like you. So when will you tell me your tale? Why are *you* here?'

'I had nowhere else to go,' Jack replied with honesty. 'Besides, I am being rewarded for doing this.'

'They're paying you to take me back to my dear old pater's side?'

'Yes.'

'And my sorry tale did not convince you to leave me alone?'

'No.' Jack placed a hand on Fleming's shoulder. 'No offence, but I still have to get you away from all this. People are depending on me. I cannot let them down. Not again.' His voice tailed off. The memory of his mother's death flickered into his mind. The flames of the campfire became those of the burning gin palace. An image of his mother's face in the moment before she died formed in his mind's eye. She was shouting at him, telling him to leave, to get away.

'Jack?'

He started. The image fled as he forced the memory away.

'They are awful buggers, aren't they? The memories.'
Fleming was watching Jack's face closely. 'You've been around
a bit. You have the same look in your eyes as some of the boys
who have served for a long time, like you're looking at
something a thousand yards away.'

Jack shook off the chill that the memory of his mother's
face had sent rushing through his veins. The notes of a bugle
call prevented him from answering. The sound came clearly in
the quiet. It signalled the end of the day and summoned men to
the first watch of the night.

He stood up and bashed the dust from his backside. 'I think
I'll leave you in peace.' He nodded towards the bubbling
cauldron. 'That smells like shit.'

Fleming laughed dutifully, but his eyes did not reflect any
sign of humour. He got up too, and held out his hand. 'I rather
think we could have been friends, you and I.'

Jack shook the hand being offered to him. 'Perhaps.' He
sighed. 'I still have to come for you.'

'You can try.'

Jack nodded. There was nothing more to be said. He had
come to find out more about the man that Ballard had ordered
him to take away, perhaps even to convince him to come
without any more fuss. He had expected to find a fool, someone
he would despise. He had not expected to find a man cut from
the very same cloth as himself.

Chapter Thirty-one

———◆•◆———

The mysterious object was almost motionless in the sky, swaying gently from side to side in the breeze. It looked like some monstrous bird flying into the wind, the unearthly calm unsettling.

'What the hell do you think it is?' Jack screwed his eyes tight against the eyepiece of his field glasses. They watered with the effort, but he could just about make out a large basket hanging from underneath the monstrous beast. He thought he could see two or three men inside it, but the distance was too great, and he gave up the struggle.

'Witchcraft?' Billy spoke in reverential tones, his voice betraying a mix of fear and excitement.

'You daft bugger.' Mary clipped her son's head for such a foolish answer. 'Jack?'

Jack laughed off the boy's fear. 'It's not witchcraft, lad, but blow me if I know how that thing works.'

'It is a balloon,' Ballard answered. He was spending a rare morning with them, and now he held out a hand. 'May I borrow your glasses, Jack?'

Jack handed them over. He had not seen a contraption like the one ahead before, and he was intrigued.

'Ah, that is better. This really is a fine pair of glasses, Jack. The man you stole them from must curse you daily for their loss.'

'I pinched 'em, not Jack,' Billy piped up, puffing out his chest as he did so.

'You really should not brag about such delinquent behaviour, William. It will lead to no end of trouble.' Ballard spoke whilst still studying the balloon. His habit of addressing Mary's son as William never failed to make the boy scowl and his mother smile. 'That really is a marvel of modern engineering.' He lowered the glasses then handed them back to Jack, his expression revealing his fascination with the machine that had so concerned Billy. 'We are lucky to see—'

'Lucky?' Jack interrupted. He was trying hard to forget the close-quarter fighting in the town that he now knew was called Magenta. 'I doubt the fellows who had their guts ripped out the other day would say they had been lucky.'

Ballard flicked a hand to brush off such a dark retort. 'You know full well that I do not mean it like that. What I would have said, if you had just let me finish,' he sounded peeved as he was forced into the longer explanation, 'is that we are lucky to see a truly modern war, one where industry and engineering will play as much a part as the generals and their armies. The French seem to have grasped that fact rather faster than the bally Habsburgs. Their cannon are superior thanks to modern manufacturing methods, as are their rifles. Their ability to manoeuvre is better thanks to their use of the railways. Now the Austrians are using balloons as observation posts, and whilst that is to their credit, I do not fancy it will win them any battles.'

'Will there be another battle?' Billy asked the question eagerly.

'I very much doubt it.' Ballard smiled at the boy. 'At least not for some time.'

Jack winced at the expression he saw on his master's face. He was trying to win the boy over, but to Jack's mind the sickly smile looked rather as though he was attempting to coerce him into an unwelcome proposition.

'The Austrians are retreating.' Ballard continued his explanation. 'They show no intention of stopping this side of the Quadrilateral.'

'The what?' Jack could not help but ask the question he knew Ballard wanted to hear.

'The Quadrilateral,' Ballard repeated. 'For many years now the Austrian generals have relied on the strength of their fortresses to dominate these lands. They have four major fortresses to the south of Lake Garda: Peschiera, Verona, Legnago and Mantua. Together they make for a vast entrenched battleground. It is the opinion of the French high command that the Austrian commanders are seeking a return to this strong defensive position. No, there will be no battle. At least not any time soon.'

'There *will* be a battle.' Jack enjoyed pricking his master's bubble of confidence. 'And soon.'

'Why do you say that?' Ballard's scowl was immediate.

'I have heard that the French patrols have been coming across many more enemy reconnaissance parties than before. Now there is that blasted thing.' Jack gestured at the distant balloon. 'The Austrians are taking more notice of where the French are and where they are going. I reckon that means they aim to stop them.'

Ballard harrumphed. 'I fancy the French high command does not share your opinion. Perhaps they should ask for it. I am sure the view of a charlatan would be most welcome.' He smiled, pleased with the jibe.

'I'd be happy to tell them.' Jack met the barb with deadpan seriousness.

'I am sure you would, you scoundrel.' Ballard was enjoying himself, and not even Jack's contrary opinion could harm his high spirits.

'You don't believe me?'

'On this occasion, I shall trust to the opinion of the maréchal.'

'I'll prove it to you if you like.' Jack made the offer with a smile. He had spotted a small village that hugged the ridge around half a mile from the line of march. It was not a grand place, but he could see that it possessed a church with a tall spire. 'We could go over there.' He pointed across to the tower. 'I reckon that will let us see what's ahead. If I'm right, I think we will spot the Austrians. I would say your friend the maréchal would be rather impressed if you were the one to tell him what was what.'

Ballard's eyes followed the direction of Jack's pointing finger. A thoughtful expression crept over his face as he contemplated the suggestion. 'I think it might be worth the effort.' He turned and nodded to Jack. 'How lovely it would be for a British observer to point out the facts of the matter before the maréchal's own reconnaissance forces.' He paused as he made up his mind. 'I think we shall do it. Mary, I shall leave Palmer to watch over you and young William.' He gave his orders quickly before rewarding Jack with one of his odd smiles. 'I say, Jack, shall we go for a little stroll?'

* * *

The village was quiet. It was mid-morning, and most of the locals would be out working the fields, but there were still enough around to stare at the two men who walked along the main road that passed through the village's centre. By the time Jack and Ballard had reached the small square to the front of the church, a priest was waiting for them.

'*Bonjour, messieurs.*' The priest opened his arms as he greeted them in French. He was not old, but his hair was thin, and he was thick enough around the waist to be well into middle age.

'Good afternoon, Father,' Ballard replied. 'I'm afraid we are English, not French.'

'Ah, then in that case perhaps I should say welcome, gentlemen.' The priest's English was good, his Italian accent barely noticeable.

'Thank you.' Ballard walked towards him. 'I am Major Ballard of the British Army, currently serving Maréchal MacMahon of His Majesty's French forces. This is my man Lark.'

'A good morning to you both.' The priest bobbed his head in greeting. 'My name is Father Danese and I welcome you to our humble village.'

'Thank you for such a warm greeting.' Ballard was clearly enjoying the formalities. 'Your English is very good indeed.'

Danese inclined his head at the compliment. 'I was fortunate to spend some time in your beautiful country when I was a younger man. At Canterbury, a most beautiful city. Now,' he clapped his hands together, 'perhaps I can offer you a little food, or is it accommodation you are searching for?'

'Thank you, Father, but all we require is the opportunity to climb your tower.'

'Ah, a reconnaissance!' The priest seemed relieved that his visitors could be pleased so easily. 'Yes, of course, I shall show you myself. Please, if you will, follow me.' He beckoned for Jack and Ballard to follow as he set off towards the church.

'So I'm your man now?' Jack spoke out of the side of his mouth as they trailed after the priest. 'Who knew promotion could be so rapid?'

'Do be quiet, Jack, there's a good fellow.' Ballard could not help a half-smile from creeping on to his face. 'We were getting on so famously, it would be a shame to spoil it with your recalcitrance.'

The steps that led to the top of the tower smelled of damp and mould. The priest went first, his feet kicking up a fine cloud of dust. The climb was long enough to have their breath catching in their throats and their knees and thighs protesting, but the view when they emerged from the gloom of the stairwell was spectacular.

Danese led them to the edge of the narrow parapet that surrounded the pinnacle of the tower, his face creased into an indulgent smile as he saw their delight.

'It is beautiful, is it not? A reminder of God's hand at work, I think.' He clasped his hands together and stood back so as not to interrupt his guests' view of the landscape.

For once, Jack did not disagree with the invocation of God's name. The tower was the perfect vantage point, and the priest was right to be proud of the vista. In the bright morning sunlight, the countryside looked pristine and tranquil, the patchwork of wheat fields, grassland and woods simply stunning.

He moved to the side facing east, the direction in which the

French army was advancing, careful not to lean against the rough-hewn stone parapet that was all that stood between him and a fatal plunge to the square below. A steep ridge ran west to east, its slopes covered with vines, mulberry trees and great fields of wheat. A handful of small villages broke up the lush countryside, their red roofs bright against so much greenery. It was a picture of rural bliss, the scene likely to have been unchanged for centuries.

'Permit me to tell you what you see.' The priest had followed Jack and now held out an arm, his finger pointing towards the first of the villages nestled so perfectly into the countryside that it appeared it had formed there naturally.

'Let us start on our left. The village you can see closest to us on the western side of the ridge is Castiglione. There to its right, nestled into the foot of the slope, is Grole. The larger one, up on the centre of the crest, is Solferino. You see the tall tower at its centre? That is called the Spia d'Italia, the Spy of Italy, you would say. I have to confess that the view from there is perhaps finer than the one you see before you, but please do not tell Father Bellini if you meet him that I admitted to that.' Danese chuckled at his own humour before continuing his description. 'To the south of Solferino and on the slope of the ridge itself is San Cassiano, with Mont Fontana just behind. Then at the end of the ridge, just before the last hilltop, that is Volta. The view across the Campo di Medole to the south is magnificent from there.'

Jack did his best to remember the names. On the slope that led up to the village that Father Danese had named as Solferino were a handful of small streams, their banks lined with thick bands of vegetation. A single minor road led directly along the ridge line from Castiglione to Solferino, and another, larger road ran along the base of the ridge before heading south-east. He turned his head, following the path the road took as it meandered away. It led him to look out to the south, where the great plain that Danese had called the Campo di Medole stretched for miles. There the ground was wide and open and covered with vast fields of maize, wheat, barley and rye that rippled in the breeze that washed across them.

'It is a beautiful view.' Ballard had come to stand at Jack's side.

'It is that.' Jack had seen enough. The view from the church tower was indeed spectacular, and the ridge, with its charming villages, lush greenery and pretty meandering streams, was a classic example of the beauty of Lombardy.

He reached down to his hip to free his field glasses from their leather case and lifted them to his eyes. Within a few seconds he had spied the first Austrian troops, clustered around the villages of Solferino and San Cassiano. It did not take him much longer to pan along the ridge and see the preparations that were being made.

He lowered the glasses and handed them to Ballard. 'Take a look at Solferino.' He pointed out the village, then stood back slightly to give his commander a better view.

'I see them.' Ballard moved slightly as he studied the ridge. He lowered the field glasses, then gave Danese one of his odd little smiles. 'Father, could we have a moment?'

'Of course, you have military matters to discuss that even a man of the cloth should not overhear.'

'I thank you for your understanding.'

Danese inclined his head to acknowledge Ballard's politeness. 'I will leave you now, but please take care on the way down. The steps can be treacherous, and I would not have it said that I was the cause of injuring a British officer, or his man.' He gave Jack a half smile as he backed away and made for the stairs.

Ballard waited, his head cocked to one side as he listened to the sound of the priest's footsteps on the stone stairs. Only when he was satisfied that they were truly alone did he fix his gaze on Jack. 'So they have turned.'

'It looks like it. It makes sense, too. Each one of those villages makes a perfect strongpoint to anchor their line.' Jack was running his eyes over the ridge. He could see the places where the Austrian generals would deploy their men. There was little room for Napoleon to manoeuvre. The French could advance as far as Castiglione. From there they would be forced to move on to Solferino, which appeared to be a natural fortress. The road that led there narrowed on the approach, tottering along a knife-edged ridge, the last few hundred yards overlooked by a series of high walls and what appeared to be some sort of church or castle. The walls looked solid, even from a distance, and the Austrians would be sure to prepare a strong defensive position.

The ground to the south of Solferino looked more inviting. The great open plain of the Campo di Medole favoured cavalry and horse artillery. It would also give the French infantry space to manoeuvre. With the ridge too narrow to support a wide advance, Napoleon would be forced to commit troops to the plain. Any fighting there would be more in the classic style, with all three arms of both armies working in unison.

Jack looked northwards. He could see little of the terrain on the far side of the ridge, save for another village perched high on a hilltop far in the distance. He could only guess that Napoleon would send more troops in that direction, the fight for the ground to the northern side of the ridge forming the French army's left flank. With Solferino in the centre, and the great plain on the right, Jack got a sense of the ground that he believed would likely see a battle in the coming days. The enormous swathe of land looked serene and peaceful in the morning sunshine, but if the armies did fight, the beautiful countryside would be devastated.

'It'll be a bugger of a job to shift all those bastards off that ridge.' He gave the verdict solemnly.

'I do see what you mean,' agreed Ballard.

'Their men will still need to stand. It all comes down to that at the end of the day.'

Ballard nodded. 'Let us see what else we can see, shall we?' He gestured for Jack to follow him to the other side of the tower.

'Goodness me, would you look at that?' He had not placed Jack's field glasses to his eyes for more than a few moments before he made the exclamation.

Jack did not need the fancy glasses to make out what had caused such a reaction. As far as the eye could see, the roads were clogged with men and the materiel of war. The French army was simply enormous, with great columns of men, horses, artillery wagons, limbers, commissary carts and ambulances stretching back for miles.

'So the Austrians are being bold.' Ballard had seen enough. He lowered the field glasses and handed them back to Jack. 'And therefore there will be a battle. If the French numbers, and their estimates of the Austrians' strength, are accurate, it could be the biggest battle the world has ever seen.'

Jack stared at the huge French columns. He could not contradict Ballard's claim. Nothing he had ever seen had been on this scale. If the Austrian army was as vast as the French horde, the forthcoming battle would indeed be cataclysmic in scale.

'We shall have our chance.' Ballard came to stand nearer to Jack. 'You can do what you were brought here to do.'

Jack could feel the wash of breath on his cheek. His commander was uncomfortably close.

'Do not let me down again, Jack.' Ballard lowered his voice, speaking barely louder than a whisper. 'You must get the boy away. He will be in dreadful danger.' His words caught in this throat. 'You must find him and you must keep him from harm!'

Jack felt a chill at the back of his neck. Tens of thousands of men were marching to their deaths. And he would have to take his place in their ranks.

Chapter Thirty-two

The French army awoke long before dawn. It did so quietly, the men silent, and the sergeants and corporals limiting themselves to hoarse whispers as they made sure their troops were ready. Even the musicians' instruments were mute, the army rousing itself without any of its usual fanfare.

The men drank a hasty morning coffee before leaving their knapsacks behind. Many looked wistfully at their belongings, their worldly goods abandoned save for a keepsake or memento kept for luck. To a man they wondered if they would see them again; how many knapsacks would be left in the heap unclaimed and free to be rifled through by those left alive?

'Good hunting, Jack.' Ballard offered his hand. It was still dark. The only light came from their campfire, and it left much of their faces in shadow. The two of them were standing alone underneath the black flag of a first aid station. They had spent the night in one of the buildings that had been requisitioned as a temporary hospital for the following day. One of the pair of French surgeons assigned to the station had arrived in the early hours, demanding that they vacate the space that would shortly be used to shelter the wounded.

Jack was forced to switch his mug of coffee to his left hand so that he could shake his commander's hand.

'You know what you are about?'

'Yes.' Jack sipped at the coffee, wincing at the bitter taste. He wanted to be away and put an end to the interminable waiting.

'Good. Keep close to Palmer.' Ballard felt the need to repeat the plan that he had outlined the night before. 'When the moment is right, you can change into your new uniforms. Find our man. Stay at his side, then get him out of there as soon as you can. I don't care how you do it. Just bring him to me here.'

Jack looked around him, making a mental map of the place he would need to find later that day. 'What happens if you have to retreat?'

'Then we shall stay close to MacMahon's headquarters. Find that and you will find us.' Ballard's reply was clipped.

Jack nodded. He saw Mary busy around the fire. 'You'll keep Mary safe?'

'I will.'

'Whatever happens?'

'Of course.' Ballard glanced across at Mary. 'She is a fine woman.' He looked back to meet Jack's gaze. 'Whatever happens to you, she will be taken care of.'

Jack's eyes narrowed as he heard something change in Ballard's tone. But it was not the time to wonder at the goings-on in his master's mind. 'What if we cannot get him out?'

'You must. You have to find a way.' Ballard scowled at the notion, then took a deep breath. 'This boy is important to his family. Our sponsor needs him back. We cannot let him down.'

He fixed Jack with a hard stare. 'And you have been well rewarded for your efforts, or have you forgotten?'

'No.' Jack refused to let the memory of the burning gin palace into his mind. Ballard had taken him from the gutter, and had given both him and Mary a future. It had come at a price. That price was currently in the ranks of the French Foreign Legion. 'What if we don't get him away? Or if he's killed before we can get to him?' He watched his commander closely as he asked the questions.

'Then there is no need for you to return.'

'I see.' Jack drained the last of his coffee. He understood well enough. Without Fleming, Jack had no name and no access to the money deposited in his real name. Mary and Billy's future would look as bleak as his own. He dug deep for a smile. 'Do you always get what you want?'

'Oh yes.' Ballard smiled at the notion. 'I make sure of it.'

Jack was given no chance to reply. Behind Ballard's back he saw Palmer get into the saddle. The major had been able to requisition three horses from MacMahon's headquarters; one each for Jack and Palmer, and one for Fleming. Palmer beckoned to him. It was time to go.

'I'll see you later, then.' Jack tossed the dregs of his coffee to one side.

Ballard did not answer. Mary came over to take his mug. He could see the concern on her face, her lips showing white as she pressed them tight together.

'Look after my Billy.' She cradled Jack's mug. 'You bring him back safe.'

It's a battlefield.' Jack understood her pain, but he would not lie. 'I cannot promise you that.'

Mary glanced at Ballard, who was watching a column of

French infantry march along the road close to the aid station. 'Yes you bloody well can.' She hissed the words through gritted teeth. 'And you will.'

Jack held her stare. He saw her fear. It was no small thing to let her child go with the two men. But someone needed to look after the horses when Jack and Palmer went to get Fleming.

'He's a bright lad. He'll stay out of trouble.' Jack would not tell her what she wanted to hear. He had already broken enough promises to blacken his soul for all eternity. He would not add to it by making another he could not be certain of keeping.

'Mary.' Ballard had turned back and now placed a hand on her shoulder. 'William needs to do this. He is not going to fight. He will just look after the horses. Jack will see that he is left somewhere safe.'

'I will.' Jack saw the interplay between the two. It was not like Ballard to touch anyone, let alone a woman. He wondered how much he had missed.

'He had better.' Mary allowed Ballard's hand to rest on her shoulder, but its presence did not lessen the emotion behind the glare that she sent Jack's way. 'If he doesn't come back, then so help me, Jack, I will track you down and throttle you with my own bare hands.'

'I hear you.' Jack felt his anger start to rise. He swallowed it with difficulty. It appeared half the damn world was making demands on him. Doing his best to ignore the twin stares he could feel boring into his spine, he went to find Palmer.

Jack sat easily in the saddle, Billy's warm body pressed close against his back, the boy's arms clasped tight around his middle. They had three horses, but a childhood in the rookeries of east London was not one that gave a lad the opportunity to learn to ride.

Palmer rode at his side, the two saddlebags containing the uniforms of the French Foreign Legion strapped behind him, and the lead rein of the spare horse held loosely in his left hand. Whether Fleming would ride it, or would simply be draped across its saddle, was yet to be discovered.

The two men and one boy sat watching the French army prepare for the battle. Jack was impressed by what he saw, the troops going about their business without fuss. The long columns marched well, the ranks ordered and precise, the faces of the soldiers hardening as they made ready for what was to come.

Other than the sound of an army on the move, all was peaceful. In India it was called the *hawa khana*, the breathing of the air. The quiet moments before battle were a time for prayer and for ritual, for the final taking of a breath before the struggle to stay alive began. Jack was reminded of another dawn, on another day. Then he had been at the fore, his place at the side of the commanding general dictating that he would be in the front ranks of the fighting. Now he would advance behind the attack, biding his time and waiting for the opportunity to strike.

The army marched in darkness, shrouded in mist, the thud of boots hitting the ground the only sound disturbing the still air. Jack waited patiently for the men of the Legion to pass by. He did not bother to scan the massed ranks to see if he could locate Kearney or Fleming. There would be time enough to find them once the fighting began in earnest. Instead he looked to the east, searching for the first trace of dawn, and for the start of the day that would see many of those in the ranks marching past him left broken on the ground.

* * *

The first sounds of distant fighting came from the direction of Solferino, where the initial French attacks were taking place. The men of II Corps were marching south on the road that ran along the foot of the ridge to take up a position on the French army's right flank. Every head turned to the left, even the eyes of the sergeants and the officers drawn to the telltale echo of combat. Nothing could be seen, the distance too great and the watery light of dawn too dim. Yet each man, veterans of the campaigns in North Africa and the Crimea, could picture all too well what it was they heard.

Jack, Palmer and Billy did their best to keep close behind the Legion. Twice they had been turned back, the staff officers galloping between the French regiments ordering the civilian observers away from the fighting. Both times the orders had simply been ignored, but they knew they were pushing their luck. Eventually they would be kept away more forcefully, so they would soon have to find a convenient spot to change into the uniforms Ballard had secured for them.

Billy squirmed for the umpteenth time, his warm body fidgeting against Jack's back. Jack did not berate him for it, allowing the lad his excitement. It would not last. There would be time enough for the boy to feel far worse emotions, the reality of the sights and sounds found on a battlefield bearing no comparison to any boyish dreams of glory he might be nurturing. Jack would rather he was not there, but Ballard had insisted. At some point they would have to dismount, and the horses were too valuable to abandon.

'You all right, lad?' Jack whispered the question over his shoulder.

'Course.' The reply was quick.

'You do as I tell you, or so help me I'll tan your damn hide. You understand me?'

'Yes, Jack.' The boy's contempt for the unnecessary warning was obvious. 'When will it start?'

'Soon enough.'

'It had better. I've had my fill of being pressed up against your sweaty arse.'

'Watch your tongue.' Jack tried not to laugh. 'You're not going to see any of it anyway.'

'That ain't fair.'

Jack twisted in the saddle so he could look at Billy's face. The boy was scowling. 'A battle isn't the place for a child.'

The scowl deepened. 'I ain't a child.'

'You think you're a man?'

'I think I could fight. There's boys my age with those Frenchies.' Billy nodded towards the drummers buried in the heart of the column.

'They don't fight.'

'They might.'

'No, they just shit in their breeches and run away.'

'You don't want me to see anything just so my ma don't scold you.'

'Maybe.' Jack acknowledged the truth of the statement. 'But you'll see plenty that you wish you hadn't, believe me.'

'I ain't bothered. I've seen bad things before. Like when old George the sweep had his belly slit open by that whore. Those guts of his were bright blue and he sat with them in his lap like they were that little dog Maggie had for a while.'

'I don't care what you've seen. Your ma wants you out of the way, so that's where you'll be.' Jack smiled at the lad's belligerence. The rookeries were a hard place, but they did not compare to the battlefield.

Anything more he wanted to say was lost in the urgent sound of the first bugle of the day calling the column to a halt. The heavy drums followed, rattling into life. The lads had snatched away the covers that protected the instruments' skins from the damp morning air, and now brought their sticks down sharply, beating out the time that would provide the tempo as the column changed formation.

The men knew what they were about. To the beat of the drum the rear of the column marched outwards to form a line, the rearmost files walking the furthest, to the extremities of the new formation.

Jack pushed ahead as the Legion's frontage widened.

'Hold up, Jack.' Palmer had stopped his mount and the one he still led, and now he called across to Jack as he saw the first enemy soldiers emerge from the mist-shrouded land ahead. 'You see 'em?'

Jack had been watching the Legion. Now he peered through the fog. He saw what Palmer meant immediately.

'My eye.' He leaned to one side, letting the boy clinging to his waist have a clearer view. 'You see those, lad?'

'Blow me tight.'

Jack laughed at Billy's reverential tone, the lad's bold claims forgotten the moment he clapped eyes on the enemy.

For the Austrian army was not sitting back and waiting for the French to attack. Instead, it was advancing. Huge columns of infantry were marching towards the French army's right flank, each one made up of a whole battalion.

And they were heading straight for the Legion.

* * *

The French waited for the enemy. This would be no close-quarter battle like the cramped fight in the confined streets of Magenta. Rather it would be a set-piece affair, with the Austrian conscripts packed tight in a series of columns aimed directly at the French line.

The ground was made for such a battle. The Legion had deployed into a line at right angles to the road, facing south. The ridge of high ground anchored their left flank. In front of them was the great plain, the level terrain covered with wide fields of wheat. The Austrian infantry would have a fast and easy march as they headed northwards, with no obstacles in their way or rising ground to sap their strength.

'Those things are bloody big.' Billy stared in awe at the enemy columns.

'You wait until they get close.' Jack could not help but smile at the way the lad's eyes widened as the Austrians emerged from the early-morning mist.

But Billy's eyes narrowed again as he peered at the French line. Two men deep, it looked fragile, stretched thin across the front of the enemy attack. 'They can't stop those bloody great things like that.' He looked at Jack. 'Why are they just standing there?'

Jack offered a tight smile. 'That line doesn't look much, I'll grant you, but it will stop them well enough. If they stand.' He had seen columns before. He had known the fear as he had watched the seemingly relentless tide of humanity surging towards him. And he had seen them stopped, ranks gutted and torn, the thin lines of British redcoats bludgeoning them to a halt with volley after volley of accurate rifle fire.

'Those buggers will march to the sound of their drums.' Jack smiled as he spoke softly to the lad clutching around his middle. 'They'll keep coming, and that noise, why, it won't ever stop.'

The columns came on, steady and calm. Drums deep in their midst beat out the tempo of the advance, the mesmeric, hypnotic rhythm driving the white-coated Austrian infantry forward through the great fields of wheat still wet from the morning dew.

'Then they'll cheer. They'll cheer so loud that you'll feel it deep down in your belly.' Jack warmed to his tale. He saw the boy hanging on his every word, his eyes riveted on Jack's mouth as he foretold what was to come. 'Their officers will lead them on, waving their swords over their heads and shouting at the lads in the ranks. They'll goad them, daring them to kill every last one of us. Closer and closer they'll come, those drums beating all the while. They'll seem unstoppable then. It'll look like there are so many of the buggers that it won't be possible to kill enough to make a difference.'

The French line settled, then began to load their rifles, the commands of their officers and sergeants rippling up and down the companies as they prepared to make their stand against the massive columns.

Jack smiled. 'And then that fragile line will open fire, and it'll all be over in a couple of minutes.'

'How so?' Billy scoffed at his words. 'How can that,' he pointed at the Legion, 'stop those.' He waved at the Austrian columns moving purposefully towards them.

'Did your ma teach you to add up?'

'Course.'

'Then do it now. How many rifles are in that line?'

Billy twisted in the saddle as he looked at the French soldiers. 'A lot.'

'How many men in those columns can return fire.'

Billy screwed up his eyes as he peered through the mist. 'Just those in the front.'

'So who wins?'

Billy's lips moved as he did his calculations. Every man in the French line could fire, whereas only the Austrians in the front two ranks of each column could hope to return it. He did the sums, and for the first time in a while he smiled. 'We do.'

'It's simple, isn't it?' Jack nodded as the boy reached the correct conclusion. 'Those columns look bloody frightening, I give you that, but when they're close enough, our boys over there will open fire. The first volley will cut down the front ranks, maybe the second and perhaps even the third. The white coats will still come on, even if they have to tread their mates into the dirt to do it, but then the second volley will hit them. The front of that column will be like a bloody butcher's yard. They'll be screaming then, those whose arms have been torn off, or whose guts are spilling into their hands. They'll get in the way, stopping their mates coming up behind. The French, well, they'll keep firing, keep killing and maiming, and they won't be able to miss, will they, seeing as how those bloody things are so damn big.'

Jack tasted something bitter as he predicted what was to come. 'If those Austrian boys have any sense, they'll turn tail right here and now. If they're brave, or foolish,' he shook his head, 'or both, then they'll still try to come on. But they won't stand, not for long. When they break, they'll be nothing more than a mob of frightened bastards running for their lives.'

He looked at Billy, his smile stretched thin. 'So don't be frightened. Those poor buggers are marching to their deaths.'

Chapter Thirty-three

⸺•◆•⸺

The Austrian columns came on in fine style. The noise assaulted the French line, the bugle calls and the beat of the drums getting ever louder. The advance of the great blocks of men seemed inexorable, the French line far too fragile to stand against such power.

The Austrian conscripts saw it too. They cheered with every step, whilst their officers bellowed encouragement. The great yellow and black flags waved at the columns' heads, the proud imperial eagles revealed to the men packed tight in the ranks as the breeze caught the huge squares of silk.

Jack watched, grim-faced, as the men of the Legion finished loading their Minié rifles. It was the same weapon he had used in the Crimea, a fine gun for an infantryman. The barrel was rifled, the long grooves etched into the inside spinning the bullet to make it vastly more accurate than the smoothbore muskets it had replaced. But it was not the rifling that made the Minié one of the most deadly weapons ever used on the battlefield. The real genius was in the bullet.

Unlike the round balls fired by the rifles used when the first

Napoleon was emperor, the conical bullet fired by the Minié was smaller than the weapon's barrel, allowing the men to load quickly and easily. When the charge was ignited, the base of the bullet deformed and expanded to grip the rifling. This expansion also contained the power of the charge's detonation, ensuring that all of it was delivered behind the bullet.

It was dreadfully effective. In the Crimea, Jack had seen five or even six men hit by a single bullet. Now he looked at the advancing columns and felt something close to sympathy for the Austrians approaching the French line. He had no doubt what would happen, what fate awaited the men packed together in the tightly spaced ranks. He knew what was to come, and he felt angry. For the Austrian commanders had learned nothing of the wars already fought in the era of modern weaponry.

The French general would still take no chances. He saw the might of the columns, and he sent his artillery to support his infantry. Jack watched as the French artillerymen bustled around their guns, the air filled with the shouts of their officers and sergeants as they prepared to fire. The men knew what they were about, and it did not take long for the teams of horses to be sent to the rear, the guns lined up so that their great gaping muzzles pointed towards the enemy.

The columns were getting closer. The white-coated ranks advanced with discipline, the formation maintaining its cohesion even as they came into range of the French gunners.

With a great roar, the guns opened fire.

Jack felt Billy flinch as the thunderclap of sound pounded into them.

'Watch, boy, watch!' He snapped the instruction, his own eyes fixed on the columns.

Soil and dust was thrown up in great fountains of dirt as the first shells smashed into the ground just ahead of the closest column. The French gunners were firing at what seemed to Jack to be an impossibly long range, but they had still nearly found their mark with their first volley.

The gunners did not pause to celebrate. The gun line was a hive of activity as the artillerymen went through the tightly choreographed routine of reloading.

The second volley seared out across the plain less than half a minute later. This time the barrels were warmer and the shells went further, tearing into the Austrian columns. Even from a distance, Jack saw great gaps ripped in the enemy's ranks before a thin cloud of powder smoke obscured his view. The familiar stink stuck in his throat, the rotten-egg stench filling his mouth. He leaned from the saddle and spat, the taste bitter.

When his head lifted, the powder smoke had rolled away enough for him to see a battery of Austrian guns deploying to return fire. From so far away the enemy gunners looked tiny, swarming around their cannon like so many ants disturbed from a nest.

The French fired two more volleys before the enemy gunners were ready to reply. Jack saw great gouts of flame sear from the Austrian cannon as they replied, the sound very different to the great roars of the French salvos. He tried to trace the path of the shot, but the range was simply too great, and all he saw was a series of crevices being gouged in the ground well to the front of the French line.

The French gunners did not pause. They poured on their volleys, their rifled barrels so much more effective than the smoothbore cannon used by the Austrians. Shell after shell hit the infantry columns, each one tearing another great gash in the ranks.

'Jesus Christ.' Jack had never seen an artillery barrage like it. The French gunners were destroying the Austrian columns. Barely a shell was missing, even at such long range, and already the advance was grinding to a bloody halt.

A battery of Austrian horse artillery rushed forward. It was a courageous move. Jack could see the gunners lashing at their horses to drive them on. The limbers scrabbled across the ground, the cannons behind bucking like wild creatures. The Austrian artillerymen were gambling on a fast advance to allow them to close the range and bring their cannon to bear on the French guns that were wreaking such havoc on their comrades.

Jack heard the shouts from the French gun line as the enemy horse artillery was spotted. It took little time to turn a battery of the French guns towards them, the gunners hallooing joyously like a hunter getting his first glimpse of a fox.

Still the Austrian horse artillery came on, flaunting their courage. The men in the columns cheered them loudly, even as another salvo of shells ripped into their ranks.

The French battery finished realigning and opened fire. Their gun sergeants had taken their time aiming, their skill challenged by the bravery of their peers in the enemy's ranks. Jack tried to gauge the range. It had to be at least a thousand yards, much too far for a smoothbore cannon to hope to hit its target, but well within the range of these new French guns that had been manufactured and designed for just such a moment as this.

The French salvo hit. Not one shell missed. One moment the Austrian guns had been galloping forward; the next they were destroyed.

A lone gun emerged from the destruction. Five had been hit and now lay in smoking ruin, the ground around them smothered with dead horses and broken men. The single gun to survive swerved around and charged for the rear. The cheers of the Austrian infantry died away.

Jack turned his gaze from the slaughter. It was a dreadful demonstration of the power of the modern cannon. Warfare was changing in front of his eyes.

To the left of the French line, the ridge was wreathed in smoke. Maréchal MacMahon's II Corps was just one of the five French infantry divisions at the emperor's disposal that day. Whilst Jack was witnessing the fight on the southern flank of the battlefield, other French divisions were assaulting the ridge itself. From where he sat, it was impossible to know if these assaults were succeeding, or if they were being destroyed as easily as the Austrian columns.

'Those are brave boys.' Palmer voiced his opinion softly, drawing Jack's attention back to the great blocks of infantry that were still struggling forward. It was indeed a courageous display, the men in white uniforms forced to pick their way over the dead and the dying, the ground behind them littered with broken bodies.

The French guns fired without pause. Every shell hit. Every shell killed.

The columns were nowhere near the French line when the inevitable happened. With hundreds slaughtered, the survivors could advance no further. The formations broke, the men turning and streaming towards the rear in sudden, desperate haste. The French gunners kept firing, killing and maiming even as their enemy ran.

The men in the French line did not cheer. The legionnaires

had watched fellow infantrymen butchered by the artillery fire, and more than one face turned to stare in loathing at the gunners, the foot soldiers' sympathy firmly with the men in the white uniforms.

The guns fell silent, the broken enemy ranks now too far away even for the power of their precious new cannon. The first Austrian attack had been repulsed without the French infantry firing a single volley.

Jack shifted his aching buttocks as he sat on the ground. He looked around, trying to see if anything was happening, but he could see nothing save for French troops standing patiently in their ranks as they waited for fresh orders. He could hear the sounds of fighting, but they came from far away on the ridge, and were not close enough to warrant his attention.

'Going to be a storm.'

Palmer was sitting on the ground next to Jack whilst Billy held all three horses. He was looking up at the sky. The day was already hot, the air muggy and close. The skies overheard were grey and smudged with an inky darkness, the telltale signs of a storm building over the top of the battlefield.

The Legion had not moved for several hours, the morning dragging by with excruciating slowness. There had been some activity. Austrian cavalry had threatened II Corps's right flank, the hostile detachments probing the joint between it and III Corps. MacMahon's cavalry had seen them off easily enough. The fighting had been too far away for the men in the Legion to see very much of it at all, and Jack was feeling thoroughly bored.

'Looks like it,' he agreed. He looked across at his comrade. 'I've never seen columns beaten back like that.' He had been dwelling on the fate of the Austrian infantry.

'No.' Palmer's expression was as dark as the sky. 'Those poor boys didn't stand a chance.'

Jack denied any notion of sympathy. 'At least it was over quickly.'

'Hark at you. You don't know shit, Jack.' Billy was standing close enough to overhear, and he interrupted with laughter. 'It was nothing like you said it would be.'

Jack ignored the comment, but the boy was correct. He had seen war, had fought in enough battles to know what to expect. But his experience bore little comparison to what they had just witnessed. War was changing, the men far away in the factories designing and manufacturing weapons that made a mockery of the tactics used on every battlefield since the previous century.

'Here we go.' Palmer spotted the arrival of a galloper, a young officer in sky blue who rode fast along the line towards a group of officers. As he came closer, they turned as one to face him.

'At last. I reckon we'll go north.' Jack glared at Billy, who pulled a face as he heard a fresh prediction. 'That way.' He nodded towards the ridge.

'I reckon you're right.' Palmer stood up to get a clearer view. He sat down quickly enough, shaking his head. 'I can't see fuck all.'

Jack grunted in acknowledgement. It was always the way. Once the battle started, a soldier could only see what was going on around him, and even then it was hard to know anything more than what was happening right under his own nose. No one knew the whole picture, not even the general commanding the army. It was only afterwards that some overall sense of events could be gleaned. During the day, all a man could do was beat the enemy in front of him, and pray to God that everyone else was doing the same.

A series of bugle calls followed within a minute of the galloper's arrival. Almost immediately the long line of infantrymen started to break up, returning to the column formation that was more suitable for manoeuvres, re-forming to face northwards towards the ridge that dominated the centre of the battlefield.

Ahead of them was San Cassiano, the village spread across the slope of the ridge to the south of Solferino. Thus far, the men of the Legion had been spectators, their role in the battle limited to standing by and watching as the Austrian columns were destroyed. But the day was young, and now it would be their turn to go on the offensive.

Chapter Thirty-four

*J*ack guessed that it was early afternoon when the French columns marched for a second time. The officers took their time. The columns had no sooner moved off when they were stopped again, the sergeants and corporals running around the ranks to ensure that every file was perfectly spaced and every rank aligned with those around it, so that the column was ordered and formed correctly. Only when they were satisfied did the men move off again, the drums beating out the rhythm of the advance.

Jack, Billy and Palmer followed the rear ranks of the Legion. They rode easily, their borrowed horses taking the strain as the ground sloped up sharply once they reached the lower reaches of the ridge.

Now the column stopped again. This time it was to redeploy. With the drums beating out the time, the men moved into a new formation. In the days of the first Napoleon, the French army had attacked in great columns, a dozen or more battalions formed into one massive body of men. Reform had been slow, but defeat at the hands of the British and their European allies had taught the French that such tactics needed to be consigned to the past.

Now the Legion redeployed into mixed order. There were eight battalions committed to the attack on San Cassiano. They were ordered into two groups of four. In each formation, two battalions would form line, the men arranged in two long ranks, one battalion beside the other. The other two battalions would advance in a battalion column, one on each flank of the line. The formation was designed to lessen the effect of enemy artillery fire whilst having the firepower of a line, but with flanks secured by the denser columns.

The Legion would form the right-hand column on the southernmost formation. Each of the battalion's eight companies moved into a two-man-deep line arranged one behind the other. Once in place, the men fixed their bayonets, the air filled with purposeful clicks as they twisted the steel blades into place.

With the French assault paused, Jack had time to pull his field glasses from their leather pouch and use them to see what lay ahead. It did not take long to bring the slopes around San Cassiano into sight. The ground the French were attacking was smothered with white-coated Austrian infantry formed into long lines on the slopes below the village.

It would be a hard fight. The French battalions would have to advance against the Austrian line with the slope sapping their strength. They would be under fire every step of the way, the Austrian line able to pour down volley after volley. The ridge was a strong defensive position, and this time the Austrian line held all the advantages.

'This is close enough.' Jack twisted in the saddle so he could face Billy. 'Down you get, lad.'

The boy needed no further urging. Jack felt the cold breeze on his back as Billy's warm body slipped from the saddle, to land sure-footed on the ground. Jack dismounted too, immediately handing the reins to Billy. Palmer had already done the same and now tossed a sack in Jack's direction.

Jack slipped his worsted jacket from his shoulders. He dipped into the sack and pulled out the blue tunic of the Legion. It was time to lose the civilian garb and become a soldier once again.

'Stay here and don't bloody move. We'll need to come and find you, and we can only do that if we know where you are.'

Billy nodded earnestly in reply to Jack's instructions. They stood in a sparse copse of cypress trees. It would offer little in the way of shelter, but it was a decent landmark, one Jack was reasonably sure he could find again with no trouble. He did not know how the day would play out, but if Ballard's plan went off perfectly, he and Palmer would be back soon enough, the errant son reclaimed.

'He'll be all right.' Palmer walked over with an oddly stiff gait. His legionnaire's tunic was too tight and pulled badly across his shoulders.

Jack smiled at the effect. 'You look about as French as boiled beef and carrots.'

Palmer chuckled at the comment. 'I don't plan to wear this get-up for long.' He nodded at Jack. 'At least yours fits.'

Jack made a show of preening. 'I quite like it.' He had worn both the bright scarlet of a British officer and the plain red wool of an ordinary soldier. He had worn the dark blue of a British hussar, the dusty khaki jacket of an Indian irregular, and even the fabulous sky-blue tunic of a maharajah's general.

The legionnaire's blue coat was just another to add to the list.

He settled the kepi on his head. Ballard had done well to find them the uniforms. The battle to come would be quite unlike the confused close-quarter fighting in Magenta that had allowed them to find Fleming without being turned away. This time it would be hard, if not impossible, to get close to him, the Legion sure to fight in a tight, organised formation. Ballard's stolen uniform gave them a chance of getting amongst the ranks, a chance they would need to take if they were to have any hope of completing their mission.

Jack turned to jab a finger against Billy's chest. 'Repeat your orders?'

'Stay here.' The boy bit his lip. It was no small thing to be left alone on a battlefield. 'Until you come back.'

'Good lad.' He bent down to retrieve his discarded clothing, then shoved it into the hemp sack. He paused as he picked up his revolver. He was tempted to buckle the weapon around his waist. He hefted it in one hand, then looked at Billy.

'Here.' He held the revolver by the barrel and offered it to the boy. 'Take it.'

Billy took the gun and looked at it with wide eyes.

'You know how to use it.' Jack was watching him carefully as he handed over the revolver's cartridge pouch. 'You remember everything I taught you?'

'Course.'

'Only use it if you have to. If you do something bottle-head stupid with it, I will give you a hiding the likes of which you have never seen. Is that clear?'

'Yes, Jack.' Billy was busy stuffing the pouch into his pockets.

'You hear me?' Jack injected more force into his voice.

Billy slid the revolver into the waistband of his trousers, then looked at him with solemn eyes. 'Yes, Jack.'

'Good.' Jack jabbed the lad with his finger. 'And don't let anyone take the bloody horses.'

'I won't.' The boy's chin lifted in defiance.

'Good lad.' Palmer reached across to ruffle Billy's hair before turning back to make sure that all three horses were safely tethered to a couple of sturdy trees. Satisfied, he unbuckled a pair of Minié rifles that he had tied to his saddle, handing one to Jack. 'You know how to use a bundook?'

Jack took the rifle with a tight-lipped smile. He had left his sabre in its scabbard tied to the saddle of his horse, and now Billy had his revolver. But he would not go on to the field of battle unarmed.

The rifle's weight was both reassuring and familiar. It had been many years since he had carried a long arm into battle, but he knew that the drills he would need to use it were buried deep inside him.

Palmer handed over a black leather belly pouch full of cartridges, followed by a cap box that Jack could wear around his waist. Jack took his time with the new equipment, making sure that both items sat snugly against his body. Only when he was happy did he reach over to take the final item that Palmer had brought for them both.

The bayonet was heavy. Jack held the weight for a moment, his fingers lingering on the steel blade, the metal cool to his touch. He could feel the sheen of oil under his fingertips, its stink just as he remembered.

With a purposeful action he slotted the bayonet into the end of the rifle's barrel before giving it a firm twist to lock it in place.

Palmer nodded in approval. He offered a half-smile. 'Shall we go?'

Jack nodded. It was time to find Fleming.

It felt odd being on his feet after riding all morning. The heat was getting oppressive, and Jack was sweating freely. They were walking fast, closing the distance between them and the column of legionnaires, which was already a fair way ahead.

Neither of them had said a word since they had left Billy and the horses. Jack needed his breath for marching, the steep slope already pulling at his calf muscles. But he still had enough strength to turn as they pressed on, the rising ground presenting him with a good view over the ground to the south and east.

It was easy enough to spot the place where the Austrian columns had been turned. The ground was churned up and scarred. Hundreds of bodies lay where they had fallen, and he was glad to be far enough away to be spared the details. Further to the south, he could just about make out a number of other French troops holding their ground. From their numbers, he supposed he was looking at the best part of a whole corps. A wide band of cavalry protected the joint between the men attacking the ridge and those still on the plain. The horsemen would cover both divisions' flanks, their presence enough to prevent any Austrian attack from severing the link between them.

The pace of the French drums increased. The Legion was moving briskly, its commanders eager to see it close on the Austrians holding the slopes around San Cassiano. No one turned to shout at the pair of straggling legionnaires running after the column.

Jack's breath was rasping in his throat by the time they

reached the Legion's rearmost company. He felt as if his face was on fire. His palms were slick, and when he lifted one from his rifle, he saw the sweaty imprint left behind.

The drummers picked up the pace yet again. Now they sounded the pas de charge, the rhythm that had propelled the French army into the attack since the days of the first Napoleon. The legionnaires greeted the change in tempo with a great roar. It was a feral sound, a snarl of anger and fear released. The column surged forward, the beat propelling them on. Jack and Palmer went with it, their legs pumping hard as the slope steepened beneath their boots.

Jack could no longer see the enemy line that waited ahead. But he could imagine it. The Austrian infantry would be standing in a line three men deep, the front two ranks ready to fire, the third ready to step forward to take the place of any that fell. Their skirmishers would be running forward, whilst the officers and sergeants stationed on the flanks and behind the line would be shouting themselves hoarse as they readied their men to fire their first volley.

He flinched as a battery of enemy artillery opened fire. The roar of their volley echoed over the heads of the Legion in the moments before the first roundshot ploughed into their ranks. The Austrian cannon might be old-fashioned, but the solid iron shot still cut a swathe of death through the neatly ordered ranks.

The Legion pressed on, the damaged ranks closing up, the sergeants in charge of the broken files shouting at their charges to keep going. Another volley of roundshot smashed into the column with appalling force. Men were punched to the ground, their bodies shattered. Their mates could do nothing but march on, the dead and dying ignored.

Jack stepped around the first body he saw. A young legionnaire lay face up, his sightless, staring eyes betraying the shock and surprise of being hit, his left arm, shoulder and much of his side ripped away by a fast-moving roundshot.

The bitter taste of fear was on Jack's tongue. He had stood and watched as the Austrian columns were gutted by artillery fire. Now the Legion faced the same fate, and he was no longer a dispassionate observer. This time he marched in the ranks being targeted by the enemy's guns. This time it could be his body left broken and torn for others to trip over. This time he could die.

Something roared past overhead. Another similar object followed almost instantly, followed by yet another. Each cut through the air with a strange fizzing sound, a long trail of smoke surging out behind.

'Rockets!' Palmer had to bellow to be heard.

'Shit!' Jack could not help ducking as one of the devilish missiles seared by just above his head. It ploughed into the company ahead, exploding on impact, cutting two men in half and showering the rest with red-hot shards of steel. Six men fell as the shrapnel tore into them, a great hole blown in the files.

'Fucking hell.' Jack lowered his head. He did not look at the ruined flesh that passed by his boots, the remains of the men hit by the rocket now scattered wantonly across the blackened grass.

The sound of muskets firing came in between each volley of artillery. He knew that the skirmishers from both sides would be in the fight now, the light troops picking at one another to keep their opposite numbers at bay. It was a bitter fight fought in the dead ground in front of the Austrian line. It would not decide who won, but men still died lest the other side find an advantage.

He sucked down another lungful of scorching air. The legionnaires advanced steadily, ignoring the gaps blown in their ranks. Officers shouted encouragement, whilst sergeants screamed threats. The beat of the drums was unfaltering and constant, the pas de charge goading the ranks into the attack no matter how many of the young drummer boys were slain.

They were close to the Austrian line now. The air was full of the dreadful cacophony of battle: explosions and screams, the roar of cannon and the crackle of musketry. They marched as if into a storm, hunched and bowed. Jack went with them, his senses battered by the tempest.

The main Austrian line fired their opening volley. The air was filled with a dreadful storm of musket balls that cut into the leading ranks of the column, scything men down by the dozen. For a moment the Legion shuddered as it absorbed the dreadful punishment. Then it lurched back into motion, the damage it had taken shrugged off as if it meant nothing.

The officers still led the way, swords waving as they exhorted their men to follow. Jack could only marvel at their bravery. Many died, their bright epaulettes and golden buttons marking them out as targets for the enemy infantry, but enough stayed standing, and they ran at the Austrian line, setting the example the battered ranks needed

With a great roar, the Legion stormed forward, following their officers as they charged at the enemy. Jack went with them, forcing his way deep into the ranks, his eyes scanning the faces around him for the man he sought. He could see nothing of the other battalions in the attack, his world reduced to little more than the men around him.

The Austrian line fired a second volley. Dozens of legionnaires were cut down, but the men were past caring and they swept past the broken bodies without pause.

Jack shouted as he went with them. He felt nothing as his boots slipped on a man's spilt guts, his only thought not to lose his footing. To his front an officer died, his face smothered in blood. He fell away, a legionnaire shoving his body to one side without mercy.

The Legion had taken its casualties. It had advanced no matter how many of its men had fallen. Now they charged, bayonets at the ready. It was time to exact a bloody revenge.

Chapter Thirty-five

⁌⬥⁍

*J*ack bellowed his war cry as the Legion charged. Around him, the ordered ranks were breaking up. These were the hard yards, the bloody yards, when there was nothing to be done save to keep going forward, no matter what horror was inflicted upon those around him. Time was slowing, each moment taking an age. The ground passed under his boots with stubborn slowness, every step an effort of will.

He glimpsed the Austrian line. He was close enough to see the look of horror on the faces of the young conscripts ordered to face the charging legionnaires. As he watched, he saw them lift their muskets to their shoulders. He could not hold back another cry as a tongue of fire leaped from every muzzle. The air around him snapped and crackled, musket balls zipping past close enough for him to feel the air shake. The cry turned into a cheer as he realised he was still whole.

The legionnaires ignored their casualties and surged forward. They were close enough to know that the Austrians had no time to reload. Time accelerated to pass at breakneck speed, the last yards flying by in a blur.

Jack spotted a blond-haired legionnaire to his left. He angled his run, sliding past another soldier then following the man he had sought even as he charged at the Austrian line.

The legionnaires hit the enemy at full tilt. They had taken heavy casualties, but these were men who had been hardened on the battlefields of the Crimea and North Africa. They tore into the Austrians like a whirlwind.

Their sergeants led the way. With so many officers gone, it was down to the non-commissioned officers to show their men what was expected. Now the most experienced soldiers fought their way into the enemy line, their bayonets thrusting at the men standing against them. The legionnaires followed, keening for blood.

The Austrians held their ground. They might not be veteran soldiers, but they understood pride. Their own bayonets rammed forward. Many legionnaires died at the point of the charge. The Austrian conscripts had been well drilled, and they fought with the relentless purpose of automatons. Time and time again their bayonets found their way into a legionnaire's flesh, the advantage of the higher ground making their grim task all the easier.

Yet the French soldiers would not quit, the despairing cries of the fallen goading their comrades on. All along the line they gouged gaps in the Austrian formation. Wherever a white-coated defender fell, two or more legionnaires threw themselves into the breach. The line was slowly ripped apart, the French bayonets exacting a dreadful toll on the enemy ranks.

Jack saw Fleming enter the fray. To his front the enemy line was still whole, and three legionnaires died almost at the same instant as Austrian bayonets cut them down. Fleming threw himself into the gap. Jack saw him batter aside a bayonet aimed at his stomach then thrust his own weapon forward, an animal snarl of anger exploding from his lips.

Jack pounded up the slope, forcing his way through the men in front of him. The pain in his lungs and in his legs disappeared as he followed Fleming into the Austrian line.

An Austrian conscript screamed as he lunged with his bayonet. Jack spotted the blow coming. He battered it to one side with the barrel of his rifle. He saw his foe's eyes widen in sudden fear before he slammed the rifle's butt into the man's face.

'Come on!' He bellowed his challenge as he stepped forward, keeping close to Fleming. He had lost sight of Palmer, but there was no time to wonder if his comrade had survived the bloody advance.

More legionnaires pressed around him. They went forward in a wedge, each man trying to protect the others. Fleming led the way. He fought hard at the point of the wedge, leading his comrades deeper into the enemy formation, his bayonet already bloodied to the hilt.

An Austrian officer came at Fleming from the side, his curved sword slashing at the legionnaire's face. Jack saw the danger so raised his rifle, knocking the sword away. The Austrian snarled and turned on Jack, lunging again, his sword cutting a thick splinter from the barrel of Jack's rifle. Another attack followed, then another, the officer shouting incoherently with every blow.

Jack saw the man's lips pull back into a grimace as he came at him again. The Austrian was young, but he was quick and used his sword well. Jack staggered as he only just blocked a thrust aimed at his groin. The man recovered fast, leaving him no time to counter, and lifted his sword before darting forward in a swipe at Jack's throat.

Jack lowered his rifle and swayed back. The blade rasped by, close enough for him to feel the wind of its passing. It went wide and he roared as he lunged his bayonet into the soft flesh beneath the Austrian's chin.

The officer tried to scream, but Jack twisted the bayonet, tearing the gristle of the man's throat wide open so that blood gushed from the horrible wound, smothering the cry before it could be formed. He pushed hard, forcing the body backwards and off his bayonet. He felt nothing as the Austrian officer fell away, his sabre dropping from his grasp.

Jack looked around. The Austrian line had stood firm, the conscripts in its ranks fighting long after other, more experienced men would have run. But against the veteran legionnaires they could not hold for ever, and now they broke.

Jack sucked in huge draughts of air. Each breath scorched his lungs, the air heated as if from an oven, but he pulled it down nonetheless until he could breathe almost normally. The legionnaires around him were doing the same. Each face mirrored the same expression of relief and exhaustion.

He looked back the way the column had come. The ground was littered with bodies. Some lay in groups, half a dozen bundled together, twisted into a single grotesque shape. Others were alone, serene and peaceful as they stared at the sky through sightless eyes. Everywhere the ground was torn and blackened, the pits and rents from exploding shells scarring the landscape.

He saw artillery advancing up the slope, the French commanders seeking to consolidate the position the legionnaires had paid for with their blood. The slope was too steep for the gunners' horse trains, and so it was down to the strength of the men in the regiments held in reserve to drag the guns into position. Whilst lines of men hauled the cannons up, others stood in long chain gangs, passing up ammunition from the caissons left at the foot of the slope.

With his body recovering, Jack picked up his rifle and walked towards the man he had come so far to find. Fleming was squatting next to a legionnaire stretched out on the ground. His eyes lifted as he saw Jack approach. For a moment there was the flash of recognition, then he turned his attention back to his fallen comrade, his lips moving as he offered comfort to the dying man.

'Do nothing foolish.'

Jack turned at the sudden command. Kearney had come up behind him. The legionnaire sergeant looked like he had just returned from a day working in the slaughterhouse. His blue uniform was covered with dark stains, his sleeves bloodied to the elbow. Drops of blood speckled his face like engorged freckles, and five streaks of red lined one cheek from where an enemy soldier must have clawed at his face. His bayonet was dripping blood, and it was pointed at Jack's heart.

'Leave him be.' Another voice made itself known.

Jack saw Palmer coming towards him. His uniform was just as grim, and a great tear had been ripped down one side. It was a relief to see the large man still standing, especially as he now approached Kearney with his rifle held ready to strike.

Kearney glanced over his shoulder at Palmer. If he felt any emotion at the threat, he did not show it. He looked at Jack. 'I saw you fight.'

Jack kept his eyes on the bayonet aimed at his heart. The blood was already blackening and congealing. It would not stop the blade if Kearney chose to drive it forward.

'You're good.' The sergeant gave the praise with a trace of a smile. 'You've done this before.'

'Once or twice.'

Eyes still on Jack, Kearney lowered his rifle. 'You cannot take him away. Not yet. I still need him.' He turned to glance at Palmer. 'Drop your weapon, my friend. There will be enough killing today without you adding to it here.'

Palmer grunted, but he did as the legionnaire sergeant said. He walked easily to Jack's side, the rifle held casually in one hand. 'Where's our man?'

Jack nodded towards Fleming, who had not yet moved. He still crouched next to his dying comrade, his hand on the man's shoulder.

'You two are persistent.' Kearney stood between them. 'Will you ever give up?'

'No.' Palmer said the single word, then turned to spit out a wad of phlegm. 'Like it or not, that little shit is coming with us.'

Kearney smiled at the bold claim. 'You must want him badly.'

'Not us. It's my master that wants him back.' Palmer wiped a hand across his face. 'He wants to take the dolt back to his father.'

'You will return him to his family?' Kearney asked the question quietly.

'That's the plan,' Palmer answered.

Kearney nodded slowly. 'I have your word?'

Palmer scowled. 'I said it, didn't I?'

'Then you can take him.' Kearney looked at them both in turn. 'After the battle, he can meet with this master of yours. But I need him until it's over.'

Jack considered the notion. 'He might die.'

Kearney shrugged. 'So keep him safe. From what I saw, you both know what you're doing. And you appear to be wearing our uniform. So stay. Fight with us. Keep him safe and then you can go. All three of you.'

Jack looked at Palmer. The larger man's expression was unreadable. 'What if we say no? What if we take him now?'

Kearney laughed at the notion. 'Look around you.'

Jack did as he suggested. A dozen or more faces were staring at him, each sharing the same calm look. Enough had understood the conversation. Those who had not were being given a rapid translation, the men of Kearney's company all aware of the deal their sergeant was striking with the two impostors dressed as legionnaires.

He had no doubt that these men would kill him at a single word from Kearney. His would be one more body amidst the hundreds, the thousands, that already littered the ground. The battlefield was the perfect place for a quiet murder. For who would notice one more on a day of ten thousand?

Kearney smiled as he saw understanding appear in Jack's expression. He stepped forward and clapped a hand on the Englishman's shoulder. 'I need more men. We have lost too many taking this damn hill. Stay and fight with us. If you live, you can take Fleming to your master. If you die . . .' He left the last part of the sentence unsaid.

Fleming stood up. His comrade on the ground was dead. He saw Jack and Palmer standing with Kearney. For a moment it looked like he would come to join then. Instead he hefted his rifle in his hand and went to rejoin his mates.

'Decide, quickly now.' Kearney had spotted movement amongst the legionnaires. Two young officers were striding along the ranks, bellowing fresh orders at the men who had won them the high ground.

Kearney cocked an ear, then gestured to his men. '*En place!*'

The legionnaires sitting on the ground responded immediately, lumbering to their feet and shuffling towards the line that was being formed across the crest of the ridge facing east.

'What's it to be?' Kearney snapped the question at the two Englishmen.

Jack looked at Palmer, then shrugged his shoulders. There was no choice. If they were to obey Ballard and keep Fleming safe, they had to stay close to his side. That meant going wherever he went.

For better or worse, the Legion had two new recruits.

Chapter Thirty-six

*M*ary stood outside the aid post and fretted. She stared into the distance, trying to make sense of the noises that echoed towards her. The rattle of rifle fire underscored the constant boom of artillery. At times the din was relentless, the sounds blending together like a concerto in full flow. Then it would quieten down, the deep bass blasts of the cannons coming alone before the sound of rifle fire returned, sometimes in single shots, at other times in long bursts that sounded like a child running a wooden rod along a fence. She was mesmerised by it all.

She wondered if Billy was hearing the same noises. Did they frighten him, or did the roar of battle excite him? For the umpteenth time she regretted letting him go with Ballard's men. She cared nothing for their great quest. The fate of one man meant nothing against the safety of her only son.

'He will be fine.' Ballard had approached silently, and now he spoke softly, interrupting her thoughts.

'How can you say that?' Mary spat out the reply.

Ballard's eyes narrowed. 'I trust Palmer. Jack too, I suppose.

I am certain that they will not allow anything to happen to your boy.'

'Then you are a fool.' Mary crossed her arms. 'No man can promise something like that. Listen. You hear that? You think those two clots can do anything against that?'

'No.' Ballard bowed his head as he made the admission softly. His fingers lifted to toy with his moustache. 'I should not have ordered him to go.'

'It's too late for that.' Mary sighed. 'We just have to pray that he comes back.'

'I understand.' Ballard's hand moved as if to touch her shoulder, but he hesitated so that it was held awkwardly in mid-air. 'I know what it is to fear for a child.'

Mary looked at him sharply. 'You have a child?'

Ballard nodded, his lips pressed together. 'A boy. I let him down rather badly. I was not the father I should have been.'

'Few men are.'

'Perhaps.' He offered a tight-lipped smile. 'Perhaps I have time to rectify it. To make amends.'

'Well, that would be nice.' Mary's reply was caustic.

'You don't believe me?'

Mary considered the notion. 'Maybe you will. Jack told me you always get what you want.'

'Did he now?' Ballard chuckled. 'I confess I do not understand that man, but I do respect him. He is a good man to have on one's side, especially in a place such as this.'

'Jack is a fool. He believes he can make a difference.' Mary shook her head. 'He's a good man, I suppose, but he is driven by his demons. He won't ever be happy, won't ever make a home. He'll just keep wandering. Oh, he does what he thinks is best, I'll give him that. But when things get hard, he walks away. Leaves others to deal with the mess he creates.'

'Yet you rely on him for your future.'

Mary scowled. 'He took my future away from me. If he hadn't come back, I'd still be working in the ginny and my son would not be on some godforsaken battlefield.'

'So he owes you?'

'Damn right he does.'

'And you trust him to deliver.'

Mary's scowl deepened. 'I don't have much of a choice.'

Ballard's mouth formed to make a reply, but stopped. He looked at Mary, then at his boots. 'You do have a choice. At least, I would like to think there is another option for you to consider.'

'And what's that?' Mary had looked away. She was staring towards the front. The rate of cannon fire had increased. She could feel the ground shaking, the very earth beneath her feet trembling as it too heard the sound of battle and was afraid.

'Me.' Ballard spoke gently, the word barely audible over the din of distant fighting.

'You?' Mary could not hold back the exclamation.

'I have come to admire you.' Ballard winced as he spoke, as if the words were being dragged painfully from the very depths of his being. 'I would like you to stay with me.'

'You want me to work for you?' Mary stalled for time. She had tried not to think of her future, but relying on Jack alone to fend for her and her son was not an attractive option. She knew he would not stay with them, at least not for long. He would claim that he would, that he would not shirk his duty towards her. But she knew him too well to believe him.

Ballard cleared his throat. 'No. I was thinking of an alternative situation.'

'Well, what then?'

'I would like you at my side. I would like to ask you to marry me.'

Mary was struck dumb.

'Of course, you would not consider such a notion.' Ballard quickly filled the silence. 'It was a foolish idea. I should not have mentioned it.'

'No.' Mary reached out to hush him by laying her hand on his arm. She smiled as she saw the way his expression changed as she touched him. 'It's not foolish. It is generous and kind, and I am honoured you would think of me in that way.' She laughed then, the idea that she could wed a respectable gentleman like Ballard striking her as the queerest thing she had ever heard. She was a back-street whore with a bastard child, not some princess in a fairy tale.

Ballard misunderstood her laughter. His face coloured and he pulled away. 'I am sorry that you find my suggestion ridiculous.' He puffed up with precious dignity.

'It's not that.' Mary swatted his arm, then composed herself. 'It's a lovely offer, really,' she sighed, 'but I cannot accept it. At least, not for now, not with this going on, not with my boy out there.' She offered a smile. 'Let's get through the day, shall we? Then we can think on the future.'

'Of course.' Ballard was quick to seize on her suggestion of a delay. 'It was thoughtless of me to bring the matter up at this juncture.' He paused. 'But you will consider it?'

'I will,' Mary replied seriously. 'But for now I think we should get to work.' She looked past Ballard's shoulder. A commissary cart was pulling up beside the mast that flew the aid station's black flag. The first wounded were being brought in. 'We promised we would wait here, but that doesn't mean we cannot lend a hand.' She smoothed down her skirt. It would be good to help with the wounded. It would take her mind off worrying about Billy. 'Come on, Mr Ballard. Let's see what we can do here.'

Billy hated thunderstorms. No one knew it. Not his mother, and most certainly not Abigail, the girl who used to come to the gin palace every night to ply her trade. It was probably the only thing about him that Abigail did not know. He smiled as he remembered the nights spent sitting with her as she waited for custom. He had told her everything, and in return she had held his hand and, on a few, very rare occasions, let him lay his head in her lap.

Now he sat on the ground listening to the dreadful cacophony of battle, wondering how he could ever have been frightened of something as gentle as thunder. Each blast of cannon fire sent a shudder running through his body. It reverberated through him, every bone jangling with each concussion. The fear was like a creature that lived deep in his guts. It fought like it was cornered, tearing at his bravery so that it ran into his bowels, churning and twisting as it fought to escape.

To ward off the fear, Billy tried to conjure an image of Abigail. He thought of how she smelled, how she giggled at his attempts to make her laugh. He needed her then, more than he could ever have imagined needing anyone. Yet she refused to come, his mind failing to picture the girl he dreamed of every night.

The noise of battle grew louder. It was coming closer. For the first time he heard the screams, the dreadful banshee wails of men meeting death. His fear built. He wanted to run. To flee from the copse of trees where he had been left.

He looked back at the three horses. They were as frightened as he was. They stood with ears alert and twitching. Every so often they tossed their heads, or pulled against their tethers, hooves pawing nervously at the soil. The animals shared his desire to run, their own instincts urging them to flee. Yet they were tethered firmly, Palmer's knots holding them fast. Billy was tied to the spot just as securely. He would not give in. He would not run. He would not let Jack down.

There had been few men in Billy's life. He had no idea who his father might be. He was well aware of what his mother had done before he had come along, and he knew better than to ask about the man who had sired him. His life had been run by women, both his mother and Maggie Lampkin taking care of him as best they could. His friends had been whores like Abigail, the young girls who paid Maggie a shilling to work the gin palace's meagre crowd. The only men he knew had been punters, the customers of either the palace or the girls. None had paid much attention to the skinny boy gathering dirty glasses, or snapping off a measure or two if his mother and Maggie were especially busy. Then Jack had come along.

Billy did not think he had ever known someone like Jack. He had met strong men before; men with big arms and wide shoulders who would start a fight as quickly as they would order a pennyworth of gin. None had carried themselves as Jack did, his quiet confidence so different to the bawdy gobshites Billy was used to. He had seen the way other men looked at Jack, the sly, furtive appraisals as they compared themselves and were invariably found lacking. He had also spotted the way women stared at him, with hooded eyes, their lust as easy to read as a man's fear.

Billy wanted to be just like Jack.

He stayed sitting on the ground, controlling the shakes and the shudders as best he could. He would not run. Not for anything.

Chapter Thirty-seven

The Austrian columns came on haphazardly. Their ranks were ragged, their officers unwilling to waste time in forming them up properly. The Legion had formed a two-man-deep line across the slopes around San Cassiano. They were determined to hold on to the high ground they had fought so hard to capture. The Austrians had rallied quickly, their counter-attack coming before the French could get their artillery in place. It would be down to the battered foot soldiers to hold on to what they had won.

'That was fair quick!' Palmer made the observation as he elbowed his way into the French line. A swift glare silenced the legionnaire he had barged to one side, the man's loud protest shut off before it was fully formed. Palmer took his place in the front rank directly beside Fleming, then nodded a friendly greeting.

'How you faring, old son?'

'I wish you would leave me alone.'

'Now, now, less said, sooner mended.' Palmer was checking his rifle, his hands moving over the weapon with practised ease.

'Like it or not, when this shindig is over, you and I are going to take a little walk.'

'I am not going anywhere.'

'You'll do as you are damn well told.' Palmer had finished with his rifle and now checked that his bayonet was still securely locked in place. His hand came away bloody.

Jack said nothing during the short exchange. He was watching the Austrian infantry as they started to swarm up the reverse side of the ridge. Their white uniforms looked splendid against the lush greenery. Even in half-broken ranks, there was something glorious in their advance. Their colours led them, the great eagles showing them the way. Men who had been running just a short time before found heart as they followed their regiment's pride back up the slope.

The first order was shouted from the middle of the French line. Hundreds of rifles were pulled in to shoulders, the men obeying instantly. Jack had not understood the command, but he knew an infantryman's job as well as any. The rifle Palmer had given him fitted snugly into his shoulder. He squinted down the barrel, aiming above the head of an Austrian infantry-man to allow for the drop of the shot as he was firing downhill.

The second order came and Jack braced himself, curling his finger around his rifle's trigger. He held his breath, every muscle tensed.

'*Feu!*'

The sound of hundreds of rifles firing in unison roared out. Jack barely felt the kick as his rifle thumped back into his shoulder. He let it fall to the ground the moment the trigger was released. Every man did the same, the routine of reloading deeply ingrained in each of them.

He snatched a fresh cartridge out of the pouch on his belly

and bit off the top, spitting it to one side as he poured the powder into the barrel. He followed the powder with the bullet. With deft fingers he slipped the ramrod from its loops and used it to force the bullet to the bottom of the barrel, giving it two slight taps to make sure it rested on the powder. The ramrod went back into its place beneath the barrel before he slipped a fresh cap from its pouch and pressed it into place. It felt like just moments had passed since the first volley. The motions were instinctive, the rifle pulled to the shoulder for the shortest pause before the command to fire was bellowed out for a second time.

'*Feu!*'

He did not bother to select a target. He had the briefest impression of another white uniform falling away before his eyes were back on his rifle as he reloaded.

The men from the Legion poured on the fire. A third volley seared out, hundreds of spinning rounds tearing into the attacking Austrians. Dozens fell, the men crumpling as the heavy Minié bullets found their marks.

Jack repeated the routine again and again. His fingers hurt and the taste of gunpowder lingered on his lips, his thirst building with every cartridge he bit open. Volley followed volley, the Legion killing and maiming as the Austrians refused to turn away.

There was no time to marvel at such a brave display. Jack's world had reduced to his rifle and the men around him. His only thought was to reload as fast as he could, then send another bullet on its deadly path. He had no sense of the fight other than his minute role in it. He was just a single part of the machine that was inflicting such terrible damage on the men in white coats.

A different order was shouted. Jack stiffened, knowing what was to come.

'*Chargez!*'

The Legion snarled into motion. Jack went with them, the battle madness coursing through him once again. It took him swiftly and completely, the need to kill overwhelming his senses so that he roared with fury as he pounded towards his newest enemy.

The battered Austrian infantry had advanced to within fifty yards. They had taken heavy casualties, but somehow they had come on, the conscripted infantrymen not knowing when they were beaten. Now they tried to make a line of their own. It was a ragged affair, and many of the men stopped in mid-evolution to stare in horror as the legionnaires were unleashed against them.

Jack saw enemy muskets lifted to shoulders. He knew what was to come, but he cared nothing for the danger. The madness had him, and he screamed as he charged.

The Austrians fired.

It was the legionnaires' turn to die. The Austrian muskets may have lacked the power of the French rifles, but the range was short and the volley cut down the attackers in swathes.

Jack could not hold back a cry as a musket ball seared through the soft flesh above his hip. The pain flashed brightly, then he hit the line.

An Austrian conscript lunged at him. It was a weak blow, the man's terror stealing the strength from the attack. Jack laughed as he battered it aside. He was still laughing as he hit the man with his rifle butt. It took him barely a second to ram his bayonet down before he was moving on, the Austrian soldier left clutching the terrible hole that had been torn in his belly.

Within moments, the Austrian line had been splintered. Dozens died, the legionnaires ramming home their bayonets with ruthless precision. Some Austrians turned to run, but they were cut down. Jack felt no mercy as he stabbed his bayonet into the joint of a man's neck and spine. The man screamed, twisting as he fell so that he landed on his back. He lay there floundering like a recently landed fish until Jack silenced him with an efficient thrust through the heart. His bayonet stuck fast, and he cursed as he was forced to stamp hard on the man's chest to free it.

The delay nearly cost him his life. The fight had broken up into a hundred vicious melees where death could come from any direction. Jack ripped his bayonet free just in time to see a white-coated soldier preparing to smash in his skull with a rifle butt.

He threw himself to one side. The rifle butt caught him a glancing blow on the shoulder. Pain seared through him, but still he thrust his bayonet into the man's gut. This time he twisted the steel cruelly, freeing it before it stuck fast.

The fear came then. Men were falling in droves, many cut down from the side or rear so that they died without knowing who had killed them. His nostrils flared as the familiar stink of battle caught in his throat: the sour odour of blood and shit, mixed with the stench of opened guts and torn flesh.

He lunged, bellowing with rage. An Austrian officer was on the point of cutting into Kearney's unprotected neck. Instead of landing the blow, he turned, a scream escaping from his lips, his face revealing a horrible mix of terror and surprise as Jack drove his bayonet into his side.

The legionnaire sergeant whirled on the spot, finally alive to the danger. The Austrian was already falling away, his hands scrabbling frantically at the gaping wound. Kearney's face twisted into a vicious snarl as he realised how close to death he had just come. He hammered his rifle butt down, finishing off the officer who had so nearly killed him.

An Austrian conscript came at Kearney from behind, crying out as he lunged. His bellow turned into a scream as Jack's bayonet took him in the throat, the long steel blade erupting from the back of his neck as Jack drove it home.

'That's twice!' Jack shouted the words as he pushed forward so that he could cover Kearney's back.

Kearney had no time to reply. Another Austrian attacked, using his bayonet in short, efficient thrusts. The sergeant battered each one away, keeping the man at bay long enough for Jack to come at him from the side. His bloodied bayonet ended the disciplined attack with a single strike to the heart.

It was their last fight. The Austrians broke for a second time. A few legionnaires cheered as the enemy fled, but most just sucked down huge draughts of air before starting the hideous task of pulling the wounded from the piles of bodies that lay around them.

They were not given time to do much. The worst of the wounded would be left behind as fresh orders rallied the ranks and recalled them to their position on the ridge's crest.

Whilst they had been fighting off the Austrian counter-attack, the first guns had finally been manhandled into position. Now the artillerymen opened fire, their shells smashing into the fleeing troops.

'Fucking bastards.' Jack cursed under his breath at the merciless French gunners. He sucked in a lungful of air, then started to retrace his steps back up the slope. A heavy hand on his shoulder stopped him.

'I owe you my thanks.' Kearney's face was serious.

'You'd have done the same for me.' Jack had not fully caught his breath, so he gasped his reply.

'Would I?' Kearney's face creased into a smile. 'I'm glad you think so.'

Jack tried to laugh, but it came out more like a sob. He took a moment to catch his breath before he replied. 'I know your type. You cannot help playing the hero.'

Kearney slapped him on the back. The fight seemed to have barely affected him at all. 'Come on, Jack, that's enough of your crap. Let's get you back safe.'

The two men started the long trudge up the slope. Neither looked at the pile of bodies left behind, the pathetic heaps that marked the high tideline of the Austrian counter-attack. Palmer and Fleming passed them. From the look on the legionnaire's face, he was not enjoying Palmer's presence. It appeared that Ballard's enforcer planned not to go more than a yard from Fleming's side.

Jack looked at the sky. It was dark, and heavy black clouds shrouded the sun, but he guessed it could be no later than mid-afternoon. There was plenty of daylight left. Plenty of time for more men to die.

Chapter Thirty-eight

'You're still alive, then.' Palmer greeted Jack as he made it up the last yards of the slope. Around him the exhausted legionnaires were slumping to the ground. For the moment, both the Austrians and their own officers were leaving them in peace. It was time for a moment's rest, to give thanks for being alive, and to relive the moments of the chaotic fight.

'Takes more than a little scrap like that to kill me.' Jack wanted nothing more than to lie on the ground. He was out of condition, a fact made all the more evident as Kearney came striding past him, his breathing unaffected by the events of the last half-hour. He forced as deep a breath as he could manage into his lungs, then stood straight. 'Blow me, but it's hot.'

'Not as hot as India.' Palmer pulled his canteen from over his shoulder and took a long draught.

Jack gave his own canteen a shake. It was still half full, so he had a drink, careful not to take too much. He knew how badly he would need it later on. Good water was as scarce as mercy on a battlefield.

'Hot? This isn't hot,' Kearney scoffed. 'In Algeria, it was so hot you could feel your brain frying in your skull, during the day at least. The nights were cold enough to freeze your balls for all time.'

Fleming chuckled at his sergeant's mockery. 'Best be kind to them. They're just new recruits.'

'Hark at you. I was killing men when you were still shitting in your breeches, old son.' Palmer did not care for the abuse.

Fleming shrugged, then looked to Kearney. 'Sergeant, we should show the old man some respect.'

'Old man indeed!' Palmer rose to the bait. 'I didn't hear you calling me that when I killed that white-coated bastard who was about to shove his bayonet up your fucking arse.'

'That was kind of you,' Fleming was enjoying himself, 'just as it was kind of you to leave that other fellow to me. You recall him? The one about to ram a bayonet into your balls before I killed him.'

The two men laughed. It earned them a few stares, and some glares, the English voices clearly grating on finely stretched nerves.

Kearney spotted the reaction. 'Enough. There'll be plenty of time for those tales. That time is not now.'

'No, but it is time for us to leave.' Palmer's smile disappeared quicker than a routed Austrian. 'Old son,' he wrapped his hand around Fleming's elbow, 'I'd be grateful if you'd walk with us.'

Fleming shook his arm to free it, but Palmer's great paw stayed in place. 'Don't be foolish. I cannot leave now. The day is not done.'

'We can slip away all quiet like. Even these French buggers will let you go for a shit. We can go and not come back. We have horses over yonder.' Palmer looked at Kearney. 'We've all done our bit for today.'

Kearney nodded. 'I won't stop you.' He glanced around at the tired men sitting on the ground. There were far fewer than there had been an hour earlier. Those left alive did not care if Fleming and the Englishmen left, and the handful of officers still on their feet were too busy to notice.

'There you have it.' Palmer kept a firm grip on Fleming's elbow. 'Now you behave yourself and come with us.'

Fleming shook off Palmer's hand. 'I am a legionnaire. I will not leave my comrades.'

Palmer was unimpressed by such passionate loyalty. 'I need you to put an end to all this, one way or the other.'

Jack watched the exchange in silence, content to leave the negotiations, such as they were, to Palmer. The older man was having no more luck than he himself had had when he had tried to convince Fleming to come with them.

'Hold fast.' Palmer was about to grab Fleming with more force when Jack spotted a French officer riding down the line towards them.

'What the devil does he want?' Palmer glared at the unwanted interruption.

The officer's horse was lathered in sweat, great globules of foam at the corners of its mouth, but it still had enough energy to toss its head as the few surviving Legion officers stepped towards the man on its back.

The exchange that followed was curt. The mounted officer spoke quickly and urgently, his left hand thrust out to point to the south.

'Do you understand what he is saying?' Kearney stood at Jack's shoulder.

'No idea.' Jack gave a half-smile as he admitted it.

'The Austrians are trying to turn our right flank.' Kearney spoke softly, one ear turned to listen to the conversation. 'While we have been fighting up here, the men down on the plain have been under heavy attack. He says every man is needed, otherwise the day is lost.'

Jack twisted and looked in the direction the officer was pointing. From their place on the high ground, he could see a fair way to the south and east. The plain stretched away for miles. Most of the great expanse was wreathed in powder smoke. The men of the Legion had started their day down there, watching as their artillery had turned back the first Austrian columns. They had then moved on to assault the ridge, but it appeared that the Austrian commander had not been so quick to divert his attention from the ground that formed the French army's right flank.

Through patches in the smoke, Jack could just about make out the dark blue uniforms of the French infantry. They were in line, and he could see the flashes popping out from each musket as they fired a volley at some unseen enemy.

'Here we go.'

Kearney brought his attention back to the French officer. The man had finished speaking and was in the process of wheeling his mount around. Without ceremony, he kicked hard, forcing the horse into motion.

'*En place!*' One of the Legion's officers shouted the order to his reluctant troops. '*Marche ou crève.*' He strode down the line, urging his tired men to their feet.

Kearney gave Jack a tight-lipped smile. 'Looks like we aren't done yet. You still coming along?'

Jack nodded but could not return the smile. He had no

choice. He would follow wherever Fleming went.

'Then let's go. You heard the man. We march or we die.'

The Legion had fought hard. But their day was not yet done.

The Legion marched down the slope, keeping the pace slow and steady until they hit the flatter ground of the great plain. The legionnaires were tired, but they had formed into column without a murmur. The regiment's colour led the way, the red, white and blue of the tricolour gaudy against the bruised sky.

For the second time that day, Jack advanced with the French. This time he was in their ranks, rather than following behind, marching to Kearney's left, with Palmer and Fleming on his other side. It did not feel odd being in the midst of the French unit. It had been a long time since he had walked in the rank and file of an infantry column, yet he felt at home in a way that he hadn't for as long as he could remember. He might have been an Englishman hiding in the French army, but he was a soldier amongst comrades, the legionnaires around him accepting him without complaint.

The pace increased as the column came down off the high ground. The officer leading the way turned them on to the road that took them along the bottom of the ridge. From somewhere just ahead, a legionnaire began to sing. The man's voice was deep, and others joined him almost immediately. They sang sombrely, each word resonating through the column. It was a sound quite unlike any Jack had heard from an English regiment.

The song died away, the only sound left the thump of the men's boots hitting the road's surface in unison. They marched with their heads held high, the élan of the Legion restored by the deep, melodic song.

They did not keep the pace up for long.

Ahead, the road was almost completely blocked. A convoy of wounded soldiers was heading towards them, the long line of wagons and ambulances stretching back for hundreds of yards. Orders were shouted and the column stopped, then filed off the road, scurrying out of the way of the miserable procession.

They stood at the roadside as the convoy passed by. Every wagon and ambulance was packed full to capacity, with the less grievously wounded clinging on to any spot they could find. Dull, listless eyes stared down at the legionnaires as they passed, from faces etched with pain.

Those unfortunate souls unable to secure a place in the transport plodded along at the road's edge. Many bore dreadful wounds, their proud uniforms now soaked in gore. A few sported bandages, or had wounds stuffed with lint, but most were untreated, the tears and rents in their flesh left open, bloody and oozing.

Some men came alone. Jack saw one marching along at a fine pace, his severed arm clutched across his chest whilst blood pulsed freely from the stump just below the shoulder where the limb had once been. Others came in small groups, those with lesser wounds supporting those who could barely walk. All bore the same haunted expression, their assumption that it would be other men who would be hit proven to be the false hope that it had always been.

Then there were the bodies of those for whom the march had been too much. As the convoy thinned out, Jack looked along the path it had taken. Corpses were being treated without dignity. Some of those who had fallen had been dragged to one side, their broken flesh abandoned and forgotten. Others were simply left to lie where they landed, the boots of the men and the wheels of the wagons and ambulances grinding them into the dirt.

Jack watched it all, holding his emotions tight. He had seen such sights before, but there was something in the numbers that came close to overwhelming him. Even the breach at Delhi had not been as bad.

The last of the wounded went past, the road now empty once again. The column re-formed silently. Even the officers were subdued, their orders called out just loudly enough to set the men into motion. The Legion marched once more, picking up pace now the road was clear. This time no one sang.

Eventually the officer at their head turned them from the road and led them south, towards the sounds of fighting that continued unabated out on the army's right flank. They soon passed an aid post, its black flag hanging listless in the heavy air. Bodies smothered the ground in every direction. There was little way of knowing who was alive and who had died, the men lying in long lines that were being tended to by a mere handful of orderlies. Other bodies had been heaped into a single great mountain, the forms twisted and broken, the glazed eyes of the slain staring in accusation at those still clinging to life.

A few local women were tending to the wounded. They offered water, the canteens they had filled taken greedily by men half crazed by thirst. There were far too few to cope with the vast swathe of humanity dumped upon them, but that did not quench their desire to help, and as the column walked past, Jack saw them working tirelessly to give some succour to as many men as they could.

The column left the bitter scene behind and moved across a

great field of wheat, now trampled into dust. They passed behind an isolated farm packed full of French troops. The area had clearly seen much heavy fighting already that day. The buildings that made up the farm had been nearly destroyed, the ground around them ripped and torn, and covered with scorch marks from where Austrian artillery shells and rockets had fallen. Bodies lay in every direction, the dead carpeting the ground.

A staff galloper rode up to the officer in command. The conversation was short, the galloper riding away almost immediately. The Legion pressed on, marching towards three regiments of line infantry forming up to the south of the battered farmhouse.

'I know those men, they are from Bataille's brigade, part of III Corps.' Kearney marched at Jack's side. Neither had spoken for some time, but now the American sergeant broke the spell that had fallen over them both.

To their front, Jack could see a village, one that he could only assume was still held by the Austrians. 'What is that place called?' He strained his eyes, but they were too far away for him to be able to see any enemy troops.

'Hell, I don't know.' Kearney peered ahead. 'These damn places all look the same to me.'

'Well whatever it's called, it's about to be attacked.' Jack saw French cavalry moving up to cover the flanks of the infantry. At least six battalions were on the move, their bright tricolours creating a splendid sight.

The officer leading the Legion turned to shout at his men. They picked up the pace immediately, heading towards the French infantry beyond the farmhouse.

They had arrived in time to join the attack.

Chapter Thirty-nine

———◆———

*B*allard held the wounded hussar down, pinning him by the shoulders. The man fought against him, and it took all of Ballard's strength to keep his back pressing against the tabletop.

The surgeon who worked at his side swore under his breath and spat out a wad of phlegm. Neither altered the pace of the saw that was moving back and forth at a steady, even pace. The noise as it cut through bone set Ballard's nerves on edge. It grated in his ears and echoed in his skull. He had already listened to it a hundred times, yet familiarity had not dulled its horror.

The surgeon gave a short gasp. It was followed immediately by the solid thump of the severed leg hitting the ground. Ballard felt the hussar give a great shudder, his body twisting with one last lurch before going still.

'*Merde.*' The surgeon leaned forward and peered into the hussar's face, a bloodied finger poking at the man's eyes. There was no reaction to the clumsy touch, so he bellowed for his orderlies to come and collect the fresh corpse.

Ballard stood back as the two overworked assistants dragged the hussar away. There was no time to reflect on the man's passing. Another pair of orderlies bustled over, a white-coated Austrian soldier held awkwardly between them. No distinction was made between the soldiers of the two armies. Here, in the hell of the field hospital, they were just men.

The foreign soldier was shrieking as they carried him, his arms and legs jerking uncontrollably. The moment he was laid on the table, he jackknifed, his hands clawing at Ballard as he tried to escape the surgeon's knife. He was pushed down cruelly. There would be no escape.

One of the two orderlies stayed to help Ballard hold the patient down. Both of the Austrian's legs had been crushed below the knee. There was little left except for a pulsating mass of flesh and bone that had twisted and fused together so that what remained barely looked human. Ballard could only suppose that the man had been run over by an artillery limber, or the wheel of a cannon. He had seen a similar wound in the Strand when a young boy had been run down by a hackney carriage. That boy had died, and he held out little hope for the Austrian soldier.

The surgeon snapped a command and Ballard pressed down with his whole body weight on the man's chest. His arms were shaking with the effort, but somehow he managed to pin the Austrian in place long enough for the surgeon to take off first one leg and then the other. The second severed limb hit the ground and an orderly returned to help haul the Austrian away. The man still fought against them, his cries unaltered throughout the whole dreadful process. To Ballard's surprise, he had survived the double amputation, whereas the French hussar had died when having just a single limb removed. He wondered why that would be, what force there was hidden in the Austrian's physical form that was lacking in the hussar's.

He stood back and wiped his sleeve across his face. It was sweltering in the farm outbuilding that had been requisitioned as a hospital, and the sweat was running freely down his face. His blue uniform was streaked with ordure, the sleeves bloodied and the golden lace on its front half hidden under a sheet of gore. He had never felt so dirty. It was as if the blood and the filth was somehow seeping inside him, polluting his soul for all time.

The orderlies were slow with the next wounded man. It gave Ballard an opportunity to look for Mary. He saw her almost immediately. She was crouched next to a wounded French soldier, carefully spooning water into his mouth. The man clutched at her arm as he sucked on the wooden ladle, holding on so tightly that she had to force his fingers loose before she could shuffle over to the man lying next to him.

There were so many wounded. The ambulances, limbers and carts arrived non-stop, each packed full. Still more men staggered in, those able to walk drawn to the aid station by the sight of its black flag. The buildings had been filled in the first hour; now the wounded lay in long lines outside. There was no shade or respite from the heat. Their only comfort came from a handful of local women, who were offering what aid they could. The wounded were desperate for water, and many of the volunteers were pressed into service hauling bucket after bucket from a stream a few hundred yards away, so that at least some of them could have a mouthful or two.

Mary felt his gaze and turned to look at him. From somewhere she summoned a tight-lipped smile, the gesture fleeting but one he appreciated greatly. He hoped he was winning her approval, that his efforts as surgeon's mate were improving her opinion of him.

His reverie was brought to an end as the next body was thumped on to the table. He pressed down, not caring that his hands slipped across a man's chest sheeted in blood.

The rasping sound of the bone saw at work came almost immediately.

Billy hid behind the tree. He did not know how long he had been there. He had moved to screen himself from view when the first men had come past. It had seemed a wise thing to do, even though he could not do the same for the horses, which were still tethered where Palmer had left them.

He had mastered his fear. Cannon fire still thundered out, the noise ever-present, but he could not maintain his terror for ever. Somehow it had dulled, the unceasing pounding fading into the background so that now he barely even heard it, even when it intensified so that the individual blasts blurred into one great roar.

Safe in his hiding place, he had watched the first wounded stagger past. Two men had walked together, their arms intertwined. He had heard them laughing, their loud voices reaching him as he cowered away.

Since then, he had seen a steady stream of men descending from the high ground. Most came in ones or twos. All had been wounded. It was not hard to see where they had been hit. Some were dragged, their legs shattered or even missing completely. Others staggered along by themselves, pressing their hands into open wounds, or cradling an arm or shoulder shattered by an enemy bullet.

Some had not made it past his vantage point. He had

counted at least a dozen who had either collapsed or been left by their comrades, their attempt to reach help ending in death. The bodies lay where they had fallen, untended and ignored.

A fresh wave of men came past. He peered at them, trying to see their injuries. He frowned. These were the first he had seen who appeared whole, their uniforms unblemished. They were moving faster too, pressing forward urgently.

He did not recognise their uniform, but he could see that it was not the same one that Jack and Palmer had donned before they had left him. He shrank deeper into his cover. He did not know whether these men were French or Austrian. The idea that they could be the enemy both frightened and excited him. He slipped his hand into the waistband of his trousers and pulled out the revolver. He knew how to use it; Jack had taught him on the journey. He remembered Jack's hand ruffling his hair as he declared him to be a fine shot, the memory making him smile.

The weapon was heavy in his hand. It felt solid. Powerful. Reassuring. He squinted at the men running past. He imagined them rushing towards him as they spotted the horses. In his mind's eye he pictured himself standing, the revolver in his hand. He saw their faces twist in fear before he gunned them down, one after another, not a single bullet missing.

A shout shattered his imaginings. It came again, louder this time, the voice horribly close. He shrank away, his childish notion of fighting swamped by a sudden rush of fear. Heart pounding, he peered around the tree. Four men were running directly towards him.

The shouting came louder then. He knew it was directed at him, that the men had spied the horses and were coming to take them for their own. He rose up on his haunches, the instinct to run taking over before the thought had fully formed. Yet he held himself back, refusing to obey the urgings. Jack would not run.

He stood, even though his legs were shaking so hard they were barely able to support him. The four men saw him immediately. They shouted at him. He understood nothing, but he heard the anger in their voices. And he heard their fear.

'Go away!' The command emerged with little force. 'Go away!'

The men were coming on fast. They showed no sign of heeding him.

'Go away, or I'll shoot.' He lifted the revolver, holding it in both hands. He swallowed to clear the knot that had tied itself in his throat. His fear was surging through him. He felt weak, and his backside puckered and quivered. Yet he stood his ground, holding the revolver as steady as he could.

There was no more shouting. The men were thrashing through the undergrowth at the edge of the copse. They were close now. No more than twenty or thirty yards away.

A face appeared over the end of the barrel. Billy saw reddened cheeks above a thick black moustache, and brown eyes that blazed in anger. It was the face of the first man he would have to kill.

The man was saying something. The words spewed forth. He came closer, moving fast.

Billy's finger tightened on the trigger. He felt sick; fear choked him. The moment to fire came. And passed.

The man was upon him in an instant. The gun was snatched from his grasp. He had time to cry out before a fist slammed into his face.

He fell hard, blood pouring from his nose. He cried then,

the fear and the pain mixing inside him. He was still crying when the boot caught him in the pit of his stomach.

The blows came fast. The man he had come close to shooting attacked relentlessly, kicking and punching without pause.

Billy screamed. He could not hold it back. He screamed again, even as his mouth filled with the blood that streamed across his face. The noise goaded his attacker, and he lashed out with his heavy boot, catching the boy in the side of the head.

The screaming stopped as the blackness took Billy away.

Chapter Forty

The French did not linger. With the Legion reinforcing their battered ranks, the men of Bataille's brigade went on the attack. The Legion had regrouped into a mixed formation, with four companies forming a two-man-deep line supported by two companies on either flank arranged in column. All the battalions in the attack were arranged in a similar fashion, and they advanced *en échiquier*, spaced as though each was on a separate square of a chessboard. Hundreds of men in tightly packed ranks were committed to the assault on the Austrian infantry divisions that had come so close to folding the French army's right flank.

The Legion marched through clouds of dust. It blinded the troops, the wind whipping it across their faces so that they were forced to advance with their eyes screwed almost shut. It scoured their faces dry, leaving them red and sore.

'We still need to keep an eye on this one, Jack.' Palmer protected his mouth with his hand as he called across from where he was walking on the far side of Fleming, their company marching in line in the heart of the Legion's formation, on the left of the advance. 'Remember our mission. We keep this fellow safe, come what may.'

'I'm right here, you know.' Fleming laughed. Palmer spoke as if he were incapable of understanding the conversation.

'I know, old son, and I intend to keep it that way.' Palmer marched easily, even as the Legion picked up the pace.

Jack had no time to listen to Palmer. He was watching the large body of French cavalry that was rushing to form up on the infantry's left flank. He saw three different uniforms in the mix as the cavalry manoeuvred into two long lines. Two regiments formed the first line, with the second consisting of just one.

He was pleased to see the French horsemen. Now that they were on the wide expanse of the plain, their flanks were vulnerable. If the Austrians got the chance, they would send their own cavalry to attack the advancing French infantry, who would then be forced to form square, the only defence they had against rampaging horsemen. The formation would keep the cavalry at bay, but it would leave the infantry in tightly packed ranks, unable to either advance or retreat. They would then be at the mercy of the Austrian artillery. The enemy roundshot would be sure to massacre them where they stood. The walls of bayonets would be ripped apart. Then the cavalry could ride them down unopposed, any man left standing certain to be butchered by the merciless Austrian riders. The French cavalry would protect them from such a fate, their role vital if the assault was to result in victory.

The cavalry did not take long to form up, and Jack kept watching them as they began to advance, their ranks ordered and steady.

'There they go.' Fleming was watching too. He flashed a smile in Jack's direction.

Jack kept his eyes on the horsemen. The three regiments were picking up the pace and were already advancing faster than the men they were there to protect.

'Where the hell do they think they're going?' He did not understand the cavalry commander's decision. 'They should be guarding our bloody flank.'

Fleming gave a very Gallic shrug. 'They do as they please.'

Jack shook his head as the cavalry started to canter. It was folly. He looked to their front. He was taller than most of the legionnaires. At that moment, all he could see of the Austrians was a skirmish line; a thin, dispersed chain of light troops whose job it was to screen the main line from any scouts the French sent forward. The French cavalry had seen the same and now pressed forward to ride the light troops down.

'Fucking plungers.' Palmer spat as he saw the same as Jack. 'They should stay on our flank.'

Jack could only agree. The French cavalry were already moving fast, the noise of hundreds of hooves drumming into the ground washing over the slower-moving infantry.

'What a damn waste.' There was time for him to give his own verdict before the French cavalry swept into the line of enemy skirmishers.

It was not a fight. The French riders in the first line attacked stirrup to stirrup. They rode over the thin screen of skirmishers like a wave washing on to a beach. The Austrian light troops simply disappeared, with not one French rider unhorsed.

Buoyed by their success, the French cavalry pressed on. Bugles blaring, they inclined to the left then galloped on, now heading for the main enemy line. The horses were at full speed and they hurtled over the ground, their riders cheering, swords raised high.

The enemy infantry had witnessed the destruction of their skirmish line. They were no fools. They knew the fate of infantry caught in line by cavalry.

'They'll form square.' Jack was watching the fight even as the Legion marched forward. He knew what was about to happen. A tight knot had tied itself deep in his gut as he bore witness to what he was certain would be the destruction of the French cavalry.

It was now a race, one where the loser would die. Already the French cavalry were closing in on the enemy line. Their horses were slowing, the long gallop sapping their strength, but the momentum of the charge was with them and they powered towards the closest Austrian regiment.

The men in white coats knew what they had to do. The line was already breaking up, the infantry rushing into the formation that would save them from the rampaging cavalry. Once the four walls of the square were formed, they would be safe. Each wall would be at least four ranks deep. Those in the front rank would squat down, the butts of their muskets ground into the earth so that the bayonets pointed up, ready to disembowel any enemy horse that should come close. The men standing in the ranks behind would thrust out their own bayonets, forming an impenetrable wall of steel that no cavalryman, no matter how brave or foolish, could hope to cut their way through. With their attack thwarted, the cavalry would be easy targets for the infantry's muskets. They would be shot down as they milled around outside the square, their attack over the minute the infantrymen closed the last gap in the formation.

The Austrian infantry knew it as well as he did. Already the first battalions were nearly fully re-formed. Jack could almost hear the howls of frustration coming from the French cavalrymen, their charge about to end in either death or the ignominy of a long gallop to the rear.

But one Austrian battalion was too slow.

Jack spotted them first. They were just to the left of the French cavalry's line of attack. He could see no reason for their tardiness. Perhaps they were new recruits, not yet adept at the manoeuvre. Perhaps their officers had delayed, the order coming too late to give their men enough time to get into the new formation. Whatever the reason, they were now doomed.

The French cavalry swerved to the left. Their pace seemed to increase as they saw a target for their charge. Their bugles blared, the sound urgent and demanding, and the line of riders hurtled towards the half-formed square, their horses spurred hard for every last vestige of speed.

'The poor bastards.' Jack could not hold back the verdict.

'The stupid bastards.' It was Kearney who had the last word.

The cavalry hit the enemy hard, driving deep into the half-formed ranks. It was bravely done. Some of the horsemen were unseated, the enemy fighting on even in the face of death, but most rode the white-coated infantrymen down, hacking at any man standing. Many Austrian soldiers tried to flee. Their attempt turned the massacre into sport, and the French cavalrymen competed to ride the runners down.

The destruction of the enemy battalion was hard to watch. No foot soldier could look on easily as the men on horses butchered others who fought on their own two feet. Not one man in the Legion cheered as their comrades in the cavalry won their victory.

Within minutes the fight was over. Hundreds of Austrian soldiers lay dead or dying, the ground smothered with bodies.

The French cavalry were in disarray, the ordered ranks of the charge long since broken. Their horses were blown, their strength spent. It was time to retreat, to re-form the ranks and return to the flanks of the infantry columns.

But the Frenchmen wanted more.

'Come back!' Jack was the first to shout. The cry was picked up as men throughout the Legion beckoned to the cavalry. It was to prove a futile gesture.

As the French horsemen milled around the bodies of the men they had slain, the bugle called, summoning them back to the charge. The riders responded, surging away from the remains of the slaughtered battalion. They rode in a mob, any last vestiges of cohesion lost, cheering as they charged for a third time. They brandished swords that were bloodied to the hilt and kicked hard with their spurs, forcing their mounts on as they sought another victory, another target for their insatiable desire for glory.

The closest Austrian battalions waited in fully formed squares. They had stood by, powerless to intervene, as their comrades were butchered. Now they were being given a chance for revenge.

The French cavalry advanced gamely. Their horses laboured along, lathered in sweat and covered in blood. Yet still they managed to pick up the pace, the wild joy of the charge driving them on.

The Austrians watched them come. Their ranks stood firm, the wall of bayonets presented, the men ready to fire.

The Legion was still marching towards the enemy line. They were too far away to be anything other than spectators. Their ranks were silent as they watched the cavalry ride to their doom, every legionnaire certain of what was to come.

The first Austrian square opened fire. First one wall, then another fired a volley. At close range, even the outmoded muskets were brutally effective. Each volley cut down swathes of riders.

The cavalrymen rode on. They were committed to the charge now. Their momentum drove them past the first square and into the face of the next. Another volley roared out, cutting down the leading riders before they were even close to the wall of bayonets.

The pace of the charge was slowing. Some horses fell as they stumbled over the bodies of the slain. Others baulked as their riders rode them at the squares, the animals refusing to obey no matter how hard they were spurred.

The Austrian soldiers stood firm. Volley after volley seared into the broken ranks, killing men and horses alike. The French cavalry had won a great victory, yet now they died in droves. Those left standing tried to escape the vicious close-range fire that was decimating their numbers.

At last the cavalry turned for the rear. The survivors of the charge streaked away from the slaughter, riding hard. The Austrians cheered as the French broke. The sound rippled from one square to the next, reaching the men in the French columns as they marched to fight on the same ground.

The cheers continued even as the squares broke up, the Austrian infantry quick to return to the formation they had started in. The long three-man-deep line reappeared almost as if nothing had happened, the lost battalion forgotten as the ones on either side closed the gap in the line.

The French cavalry had tried to win the battle by themselves. Many of their number had died for such foolishness. Now it was down to the infantry. The men marching to the beat of the drums did not hope for glory, nor did they seek to write their names in the history books.

They marched to fight.

Chapter Forty-one

———— •◆• ————

The infantry pressed on, the drums driving them forward. Their officers understood the need for speed now that the foolishness of the cavalry had left their flanks exposed. Without their protection, the infantry had to press home the attack before the Austrian commanders saw an opportunity to send forward their own mounted troops.

Deep in the heart of the Legion, Jack felt the pulsating rhythm of the drums resonate in his soul. The men around him advanced with a relentless purpose, the young drummers beating out the staccato rhythm of the march without pause.

They were approaching the small village that Kearney had been unable to name. Ahead, the Austrian line was interspersed with lines of cannon standing wheel to wheel. Now these guns opened fire, the large French formations offering a fine target.

Jack heard the roar of the first massed volley. He stared at the sky, picking out the pencil-thin lines that raced towards the Legion at breakneck speed.

'God keep us.'

There was time for the muttered prayer before the fast-moving roundshot hit. The iron balls tore into the ranks, ripping through bodies before slamming into the ground with ferocious violence and skipping back into the air, the collision with the earth doing nothing to stall their progress.

The screaming began.

Every roundshot had found a mark. Men were flung to the ground, their bodies torn by the solid shot. Huge gaps were gouged in the line, dozens falling to just the first volley.

The Legion's sergeants bellowed the orders that closed the ranks, the litany of battle that would continue unabated as the infantrymen walked into the face of the enemy fire. The dead and wounded were left behind, their fellows deaf to their cries.

The second volley seared out across the plain. Jack could not help but flinch as the roundshot ripped into the Legion. Somehow it kept grinding its way forward. Another volley tore through them, followed by another. Jack saw men die just feet away from where he walked. A roundshot hit a sergeant five files to his right, the man's head disappearing in a shower of blood and bone. The body tottered on, marching in time by itself for at least five or six paces before it fell, the legionnaire in the rank behind using his rifle to lever it to one side.

Jack focused his gaze on the back of the man in front. His body was on fire, and every nerve screamed at him to run from the merciless bombardment. Somehow he controlled his mind, forcing himself to keep placing one foot after the other.

He stayed close to Fleming as the ranks closed to fill the gaps torn in the line. Everything was happening in a rush now. They were still moving forward, but every other step seemed to be to the left as more and more gaps opened up.

'Hungarians.' Fleming bellowed the word at him.

'What?' Jack didn't understand.

'Those bastards are Hungarian.' Fleming fired back the answer.

Jack stared at the men to his front. He did not know if Fleming was right, but he could see that although they sported the same white coats as the other enemy troops he had seen, their trousers were tighter than those worn by the men he had fought on the slopes near San Cassiano. The Hungarians were a part of the great Austrian empire, and its soldiers had a reputation as vicious, merciless fighters who took no prisoners.

As he stared, the Hungarian line seemed to take a quarter-turn to the right and raised their muskets. He was close enough to hear the enemy officers shouting their orders, the foreign words coming clearly enough even over the bellows of the French commanders.

With a great roar, the Hungarians opened fire.

Jack held back the cry that sprang to his lips. The air around him was filled with a violent storm, as if a thousand snapping, biting insects had been released. Men to his left and right screamed as they were hit. Some fell; others reeled away, the force of the impact knocking them backwards.

The Legion was ordered to halt. Jack glanced to his left. Palmer and Fleming were still with him, as was Kearney. The legionnaire sergeant was hauling more men into position, plugging the gaps as the Legion prepared to return fire.

'*Ajustez la visée!*'

Jack could not see the men who gave the order to prepare to fire. But the legionnaires around him raised their weapons and it was easy to copy them. He pulled his rifle snugly into his shoulder. There was time to squint down the barrel, to line up a Hungarian face above the sights.

'*Feu!*'

Every man in the line fired instantly.

Jack saw the white-coated ranks showered in a red mist. Dozens fell, the neatly formed ranks gutted by the legionnaires' close-range volley. Then he looked down, the rifle already falling from his shoulder, his hand reaching for a fresh cartridge.

The Hungarians fired again before he could get more than halfway through reloading. The power of the enemy volley was as nothing when compared to their first. Still dozens of Frenchmen were hit, their screams adding to the chaos. He paid them no heed, the air around him wonderfully still, and worked to reload with as much speed as he could muster.

Then the Hungarian cannon opened fire once again. If their infantry's first volley was dreadful, the cannon fire was hell unleashed. With the range closed, the gunners had switched to canister shells, metal cases packed full of musket balls that turned the cannons into glorified shotguns. The volley scythed through the French ranks, killing and maiming with wanton destruction. Men were torn apart, their lives ripped out of their bodies in an act of impossible violence.

It was as if the line simply ceased to be. Groups of men were left standing, but in between, great swathes of empty space showed where each canister shell had been aimed.

The legionnaires paused in their reloading and stared at one another, the shock of such destruction reflected in every expression. Veteran soldiers who had fought a dozen battles wept as they saw their precious regiment wiped out around them, the scale of the slaughter beyond comprehension.

Jack glanced at Fleming, checking that he was unharmed. The Englishman stared back, eyes wide, his mouth open in a silent scream of horror.

The Legion stubbornly stood fast. Those men still alive

pushed away the horror, then raised their rifles and fired at the enemy.

More men in white coats fell, the heavy French bullets cutting them down all along the line. The legionnaires cheered then, goading the Austrians, throwing insults after their bullets. It was a fine display of courage, the battered, bleeding ranks roaring in defiance. The cheering intensified, men baying with anger and fear, the sound taking on an unearthly tone.

Then the enemy guns fired a second volley of canister.

Jack flinched. The clumps of French infantry were gutted, the last of their cohesion shattered. Many died, their bodies falling alongside those already shot down, the firing line now composed more of corpses than of living men.

With a great cheer, the Hungarians charged.

Jack saw the enemy's faces as they were unleashed to the attack: twisted, sneering, teeth bared and lips pulled back. They ran hard, bayonets thrusting forward, their officers' swords pointing at the remains of the French line. The air was filled with their battle cry, a dreadful banshee wail that grew with volume as they charged.

The last legionnaires stood firm. There was no order to retreat. No thought of running. The men of the Legion would stand and fight.

Chapter Forty-two

⸺◆⸺

'*Chargez!*' The command came when the Hungarians were no more than twenty yards away.

Jack did not know who gave the order. As one, the remains of the Legion threw themselves forward. They did not care that the Hungarian line contained at least twice as many men as their own. They did not care that their flanks were exposed. They cared only for violence; for revenge.

Jack bellowed as he ran forward. He released his fear and let the fury of battle fill his head. Nothing mattered. Not Fleming. Not Ballard. Not even his own life. He just wanted to kill.

The two sides closed in a rush. Jack picked his target, his eyes flickering from the Hungarian's bayonet to his face. There was time to look into the other man's eyes and see fear. His first victim was young, little more than a boy, his pale cheeks darkened with a thin pelt of hair and his expression revealing his terror at finding himself in the front rank.

The boy's mouth opened as the two lines collided. It was still open when Jack battered his opponent's musket to one side and thrust his bayonet into his throat.

He felt nothing as he killed. It was too easy, the boy no match for the brutal skills he had honed on the battlefield. The Hungarian fell, hands clasped to the ruin of his throat, the blood already gushing from his mouth. Jack ignored him and drove forward, ramming his bloodied bayonet at a man in the second rank. Kearney fought at his side, the legionnaire sergeant killing with ruthless efficiency.

Jack's next blow was parried, his bayonet pushed wide. The second man he fought roared in triumph as he deflected the seventeen-inch blade. The roar was shut off as Jack slammed his rifle butt forward, using his momentum to deliver the blow with enough force to smash his target to the ground.

'Come on!' Jack screamed his wild challenge. He pulled his rifle back then thrust it forward, driving his bayonet into a man's stomach. Then he turned to batter his elbow into a Hungarian's throat, following the blow with the end of his rifle's butt, which he drove into the man's face.

The fight was descending into chaos. Jack grunted as someone hammered his shoulder with a musket barrel. He turned, flailing his rifle around only to find the man who had struck him already dying with Kearney's bayonet in his heart.

A Hungarian thrust his bayonet at Jack's side. The blade slipped past his hip, the steel barely an inch from his flesh. He counter-attacked, roaring in triumph as he punched his own blade through the man's open mouth. The Hungarian dropped his musket, his hands clasping to the dreadful wound. Jack cut him down without mercy, driving his bayonet into his chest then kicking the body away to free the blade.

He was given no time to aim another blow. A Hungarian came at him from the left, bayonet thrust at his chest. He twisted away, letting the bayonet slide past, only to nearly impale himself on another that came at him from the other side. The melee was swirling all around him now. The outnumbered legionnaires were fighting hard, but they were being cut down in droves. Jack could only defend, parrying blade after blade. Kearney fought at his side, the two men fighting to stay alive.

The Legion sergeant staggered as a rifle butt caught him on the thigh. He blundered into Jack, pushing him forward. A bayonet came for him. It sliced through his upper arm, the sharp steel cutting through his uniform jacket with ease. He jerked away, ducking under a swinging musket but losing his balance in the process.

He fell, landing awkwardly on his right side, his rifle trapped beneath his body. A wild-eyed Hungarian punched his bayonet down, seeking to kill him as he scrabbled on the ground. Before the blow could land, Jack kicked out and caught the man's knee. It was a cruel blow, and the man shrieked as his limb buckled. He tumbled forward and Jack reached up, grabbing him by the throat, pulling him downwards.

The Hungarian sprawled on top of him. Jack kept his fingers locked around the man's throat, even as his cheek pressed against his foe's face, desperate gasps for breath filling his mouth. He rolled his enemy over, fingers still digging into the soft flesh under the man's chin. As soon as his weight was on top, he lifted the Hungarian towards him then smashed him violently back into the ground, all the while throttling him with every ounce of strength he possessed. The Hungarian died quickly, his eyes staring up in accusation even as his last breath left his body.

Another rifle slammed into Jack's back, throwing him forward over his victim's body. As he rolled on to his side, there was time to see the man who had struck him preparing to lunge down, to see the bloodied bayonet that was about to kill him.

The blow never came. The tip of another bayonet erupted from the man's neck, the enemy soldier killed before he could plunge his own blade into Jack's gut.

'Get up, you fool!' Kearney bellowed.

Jack did not need to be told twice. He grabbed his fallen rifle and lumbered to his feet. The moment he found his balance, he killed a Hungarian soldier, striking him down just before the man thrust at Kearney from behind.

He looked for other legionnaires. The fighting blocked much of his view, but he could see their ranks were dreadfully depleted. Even as he tallied their numbers, the first broke and ran. It was the final confirmation he needed.

'Run!' he bellowed into Kearney's ear. He did not wait to see if the command was heard. Instead he grabbed the legionnaire sergeant's arm and pulled him backwards.

A Hungarian howled in frustration as Jack hauled Kearney out of reach. The howl turned into a shriek of horror as Jack drove his bayonet into the man's groin.

'Go! Go!' Jack ripped his blade out of his victim's flesh and smashed the rifle's butt into another Hungarian's bayonet, knocking it to one side. Then he was running, legs pounding into the ground, heart hammering in his chest.

Kearney came with him. The two men ran hard. Other legionnaires followed, the remnants of the Legion finally giving way to the enemy's superior numbers. They fled the melee, many dying as the frustrated Hungarians cut them down the moment they turned their backs.

Jack tried to look around him as he ran, searching the chaos for a sight of either Palmer of Fleming. He saw neither.

The other French battalions were retreating, mostly in good order, their ranks still formed. The Hungarians who had beaten the Legion did not give chase. The fight had been short and sharp, and those who had survived had no appetite to run after the broken French regiment. Jack saw the enemy soldiers checking the bodies on the ground. Any wounded legionnaire they discovered was greeted with a cheer before a bayonet was rammed down, the Frenchmen dispatched without a qualm.

Jack stumbled, his tired legs weak.

'Run.' Kearney grabbed his shoulder, pulling him on. The instruction came in between gasps for breath.

Jack did not look back again. 'Where the hell are they?' He found the breath to shout the question at Kearney even as they ran.

He was roundly ignored. Kearney was pulling away. Jack was struggling. The humid air rasped in his throat. His chest felt as if an iron band had been pulled tight across his ribcage. It took all his willpower to stay on his feet.

To his relief, Kearney slowed. As he eased up, his legs almost gave way.

'Crap.' The sergeant twisted as he spat out the single world. He grabbed at Jack, taking tight hold of his shoulder.

Jack's relief at the slower pace did not last. His breath echoed in his ears, and his heart thumped as if it was about to burst, but still he heard the ominous drumming on the ground that he recognised in an instant.

'Fuck.' He turned and looked over his shoulder. The Austrian cavalry were thundering past their Hungarian allies. Hundreds of riders had been unleashed to the slaughter, the broken ranks of the Legion the kind of target every cavalryman dreamt of. In open ground, the legionnaires would not stand a chance.

'This way!' Kearney pulled at him. 'Come on!'

Jack needed no urging. The pair ran, changing direction. He trusted Kearney, sensing that the sergeant had spotted something that might offer them a chance of survival. He hoped he was right. He had not seen any cover of any sort. On the plain, the scattered infantry would be easy pickings for the rampaging Austrian cavalry.

Around them the legionnaires fled in every direction, each man making his own bid for survival. He saw some banding together, a rough-and-ready square drawing in some of the survivors. But it was too far away for him to consider running to join it. He tried and failed to see if Palmer or Fleming had made it to the group's relative safety. All he saw was the Austrian cavalry increasing their speed, the riders gouging back their spurs as they urged their horses into the charge. It was time to forget any notion of looking for the two men. They would have to fend for themselves.

The sound of the Austrian horses was getting louder. Jack heard the first screams as the slowest legionnaires on the far left flank of the attack were cut down without mercy.

Kearney had kept hold of his arm. They ran together, both blowing hard. The screams got closer. Legionnaires who had run at their side were being slain, their wrong choice of direction costing them their lives.

Jack searched the ground ahead, trying to spot something that would give them shelter. He saw nothing but open ground, a great field of trampled rye stretching away in every direction.

Cheers came from behind them. Austrian voices bellowed as

they killed. The cheers turned to hoots of glee as some spotted the pair of blue-coated legionnaires still trying to escape.

'Where the hell are we going?' Jack choked on the words. He clasped at the arm that was grasping his own. He felt Kearney falter, his strength fading.

Hooves drummed on the ground. He could not look back to see who would be the one to kill him. The noise was relentless, the drumming coming at pace. It was all he could hear, his ears filled with the sound of oncoming death.

'There!' Kearney gasped out the single word. His gait had become uneven, and Jack had to pull hard to keep him moving.

Again he searched the ground ahead. Finally he spotted what Kearney had found. A drainage ditch had been dug along one edge of the field. It was not deep, perhaps just three or four feet, but it was all they had.

'Come on then!' He hauled on Kearney's arm. The man was heavy and was slowing fast. Together they stumbled on, neither able to look back at the Austrian cavalrymen spurring after them.

'Get down!' Jack roared the order, then dived forward.

They fell together, hitting the ground hard. Momentum tumbled them into the ditch, their bodies tangled together. Jack felt the air rush from his straining lungs, then Kearney's elbow caught him just above the ear, knocking him half senseless.

The fall saved them. He had pulled them down moments before the Austrian cavalrymen would have reached them. Instead of cutting at the two fugitives, the pair of riders had to force their horses to jump the ditch. Even as Jack and Kearney were still rolling to its bottom, the horses' hooves were passing by just a matter of feet above their heads.

Chapter Forty-three

———◆———

Palmer punched his bayonet into a white-coated soldier's chest, twisting the steel hard lest it be trapped in his victim's flesh. Another man, an officer, came at him almost instantly, sword lunging towards his head. He parried the blow, ignoring the splinter of wood cut from the rifle's barrel that drew blood as it seared across his cheek. The Austrian officer died a moment later with Palmer's bayonet in his heart, his shriek of horror lost in the bellows and grunts of men fighting for their lives.

Fleming still fought at his side. He had lost his kepi, and his face was streaked with blood from where a bayonet had cut through the soft flesh of his cheek. Palmer did all he could to protect the younger man, but in the swirling hand-to-hand combat he could only do so much, and Fleming was fighting hard just to stay alive.

Palmer parried another attack, then another. He wanted to spit, the stench of blood and shit sticking in his throat. All he could do was batter away the bayonets that came at them, the enemy swarming around the handful of legionnaires that still stood.

The first men began to run. He saw them go, the remains of the line breaking up fast. He turned, swatting aside another steel blade aimed at his guts, and looked for his comrades.

He saw Jack almost immediately. His fellow impostor was fighting hard, but the Hungarians were pressing all around him. Even as he watched, Jack went down, his body swallowed up by the sea of white uniforms.

Palmer had seen enough. He turned his attention back to the melee, snarling with anger as a bayonet reached for his throat. He ducked, letting the weapon come past, before stamping forward and driving his own blade into his attacker's heart.

Another Hungarian came at him, his bayonet held low. Palmer gave him no time to use it. He sidestepped the inevitable thrust, smashing the man to the ground with his rifle's butt. The man fell, yet dozens more immediately pressed forward, the tide of white-coated soldiers relentless and seemingly without end. He thrust his bayonet forward repeatedly, keeping the enemy at bay a moment longer. The Hungarians nearest to him backed away, giving him time to turn once more.

'Come on, old son.' Palmer had fought in enough battles to know when one was lost. He reached forward to grab Fleming by the collar, hauling him away.

Fleming needed little urging. He was facing two Hungarian bayonets, both already bloodied to the hilt. They came for him as Palmer pulled him backwards, thwarted as their target was dragged away.

The two men turned and ran. They paid no attention to the howls of frustration as they escaped. Instead they put their heads down and pumped their arms, finding the strength to sprint away. They ran with a few dozen other legionnaires, survivors of the bitter fight clinging together. Together they pounded back over the ground they had advanced across, their path taking them past the bodies of the men struck down by the enemy cannon fire.

'Horses!' Fleming heard the Austrian cavalry first and shouted the warning.

Palmer glanced over his shoulder. He saw the threat as the Austrian cavalry came cantering around the side of the Hungarian line and slowed his pace, head twisting from side to side as he assessed their options. He saw no place to hide.

'On me!' He bellowed the order, not knowing if anyone would understand, let alone obey. He grabbed at Fleming, forcing the younger man to his side. 'Tell them!'

For a moment, Fleming stared at him. Then he started shouting in loud, rapid French, summoning the running legionnaires to join them.

The retreating French soldiers understood. These were no raw recruits. Most had fought before, and they knew there was only one way to survive against marauding enemy cavalry. Dozens of battered legionnaires formed around Palmer. This was no organised square, just a huddle of tired, bloodied men who did not know when they had lost.

'*Ici!*' Fleming bellowed the order, summoning more men from the rout. Some heeded him, changing course to join the group who stood in a rough circle, bayonets held outwards. Others simply ran on, unwilling to stay on the field of battle a moment longer.

Palmer concentrated on loading his rifle. Others followed his lead, the men skinning their knuckles on their bloodied bayonets. He lifted the weapon the moment it was loaded. The

Austrian cavalry were close now. Their swords rose and fell, the slowest legionnaires cut down as they tried to evade the men on horseback.

'Here they come!' he sang out in warning. Men still halfway through reloading stopped and presented their bayonets, holding them out to force the enemy riders away.

Just over fifty men stood with Fleming and Palmer. Their square bore little comparison to the well-formed ones that had defeated the French cavalry. But it would have to do.

Palmer squinted down his barrel, aiming at one of the leading Austrian cavalrymen. He held himself still, then pulled the trigger. His target's head snapped backwards, the rifle bullet finding its mark in the centre of his face.

'Got the bugger,' Palmer hissed as he saw the horseman fall. There was no time for him to say anything else.

The first Austrians pressed close. A handful of other legionnaires fired, emptying some of the saddles nearest to the square. It was enough to remind the Austrians that not every man was an easy target. Many of the cavalrymen swerved away, their horses shying as the ragged square opened fire. But not all.

One officer rode close before hauling hard on the reins to bring his mount to a halt. His arm straightened as he aimed a revolver at the men huddled behind the wall of bayonets. He roared once in anger, then began to fire.

At such close range, the revolver was an effective weapon. The first bullet hit a legionnaire just to Palmer's left in the very centre of his chest. The Frenchman crumpled, his cry of anguish lost in the noise of the fight. The second and third bullets both hit the man standing next to the one already shot. He fell backwards, his arms windmilling in the air as the heavy bullets cut him down. Two men had been killed. A gap had been opened in the front of the square.

The Austrian officer saw the opening his revolver had created. He spurred his horse hard, throwing the animal at the gap. His shout of victory was loud enough to be heard by every man in the ragged formation, the cry summoning more cavalrymen to the fight.

Palmer saw the danger. He knew what would happen if the Austrian cavalry broke in. He stepped into the gap, hefting his rifle as he placed himself directly in the Austrian cavalry officer's path.

'Fuck off!' He bellowed the curse as he swung his rifle. He made no attempt to hit the rider. Instead he smashed the rifle's butt into the horse's mouth. The contact was brutal. The horse reared, its mouth gushing with blood, its terrified scream horribly loud. As its front legs lifted from the ground, a legionnaire rammed his bayonet into the animal's chest, driving the steel deep. The officer was thrown, his body hitting the ground an instant before the wounded beast turned and galloped away.

Palmer gave the Austrian no time to stand. He stepped forward and drove his bayonet into the man's heart, ramming it down hard before tearing the steel away.

The legionnaires cheered then. They roared their defiance, daring the Austrians to come against them. A few more had loaded their rifles. Now they fired, knocking men from their saddles or killing the horses that came close. The fire was ragged, but it was effective, and the Austrians nearest the square pulled away, looking for easier targets .

'Where's Jack?' Fleming had to press his lips to Palmer's ear to make himself heard. 'We need to find him.'

'No.' Palmer was having none it.

'We can't just leave him.'

'Yes we fucking can,' Palmer shouted back. 'I saw him go down. He's dead or dying. Either way he's no use to us now.'

Fleming shook his head. 'I'm not leaving him.'

'Yes you fucking are.' Palmer growled the words then slammed his rifle butt into the side of Fleming's head. He had held back some of his strength, but the blow was still powerful enough to knock the young man from his feet. He fell to the ground with all the grace of a sack of horseshit.

Palmer turned on his heel, holding out his bayonet, wary of any legionnaire who wanted to intervene. A few looked at him, but none stepped forward to come to Fleming's aid. Many had been present to hear Kearney make his promise that Fleming could leave once the battle was done. None would deny him that reward now.

Seeing that no one would stop him, Palmer left Fleming on the ground. An Austrian cavalryman's horse was nearby, standing loyally by its master's corpse. Palmer walked towards it slowly, cooing at the animal, the soft sounds soothing and calm. He stepped past the body, barely glancing at the ruined face that had taken a Minié bullet right through its centre.

The horse's ears twitched and it shied away. But it was well trained, and it stayed in place, waiting dutifully for its next command. Palmer took its reins easily enough, then led it back to where the square was slowly breaking up, the exhausted legionnaires slumping to the ground, too tired to even start picking through the bodies of the enemy for their valuables. It took little time to haul Fleming's unconscious body across the saddle.

Finally Palmer had his man.

Chapter Forty-four

———◆◆◆———

Jack scrabbled in the thin trickle of water that lay in the bottom of the ditch. Everything hurt, but he knew he could not give in. He found his footing, then pushed himself up, his muddied rifle in his hand.

'Get up!' he shouted at Kearney. The legionnaire sergeant was on all fours, gasping for breath. 'Get up, for God's sake.'

There was no time to see if he would obey. The two Austrian cavalrymen were now hauling hard on their reins. In seconds they would be spurring back towards the ditch. Jack braced his legs. He had no idea how to fight two men on horseback whilst standing ankle deep in mud. He and Kearney would die like rats trapped in a bucket.

He kept his eyes on the enemy horsemen even as he sensed the sergeant struggling to his feet. He could taste fear. It lingered on his tongue, bitter and acrid.

Kearney staggered upright, then pushed one leg forward so he could brace it on the front bank of the ditch. He raised his rifle, the butt pulled snugly into his shoulder.

'You loaded?' He spoke out of the side of his mouth as he squinted down the barrel.

'No.' Jack spat out the word.

'Then you really are a useless damn lobster.' Kearney's lip curled into a sneer, then stilled as he held his breath.

The sharp retort of the rifle firing echoed around them.

The Austrian cavalrymen were no more than twenty yards away. Kearney's bullet hit the leading man in the face. Jack saw the spurt of blood erupt from the back of his head as it smashed through his skull. The Austrian's horse was at full speed when he was hit. It tripped, the sudden change of weight on its back throwing it out of stride, and hit the ground hard. The bones of both rider and horse snapped like twigs, the animal's sudden scream of terror cut off as the confused jumble of man and beast came to a shuddering halt ten yards from the ditch.

The second rider spurred hard, his pace unaltered by the death of his comrade. His sword lowered, the blade held steady even as his horse thundered towards the two stubborn legionnaires.

'Come on!' Jack screamed his futile challenge. He would not go down without a fight. The Austrian cavalryman was charging towards him at full speed. The desire to run was overpowering. Fear surged through him, every fibre of his being trembling. But he planted his feet, bracing his rifle with the bayonet held out. He would not run.

The distance closed with terrifying speed. There was no time to think. Jack sensed Kearney at his side, the American presenting his own bayonet-tipped rifle outwards. They stood shoulder to shoulder, teeth bared in defiance, neither flinching from the inevitable collision.

Then the Austrian swerved.

It was well done. One moment the rider was thundering towards them, the next he kicked hard and twisted his mount to one side. He flashed past them, the horse stretching its legs as it leaped the ditch for a second time.

'Shit.' Jack turned on the spot, his eyes fixed on the enemy cavalryman. 'Come on, you bastard,' he hissed as he rammed his boot hard into the opposite side of the ditch, preparing to stand against the next charge. 'For fuck's sake turn around, you dolt.' He snapped the order at Kearney, who was still facing the other way.

The American did not move.

'Kearney!' Jack shouted angrily. He could not hope to stand alone. He tore his eyes away from the Austrian rider for long enough to berate the American for being so slow. 'For God's sake . . .' The words died on his lips.

Kearney dropped his rifle, then fell to his knees, his hands clasped to his neck, fingers scrabbling over the huge gash that had been ripped in its side. The Austrian's sword had cut him without mercy, the blow coming in the span of a single heartbeat as the rider galloped past.

For one dreadful second Kearney looked back at Jack, his eyes wide. Then he fell forward, turning so that he landed on his back. He lay in the dust, his body convulsing, hands clawing at the dreadful wound.

Jack's soul froze, every emotion scoured from his being.

Then he ran.

His boots slipped as he scrambled free of the ditch, then he was up and running.

Ahead of him, the Austrian cavalryman was still turning his

mount around. The beast was tiring, and its rider had to work it hard to get it facing towards the lone soldier he had left in the ditch.

Jack felt nothing as he ran. There was no fear. No rage or anger. He felt numb, empty, his soul barren.

The Austrian saw him coming. He kicked his horse hard, forcing it back into motion. It lurched forward, its great muscles straining as it tried to increase speed.

Jack just ran, legs pumping hard, mouth open in a silent war cry.

The Austrian's horse was slow. It had been pushed past the point of exhaustion and it was struggling. It had reached no more than a laboured trot when Jack attacked.

He did not hesitate. He picked his spot even as he ran at full speed. When the horse came at him, he was ready. He dodged to one side, then rammed his bayonet forward with every last ounce of strength he possessed. It was a cruel blow, driven by grief, and it pierced the horse in the neck, the steel driven deep. Jack pushed his weight behind it, not caring that the bayonet would be stuck fast.

The horse screamed. It was a dreadful, feral sound, the stricken beast driven mad by the sudden agony. It staggered on, its momentum driving it forward before it fell, blood pumping from the horrific gouge in its flesh. Its rider was thrown forward, all balance lost.

Jack let his rifle go and threw himself at the Austrian. His hands clawed at the man's leg, blackened fingernails tearing at his breeches. The rider stood no chance. Jack tumbled him from the saddle and threw himself on top of him. He used his weight to pin him in place, hands locking tight around the Austrian's throat. He kept them there even as the man jackknifed underneath him, his body convulsing as he strained to get free.

Jack leaned forward, fingers digging deep into the soft flesh of the man's throat. Still the Austrian struggled, even as Jack throttled the life out of him, his fists battering at Jack's head, every blow weaker than the one before.

It took him a long time to die.

'Kearney?' Jack asked the question gently, as if waking the American from sleep. He squatted down, then reached forward, the touch of his bloodstained finger as gentle as he could make it. Kearney's eyes popped open.

'Take it easy.' Jack breathed the words. He took hold of Kearney's hands, which were locked tight around his neck. 'Let me see.'

Slowly and carefully he eased the sergeant's hands to one side. The wound was oozing blood. Thick strands of gristle were clearly visible amidst the gore. The Austrian's sword had cut deep.

Kearney sucked down a breath. The blood in the wound bubbled up, pink and frothy, then he choked, more blood gurgling in his throat.

Jack could find no words. He reached into Kearney's jacket and pulled out a pale blue scarf he must have picked up in Genoa, his first thought to bandage the wound. But the American would not lie still. His hands scrabbled against Jack's, fighting his attempts to fix the scarf in place. It took several minutes before the grotesque gash was finally hidden from sight.

'There you are. That should do.' Jack spoke in little more than a whisper. He rocked back on his haunches, looking at the fresh blood streaked across his hands. He wanted to run. To flee from the horror of Kearney's wound. Instead he just sat there, powerless. He had never felt so impotent.

Kearney's right hand jerked across his chest, trying to get inside his blood-soaked jacket. It fumbled with the buttons, the fingers clumsy.

'Rest easy.' Jack reached forward to take hold of the sergeant's wrist. 'I'll do it.' He gently placed Kearney's hand on his breast, then reached inside his jacket and pulled out a thick wedge of what looked to be letters held together with string.

'Give them …'

Blood rattled in Kearney's throat, making the words barely audible, but Jack understood them well enough. He glanced at the uppermost letter. An address was written on the envelope in pencil. He did not bother to read it. Instead he shoved the bundle into his own pocket, not caring that he left dark streaks of blood across it.

'You can deliver them yourself.' He offered the lie with a flicker of a smile.

Kearney tried to speak, but no sound emerged. Blood flecked his lips as he tried again. When they came, the words were so quiet that Jack could hardly hear them.

'Kill me.'

For a moment, Jack could not breathe. Kearney's eyes bored into him. The stare was fierce, and it was proud.

'Kill me.'

The words were almost completely drowned by the constant flow of blood that filled Kearney's throat. But Jack had heard them well enough. He knew what Kearney wanted. He understood what was being asked. It was what he would want were the roles reversed. He had seen enough wounds to know which would kill. The American faced a long, agonising and drawn-out death.

Kearney gasped as he fought against the pain. He was shaking now, every muscle trembling. Somehow he managed to lift a hand. It clutched clumsily at Jack's, then pushed it lower so that it rested against the short sword at his waist. He shuddered, and his grip tightened around Jack's wrist, the fingers digging in like claws, before it fell away.

Jack let his own hand stay on the hilt of the short sword. It was not a weapon made for fighting. The Legion's sergeants wore it as a badge of their rank, the tradition of more importance than the blade itself. But Jack knew that Kearney would have kept the edge sharp. It would do the job well enough.

It was easy to draw the blade. It fitted snugly into his hand. It did not weigh much, not like an officer's sword, or a maharajah's talwar. But it would be enough to kill a man.

He held it beside his thigh and out of Kearney's sight. He understood what had to be done, but still he hesitated. He knew that killing the American would be a mercy. He had heard such pleas before, just as every survivor of battle had. Wounded men, crazed by suffering, would beg for a bullet to put an end to their misery. Often they were given it, their fellow soldiers willing to do that one last thing for their comrades in arms.

Jack knew what had to be. It was a soldier's duty to a comrade. At the very last, a man had the right to die.

Kearney's eyes had closed. He was still alive, his chest rising and falling with every shallow gasp of breath. His face was screwed tight against the pain, and a thin trail of blood snaked from the corner of his mouth.

For a moment Jack hoped the American would just die. The

notion tempted him. He could simply sit and wait for the inevitable. It would surely take a long time, but at least he would be spared from having to act, from having to be the one to end another life.

Kearney shuddered. He was suffering, every breath laboured, every second lived in agony.

Jack sucked down a breath, then held it. He looked at Kearney. The American's eyes flickered open and locked on to Jack's as he began to move the sword. They stayed there even as the blade pressed against his heart, the tip sliding through cloth and then into flesh. Then they closed for the last time, the window to his soul shut off for all eternity.

Jack threw the sword away. He could feel the warmth of fresh blood on his hand. He did not have the will to wipe it away.

Chapter Forty-five

―――●◆●―――

Palmer led the borrowed horse away from the fighting. The Austrian cavalry were still cutting down the stragglers, but the French retreat had been halted, the battered battalions in the brigade strong enough to ward off the enemy riders.

No one paid him any attention. The wounded were streaming to the rear, absolved from the need to fight. They staggered, limped and lurched towards some half-understood notion of safety, their bloody, torn bodies the defining emblem of courage. Many would not make it. They fell to the ground, ignored and forgotten, their battle, and their lives, ending on a churned-up field.

Palmer walked past them all. He paid no heed to the entreaties for aid. He had no water left to share and his well of compassion had run dry. He thought only of his duty, and of delivering Fleming to Ballard.

As he walked, he looked at the man draped across the saddle. For a moment he worried that he had hit Fleming too hard, a thin trickle of blood running down from the man's temple. Then Fleming stirred, his eyes fluttering open for a half-second as he drifted in out and out consciousness before closing again. It was reassuring. It meant he would live.

Palmer found it hard to understand why Ballard had declared Fleming's life to be worth so much more than Jack's. He had felt a moment's sorrow when he saw Jack go down, the death of the younger man reaching a place inside him that he had ignored for so long that he had believed it to be gone for ever. He had enjoyed working with a partner, even one as cocksure and strong-willed as Jack had been.

Such thoughts were interrupted as he heard shouting coming from behind him. At first he paid them no attention. Then the shouts and the screams intensified, and he found the energy to glance over his shoulder.

The remains of the Austrian cavalry had turned from the squares that the other French battalions had formed. Their horses were tired and their arms were bloodied to the shoulder. But they still had the desire to kill. They left the hastily formed squares behind and turned their attention to the last men still in the open.

Palmer had turned in time to see the cavalrymen cut into the wounded stragglers behind him. The enemy regiments no longer rode stirrup to stirrup, their formed ranks long since disrupted by the fighting. But they still hit the fugitives in style, the defenceless men dying in droves.

The screams stopped almost immediately. Those still strong enough to run did so in silence, the time for cries of terror now long past. Those without that strength died where they were, their final moments spent in soundless horror.

Palmer looked at the battered rifle he still carried. Its bayonet was bloodied to the hilt, and the tip had been bent out of shape. Both the barrel and the stock were pitted and scarred, and the butt was caked in blood. He had not bothered to reload, the thought that he should have done so a fleeting regret. It did not take him long to tie the reins across the saddle, the temporary lashing the best he could hope to do in the time left to him, then he slapped the horse hard across the flank, goading the tired animal into motion. It lurched away at little more than a half-arsed trot, Fleming's body bouncing in the saddle.

Palmer sighed as he turned to fight one final time. The Austrian riders were close now. The enemy's horses were on their last legs, but he did not doubt that they would come for him. There would be no reprieve, no miraculous escape like at the end of a great fable. He knew what fate had planned for him. He planted his feet and hefted his rifle in both hands. At least he would go down fighting.

He felt a few heavy raindrops land on his head. The rain that had threatened to fall all day was finally making a belated appearance. It heralded the arrival of a storm that would likely put an end to the fighting. But it would come too late for him.

An Austrian cavalryman spurred towards him. Palmer saw that the man had lost his shako so now rode with his hair ruffled by the wind. He tensed, thinking to repeat the blow to the horse's mouth that had served him well so many times before.

But he was tired. And he was slow.

The Austrian rider gave his mount the spur, urging the beast to find a final burst of speed. Palmer saw the change in the horse's motion. He started to swing the butt of his rifle, trying to time the blow so that it would land square and true.

He was too late. The Austrian rider was already on him.

The man's sword tore into his chest, the notched blade gouging a deep crevice across his front before the horse's momentum ripped the blade free.

Palmer fell to his knees, his rifle dropping from his hands. There was time to look down, to see the rush of blood that smothered him from nipple to navel, before he crumpled over.

The storm that had threatened all day burst across the battlefield with biblical ferocity. Day turned to night as thick grey-black clouds smothered the sun. The rain came down in a torrent, any notion of carrying on the fight washed away by the downpour that soaked the combatants to the skin in minutes.

With the rain came great gusts of wind. Whirlwinds of yellow dust billowed across the plain like powder smoke, reducing the visibility to mere yards. The few trees were battered, branches torn from their trunks like arms and legs ripped from bodies by fast-moving roundshot.

Jack looked up and let the rain wash across his face. It felt cold as it drummed on his skin, but the sensation revived him. He did not know how long he had sat on the ground next to Kearney. He barely felt the cramp in his legs, or the pain in his back. His mind had been emptied of all thought. His soul was as numb as his flesh.

A great bolt of lightning seared across the heavens. It was followed by a peal of thunder that would have overwhelmed the heaviest artillery barrage. The sound resonated through him, lighting the spark of life that had been nearly extinguished in the fighting.

It was time to move.

Gingerly he eased himself to his feet, slinging his rifle on to his shoulder. His back ached abominably, the pain searing up and down his body to leave his legs trembling. The wounds he had taken in the fight made themselves known, the aches and bruises interspersed with brighter flashes of pain caused by Austrian bayonets. He stood in the rain, letting the storm wash over him until the first chill came, the single shiver that ran through his abused flesh a delicious torture that reminded him he was still alive.

He could not bear to look at Kearney's corpse.

He went north, walking through a field of flattened rye. The local population would likely go hungry that winter. Hundreds of acres of grain had been destroyed by the battle that had been fought on a front many miles wide. Yet there was a new crop that now smothered the ground, one that would improve the soil for generations.

He steered clear of any formed bodies of French infantry that he saw. He supposed the French would claim victory, their occupation of the battlefield all the proof their eager generals would need to proclaim their success. For his part, he did not care who had won, or who had lost. He was indifferent as to how the French would write of their great success, or the strategy and manoeuvres they would claim had earned it for them. His part in the struggle meant nothing. His was no tale of a valiant hero, a fable where one man decided the fate of a battle. His was a tale of horror unleashed, where men died screaming and friends begged for death.

He walked through a field of corpses. Many wore the same blue uniform he had borrowed, the colour now turned almost to black by the rain. The men from the Legion lay in every direction, some alone, others in small groups, cut down by the Austrian cavalry in the same desperate flight that had seen Jack and Kearney left cowering in a muddy ditch.

A few bodies moved. Hands lifted towards him as he approached, voices begging for aid, for water, or simply for a bullet to put an end to their suffering. He ignored them all. There might be a time to try to help, but it had not yet arrived. He still had a mission, a purpose that he clung to lest his soul be suffocated by the suffering that surrounded him.

He picked his way past the heaps of the dead and the dying. His boots caught against discarded equipment, the fields littered with knapsacks, mess tins, shakos, kepis, belts, bloodstained clothing, broken weapons and abandoned rifles. The rain fell constantly, driven by the wind so that at times it was almost horizontal. All the while great flashes of lightning were interspersed with the deep booms and crashes of thunder. It was as if the gods had been angered by the battle and now raged in the heavens, their display a vivid demonstration of their superiority over the struggles of man.

Jack did not know where to search first, so he retraced the path of the Legion's retreat as best he could, towards the scene of the hand-to-hand fight with the Hungarians. The enemy were close by, but the rain shrouded him, hiding him from view. He trod carefully amongst the bodies, always looking down as he searched the grey, lifeless faces of the dead. He did not find either of the men he was looking for.

He closed his eyes, picturing the flight from the Hungarians. He remembered seeing a group that had stood together, a square that he had glimpsed forming amidst the chaos. Angling northwards, he found the place easily enough, half a dozen dead enemy horses confirmation that at least some of the legionnaires had managed to hold their ground. There were a few French bodies, but here the wounded had gone, a sign that the men had been able to retreat in good order, taking their comrades with them. None of the dead legionnaires were familiar to him.

He stood amidst the corpses and thought about lying down. It would be a sweet relief to let it all end, to close his eyes and allow oblivion to claim him. The temptation was strong, but he knew he would not give in to it. For the mission was not yet done. No matter what, he had to know what had happened to his comrades.

Chapter Forty-six

———◆◆◆———

Ballard stood outside the aid station, staring into space. The rain was lashing down, the drops jumping a good two feet back into the air as they hit the ground with all the force of a canister shell. It drummed off his head and shoulders, his hair slick to his scalp and his dark blue jacket doubled in weight as it absorbed the deluge. Yet standing here was a relief after enduring the cloying atmosphere inside the aid station for so long. The rain felt wonderfully clean, and he prayed that it would scour the stains from his soul as effectively as it was cleaning the blood and the sweat from his skin.

'Mr Ballard! Mr Ballard, help me over here.'

Ballard turned on command. A fresh wagon had pulled up outside the aid post. He could no longer tally how many had come in. One hundred? Two? Whey-coloured faces lifted in hope as they reached their destination, the wounded men looking down with wild eyes as a single orderly walked towards them with Mary at his side.

It had been Mary who had summoned him. The apron she

had borrowed was covered with gore, as were her bare arms, the streaks of blood smearing in the rain. She paid the storm no heed and trudged through the puddles with determination, her eyes fixed on the men waiting for her aid.

Ballard watched her as she walked. Her dress had quickly become soaked and now clung to her body, and her hair was flattened against her head. She was covered in filth, and her face was puffy and haggard after so many hours doing all she could for the wounded. Yet to Ballard's eyes she had never looked as beautiful.

He found he did not regret making his offer. He had considered the idea of marrying again before, but he had always been so busy. Suggestions had been made. Once or twice a year, he would receive a letter from a distant family member, or an associate, which would gently mention some worthy woman in search of a husband. He had never paid them much heed, the itch for a wife one that he never seemed to have the time to scratch. Until he had met Mary.

'Mr Ballard! Mr Ballard!'

Another voice called for his attention, one that scattered his foolish musings to the wind. He was moving towards it before any thought to do so fully formed in his mind. He walked fast, lifting a hand to shelter his eyes from the rain. His heart raced, the voice bringing hope that it heralded the arrival of the man he had come so far to find.

His hope died. There were no horses. There were no strong men bringing in their quarry. Just a sorry-looking boy walking alone through the rain.

'William!' Ballard called out, shouting to be heard over the deluge.

The boy came to stand in from of him. Ballard took him by

the shoulders, holding the exhausted lad upright. 'Where are they?'

'I don't know.' The reply came back as little more than a sob.

'The horses? Did they take the horses?'

Billy bit his lip, then shook his head, the motion flinging water to either side.

Ballard saw the bruises on the boy's face, the flesh around his ear and across his cheek blackened and blotchy. The lad had taken a beating.

'Did you see them? Did you see them at all?' Ballard shook him as he fired the questions.

'No.'

He let go of the boy then. The hopelessness of his situation was nearly more than he could bear. Exhaustion engulfed him and left his legs shaking with the effort of keeping himself upright.

He gazed past the boy, no longer able to look at the bearer of such bad tidings. Another wagon was making its way along the track that led towards the aid station. Another cargo of ruined bodies about to vie for the scant attention that the handful of orderlies and surgeons could provide.

'Billy!'

Ballard did not turn to look at Mary as she spotted her child. The joy in her tone hurt him, her love displayed even amidst the foulness of a battlefield. He heard their voices, but could not bear to listen to their exchange. Jealousy ran through him with enough force to leave him shaking.

With a sigh, he approached the wagon that had just arrived. Like all the others, it was badly overloaded. The men who could still do so slipped over the sides, leaving behind only those unable to move. Ballard saw their uniforms for the first time. Their trousers were white and their dark blue jackets had green epaulettes. It was the same uniform he had given to the two men charged with finding his target. The familiar sight brought him up short, a last flare of hope surging deep in his belly. It pushed away the exhaustion, his body responding to the warm rush the emotion created.

Quick, urgent steps took him into the crowd of men that milled around the rear of the wagon. He moved through them, searching faces, looking for the flicker of familiarity that he longed for. It did not take him long. He reached the wagon and pulled himself up. Four men were stretched out on the floor. Two were dead, their faces waxy and grey. One of those still alive had lost the right-hand side of his chest. The dreadful wound had been stuffed full of lint, then bound with what looked like part of a bed sheet. The whole was smothered with blackened blood that glistened and pulsated in the rain. The last man's wounds were hidden from view, but Ballard could hear his soft moans and sobs even over the noise of the rain. None of the four was the man he sought.

He turned, hopelessness fighting for control of his soul. Another wagon was pulling up behind the one he was on. It too was full of men from the Legion. He jumped down. The ground was slick, the wheels of the wagons churning it to so much slurry, but still he moved quickly, sending up fountains of water with every urgent pace.

Once again the lightly wounded disembarked first. The men ambled away, moving slowly, their expressions revealing the strain of their journey. He pushed through them, pausing to look at every face. None bore the resemblance that he wanted so desperately to see.

He looked hopefully down the road, searching for another wagonload of wounded legionnaires. For the first time in as long as he could remember, the road was empty. The temptation to end his search was strong, but he hauled himself up on to the second wagon nonetheless. He would see it through to the bitter end.

There were only two men left on the wagon bed. Both appeared to be alive. One had been hit in the guts, his uniform ripped open, revealing the grey-blue mess of his belly. His hands clasped around his innards, holding them in place with trembling fingers that were covered to the wrists with gore.

Ballard checked the man's face, a fleeting moment of joy that it was not his target replaced swiftly by disappointment that the search was not over. The second man lay on his side, his face pressed against the wooden floor of the wagon. Ballard squatted, then picked his way forward, trying not to jar either man with his mud-splattered boots. He no longer noticed the thin river of blood that ran freely across the wagon bed.

The rain had darkened the man's blond hair. It lay tousled against his scalp, with thick strands glued to his forehead. His eyes were shut, yet the pattern of his features was easily recognisable.

Ballard could barely breathe. He stayed where he was, staring at the face he had not seen for so long, unable to believe that the moment had finally arrived. He reached out, a single finger moving to ease the hair out of the man's eyes. The touch sent a jolt running through him. It was enough to make him gasp, and he had to take hold of the wagon's side lest he fall.

The man's eyes flickered open. For a moment they looked up unseeing, then they focused. He gazed up at Ballard, dazed and unsure.

'Father?'

'My boy.' Ballard choked on the words. His hand lowered for a second time to push the hair out of his son's face.

'Father?' Fleming's voice wavered with disbelief.

'Hush.' Ballard smiled. 'Rest there.' He straightened up. He no longer noticed the rain or the cold. He no longer smelled the acrid stink of powder smoke amidst the stench of old blood and torn bowels.

He had found his son, and nothing else mattered.

'We are leaving. Immediately.' Ballard had steered Mary out of the dressing station. He held her under a tree, sheltering her from the worst of the storm.

'Now?' Mary wiped a hand across her face. It left a trail of watery blood.

'Yes, now. I have him.' Ballard could not hide his delight.

'What the devil do you mean?' Mary was exhausted and struggling to comprehend.

'I found him.' Ballard took hold of her elbow and turned her to face the other direction.

A short distance away, a man was squatting on his haunches beside a bucket. The water it contained was the colour of blood, but he was still using it to wash his face as best he could. Sensing Mary's scrutiny, he got slowly to his feet and walked towards her.

'That's him?' Mary finally understood Ballard's reaction. 'That's the man you've had everyone looking for?'

'Yes.' Ballard kept a firm grip on her elbow. 'He is my son.'

'Your what?' Mary shook off the guiding hand. 'We came here for your son?'

'I will explain, I promise. Now is not the time.' Ballard

spoke urgently. He lifted an arm as he ushered the man into the conversation. 'Mary, may I present William Ballard. My son.'

'No! That's not my name, not anymore.' The blond-haired legionnaire spoke quietly but firmly. 'Fleming. That's my name now.'

Mary barely looked at him. She turned the force of her gaze on Ballard. 'Where's Jack?'

'He fell.' Fleming spoke first. His words were soft, as if he were embarrassed. 'Palmer told me.'

Mary's eyes narrowed at the news. She did not gasp, or appear shocked. 'And where is Palmer?'

'He must be dead. He hit me, knocked me senseless.' Fleming looked at Mary, his eyes full of pain. 'If he was alive he wouldn't have left me.'

'And here you are.' Mary made the statement sound like an accusation.

'I'm not staying.'

'Yes you damn well are.' Ballard had watched the conversation like a hawk. Now he interjected.

'Damn your eyes, do not dare to tell me what to do.' Fleming snapped at his father, then winced, the force of his words clearly hurting him. A single drop of blood trickled from his forehead to run down his cheek like a red tear.

'You are my son.'

'Not any more. I even chose to use Mother's maiden name.' He glared at Ballard.

'Enough.' The major snapped the single word. 'Men died to bring you to me. Do not make that all have happened for nothing.'

'I did not ask you to come here.' Fleming raised a hand, then clutched at his head, swaying on his feet. The blood was running quicker now, the single drop followed by a flood. He closed his eyes against the pain, but his body betrayed him and his legs gave out. He crumpled and fell into his father's arms.

Ballard staggered as he took his son's full weight. For a moment he held him close, then he looked beseechingly at Mary. 'Mary, help me.'

Mary made no move to obey. She stared at Ballard as if seeing him for the first time.

'Help me,' Ballard gasped as he struggled to hold Fleming in his arms. 'He is my son.'

The simple words meant everything, and Mary understood. She glanced over her shoulder. Her own son was sitting on a stool, staring into space, as if looking at an object far away in the distance. The sight shamed her. She stepped forward, bracing her arm across Fleming's chest. With her help, Ballard lowered the bloodied legionnaire to the ground.

'We are leaving, right here and now.' She took control swiftly. She had watched Ballard's merry little gang for weeks now. She had not interfered with their plans, such as they had been, leaving them to their mission. The time for sitting on the sidelines had passed.

'You will do everything I say. Do you understand?' She spoke slowly, as if to a difficult child.

Ballard swallowed, then nodded.

'We will take one of these carts, one of the small ones. We will go to the rail line and get on a train, and we won't stop until we are back in London. When we are there, and only then, I will accept your offer. Is that clear?'

'Yes,' Ballard replied in an instant. There was no need to say anything more.

Mary pulled a bandage out of her apron pocket. It was

bloodstained and smeared with dirt, but it would suffice for the moment. With deft movements she bandaged Fleming's head. Then she stood, wiping her hands on her blood-crusted apron.

For a moment, she felt a pang of grief for Jack. It did not last. She could not mourn his loss. Once he had meant something to her, but that had departed with the last flushes of her youth. Her son was all that mattered now. Everything she did from that moment forth would be for his benefit.

She looked at Ballard. The major was staring at his own son, his eyes roving over the young man's face as if trying to commit every pore to memory. She knew he would give her the security that she needed, and the home and the future that Billy deserved. Becoming Ballard's wife would be the best bargain of her life.

Chapter Forty-seven

*J*ack struggled to place one foot in front of the other. The rain came down in torrents, unceasing and uncaring. Few men were foolish enough to still be walking the battlefield. Most had found their mates and had hunkered down, sitting in misery as they waited for dawn.

The rain made every step a test of endurance, yet the downpour also spared him. In the murk he could no longer see the ruined bodies that lay in every direction. With the rain pounding against his head he could not hear the pitiful cries of the wounded left to suffer where they had fallen.

He found the copse where they had left Billy. There were troops among the trees, tired men who had sought what little shelter they could find. Jack did not know what regiment they belonged to, or even what army. But one thing was certain. There was no sign of Billy or the horses

He looked around him. He saw nothing but rain. The last of the day's light was fading fast, the leaden skies cutting off any hint of evening sun. He shivered as he stood there. The chill was deep in his bones. He was tired, so very tired. But he could not rest. Not yet.

He turned his back on the copse and walked into the teeth of the gale, bending over like a redcoat advancing in the face of enemy guns. It was hard to keep moving. The rain had soaked his uniform, and he shivered with every step.

He found the road that led along the bottom of the ridge easily enough. In the darkness it was harder to see the corpses that lay on either side, and he stumbled as his tired legs caught against the dead flesh of men dragged off the road's surface.

The going was easier once he was on the road, but the storm did not let up. Above his head the skies raged with thunder and lightning, the display so ferocious that he could not help flinching every few paces.

He was nearly upon the aid station before he saw it. A few lanterns had been lit to give the place an unearthly glow. He saw shadowy figures moving around, a handful of men and women tending to the wounded through the long, lonely hours of the night that would see many of their charges breathe their last.

He walked to the far side of the buildings. He tried not to look at the great heap of bodies at the roadside, or at the smaller pile of severed limbs beside it. He turned a deaf ear to the screams and cries that echoed from within the aid station, the pitiful wails coming one after another without pause.

He spotted the place where he had bade farewell to Ballard and Mary and walked towards it, his pace increasing. He felt a pathetic spurt of something that came close to excitement as he peered through the gloom, searching the ground for the fire that he knew Mary would have kept alive even in the storm. He looked for Ballard's distinctive figure and for Billy's smaller frame.

He slowed down, scanning in every direction, certain that they would be there. He tensed, waiting for the shout of recognition. Ballard would be sure to admonish him, but he did not care. He wanted to be back in the fold, to return to people who knew him. He wanted to be home.

The excitement faded. He saw no one.

His pace slowed until he was standing by the tree. The rain fell without pause, but he no longer felt it. His tired mind tried to think clearly, to consider where they might have gone. It failed, and a feeling of such loneliness overwhelmed him that it was all he could do to hold back a cry of anguish.

He did not know how long he stood there. Everything he had done these past weeks had been at the behest of Ballard. The search for Fleming had been all. It had given him purpose when he had had none. Without it, he had nothing. Without his friends, he had no one.

'*Monsieur?*'

Jack started at the sound of the unfamiliar voice. 'Who are you?' His voice cracked. He sounded like an old man.

'Ah, you are English too.' A thin French orderly was looking up at him with concern. 'Are you wounded?'

'No.' Jack fought through the fog in his mind. 'Were there other Englishmen here? A woman? A boy?'

'*Oui, monsieur*, an English gentleman and a lady. They helped with the wounded.'

'Where are they now?'

'They left.' The orderly shrugged. 'A few hours ago, I would say. They took a carriage. They had a boy with them, and a wounded man, a legionnaire if I am not mistaken.'

'How . . .' Jack's voice caught in his throat as he tried to speak. He sucked down a draught of air, then spat, clearing the sourness from his gullet. 'How did the legionnaire get here?'

'He must have come in on a wagon of wounded.' The orderly pulled a face at the odd question. 'There are so many wounded, *monsieur*.'

'Yes.' Jack was grateful for the information. The legionnaire had to be Fleming. Somehow everything had turned out to Ballard's satisfaction. He sensed Palmer's hand in the matter, but the orderly had made no mention of the large Englishman.

'I must leave you.' The orderly interrupted his thoughts. 'There is much to be done here.'

Jack nodded. Ballard and the others were lost to him, but Palmer was still out there somewhere in the darkness. The knowledge ignited a small flame of hope deep inside him. He would try to find him in the morning. For the moment, he had discovered enough.

Jack awoke to sunshine. The warmth of the morning sun wandered across his face, its touch like a lover's the morning after a night spent in each other's arms. He savoured the feel of it, lifting his face with his eyes clamped shut. He did not want to open them. He did not want to see what waited for him.

The sun passed behind a cloud, shutting off the warmth. He sighed, then opened his eyes. It was time to face another day.

Slowly and painfully he levered himself to his feet. He was chilled to the bone and his uniform was damp, streaked with mud and stained with old blood. His whole body ached and he gasped as he stood, his head swimming. He reached out to grasp at a tree, holding himself upright.

He was also hungry. He hadn't eaten since the previous

morning, and now his stomach growled painfully. Yet he had no food with him, and so the hunger, like the pain, would have to be ignored.

He looked down at the muddy hollow next to the thin line of cypress trees that had been his bed for the night. An inch or two of water lay in the depression his body had made in the sodden soil. It had not been a comfortable place to rest, but still he had slept, the exhaustion claiming him despite the discomfort.

Somewhere in the distance a bugle sounded, summoning the battered and exhausted troops who had camped on the field of battle. It was the first sign of a return to normality, the clear notes a reminder that the men who had slept on the sodden ground were soldiers, not vagrants.

The battlefield was shrouded in mist, but he could just make out several parties of men beginning the harrowing task of sifting through the dead. They would be searching for the fallen from their own regiments, so that their comrades could at least be given some sort of burial. It would the last thing their army could do for them.

They were not the only ones searching. He could see several small groups of civilians, the peasants of Lombardy arriving to pick over the dead and the dying, their possessions enough of a lure to bring even the most timid souls in search of bounty. He did not begrudge their presence. The dead no longer had need for such things.

The bugle sounded again, the notes muffled by the heavy air. It was time for him to move, but still he lingered, trying to order his thoughts. The French orderly at the aid station had not mentioned Palmer's presence with the others. That meant he was either dead or missing. If he were missing, then Jack was certain Ballard was ruthless enough to leave his bodyguard behind. But it was hard to think of Palmer allowing himself to be lost.

Jack sighed. He could think of only one reason why Palmer would have left Fleming's side. He looked again at the groups picking through the dead. There was only one way to find out for sure if Palmer had fallen. If he were dead then he had to be found.

He retrieved his rifle from the muddy ground, then trudged away from the line of trees. He had a vague notion of which direction to take, the landscape he was now passing familiar.

He walked into a vision of hell. Bodies lay in every direction. Some were in heaps, three, four or more corpses intertwined, limbs contorted at impossible angles, open eyes bulging and staring. Many were missing limbs or even whole sections of flesh, their cause of death obvious. Others lay as if asleep, peaceful at the last.

The fields on which they sprawled had been devastated. Acres of wheat and corn had been flattened. Orchards that had been carefully tended for generations now lay in ruins, the trees mangled and shattered. Great holes had been gouged in the soil, the earth ripped and torn apart by hundreds of rounds of shot and shell. They were now filled with pools of bloody water or worse. The ground was littered with the detritus of battle. An army's worth of discarded equipment lay in every direction, some as broken as the bodies that had carried it, some simply dropped as the battle ebbed and flowed.

He walked through it all until he found the ground where the Legion had fought the Hungarians. He had searched that area the night before, so now he turned towards the west, thinking to follow the path some of the legionnaires must have taken as they ran from the Austrian cavalry.

The mist was thinning. He felt the warmth of the sun on his back as he walked. As the haze lifted, so the full horror of the battlefield was revealed. The sight of the dead was enough to sour a man's soul for eternity, but worse still was the wounded, the men who had survived the night and now faced the dawn with hope of salvation.

Most lay still, but he felt their eyes following him. A man wearing the uniform of the Zouaves stared at him as he approached. He looked like a living ghost, his skin the colour of ash. As Jack came closer, he shook with agitation and his lips moved in a silent plea for help.

Jack ignored him with difficulty. He walked to the nearest body, a man who had been hit in the neck by a shell splinter that had half severed his head from his body. The ground around him was black with old blood. He peered down at the face. It was not Palmer.

He moved on to the next. It lay on its front, arms and legs spread wide. Carefully he wedged his boot under a shoulder, then lifted the torso so he could see its face. Sightless blue eyes stared back at him over a fabulous black moustache. It was not the man he sought.

He straightened up, massaging the kinks out of his spine. He tried not to count the bodies. He moved on the next, and then the next. Some were already blackening, the flesh swollen and hideous. Flies had laid claim to many, and he was forced to flap his hands over ruined faces as he checked each one for the familiar features of the man he had begun to think of as a friend.

'God save us.' He could not help hissing the words. He had

come to stand over the body of a boy. The lad's drum lay a few feet away, the sides smashed and broken and the skin peeled back like a torn blister. He had been killed by a sword stroke that had cut through his skull so that it was opened from crown to chin.

Jack turned away, sickened to the core. It was only then that he spotted a familiar shape lying on the ground a dozen yards away from the dead boy.

It did not take him long to reach it. The man was larger than most of the bodies left lying in the bright morning sun. He wore the uniform of the Legion, but it was stretched tight across his back, the jacket not well fitted to his large frame. Jack did not need to turn the body over to know who lay face down in the muddy grave. He had found Palmer.

It was the final proof he had sought. The last of Ballard's party had been accounted for. And it confirmed that Jack was once again quite alone.

Epilogue

———◆———

ack handed over the last cigar in the box.

'*Danke.*' The Austrian Jäger breathed his thanks as
he sank back on to the ground. He lay rolling the cigar
under his nose, his eyes closing in silent ecstasy as he smelled
something other than the stench of his own corrupt flesh.

Jack did not wait for anything more. As ever, he felt wholly
inadequate when confronted by the men living with their
broken bodies. The cigars had been a good idea. He had bought
up all he could find, then handed them out to any man who
wanted them. It was a small gesture, but he did not know what
else to do.

The people of Medole were doing their best. The Lombard
villagers had opened their houses, taking in the wounded horde
that had descended upon them, the men from both sides given
the same care. There were still too many to be housed, and so
dozens lay under hastily erected awnings. Even the village
church was full, every last inch of space now a resting place for
a wounded man from the three armies that had fought just two
days previously.

Jack tossed the empty cigar box on to a grass verge, then went to find more water. The wounded men had an unquenchable thirst. They begged for water constantly, and he had spent much of the night going from man to man with whatever cruddy liquid he could find.

'*Putain!* Do not throw that away.'

Jack glanced up sharply and found himself looking at a man wearing a formal business suit that had seen better days. The man was dark-haired, with a fine set of mutton chops. He looked haggard, as if he hadn't slept for a week. At that particular moment he was glaring directly at Jack, his expression stern and disapproving.

'Do you have nothing better to do, Englishman?' He walked across and picked up the discarded packaging before thrusting it back into Jack's grip. 'It is a useful thing. It can be used to carry dressings. Leave it near the supply wagon by the church.'

Jack took the admonishment with good grace. 'Who are you?'

'My name is Dunant.'

'You're French?' Jack tried to place the man's odd accent.

'No, Swiss.' Dunant considered Jack for a moment. 'I heard a foreigner was here. The cigars, they were a good idea. A kindness.'

Jack offered a thin smile at the praise. 'I didn't know what else to do.'

'No, no one does.' Dunant plucked at Jack's elbow, then steered him to his side as he began to walk. 'There is no organisation. The men who planned this battle thought nothing of this, of what would happen to the men whose lives they ruined.' He shook his head sadly. 'They prepare for battle. They manufacture cannon and rifles, their minds focused on how to kill better, how to break more men's bodies. They do not think what to do with those bodies. If they put half as much effort into that, then think what they could achieve.' He looked at Jack, his eyes glittering with barely contained passion. 'Think what just one hundred trained nurses could do. We are overwhelmed.'

The Swiss businessman led Jack across the road, darting through the procession of wagons that crawled along at barely walking pace. Jack had learned that they were heading to a hospital in Castiglione, although he had no idea how any place, no matter how organised, could hope to cope with the vast numbers of wounded being sent there. Officers, cavalrymen and infantrymen of both sides were lumped in together. All were bleeding, torn and exhausted, and all were still covered with the dust and grime of the battlefield.

'Someone must do something!' Dunant spoke fiercely as they approached the church. 'This cannot be allowed to happen again. If the fools want to fight, they must be prepared to prevent such suffering as this.'

They paused as an orderly dragged a corpse across their path, its head bumping sickeningly against the ground as he hauled it along by the ankles.

'Come.' Dunant pulled at Jack's elbow and they followed the orderly, who had disappeared around the side of the church.

Jack went reluctantly. He did not know why he had been selected for this lecture. He supposed Dunant needed to talk, to vent his anger and frustration. He did not blame him. He himself had fought in many battles, but he had never been forced to stick around to witness the suffering that followed.

'There.' Dunant stopped as they too turned the corner of the church. 'Now you will understand.'

Jack swallowed the bile that surged into his throat. He was staring at a pile of bodies. It was like nothing he had ever seen. Hundreds of corpses, perhaps thousands, lay in a jumbled heap. At first it was hard to pick out the human forms amidst the twisted wreckage of so many lives. Then it all became horribly clear.

'We don't know how many we have put there.' Dunant was moved to tears. He turned to face Jack, holding him firmly on each forearm. 'We cannot let this happen again.'

Jack stared past Dunant's shoulder. He could not tear his eyes away from the mountain of the dead. He shuddered. He knew he was looking at his future, at the fate that waited for him. One day his own body would lie in the midst of such a heap. It would be his bulging, staring eyes that would confront an appalled witness, his limbs twisted at impossible angles, his flesh distorted, swollen and black.

The noise of a commotion came from within the church. Dunant dropped Jack's arms before bustling away. Jack followed, eager to leave the sight of the dead behind him.

The inside of the church was wonderfully cool. Dunant's boots echoed loudly on the flagstones as he marched towards the source of the argument they had heard from outside.

A French Zouave was on his feet, his fists raised as he bellowed at four wounded Austrian soldiers lying on stretchers. He was being restrained by the slight figure of a French orderly, who had placed himself between the enraged man and the target of his abuse.

Dunant strode into the melee without hesitation. He was a head shorter than the Zouave, but he got straight into the Frenchman's face, calming him down before leading him back to his own place amidst some wounded comrades, the church once again falling into a respectful silence.

The Swiss walked back to Jack, shaking his head slowly from side to side. As he came closer, Jack saw the grey pallor of his skin and the dark puffy circles around his eyes. Dunant was clearly exhausted.

'Such foolishness.' He spoke softly as he approached. 'That man, he thought those poor souls were Hungarians. Many of the French loathe them, something about their killing of the wounded. Whatever it is, it was enough to send him into a rage.' He was still shaking his head. 'How can man possess such hatred for his fellow man?'

Jack did not know how to answer. He knew hatred. He knew what it was to want to kill, to need to kill. The notion shamed him.

'Come.' Dunant was watching Jack closely. He must have sensed something of the turmoil going on inside the Englishman's mind, as he was looking at him with concern. He took Jack by the arm to steer him to the door.

It was a relief to be led back into the morning sunshine. Dunant let go of Jack's arm. 'Thank you.'

Jack pulled a face. 'You have nothing to thank me for.'

Dunant shrugged. 'You are here. You are helping. I do not think you will get any other thanks for doing so.'

'I'm not doing it for thanks.'

'No.' Dunant searched Jack's face with his eyes. 'You seem lost.'

'I am,' Jack replied with bitter honesty. He did not know what he was doing there, but he had nowhere else to go. He had once thought of returning to London, of searching for a man called Shaw. Revenge was long overdue, yet somehow the idea of another death now seemed tawdry. It meant nothing.

He thought too of Mary, and of going to find her to make sure she was well settled. He also thought of Ballard, and of finally discovering what had driven the intelligence officer to come so far to find the man he had known as Fleming. Ballard still held the key to Jack's name and to his funds. A wise man would want to make sure that both were secured now that the mission was completed. But Jack was not wise, and he found that none of those things mattered. Nothing did.

'You should go home.' Dunant had said nothing as he watched the struggle on Jack's face.

Jack snorted. 'Home.' The word mocked him. 'I have no home.'

'Then I pity you.' Dunant reached out and patted his shoulder. 'There must be somewhere you can go.'

'No. There is nowhere.'

Dunant smiled. 'Then you must do something. But make sure it is something useful. And no more littering.' His face creased into a smile. 'I am not going anywhere. Come and find me later. If you would like to help, I am sure there are good things you can do here.' He turned away, leaving Jack standing outside the church.

Jack sucked down a deep breath, then reached inside his jacket. He pulled out a wedge of letters held together with string. There was an address written on the face of the upper-most letter, the thin strokes of a pencil just about legible beneath black streaks of old blood.

He picked at the muck with a fingernail. He thought about Dunant's words. Kearney had handed him the letters. They had been the last thing he had thought of before he died. That made them important.

Jack peered at the address. It was a long way away, and it

would be one hell of a journey to get there. But he had nothing else planned. He would do as Dunant suggested. He would do a useful thing. He would deliver Kearney's letters.

Historical Note

—◆◉◆—

The Battle of Solferino involved over 300,000 men. It was the biggest battle fought in Europe since the days of Napoleon, and it directly inspired the creation of both the Red Cross and the Geneva Convention. Yet to my shame, I will admit to having never even heard of it until I started researching this novel.

The story was first inspired when I discovered a gem of an article in *The Photographic News for Amateur Photographers – Volume 2*, published in 1859. In the June edition there was a wonderful article titled 'Photographer in the Seat of War', written by a keen amateur photographer who had travelled to record the conflict as it unfurled. This was all fascinating stuff, but when I read that the correspondent had identified himself simply with the letters J and L, I knew that this was where I had to set the fifth of Jack's adventures.

It was only when I began my research that I learned that the battles of Magenta and Solferino had been fought on an epic scale. Hundreds of thousands of men took the field in encounters that were to leave nearly 40,000 of them as casualties. At Solferino alone, the French lost around 11,000 dead, wounded and missing, the Sardinians around 5,000 and the Austrians over 20,000. This truly was suffering on an unimaginable scale.

If you want to see what the battlefield looked like after the fight, then I would recommend a visit to vintagephotosjohnson. com. This fabulous website specialises in collections of photographs, many of them early daguerreotypes or collotypes. The images of the battlefield around Solferino are truly appalling and give some idea of what death on such an industrial scale really looked like.

Like many civilian observers, Henry Dunant, a Swiss businessman, was appalled by the slaughter. After the battle, he was to work tirelessly to ensure that human beings were not left to suffer in such horrific conditions again. His book, *A Memory of Solferino*, makes for powerful reading, and I recommend it to anyone interested in learning more of what occurred after the battle. Dunant was a driven man, and it was his efforts that led to the eventual formation of the International Red Cross.

The campaign in North Italy also played its part in the Risorgimento, the long, protracted and often painful process of Italian unification. The famous revolutionary Giuseppe Garibaldi was there with his men, the Hunters of the Alps, taking their place on the Allied side with the Sardinian forces.

The battles of Magenta and Solferino happened largely as described in the story. Any reader wishing to know more would be well advised to start with Osprey's *Solferino 1859* by Richard Brooks. I can honestly say I have no idea how I would manage without the Osprey books, and this one has proven itself to be one of the very best.

As ever, the needs of a fictional story necessitated a few

changes to the history of the battles, and I would like to make note of them here.

At Magenta, the Austrian troops were driven back before they reached the village of Marcallo, but I needed Jack and Palmer to find some action and so I let the Austrian skirmishers get a little further ahead than they actually did.

I also have to confess that no account of the battle of Solferino tells us of the French Foreign Legion rushing to join the fight on the other side of the battlefield after their assault on San Cassiano. But heroes need to be where the fight is at its fiercest, and so the Legion reinforced the southern flank to join Bataille's brigade's attack, one of the last actions fought before the great storm put paid to the slaughter.

The French Foreign Legion needs little in the way of introduction. It has found lasting fame both for the bravery of its soldiers and for its fascinating design. I recommend *The French Foreign Legion* by Douglas Porch as further reading on the history of this most fabulous regiment.

The notion of an American serving in the French army is not perhaps as fanciful as many would think. My Kearney is very loosely based on Philip Kearney, a US dragoon officer who had served in the Mexican war and was awarded the Légion d'honneur for his actions at Solferino.

There is little mention of British observers accompanying the French army, but there is a single image in the Osprey history of the battle that places a group of them on the battlefield after Solferino, and so I felt justified in allowing Ballard his place. Certainly the practice of sending observers to foreign wars was commonplace at this time.

Jack is still alive, having survived another battle. As ever, he does not know where the future will take him. He has undertaken to deliver Kearney's letters back to his family, but America is about to be tested by one of the bloodiest conflicts the world has ever seen. Civil war is brewing, and Jack will arrive just as the first shots are fired.

Let's see what happens.

Acknowledgments

———◆•◆•◆———

I hope it should not come as a great surprise if I confess that I thoroughly enjoy writing the Jack Lark series. Luckily for you the reader, I am not left totally to my own devices, and I would like to take this opportunity to thank those who help and guide me through the writing of these novels.

My agent, David Headley, deserves a huge thank you. I am very aware of how fortunate I am to be a published writer and to have the joy of seeing my stories made into such fabulous books. Without David's hard work and professionalism I would not be having the fun I am and for that I shall always owe him a great deal.

My editor, Frankie Edwards, has worked tirelessly on my behalf and I would like to thank her here for everything she has done. This novel would not be as good as it is without Frankie's professional and insightful advice, and I would like to thank her for her terrific support.

Jane Selley, my copyeditor on all of the Jack Lark novels, also deserves a great deal of thanks. One day I shall learn how to use a comma properly (amongst many other things), but until then I hope Jane will continue to have the patience to correct all of my many and varied mistakes.

I must also thank a group of people I have never met. The team at Headline who design my covers deserve all the credit for creating the fantastic images that adorn my novels. I think they are simply stunning and I am very proud indeed to have such wonderful covers for my books.

Lastly I would like to publicly thank my family for supporting me through thick and thin. Thank you guys.